A CIRCLE OF DEAD GIRLS

Eleanor Kuhns

severn
House

This first world edition published 2019
in Great Britain and 2020 in the USA by
SEVERN HOUSE PUBLISHERS LTD of
Eardley House, 4 Uxbridge Street, London W8 7SY.
Trade paperback edition first published
in Great Britain and the USA 2020 by
SEVERN HOUSE PUBLISHERS LTD.

British Library Cataloguing in Publication Data
A CIP catalogue record for this title is available from the British Library.

ISBN-13: 978-0-7278-9008-5 (cased)
ISBN-13: 978-1-78029-667-8 (trade paper)
ISBN-13: 978-1-4483-0365-6 (e-book)

Typeset by Palimpsest Book Production Ltd.,
Falkirk, Stirlingshire, Scotland.

For my brother Howard, the first magician I knew and the one who helped with the history of magicians and magic tricks.

ONE

A s if God Himself had taken a hand, winter abruptly changed to spring. The six inches of snow that had fallen just last week – the third week of April – was melting in the suddenly balmy air. Instead of hard-packed snow, the roads were surfaced in slush and mud. Only on the north sides of the slopes and under the trees did snow remain and even there green spears poked through the white.

Rees had already planted peas and in a few weeks he would begin plowing the rocky fields. He sighed. Although glad to see the spring, he did not like to think about the coming backbreaking toil. He would turn forty this year and his dislike of farm work had, if anything, intensified. His father had died at the age of forty-six, while Rees was away serving with General Washington in the War for Independence, and sometimes he wondered if six years was all he had left. Six years with his arms up to their elbows in mud and manure. Just the thought of it pressed down like a heavy weight. He didn't think he could bear it.

At least, with the coming warmer weather, he could look forward to a few weeks of freedom as he traveled these roads weaving for the farm wives. Besides the cash he would earn, he looked forward to what he imagined as sunlit days of freedom from the farm.

With a shake of his head, he pushed the gloomy thoughts from his mind. Now he was on his way into town. For the past several days men had been shouting up and down the lanes and byways: Asher's Circus was coming to town. Rees had brought his children to the Surry Road yesterday to watch the circus arrive. First came a man in a scarlet coat and top hat riding a bay. Bells jingled on his harness and feathers danced upon his head. Two carriages followed, the beautiful women seated inside leaning through the curtained windows to wave and blow kisses. At least five wagons followed, wagons that were unlike any that Rees had ever seen. These vehicles looked like the carriages but were bigger and taller and the curtains at their small windows were shut. On every wagon door a bright gold rearing horse glittered in the sunlight. Finally, clowns with colored patches painted over their eyes and vivid clothing walked alongside. One was a dwarf with a pig and a dog and the other a giant of a man. While the little man turned cartwheels, the big fellow walked straight ahead barely acknowledging the crowds lining the street.

Rees's children were beyond excited, jumping and shouting beside the road. Even Rees, a cosmopolitan traveler who'd visited several large cities, had been enchanted. After a long winter kept mostly inside and occupied solely with mending tack and other chores, he was ready for some entertainment.

Now he was on his way into town to see a performance. A sudden wash of muddy water splattered, not only the wagon, but him as well. He swore at the young sprig galloping by, so intent on reaching Durham that he paid no attention to those he passed. But Rees was not really angry. A circus was a grand event and he guessed he could extend a little charity to the eager farmer's boy. Rees knew Lydia would have liked to join him, and probably the children as well, but no lady would be seen at such rude entertainment, so she must rely on his descriptions.

The streets of Durham were thronged with traffic. Wagons jostled for space next to horses and mules. Pedestrians were forced to cling to the side of the buildings lest they be trampled underfoot. Rees shook his head in amazement; he had never seen the streets so crowded.

And Rouge's inn! The yard swarmed with horses and shouting men. Rees's hope – that he could leave his horse and wagon there – died. When he turned down an alley that went to the jail, he found this narrow lane almost as impassable. But he could already see a tall structure in the field that the Durham farmers usually used for Saturday market. It was so early in the season that market was just beginning. Later in the spring the grounds would be in use every Saturday.

Finally, Rees parked his wagon and horse at the jail. He watered Hannibal from a nearby trough and joined the mob streaming toward the large field. Affluent townsmen rubbed shoulders with sunburned farmers in straw hats and dirty clogs. At first, except for the arena built in the center, the fairgrounds looked exactly as normal: an occasional ramshackle hut interspersed with large areas of open ground. The farmers usually set up their wares in one of those small squares; this was how Lydia sold her butter and cheese. Rees lifted his eyes to the tall wooden structure, dazzling with colorful flags flying around the roof, that dominated the field. At first, he did not notice how peculiar the building looked. But as he approached the flimsy construction, the lack of any windows, and the slapdash roof became apparent. An arc of roofed wooden vehicles – the circus wagons – curved around the back.

At several yards distant he could see gaps between the splintered boards that made up the walls. Posters, all designed with a crude woodcut of a horse, papered over the widest of cracks. Rees directed his steps to a bill posted on the wall and paused in front of it. 'Asher's Circus,' he read.

> Mr Joseph Asher, trained by Mr Phillip Astley and Mr John B. Ricketts, and just arrived from tours of London, Philadelphia, Boston, and Albany, is pleased to present daring feats of horsemanship, the world-famous ropedancer Bambola, clowns after the Italian fashion and many more acts to amaze and delight.

Rees grunted, his eyes moving to the bottom. Names and dates scribbled in by different hands, and then crossed off, filled all the white space with the last being Durham, show time five o'clock. Since he didn't recognize most of the names, he suspected they were for very small villages, not the cities mentioned above. Mr Asher clearly had grandiose aspirations.

Rees walked around to the front. An opening was screened by a shabby blue curtain, dyed in streaks and with the same look as the boards: used over and over for a long time. Now more curious than ever, he bent down and peered through the gap at the bottom. He could hear the sound of hooves and as he peeked under the curtain he saw the skinny brown legs of a galloping horse thud past.

'I really must begin my journey.' Piggy Hanson's whiny drawl sent Rees's head whipping around. What the Hell was Piggy doing here? Rees had not seen Hanson, or anyone else from his hometown of Dugard, Maine, for almost two years, not since the magistrate had written arrest warrants for Lydia (witchcraft) and for Rees (murder). His family had had to flee for their lives. He did not think he would ever forgive the people involved, especially the magistrate who had enabled the persecution. Rage swept over Rees and he turned to look around for the other man.

He saw his nemesis – they'd been enemies since boyhood – standing in a cluster of gentlemen, their cigar smoke forming a cloud around them. With every intention of punching the other man, Rees took a few steps in his direction, but then his anger succumbed to his more rational mind. He did not want Piggy Hanson to know he lived here now and anyway there were far too many men for him to take on by himself.

'I must leave for the next town on my circuit, you know,' Hanson continued. A magistrate for a large district, he regularly traveled from town to town ruling on judicial issues. He knew Rees was innocent of murder, Rees was certain of it, but he suspected he would still be treated as though he was guilty. And he doubted he could behave with any civility at all, not with this man. He cast around for a hiding place and, quicker than thought, he dashed behind the blue curtain.

He swiftly moved away from the portal, pressing himself against the wooden wall so that no one who came through the curtain could immediately see him. Then he inhaled a deep breath and looked around.

Stones carried in from the field outside marked off a roughly circular ring. The galloping horse thundered past, a woman in a short red frock standing on the saddle. At first scandalized to see the woman's legs knee to ankle, Rees's shock quickly turned to admiration. She stood on the saddle in comfort, her red dress and white petticoats fluttering in the breeze. Puffs of dust from the horse's hooves sifted into the air.

'Pip,' said a voice from above. Rees looked up. A rope had been stretched tautly across the width of the enclosure and a woman in a white dress and stockings stood upon it. She wore white gloves but no hat and her wavy dark hair curled around her face. Rees stared in amazement as her white feet slid across the line. She was totally focused upon her task and did not give any indication she saw him. 'Pip,' she said again, and went into a flood of French mixed with some other language. Rees understood enough to know she was complaining about the rope.

This, he thought, must be Bambola, the ropewalker, crossing the sky above his head. She was one of the most beautiful women he had ever seen. As her white dress fluttered around her, all he could think of was angels.

'Bon.' A man Rees had not noticed detached himself from the wall and moved forward. He was easily as tall as Rees, if not taller, and lanky. His hair was a peculiar reddish black color. In French he assured the ropedancer that he would fix the rope in a minute.

Holding up his hand, he moved toward the ring. The equestrienne dropped down to the saddle, first riding astride and then moving one leg across so she rode sidesaddle. She pulled the horse to a stop and jumped down with none of the hesitation of a lady. She conferred with Pip for a few moments in tones too low for Rees to hear and then she went out the opening at the back. The man leaped easily into the saddle and urged the horse again into a gallop. He stood in the saddle, balancing even more easily than his female partner, and then, in one fluid motion, dropped to the saddle to stand on his hands. His lean body formed a long streak toward the sky. Rees gasped in amazement. Then the performer began jumping from one face of the saddle to the other, riding diagonally on each side with his feet pointing at the horse's hindquarters. He was even more skilled than the woman and Rees was so enthralled he forgot why he was there and lost all track of time.

Finally, Pip moved his long body into the saddle and slowed the horse to a walk. He dismounted and, taking hold of the bridle, began to walk the animal around the ring. 'You,' he shouted at Rees in a heavy French accent, 'get out. You must pay.'

Rees half-nodded, listening to the chatter floating over the wall; he could still hear Piggy talking outside, his high-pitched voice carrying over the lower tones of the other men. 'I didn't sneak in to see the show,' Rees told the circus performer in a near-whisper. 'There's someone outside I don't want to meet.'

With a grin – he could also hear Piggy – the other man turned and pointed to the curtain at the back. Rees struck across the ring for the screen. Disappointment – for now he would not be able to stay and enjoy the show – fell heavy upon his shoulders. Another crime to put at Piggy's door.

Before he dropped the cloth over the opening Rees turned to look back over his shoulder. Now the tall man was scrambling up the pole to the small landing above. Rees wondered if the talented rider was a ropedancer as well as an equestrian but he did not go all the way up. Instead, as the girl withdrew to the landing on the other side, Pip began working with fittings. The rope vibrated.

Rees dropped the curtain and looked around. He found himself in the cluster of the circus carriages, horses, and hurrying people. A dwarf wearing a clown's short ruffled red pants and with red triangles drawn in around his eyes hurried past, quickly followed by a slender fellow with oiled black hair and an aggressive black mustache streaked with gray. The performance would begin soon. No one took the slightest notice of Rees as he threaded his way through the circus performers.

Close to, the wagons looked beat up, scarred with use. Most of the gold horses on the wagon doors were simply paint and the few that were carved wood or sculpted metal were losing their gilding. Rees distinctly saw the tell-tale red of rust fringing the head of one rearing stallion.

He broke into a run. He would never have expected to meet the magistrate here in this tiny Maine town. And he prayed Hanson would leave soon. Rees would not dare to return until he could be sure that Piggy Hanson was gone.

Leaving Durham proved just as challenging as entering town in the first place. The streets seemed even more congested now than they had been earlier. Abandoning the main road once again, Rees turned down a side street on the southern side of town. There was a narrow lane, little more than a footpath, that went east, from Durham to the Surry Road. He could follow Surry Road north past the Shaker community and then to his own farm. If he could just reach the lane. The side street was packed with wagons coming from the farms on the southern side of town. It took Rees much longer than it should have to drive the few blocks before he was finally able to turn.

But from what he could see of this winding track, there was little traffic here. Because of the narrow and twisty nature of this lane most of the traffic was on foot. Only a few vehicles were heading into town. Congratulating himself on his foresight, Rees settled himself more comfortably on the hard, wooden seat of his wagon. If one were not in a hurry, this was a pleasant ride through the stands of budding trees and lichen-spotted boulders. He glanced at the sky; he'd reach home before it was entirely dark. And, although he had not been able to attend the circus, at least he'd seen enough to make a good story to tell Lydia and the children.

The wagon trundled around the last steep, sharp curve. From here the road straightened out, cutting through farmland until it reached Surry Road.

And ahead was a group of Shaker Brothers, walking towards him. Rees was surprised to see them. A devout group that rarely left their well-ordered community, they surely could not be walking into Durham for the circus. He slowed to a stop and jumped to the ground.

TWO

The group of men resolved into individual faces. One man, Brother Daniel, Rees knew well. Daniel had been the caretaker of the boys when Rees and his family had sought refuge here two years ago. Promoted to Elder since then, Daniel was beginning to look much older than his almost thirty years. He'd lost the roundness to his cheeks, his face now appearing almost gaunt, and the gray appearing in his hair made him look as though he were fading like a piece of old cloth. Rees, who'd recently discovered white hairs on his chin and chest, felt a spasm of sympathy.

Now worried lines furrowed Daniel's forehead. 'Rees,' he said. 'If I may request your assistance?'

'Of course,' he said immediately. 'What do you need?' Not only was his wife a former Shaker but the members of Zion had helped him more times than he could count.

'When you came through town did you see a Shaker lass?' Daniel's normally quiet voice trembled with fear and desperation. Rees shook his head. He had seen few women or children and none clothed in the sober Shaker garb.

'What happened? Did she run off to see the circus?'

'Yes,' Daniel said with a nod. 'With one of the boys.'

'Shem,' said Brother Aaron. Rees knew the cantankerous old man well and was surprised to see him here, searching for the girl. Although a Shaker, Aaron was not always kind or compassionate. 'I fear he was easily led by that girl,' he added, confirming Rees's judgement.

'Apparently they took off right after our noon dinner,' Daniel continued, ignoring the other man. 'We wouldn't know that much but for the fact Shem was almost late for supper.'

'Well, have you asked him where she is?'

'Shem had nothing to do with it,' Aaron said sharply at the same instant Daniel spoke.

'Of course we did. We aren't fools.'

Rees held up his hands in contrition. The Shakers were usually the most even-tempered of people. He knew Daniel's testiness was a measure of his worry. 'What did he say?'

'That they were separated.'

'Shem wanted to see the circus horses,' Aaron said.

'Leah wanted to come home,' Daniel explained, throwing an irritated glance at his fellow Shaker. 'Well, they wouldn't allow a woman to enter such a rude entertainment, would they? She was probably bored—'

'He is horse mad,' Aaron interjected.

'Please Aaron,' Daniel said in a sharp voice, staring at his fellow in exasperation. Aaron acknowledged the rebuke with a nod and Daniel continued. 'How could Leah have been so lost to all propriety as to imagine she would be allowed entry, I don't know.' For a moment his frustration with the girl overshadowed his fear. 'What was she thinking? I'm not surprised that rapscallion Shem would behave so carelessly but Leah is soon to sign the Covenant and join us as a fully adult member. The amusements of the World should hold no attraction for her.'

Rees shook his head in disagreement. He didn't blame the girl. He thought that this was exactly the time when she would want to see something outside the kitchen. After all, he was a man, well used to traveling, and seeing the circus had made him long to pack his loom in his wagon and go.

'Like all women, she is flighty,' Aaron said, frowning in condemnation. 'Attracted to sins of—'

'Did you search Zion?' Rees interrupted.

'No,' Daniel said. 'When we couldn't find the children, we suspected they'd left . . .' His voice trailed away and he looked from side to side as though expecting the girl to spring up beside him.

'Perhaps she just wanted to go home to her family,' Rees suggested.

'She has no family,' Daniel said curtly. 'Neither of those children do. Shem is an orphan and Leah has lived with us since she was a baby. Her mother brought her to us and died soon after. Leah knows no other family but us. She would not leave our community.'

All the more reason for her to want to experience something of the world, Rees thought but he kept his opinion to himself. 'I drove to town on the main road,' he said aloud. 'I did not see any children at all.'

'When was that?'

'About four,' Rees replied.

Daniel nodded and rubbed a shaking hand over his jaw. 'You were on the road too late, I think. The children left the village right after noon dinner.'

'That means they would have been on the main road between one and two,' Rees said. 'Depending on their speed.' And if Leah had parted from Shem and started home by two thirty or three, walking either road, she would have reached Zion by four. Four thirty at the latest. Anxiety for the girl tingled through him. He thought of his own children and the kidnapping of his daughter last winter with a shudder of remembered terror. 'I'll help you search,' he said. 'The more of us the better.' He already feared this search would not have a good outcome.

Daniel turned to two of the younger Brothers. 'Search along the road,' he said. 'And hurry. We have less than an hour of daylight left.' They started down the lane, moving toward town at a run.

Rees looked up at the sky. The fiery ball was almost at the horizon, and long low rays streamed across the earth in ribbons of gold. In thirty – maybe forty minutes – the sun would drop below the western hill and the pink and purple streamers across the sky would fade into black. 'I'll park the wagon,' he said, jumping into the seat.

He pulled it to the ditch on the left side and jumped down, looking around him as he did so. Farmer Reynard had planted the sloping fields on Rees's right; buckwheat probably given the sloping and rocky nature of the ground. But on the left the buckwheat straw from last year stood almost four feet high, waiting to be cut down and then turned over into the soil. Rees inspected that field thoughtfully. Tall thick stems such as that could hide a girl who did not want to be found. 'We should check the fields,' he said as he rejoined the Shakers. 'And the pastures.' When Daniel looked at him in surprise, he added, 'She might have started back to Zion and when she saw us coming gone to ground. She might not want to be dragged back to Zion in disgrace.'

Daniel nodded, pleased by the suggestion and quickly asked the other Brothers to spread out across the fields. Rees and Daniel started walking down the lane.

But before they had gone very far, one of the other Shakers called out. 'Hey, over here.' A young fellow whose yellow hair stuck out around his straw hat like straw itself, began retching. 'Oh, dear God.'

Daniel did not pause to remonstrate with the boy for his language but vaulted the fence into the field and ran. Rees struggled to keep up. Was it Leah? Was she hurt? His stomach clenched; he was so afraid the situation was far worse than that.

They arrived at the body lying sprawled in its buckwheat nest at the same time. She lay partly on her right side, partly on her back, her left arm crooked at her waist at an odd angle. Her plain gray skirt was rucked up to her thighs and blood spattered the white flesh. Daniel turned around, his face white, and shouted at the Brothers approaching him, 'Stay back. Stay back. Don't come any closer.'

'Oh no,' Rees said, dropping to one knee. 'Oh no.' Although he'd been told Leah was fourteen, she looked much younger. Under the severe Shaker cap, her skin had the translucent quality of the child. Her eyes were open, the cloudy irises staring at the darkening sky. Rees bent over her. Although it was hard to tell in the fading light, he thought he saw marks around her throat. 'She may have been strangled,' he said, his eyes rising to the worn fence that separated this field from the road that led into Durham. Leah's body had been dropped only a few yards from the fence but in the high straw it would have been almost invisible, even in daylight. Rees began walking slowly toward the main road, his eyes fixed upon the ground. There did not seem to be any path from the fence to the body; none of the buckwheat stalks were bent or broken in any way. He did not see any footprints in the soft April soil either. But in the setting sun detail was difficult to see and he made a mental note to examine this section of the field more closely tomorrow.

'The farmer, did he do this terrible thing?' Daniel cried, glancing from side to side.

'Perhaps, but I doubt it,' Rees said. He touched the girl's upraised arm to see if he could move it. As he suspected, the body was growing stiff. 'He would be a fool to leave her in his own field.'

'It was not Shem,' Aaron said loudly. Rees glanced up at the man. Why was Aaron so protective of that boy?

'She's been dead for some hours,' Rees said, returning to his examination. Then he thought about the warmth of the day. Leah would have been lying here, in the sun. 'Maybe since mid-afternoon.' And that time would be consistent with the time she'd left town.

'How do you know?' Daniel stared at Rees in shock, mixed with dawning suspicion.

'You told me she was seen at noon dinner,' Rees replied, 'so we know she was alive then.' He rose to his feet and looked at Daniel 'It must be almost six o'clock now.'

'Probably after,' Daniel said, looking around at the fading light.

'A body begins to stiffen a few hours after death and then, maybe half a day later, the rigidity passes off. I saw this frequently during the War for Independence but any good butcher will tell you the same.' Rees kept his eyes upon the other man who finally nodded with some reluctance. 'I would guess that Leah was accosted by someone on her way home.' He paused. The poor child had probably been lying here when he rode past, thinking of the circus. He closed his eyes as a spasm of shame went through him.

'She knew she was not to leave Zion,' Daniel said with a hint of wrath in his voice.

Rees sighed. This was not the first time he had seen the victim blamed. And perhaps, for a celibate such as Daniel, anger was an easier emotion right now than horror and disgust and grief as well. 'Perhaps she behaved foolishly, but she did not deserve this end to her life.'

'We will take her home—' Daniel began.

But Rees interrupted. 'We must send someone for the constable.'

'No. No. She is one of ours.'

'This is murder,' Rees said, staring fixedly at Daniel. Although shocked and horrified, he had witnessed too many violent deaths to be paralyzed by such evil any longer. His calm voice and stern regard had the desired effect. Daniel sucked in a deep breath. After he had mastered himself, he left Rees's side and joined the group of Shakers.

'Run back to the village and get a horse,' he told one of the youngest Brothers. 'Ride into Durham and fetch Constable Rouge.' His voice trembled on the final word. Rees looked at Daniel. He was swaying on his feet, his eyes were glassy and his skin pale and slick with perspiration. He looked as though he might faint.

Rees drew him away from Leah's body and pressed him down into a sitting position. Daniel was little more than a boy himself and had lived in the serene Shaker community most of his life. It was no surprise he was ill-equipped to handle such a terrible occurrence. 'Put your head between your knees,' Rees said. 'I'm going to walk to the farmhouse and talk to the farmer. Maybe he saw something.'

'I'll go with you.' Daniel stood up, so unsteady Rees grabbed him to keep him from falling.

'No,' he said with a shake of his head.

'I need to go with you,' the Brother said fiercely. 'I need to do something. That poor child!' Rees stared at the other man. Although Daniel's face was still white and he was trembling, he had set his mouth in a determined line. 'I must do this, Rees.'

'Very well.' Rees glanced over his shoulder at the body. From here, it appeared to be a bundle of rags dropped among the stalks. 'Poor chick won't be going anywhere.'

Daniel looked at Brother Aaron. 'You were once a soldier,' he said. 'You've seen violence and death. Please stay with our Sister.' Aaron nodded and, withdrawing a few steps, sat down in the row between the stalks. In the encroaching shadows he instantly faded from view. Only his pale straw hat remained, shining in the last of the light like a beacon.

Rees and Daniel set off across the fields for the distant farmhouse.

THREE

Candles were already alight inside the farmhouse. One taper sat welcomingly upon a windowsill and its flame, fluttering in the evening breeze, drew Rees and Daniel to the house. By the time they reached the front door, the sun was almost entirely down behind the horizon and only a few streaks of orange light remained. Rees glanced at the empty road behind him, a pale ribbon between the dark fields.

He knocked on the door. He heard voices inside and the sound of a child's laughter as light footsteps approached. A woman with a baby on her hip opened the door. In the candlelight behind her Rees saw a table set for supper, used wooden bowls and a number of children's heads all under the age of nine or ten. 'Yes?' the woman said, opening the door a little wider.

'Is your husband at home?' Rees asked.

'No. He and my two oldest sons went into town this morning for some kind of horse fair,' she replied. 'I expected him before now.' She peered around the two men. Rees recalled the ropedancer and thought the circus was something more than just a horse fair but it was not for him to interfere between husband and wife. The woman put down the baby. 'Go to Sarah, Mordecai,' she said. The baby toddled away. 'What's this about?' she asked, turning back to the visitors.

'A girl has been murdered in your field . . .' Daniel began.

Rees put a hand out to silence him and overrode him in a loud voice. 'We wanted to ask him if he saw anything unusual this after-noon, that's all. But since he wasn't here there's no need. I'm very sorry to have troubled you.'

'There's always traffic on the road into Durham,' said the farmer's wife. 'Many many farmers' wagons coming up from the Surry Road, sometimes,' she added, turning her face toward Daniel, 'one or two from your community.' With the light at her back her face was in shadow and Rees couldn't see her expression. But he suspected from a certain flattening of her voice that she did not care for the Shakers all that much. 'Today there were more men on horseback than usual, riding in for the fair, I suppose, and even a few carriages.'

'Was there anyone riding away particularly fast?' Rees asked.

She laughed ruefully. 'The traffic is always far too fast for my liking,' she said. 'Especially on market day. I am constantly afraid that one of my children will wander onto the road and be killed under somebody's wagon wheels.' She sighed.

'But the rider,' a boy said suddenly, coming to the door. Older than the rest, he looked to be about eleven or twelve. Rees recog-nized him from the previous summer. 'Remember: the man I told you about.'

'Oh yes.' The woman turned to look at her son, the light falling full upon her face for the first time. Although she looked tired her skin was unlined and the fair hair at the edge of her cap was untouched by gray. Rees thought she was probably close to ten years his junior.

'He rode really, really fast,' the boy said, puffing up with importance.

'What did he look like?' Rees asked. 'Could you see him clearly?'

'He was tall and had blackish hair. And he did tricks. He stood on the horse's back!'

Unbidden, the memory of the circus performer flashed into Rees's mind. The ropedancer had called him Pip. Rees nodded. 'Thank you,' he said. 'I know who that is.'

At that moment the sound of wagon wheels turning into the drive resounded clearly through the night air. Rees turned to see a wagon, lanterns bobbing at the front, coming toward the house. When it drew to a stop, the farmer jumped out. Shouting at his sons to take care of the horse and wagon, he hurried to the door.

'Mr Rees,' he said in surprise. 'What's going on?' His voice was thick with fear.

'These two gentlemen were asking about the . . .' The farmwife stopped short and looked at Rees in confusion. She did not know what to say.

'About the congregation in my field?' Reynard asked, gesturing to his right. Rees stepped back from the porch and looked. The lighted circle made by a host of lanterns shone on the heads of several men; the constable had arrived. 'What happened?'

'Thank you for your time, missus,' Rees said.

'Wait. Tell me,' the farmer demanded.

'One of our Sisters was murdered in your field,' Daniel said in an accusing tone. Reynard gaped at the Shaker.

'What he means to say,' Rees said hastily, 'is that the body of one of the girls was found in your buckwheat field. I suspect the constable is there now.'

'First my horse pasture and now my buckwheat,' Reynard said, recalling a murder the previous year. 'I had nothing to do with it.'

'We know that,' Rees said. 'I was hoping you'd seen something. But since you were in town the entire day, I realize you could not have done. Sorry to have bothered you.' He gestured to Daniel.

As they turned Reynard said, 'Wait. I should go with you.'

'Of course, you may if you wish,' Rees replied. 'But I don't think you're going to want to see this.'

The man grunted and, as Rees and Daniel started toward the field, and to the constable's lanterns, Reynard took a few steps after them. Then he thought better of following them and stopped.

With the lanterns as their guide, Rees and Daniel climbed quickly over the fences to the field. As they approached the center of the light, one of the men started toward them. 'Wait. Wait. You can't be here.'

'Simon,' Rees shouted. 'Simon Rouge.'

The constable detached himself from the group. 'Well, Will Rees, as I live and breathe. Haven't seen you for months. What are you doing here? I swear, every time we meet there's a dead body nearby. Do you make a habit of this? Or should I suspect cause and effect?'

'I just happened to be driving down the road, coming from town,' Rees said defensively.

'So, you went to see the circus too. Wish they'd never stopped here. Drunken brawls everywhere. The jail is full. And now this,' Rouge said, turning back to the gentleman kneeling by the body. 'What's the story, Dr Smith?'

'Pretty sure she's been interfered with,' said the doctor. 'And I believe she was strangled, just exactly as it appears but I'm not sure if that's what killed her. There was a struggle. Her nails are broken and her hands are scratched. Although what effort this little slip of a thing could make I can't guess. Her left arm is fractured.'

'From the struggle?' Rouge asked.

Smith hesitated. 'Could be,' he said at last. 'But I don't think so. It's a clean break.'

'Could it have occurred if she were thrown?' Rees asked. 'Say, from horseback? Or from the top of a carriage?'

Dr Smith looked up, frowning. 'You remember Will Rees, the fellow that solved the murder of that Shaker girl a few years ago?' Rouge said hastily. 'And the kidnapping of my niece last winter?'

The doctor eyed Rees sourly. 'Huh,' he said. 'I remember you. Always snooping. I daresay you're smarter than you look.' Turning back to the body, he continued his analysis. 'Yes, the child's broken arm could occur if she were thrown. She would have landed more heavily from an elevated point. But the man who threw her would have to be strong.'

'Could it have been from horseback?' Rees persisted.

'I always said you were clever,' said Rouge but not as though he meant it. Rees shot a glare at the constable.

'Maybe,' Dr Smith said. 'But I don't see how a man could twist—'

'What if he were standing on the horse?' Rees interrupted.

Dr Smith stared at him and then nodded very slowly. 'That might work. But who stands on a horse?'

'Clearly you haven't stopped by the circus,' Rouge said.

'Tell them about the farmer,' Daniel said suddenly.

'What farmer?' Rouge asked.

'Mr Reynard,' Rees said pointing.

'Ah. The Reynard family.' Rouge pronounced it Ray-no, after the French fashion.

'But the farmer didn't do it,' Rees said, turning to look at Daniel. 'He was in town all day.'

'I saw him there,' Rouge said. 'Anyway, I would never suspect him. I've known him all my life.'

'His boy saw something,' Daniel said.

'Mr Reynard's son saw a rider going fast on the road,' Rees explained.

'Doing tricks,' Daniel said. 'It sounded like one of the circus performers.'

Rees nodded. He'd seen the lanky man with the blackish hair standing on a horse. But that didn't mean the trick rider was guilty.

'Of course, it would be,' Rouge said. 'Thieves, diddlers and vagabonds all. And now rapists and murderers too. I'll talk to the lad but I've no doubt we've found our man.'

'Now, wait a minute,' Rees said. 'We don't know that yet. Shouldn't we ask around and see if the performer is innocent? I saw him in town myself around four thirty so . . .'

'The entire county saw him then. Or soon after.'

'Well then, maybe others saw him before that. Maybe he's innocent.' Rees did not bother hiding his impatience.

'You said she'd been murdered during the afternoon,' Daniel pointed out.

'I think,' the doctor said, rising and wiping his hand on a rag, 'that she was accosted earlier than four. Just a guess but I believe she could have been murdered any time from two or three on. The day was warm and the stiffening would have occurred more slowly than usual.'

Rees acknowledged the truth of that with a nod. 'So, around three?' he said. Exactly what he'd thought.

'Enough of this,' Daniel said sharply. 'I need to bring her home. We'll take care of her.' His voice broke.

'Not yet,' Dr Smith said. 'I want to take a look at her, tomorrow, at my office.' He gestured behind him. 'I brought my wagon.'

'You can have her after,' Rouge said, attempting, in his clumsy way, to be sympathetic to Daniel's grief.

And when it looked as though Daniel would still protest, Rees said, 'Dr Smith might find some clue to the child's murderer.'

Daniel stared at the three men facing him for several seconds. Then, swallowing, he nodded and stepped back.

Since violent death was almost unheard of among the Shakers, none of them wanted to touch the body. It was left to Rees, Constable Rouge and Dr Smith to carry the remains to the coroner's vehicle. The corpse was beginning to stiffen but had not become completely rigid so the transport was easier than it could have been. Rees guessed Leah had not weighed more than one hundred pounds fully clothed.

When the remains were laid carefully in the wagon and the coroner had left for the town, Rees turned to Daniel and Aaron. 'I want to question Shem so I am going to Zion. Would you wish a ride home?'

'No, thank you,' Daniel said. 'I'll go ahead. I want to inspect the springhouse and make sure we have room for . . . for . . .' He sucked in a breath and turned his face aside. Rees patted Daniel's shoulder in comfort.

'I'll go with you,' said Aaron, to Rees's surprise. 'And we'd better hurry. The light is almost gone.'

FOUR

Rees spent the trek across the dark field wondering why Aaron had accepted a ride to Zion. Not for the company. He was the least sociable of men and, unlike most Shakers, he was neither pleasant nor gentle. Of sour disposition, he could be argumentative, a trait Rees had seen more than once. The Shakers were pacifists but Rees had seen this Brother lose his temper and engage in fisticuffs although, perversely, that had made Rees like him better.

His question was soon answered. As soon as he had lit the lanterns on his wagon and climbed into the seat, Aaron spoke. 'Do you think the little hen went down the lane?' he asked.

So now Rees knew Aaron wanted to quiz him about the murder.

He took his time replying. He directed Hannibal onto the road. Although there were still some vehicles driving into town, most of the traffic was now heading east. People had finished their business in town or, more likely, were returning home from the circus.

'That would make sense,' Rees said finally. 'The lane is shorter. But the body was lying closer to the main road so I would wager that she took that way home.'

'Was it one of the men from the circus? Is that what you think?' Aaron asked.

'I don't think anything at this point,' Rees said sharply. 'We don't know enough.' He glanced again to his left, at the fields that were now invisible. In the dark the smell of freshly turned soil seemed even more intense. Without the Shakers searching for Leah she could have lain in the straw for a week or more. By then the circus would have left and the guilty man, if he were among them, could have run anywhere.

'Another week or so before that straw was cut down,' Aaron said, as though he could follow Rees's thoughts. 'Then the girl would be lying out in the open, her sin obvious for everyone to see.'

Rees almost pushed Aaron from the wagon seat. 'She was a child,' he said, turning to glare. But he wasn't surprised. He knew that Aaron did not believe in the value of women, an opinion that caused friction among his Shaker Family. Aaron folded his arms across his chest.

'She beguiled Shem into taking her to town, to that traveling wickedness called a circus.'

'I don't believe she did,' Rees said. 'We'll see what Shem has to say about that.'

Aaron shook his head. 'I don't want you speaking with him.'

'That's not your decision,' Rees said, his determination growing in the face of Aaron's obstruction. 'He may have seen or heard something.'

'He didn't. He was with the circus horses,' Aaron said in a gruff voice. 'He told me that.'

'So, you questioned him?' Rees asked, turning to look at the other man. 'And told him what to say, I'll be bound.' Although Aaron was barely visible in the gloom, Rees could see the angle of the Shaker's head. He was staring straight ahead, refusing to meet Rees's gaze.

'Tell me what you know,' he said in a harsh voice. 'Tell me.'

Aaron hesitated, chewing his lip.

At last he spoke. 'I don't have to tell you anything,' he said.

'Your own God will judge you,' Rees said.

Without speaking, Aaron jumped down from the wagon. Rees went to pull Hannibal to a stop but the Shaker, turning, ran into the darkness and disappeared.

Rees drove into the center of Zion. Most of the windows in the Dwelling House were dark but the nearby dining hall was brightly lit. It was suppertime. There was no sign of Daniel, so Rees pulled up in front of the Dwelling House and waited. After a few minutes a lantern appeared at the southern end of the main street, growing larger as it bobbed toward him. He peered at the yellow light; it looked as though there were two people approaching him. As they drew closer the shapes resolved into Daniel with Esther by his side. Esther was an escaped slave but she had lived in Zion for many years and had risen to the position of Eldress. She nodded at Rees.

'How is dear Lydia?' she asked.

'Well,' Rees said. 'And the baby is thriving.' Since Rees's little girl had been born in Zion many of the Sisters felt a bond with the child.

'You must bring them for a visit,' Esther said, smiling.

'I will,' Rees agreed. 'Now that the weather is improving.'

'We have more important issues to discuss,' Daniel said sharply.

'Indeed,' Rees said, turning to look at him.

'Go get the boy,' Esther told Daniel. As he hurried to the dining hall, she said to Rees, 'He told me you wished to speak to Shem.'

'I do. He was the last person to see Leah.'

'Other than the villain who took her life. And worse.' Esther's voice caught on the final word. Handing Rees the lantern, she went up the steps and into the Dwelling House. She had never told him what had happened to her during her former life as a slave and for the first time he wondered.

With nightfall the temperature had begun dropping and the breeze had picked up. Rees's breath turned to smoke in the chilly air. He had not worn his heavy coat and now regretted it. Wrapping his arms around himself, he walked around to keep warm.

Finally, Daniel returned, shepherding the boy before him and with Aaron drifting behind. All of them wore capes against the evening chill. Rees stared at Aaron, wondering why he had felt it necessary to come as well. What did he think Shem would say?

The boy seemed all arms and legs and his feet were huge. Rees suspected the boy would be near Rees's height when he finished growing. A shock of dark hair drooped over his white forehead. He kept his eyes down and his mouth twitched, either in fear or annoyance. Rees couldn't tell.

'Do you know why you were called out here?' he asked.

Shem nodded. 'Leah is missing.' With a sideways glance he added, 'Daniel told me. But I don't know where she is.'

But you know something, Rees thought. 'Where did you go today?'

'Nowhere,' Shem said. Rees held up the lantern, illuminating the boy's pale blue eyes. 'I was here.'

'Don't lie. We know you went to town with Leah,' Rees said, his voice sharpening.

'That was this afternoon,' Shem said. 'After I finished my chores.' He glanced pointedly at Daniel and then Aaron.

'What happened after the noon meal?' Rees asked. Shem shrugged. 'You walked into town with Leah.'

'Yeah. So what? She wanted to see the circus. Of course, they wouldn't let her in. She's only a girl.' His voice was scornful.

'What happened after that?' Rees asked when Shem did not go on.

'I saw the trick rider.' Shem's voice lifted, filled with excitement and awe. 'I went to talk to him about his horse. Could I train one of the horses here to do that?' He paused, grinning with remembered pleasure.

'You met the Frenchman,' Rees said in encouragement, his teeth clacking together. He was shivering like an aspen tree in the wind.

'Yes. Mr Boudreaux. But Leah didn't want to wait with me. She got bored and said she was going home.' Shem shrugged again. 'I didn't see her after that. What happened? Did she get lost? Of course, she did. That's just like a girl.'

'Leah is . . .' Rees began but stopped short when Daniel clutched his arm. 'What?' Daniel vehemently shook his head 'no'. Although Rees knew Shem would have to learn the truth some time, he acquiesced. For now.

FIVE

It was a slow, cold ride home and the moon was rising by the time he reached home. He could only imagine what his wife would say. And Lydia must have been waiting for him; as soon as he drove through the gate and into the yard, the house door opened and she stepped onto the porch. Holding up a lantern, she said, 'I expected you home hours ago.'

'I know,' Rees said. 'Bad news. I—'

'How was the circus?' Jerusha asked, following her mother on to the porch. Rees climbed down from the wagon. He paused with his hand still holding the reins. At almost thirteen Jerusha was within an inch of Lydia's height and quite grown up.

'I didn't see the circus,' he said.

'You didn't?' Her voice lifted in dismay. 'Why did you miss it?'

'What happened?' Lydia asked, sounding resigned.

'I'll be in shortly,' Rees said, 'and explain everything then.' He needed to consider what he would say. He didn't want to discuss the murder in front of his daughter.

While he unhitched the gelding and released him in the pasture, he struggled to come up with an explanation that would satisfy Jerusha's curiosity without frightening her. She did not need to hear about the murder, especially not after her kidnapping the previous winter. Once she'd gone to bed, he'd confide the whole to Lydia.

As he recalled Leah's delicate features, the blue veins in her eyelids clearly visible through her translucent skin, Rees felt slightly nauseous. She was so young and so vulnerable. And what if that body *had* been Jerusha? Or one of his younger daughters: Nancy or Sharon? He shuddered and ran up the porch steps to clutch his daughter to his chest. He could see he would not enjoy a moment's peace until he was an old man and all the children were grown.

When she uttered a squeak of protest he relaxed his grip and stepped back, catching Lydia's worried expression. 'What happened?' she repeated as she took Jerusha by the shoulder and drew her away.

'Later,' he said, shooting her a serious glance.

Now looking more anxious than ever, Lydia swung the door wide. 'Come into the kitchen where it's warm,' she said. Rees blew out the candle in his lantern and stepped inside.

Although the fire was banked, he could feel the heat emanating from it. A covered spider sat on the hearth, nestled up to the ashes to keep his supper warm. He pulled out a chair and sat down. 'Hanson was there,' he said as Lydia fetched a plate and dished out lamb and new peas.

'Who?' Jerusha asked at the same time Lydia said, 'The magistrate?'

She put the plate in front of Rees and cut several slices of bread from yesterday's loaf.

'He's on circuit,' Rees said, inspecting his dinner. The lamb looked dried out and the peas were mushy. 'I didn't want him to see me, to know where I lived. Where we lived.' He gestured at Lydia and Jerusha.

'Oh dear,' Lydia said, understanding his concern.

'I don't understand,' Jerusha said.

'He's from Dugard,' Rees said. 'He . . .' What could he say? 'He isn't our friend.' Jerusha's red lips parted, another question on the way. 'So, I slipped into the circus arena,' he went on quickly. 'I did see a few things.'

'What?' Jerusha leaned forward, her eyes shining. 'What did you see?'

'A woman in a frilly red dress standing on the back of a horse,' he said. 'Riding around and around the ring. But she wasn't even the best. When the groom took the horse from her – oh my, what a rider! He stood on the back as well but he also jumped from side to side. And he stood on his hands! I've never seen the like.'

'My goodness,' Lydia murmured.

'I saw a dwarf too,' Rees continued. 'A clown. But the best, the very best, was the ropedancer.'

'Truly?' Jerusha asked. 'You saw a ropedancer?'

'Indeed.' Rees said. 'A young woman in a white dress.'

'Probably no better than she should be,' Lydia said with a derogatory sniff. But she too could not help leaning forward attentively.

'She walked across a rope no bigger than my thumb as though she were crossing a stream on a line of stones,' he said, caught up in the memory.

'How did you happen to see this if you didn't attend the circus?' Lydia asked.

'When I saw Pig– Mr Hanson,' Rees said, shooting a quick glance at Jerusha, 'I slipped into the arena. They were rehearsing for the performance.'

'Maybe they'll have another show tomorrow night,' Jerusha said, her voice rising in excitement. 'If you go to that one, you can come home and tell us everything.'

'Maybe,' he said, trying to recall the dates listed on the bill posted on the wooden wall of the ring. He thought only one date had been written in for Durham but he couldn't be sure.

'It's time to go to bed now,' Lydia said, putting her hands on Jerusha's arms and steering her toward the stairs. She looked ready to argue but Lydia spoke first. 'I said you could stay up until your father came home,' she said sternly. 'He told you what he saw at the circus. Now it is time for you to retire. You have school tomorrow.'

'Please, Mama.'

'Don't argue. Otherwise I will not be so generous next time,' Lydia said. With a sulky nod, Jerusha obeyed.

As soon as her footsteps faded on the stairs, Lydia turned to her husband. 'What really happened?'

'I told the truth,' he said. 'I just didn't tell everything.' He wiped his lips with his napkin. 'I came upon Brother Daniel and several of his Brethren when I was coming home. They were searching for one of the children.' Although Lydia didn't speak, the hands folded on the table tightened until the knuckles went white. 'We found her.' He looked up to meet his wife's gaze. 'She'd been strangled, Lydia. And she-she . . .' Rees's voice broke and he took a few seconds to compose himself. 'I'll drive Jerusha to school tomorrow and pick her up after.'

'I can take her in the cart if you think it necessary,' Lydia said.

Rees had bought a mule to help with the plowing, but he spent more time hitched to Lydia's cart. 'She should be safe enough.' Jerusha and her siblings – all but Simon who now lived with David in Dugard – went to a dame school several miles distant. Most of Jerusha's peers had been taken out of school to help at home but Lydia refused to consider that. She wanted Jerusha to finish. That wouldn't be long; she already spent more time helping the younger children than studying herself. 'Do they know – do they have any idea . . .?' Her voice ran down.

Rees shook his head. 'No. The constable suspects someone in the circus.'

'What do you think?'

'I'm not sure,' he said at last. 'I mean, it could be someone in the circus but not necessarily the trick rider.' He brought his plate to the sink and put it in the dishpan. 'I'll speak to Rouge and Dr Smith tomorrow. Maybe they'll have news.' Whistling, he turned toward the stairs. 'I'm going to take a look at the loom. I'm almost finished with the cloth on it. Soon I'll be taking it off and packing up the loom to put in the wagon.'

'What? Wait. Where are you going?'

Rees looked at his wife in surprise. 'To visit the farm wives of course.'

'But I need you here,' she objected.

Rees turned around to face her. 'But spring is the best time to travel from farm to farm and weave the winter spinning. You know that.'

'Our fields have to be planted.' Her voice took on an edge.

'I can do that between trips,' he said, speaking as reasonably as he could. He could see the treat he'd promised himself, a short trip away from the demands of the farm, receding.

'The buckwheat needs to go in now,' she said. 'It can't wait.'

Rees blew out his breath in annoyance. 'I'll do one of the fields before I go,' he suggested.

'That's not enough to feed us.'

'The Shakers promised to help.'

'Really, Will,' Lydia said reproachfully, 'you can't expect them to do your work for you.'

'Why not?' Rees's voice began to rise. He stopped and took a breath. 'They'll be taking possession of this farm eventually.'

'The children will be out of school soon and I—'

'They can help too,' Rees said, snapping with temper. He'd been looking forward to taking a few trips around, just to escape the farm for a few days, ever since the weather began improving. 'The farm wives and their daughters will have been spinning all winter. This is the time to make some cash money.'

'Unless you're planning to buy a lot of our food, we need to plant first,' Lydia said.

'We'll need money for seeds and more,' Rees said stubbornly. Lydia sighed but didn't continue arguing. Rees started for the hall.

As he passed through the door, she said, 'Can you wait a few weeks at least?'

'And quarrel over this again?' He turned around, the urge to shout at her almost overwhelming. 'Look,' he said, struggling to master his irritation, 'I am too tired to discuss this now. We can talk again tomorrow.' Taking one of Lydia's fine beeswax candles, he put it in a candlestick. He lit it from the fire and started up the stairs. He almost expected her to call him back but this time she didn't.

Although he knew it was too dark to weave, he went to the weaving room anyway. He was too angry and upset to go to bed and pretend nothing had happened. He would not sleep if he did not calm down. Weaving relaxed him and besides, he told himself, he was not threading the loom but only passing the shuttle back and forth across the warp. Surely he could accomplish that even in the flickering light of one candle.

Bending over, he peered at the cloth already wrapped around the beam. He was very careful to hold the candle away; a drop of wax would ruin the cloth more than a weaving mistake. The yarn had been given to him by one of the local farmer's wives and it varied widely in thickness. She had six daughters, the youngest was only just learning to spin, and some of the skeins went from thick to thin and back again within a few inches. The cloth woven from such irregular yarn was not smooth but dotted with slubs and knots and other imperfections. Usually Rees kept a portion of cloth but this time he would take his entire payment in money.

He sat down, putting the candlestick on the windowsill. The light was dim but he could see well enough. He picked up the shuttle and stepped on the rightmost treadle. At first his mind was entirely occupied with the rejoinders he should have made to Lydia. Then, when he tried to put his anger from him, he recalled Leah and the events after the discovery of her body. But as he caught his rhythm and the faint clacking filled the room, Rees's thoughts drifted away from the horrors of the last few hours. And for a space he thought of nothing at all but the shuttle flying from hand to hand and the pumping of his legs.

He did not realize how much time had passed until Lydia came to the door and asked him if he was coming to bed. He jumped, almost falling off the bench, and turned. She was already in her night robe, her long red hair plaited and lying over her shoulder. 'In a minute,' he said.

'You've been up here for hours,' Lydia said. She still sounded cross. When he looked at his candle he saw it had burned down to a stub.

'I lost track of time,' he said, rising stiffly from the bench.

'I'm sorry we quarreled,' Lydia said. 'I did not mean to argue.'

'I know.' Dropping an apologetic kiss on her forehead, Rees said, 'I'll leave the trips to later if you wish it.' It was a tremendous sacrifice.

She smiled at him. 'Perhaps, in a few weeks, it will be a better time for you to be away. Besides,' she added teasingly, 'you will surely want to be here to help the constable with the murder.'

'That's true,' he said, adding with a grin, 'I'm going to assist Rouge whether he wants me to or not.'

'I expect no less,' Lydia said. Taking his hand, she urged him to the bedchamber across the hall. 'Now, come to bed.'

Rees realized he wasn't ready to sleep after all.

SIX

R ees arrived at Dr Smith's surgery shortly after eight the following morning. He found the coroner in the back room. Although a sheet covered the slight form on the table so the face could not be seen, Rees assumed that it was Leah. 'What have you found?' he asked.

'She's been strangled and, as I supposed,' Smith said in a self-important tone, 'she was interfered with.'

'I guessed that,' Rees said with some impatience. Smith scowled at Rees and with slow deliberation took a long draft from the mug on a nearby table. Hard cider, by the smell. 'Do you have anything else?'

Smith turned to a pile of clothing and rummaged through it with careless indifference. 'Here,' he said, pulling out the navy cape all Shaker women wore around their shoulders and tossing it to Rees. 'Take a whiff of that.'

Rees held the dark shawl to his nose. 'Wine?'

'Not any wine. That there is Madeira, and expensive Madeira too. I think the man plied her with wine, poor little hen.' He sounded sorry and Rees liked him the better for it. 'She put up quite a fight though.' He reached under the sheet and pulled out Leah's battered hand. It was so small. Rees swallowed.

'She was just a child,' he muttered. He imagined her terror and fury swept over him. He would find her murderer and bring him to justice.

'Look at the nails,' Smith said, holding up the waxy extremity. 'There's blood under them. She scratched her attacker. And I found blood on her teeth. I think she bit him as well.'

'So, I'm looking for someone with scratches and bite marks. If she cut his face we'll be able to identify him that way.'

'Look for someone with scratched and bitten hands,' Smith advised.

Rees nodded sharply, annoyed. 'That's what I plan to do. Did the constable see this?' The doctor nodded with a knowing smile. 'What?' Rees said.

'One more thing,' Smith said, choosing not to answer Rees's query. This time he pulled the sheet down to the top of Leah's small budding breasts. 'Look at her shoulders. Do you see the bruises?'

Rees bent over the purple marks. He could clearly see handprints: the blotchy marks of four fingers on the tender flesh just above her armpits. At the tops of each bruise was the indent of a fingernail; Leah's attacker had held her down with great force.

'He overpowered her,' Smith said. Rees nodded. It would not take much strength to subdue a small girl like Leah.

'Then, when he was done . . .' Smith gestured to the circlet of bruises around the girl's neck. Rees stared at the large purple ovals, both thumbprints clearly defined on the slender white throat.

'They didn't look that bad yesterday,' he said to himself. 'Why are the marks so large?'

Smith looked at Rees. 'The villain who did this had unusually large hands. Look: the fingers met all the way around at the back of her neck,' he said scornfully.

'But why kill her?' Rees asked. 'He'd already had his way with her. What was the need?'

'That I don't know. Maybe he didn't want her to identify him,' Smith said.

'But that means she knew him,' Rees said. 'Or that she might see and recognize him.'

Smith nodded slowly. 'That follows. Not that murdering this poor child saved him.'

A second or two passed before Rees, who had focused all his attention upon the body, understood what Smith had just said. 'What do you mean?' he asked, turning to the coroner. 'Who is "him"?'

Now Smith grinned. 'Rouge arrested one of the circus performers after I showed him this.'

'One of the performers?' Rees asked. A terrible suspicion began to spread through him. 'Which one?'

'I don't know. A groom, I think. What does it matter? The point is the murder has been solved.'

Rees stared at the coroner. 'Solved?'

'Yes. Solved. So, you can climb back into that wagon of yours and go home.'

Rees barely heard the insulting tone in Smith's last comment. Instead he stared blindly at the sheet covering the body. Did he trust Rouge's investigative skills? No, he did not. Rouge always tended to settle on the easiest explanation, not necessarily the correct one. And he never asked enough questions.

Without a word Rees turned and left the surgery. He went to his wagon all right but he had no intention of going home. Smith's office was but two blocks from the tavern. Rees needed to speak to Rouge immediately.

'Come to congratulate me?' Rouge asked Rees, halting the movement of his rag on the counter before him. 'I bested you this time.'

'Dr Smith told me you arrested one of the circus performers.'

Rees wished Rouge did not view these tragedies as contests to be won or lost. 'Which one?'

'Groom. The Reynard boy saw him riding down the road.'

'Ah. He told me that too,' Rees said with a nod. 'But that doesn't mean the trick rider is guilty.' He paused. He had not asked the farmer's boy when he had seen the rider, a mistake he now regretted. 'And what time did the boy say it was when he saw the groom?' Rees asked.

Rouge shrugged. 'I don't know. I didn't ask. But it doesn't matter.'

'Yes, it does. Leah left Zion after the noon meal, between one and one thirty,' Rees said, leaning forward and speaking emphatically. 'At the earliest. She could not have reached Durham until two o'clock or after. I saw that groom preparing for the performance about four thirty. And the Shaker boy said he spent some time talking to that groom before that. So, yes, the timing does matter. It may make the difference between hanging an innocent man or a guilty one.'

'So Boudreaux – that's his name – rides one of the circus nags down the road and sees the girl. When he returns to the camp the kids are waiting. After a few minutes of chat the girl leaves. Boudreaux sends the boy out and jumps back on the horse. So he had plenty of time to work his will, at least an hour.'

'Did you at least question the groom?' Rees asked.

'Of course,' Rouge said. 'Not that it made any difference.'

'What did he say?'

'That he was innocent, of course.' Rouge smirked at Rees. 'But I'm confident we have our murderer.'

Rees stared at the constable for several seconds. 'I see,' he said at last. He wanted to shake the tavern keeper and shout at him. Didn't he realize how slipshod his investigation had been? 'I'll feel more comfortable if I speak to him myself,' Rees said.

Rouge grinned, revealing his stained teeth. 'Are you fluent in French? I am and Monsieur Boudreaux does not speak English.' He burst out laughing when Rees gaped at him in surprise. Although Rees had some French – most residents in the District of Maine did – he was by no means fluent.

'I daresay you are,' he said, really wishing he could wipe the constable's insolent smile off his face.

'My mother's tongue. And my father's.' Rouge grinned. 'This time I have the better of you.'

'I think I'd like to see Boudreaux anyway,' Rees said through clenched teeth. 'Where is he?'

'In jail. What do you think?' Rouge took his knife from his belt and used the point to delicately pick at his teeth. Rees looked away.

'I want to see him.'

'Nobody's stopping you. But you won't understand him.'

With Rouge's challenge ringing in his ears, Rees left the inn.

SEVEN

L ike most jails, this was a small brick structure with one barred window and a small screened opening in the door. With the spring warmth and the number of inmates who had vomited in the small area over the last few months, the smell penetrated every corner of this square. Rees put his shirttail over his nose as he approached.

Two people were already standing in front of the door: a stocky gentleman garbed in a riding costume and a girl dressed in a light-colored cotton frock with a modest ruffle at the hem. As the man passed food and a small jug of wine through the barred door to the inmate, he spoke rapidly in a mixture of English, French and some other language Rees did not recognize. Rees could not see the girl's face under the large straw hat but as he approached, she clutched at her companion's sleeve and they both turned. He immediately recognized them as circus folk. The fellow in riding garb was the man with the large mustaches. About Rees's age, he guessed. And the young woman was the ropedancer; Bambola. With those large, liquid, dark-brown eyes and fine black hair curling around her face, she was even more beautiful in person.

'I came to speak to the prisoner,' Rees said, gesturing at the jail door.

'Why?' asked the gentleman. 'What do you want with him?' His buff breeches, leather gloves and scarlet jacket were clearly made by an English tailor and his speech confirmed England as his country of origin. But the young woman? Now with an excuse to really look at her, Rees inspected her carefully. Her hat with its burden of artificial flowers and the curled dark hair all gave off a subtle foreign aura and her pale-pink, silk frock with its straight lines looked both fashionable and exotic.

'I–I want . . .' Realizing he was stammering, Rees stopped and took a breath. 'I'm not sure he's guilty.' As he spoke, the man inside the jail pressed his face against the bars and Rees recognized the trick rider who had so delighted him with his horsemanship the previous day.

'And who are you?' asked the older man. Rees glanced from him to the girl, wondering if they were family.

'I've assisted Mr Rouge previously in these types of . . . tragedies in the past,' Rees said, carefully selecting his words. 'He sometimes requests my help.' He doubted the constable would welcome him into this investigation but chose not to say so. 'My name is William Rees.'

'Mr John Asher. This is Miss Lucia Mazza,' Asher said with a slight bow in the woman's direction. She directed an almost flirtatious glance at Rees from under her long lashes.

'Why do you think Mr Boudreaux might be innocent?' the ringmaster asked.

'Well, I can't know he's innocent; at least, I don't know yet. But more investigation needs to be done before his innocence or guilt is determined. And the first step is speaking to him and hearing his story.' Mr Asher nodded slightly.

'Do you think you might free our poor Pip?' Miss Mazza leaned forward, her lips parted.

Rees, captivated by Bambola's accent, took a moment to reply. 'I was here yesterday, between four and four thirty, and Mr Boudreaux was in the ring. So, I know that for certain,' Rees said.

'That is so,' Mr Boudreaux said in heavily accented English. A speech defect thickened his words, slurring them together and making them hard to understand. 'I'm innocent.'

'Hmm. Your constable,' Mr Asher said to Rees, 'seems to feel Pip could have murdered the girl before he returned to the ring.'

'He does think that,' Rees agreed. 'That doesn't mean he is correct.' He felt the warmth of Bambola's smile as she nodded at him approvingly. 'I'm curious to know if Mr Boudreaux saw anyone while riding on the road. And what time was he there?'

Mr Asher looked at the sunburned face behind the bars and loosed a flood of words. Rees recognized the English words and some of the French. But although the third language Asher employed sounded similar to French, Rees did not understand a word. Still, as far as he could tell, his questions were being asked exactly. Mr Boudreaux replied in such a passionate and rapid speech that Rees could barely grasp the few English terms scattered among the rest. Boudreaux spoke for some time. Mr Asher responded, speaking just as passionately at certain points and finally turned to Rees.

'Pip – ah – Monsieur Boudreaux says he only rode along that road once, out to the junction with the Surry Road and then back. He left the circus camp after one. It took him maybe forty-five minutes each way.'

'He's sure about the time?' Rees asked. If that was accurate Boudreaux could have seen Shem and Leah. Another rapid dialogue followed and then Asher turned back to Rees.

'Yes, he is sure. There were some carriages on the road as well as some people on horseback. Not many. That's why he allowed his mare her head.'

'There would have been a boy and a girl,' Rees said. 'Walking, probably on the lane. Mr Boudreaux might have seen them across the fields.' He made a note to ask Shem which way he and Leah had walked into Durham. He thought the Shakers would most likely choose the lane instead of the main road; it was both closer and not heavily traveled by vehicles, but just because he thought so did not mean the children had taken that route.

'*Oui, oui,*' Boudreaux said. '*Une jeune fille.*' Another spate of rapid French followed.

'Yes, one was a young girl,' Asher translated. 'And a boy was with her, the same one who talked to Pip about the circus horses. They were almost into town by then. And there was an older man following.' All of Rees's attention focused upon that statement in an instant.

'An older man? A laborer?' Rees asked. Asher put the question to Boudreaux.

'*Non.* He wore stout boots. Good clothes.'

Rees considered the geography of the lane. Except for Zion, and the farm across the lane from the Reynard property, there was no location nearby from which a man could walk. Could the man who had followed Leah been a Shaker Brother? 'Did he wear dark trousers and a flat-brimmed, straw hat with a black ribbon?' Rees asked. Boudreaux's head began bobbing up and down with vehemence.

'White shirt also.'

Rees turned his eyes up and stared blindly at the blue sky for a long moment. Without knowing the identity of the old man he couldn't be sure he was a Shaker but his nerves began twitching with an almost supernatural faith it was so. Did the Elders know of this other Brother's journey into Durham? Rees would bet his life they did not. What was more, he could clearly imagine how easily this unidentified older man could have overtaken Leah and soothed away her fears.

Returning his gaze to the man behind the grille, Rees asked in his poor French, 'Did you tell Monsieur Rouge?'

'*Non, non,*' said Boudreaux. 'He didn't ask.'

Of course he didn't, Rees thought.

'So, Mr Rees, what do you think?' asked Mr Asher. 'We know our Pip could never harm anyone. But you are not as familiar with him as we are.'

Wishing to hear Miss Mazza's deliciously accented voice again, Rees turned to her and asked, 'Have you known Monsieur Boudreaux long?'

'Many years,' she replied with a smile. 'I know he is not the cleverest of men but he is a kind one. Why, an injury to one of the circus horses brings tears to his eyes.'

Rees nodded although he did not find that a compelling argument. He'd known men who would treat their dogs with gentleness and beat their wives and children bloody. But he smiled at her and said, 'That is certainly one reason to defend Monsieur Boudreaux.'

'Why do you care who was on the road?' Asher asked, drawing Rees's attention away from the ropedancer.

'That older gentleman he described may have seen something,' Rees replied. Or worse. 'I'd like to question him as well as Monsieur Boudreaux. But that means I must find him first.'

'I see.' Asher threw a glance at the prisoner. 'Will Pip be free by tomorrow?'

'I don't know,' Rees said. 'But probably not.'

'By the next day then?' Asher's forehead furrowed. 'We are due in another town.'

Rees recalled the poster with its list of crossed-off village names. 'Perhaps,' he said doubtfully. 'I shall do my utmost. Let me discuss it with the constable.' As he turned Asher caught at Rees's arm.

'Wait, Mr Rees. Have you seen the performance?'

'No. Not yet. Just a little bit of Mr Boudreaux exercising his horse.'

'Please come. We are scheduled for a show tonight and, if Pip is not freed, tomorrow night as well. I will arrange for you to be let in without paying so much as a tray saulty.'

'He means three pence,' Bambola put in with a smile, seeing Rees's expression. 'It's circus talk.'

'Thank you,' Rees said in surprise.

Asher smiled, his lip curling up with a hint of bitterness. 'You must understand how grateful we are that you do not immediately assume one of our number is guilty, simply because he is circus folk. I am a good judge of character and I see you will pursue the investigation until you have found the right man.' He did not point to Rouge as an example of someone unwilling to look beyond the travelers but his meaning was clear. 'That is all I ask; that you do that. I am confident Pip will be cleared. We have no money to offer you, but we can share our show. I hope you will attend.'

Rees inclined his head, embarrassed by the praise but touched as well. 'I will. Thank you.'

EIGHT

With Rouge now in the forefront of his mind, Rees walked the short distance from the jail to the tavern so deep in thought he was barely aware of his surroundings. He was having second thoughts about the advisability of confiding all he'd learned to the constable. Although he knew he should tell Rouge that Boudreaux had seen not only the children but also an older man following them, Rees was afraid of Rouge's reactions. Either he would point to Leah and say 'of course Boudreaux attacked her; they were in the same area at the same time' or he would mount a hunt through Zion for the Shaker Brother Boudreaux had spotted.

And no doubt the constable would pull in the first old man he saw and claim the murder successfully solved.

'Rees. Will Rees.' Brother Daniel's familiar voice penetrated Rees's thoughts. When he looked around he saw both Daniel and Aaron approaching. 'Your wife said you were here,' Daniel said. Rees stopped walking and waited for the two men to approach. 'Rouge told us the murder has been solved and the guilty party arrested.'

'*Someone* has been arrested,' Rees said, involuntarily recalling Boudreaux's description of the man following Leah. Could it be one of these men? Not Daniel. Despite his graying hair he could not be mistaken for an old man. Aaron? He was older. Rees turned to look at him. Although he was within a few years of Rees's age, Aaron's hair was streaked with gray and his lined face made him seem much older still. 'Is that why you're here?' Rees asked. 'To see who was arrested?'

'We came to fetch Sister Leah from the coroner,' Aaron said.

'And we came looking for you,' Daniel added. 'The Elders wish to speak with you.'

For a moment Rees wondered if they knew one of their members had followed Leah and Shem into town but dismissed it. He had only just learned that himself.

'Why?'

'They want to ask if you'll look into this . . . this tragedy,' Daniel said.

'We are familiar with Constable Rouge's methods,' Aaron added, smiling sourly when Rees inclined his head in agreement.

'If, by some chance, his first suspect is freed, Rouge will cast around for another,' Daniel said. 'We fear he will look to Zion. Leah belonged to our community so Rouge will not hesitate to blame one of us.'

Rees nodded involuntarily. Although he wished he could argue the point, he knew better. This community was, because of its many differences, frequently suspect and occasionally persecuted. In this case, however, he planned to do exactly as Rouge would and look for Leah's murderer among them.

'One of your community might be guilty,' Rees pointed out.

'Surely none of our number—' Daniel began.

Aaron turned a look of disbelief upon his fellow Shaker and

interrupted. 'Even among the godly the wicked are with us,' Aaron said. 'Just last year we witnessed the evidence of that.'

'Yes, I remember,' Daniel said. In a non-Shaker his abruptness would have signified anger. Rees was not sure that was true of Daniel but Aaron took it as such. He frowned at his Brother and backed away, putting several feet of distance between them.

'Of course, I'll look into this,' Rees said. He'd planned to do so in any case. 'I'll stop over on my way home, if that is acceptable. I wanted to examine the body again anyway before Leah is put to rest.'

'We will stow her in the icehouse until Esther . . .' Daniel stopped, swallowing hard. 'We won't send her home to Mother Ann until tomorrow.'

Rees nodded, his throat closing up. He pitied Daniel. A young man, and sheltered, he was struggling to make sense of the murder. Rees, whose daughter Jerusha was but a year or two shy of Leah's age, could only function by walling off his horror and grief. The barrier did not always hold.

'Very well,' he said, the trembling in his voice betraying his emotion. He inhaled and held his breath for a few seconds until he was sure he could speak in a steady voice. 'I'll see you in Zion shortly.'

The three men walked back to the tavern and Rees watched the Shakers climb into their cart and drive toward Dr Smith's house. He almost – almost – walked back to his own wagon. Why should he tell Rouge anything? As usual the constable had rushed to judgment without a thorough examination of all the facts. But ultimately Rees couldn't keep this secret, not from the only officer of the law in this town. He went up the steps and into the tavern.

He could not predict the effect of the new information – the man following Leah into town – upon the constable. He guessed that Rouge would either hurry to the jail to question Boudreaux himself or hare off to Zion to harass the Brothers. He did neither. Instead, when Rees finished speaking, Rouge burst into a loud guffaw. 'You are determined to solve another murder and show me up as the fool,' he said. 'This time I caught the murderer without your help.'

'Aren't you even going to speak to Boudreaux again?' Rees asked in surprised dismay.

'Why? Why would I trust him? He didn't tell me about the man,' Rouge said.

'Maybe you should at least verify the story by asking the Reynard boy—' Rees began.

Rouge cut him off. 'I don't have to do anything. I have the murderer in my jail.'

Rees looked at Rouge, and at the few men in the tavern who had been openly listening. All of them were grinning.

'A damn circus groom,' said one of them as he spat on the floor.

'And a Frenchman to boot,' added another. 'You can't trust a Frenchman.'

Rees darted a glance at Rouge, also a Frenchman, but although he grimaced he did not speak. 'I see,' said Rees. He understood: Boudreaux was an outsider on two counts and a circus performer besides. Hanging him for the crime made a quick and tidy ending. As a traveler himself, Rees had been accused of crimes more times than he could count, simply from the accident of being in the wrong place at the wrong time. Even in Dugard, the town where he'd grown up, he'd been a target. Although he thought it was possible and maybe even likely that Boudreaux was the killer, all of his sympathy went to the groom now that he'd been assigned the blame. 'Very well,' he said to Rouge, 'I won't trouble you any further.' He spun on his heel and stalked to the door.

'And don't meddle,' Rouge shouted after him. 'This investigation is over.'

Rees did not acknowledge the command. Of course, he would not stay out of this. Although this rapid solution absolved Rouge from any further inquiry, Rees feared that an innocent man might be rushed to the gallows and a guilty man go free.

The drive to Zion did little to calm Rees's fury. When he finally pulled up in front of the stable, he sat for a moment in the seat trying to settle.

'Are you all right?' Brother Daniel asked as he crossed the street. Taking a deep breath, Rees turned with a nod. Daniel eyed him doubtfully but said only, 'I'll take care of your horse. Once you inspect Leah's earthly shell you will meet with the Elders.'

'Very well,' Rees said. After living here last year, and visiting many times before that, he was familiar with the office at the top of the stairs.

'You know where the icehouse is,' Daniel continued, taking hold of Hannibal's bridle. 'I–I can't accompany you. I just can't.' He shook his head, keeping his face averted from Rees.

'I understand,' he said. He didn't want to see the body either. But he had to; he did not want to chance missing something.

He walked to the southern end of the village and crossed the bridge over the stream. As he entered the copse of fir trees that shaded the springhouse all summer, he realized he could not smell the laundry. Of course, the Sisters would not be washing the body linens today; it was Friday. Rees guessed the Sisters were still in the laundry house, however, engaged in other tasks connected with that laborious chore.

He paused outside the springhouse for a few seconds, steeling himself for what he was about to see. Someone had vomited in the grass outside. If Rees had to guess he would bet on Daniel as the culprit. He opened the weathered, wooden door, propped it open with a stone, and went inside.

It was very cold. The movement of the stream underneath and the sawdust-coated ice blocks ensured a low temperature. Rees began to shiver. He felt almost as if he were in a dream, so similar was this to his first visit to Zion. That time too he had spent some time in this building examining the body of a young Shaker Sister.

Rees hesitated by the door. The warm sunshine outside beckoned him and for a few seconds he considered leaving the icehouse. Who would know? He would. And he would think less of himself for abandoning this unpleasant task.

He approached the body. First, he removed the cape all Shaker Sisters wore around their shoulders. Then he spent several frustrating minutes struggling with the buttons down the back of the dress – how did women manage with so many buttons! – before wrestling the bodice down to the tops of her breasts.

Although he had examined the bruises by candlelight in Dr Smith's dead room, the livid marks looked different in the daylight streaming through the open door. Longer, more oval. Huh, Rees thought. Why do they look like that? As he had noticed previously, the marks near Leah's armpits were edged with tiny half-moon cuts. Rees hoisted the body to a sitting position and examined the tiny gashes. The murderer had held Leah down with such force his nails had drawn blood.

There were more bruises on her shoulders. Rees inspected them too. These round contusions looked like blotchy palm prints. When he shifted her forward and looked at her back he found some slight bruising at the top, by the shoulders. Leah must have fought back; the murderer had been forced to change his position. Until he had strangled the girl, Rees thought, staring at the round discolorations. The well-defined bruises left by the thumbs looked as big as plums. He needed to look for a man with unusually large hands and long nails.

Because he had felt uncomfortable examining Leah's backside while under Dr Smith's scrutiny, Rees had not done so. But he turned the body over now and lifted her skirt. Although he expected to see scrapes and cuts on her back and buttocks, he did not. Instead he saw red marks that looked more like burns.

The sound of a footfall outside and the clank of a bucket caught his attention. He turned. Esther stood just outside and was peering through the door. She had maintained the toughness required to flee Georgia and walk all the way to Maine, so she was usually the Sister who dealt with the less savory aspects of living. Rees and Lydia had found her a reliable ally and ultimately, albeit surprisingly, a good friend.

'Come and look at this,' Rees said. 'Tell me what you think these marks are from.'

She came inside. When she saw Leah's body with the skirts raised she cast Rees a startled glance. But then, as she bent over the red scrapes, she concentrated.

'I thought she would have bruises and other injuries consistent with being thrown from a horse,' Rees said. 'But these look more like—'

'Burns,' Esther said. 'I think these are from fabric. Like a rug.' She raised her head and met Rees's gaze. 'She was inside when she was violated.'

'So, someone took her home, violated her and then dumped her in the field?' Rees asked, his voice rising in surprise.

'Or something like that,' Esther said.

'But how would he have had the time?' Rees wondered, mystified. Except for Reynard's farm there were no houses on the main road. Could Leah have been violated in town? But he could not see how there would have been time. And her murderer would have had to put her body in a wagon and bring her to the field. Rees would have to ask the Reynard boy if he had seen a suspicious wagon leaving town.

His thoughts then returned to the circus and its vehicles. 'But all of them are clearly marked with a gold horse,' he muttered.

'Have you seen everything you needed to see?' Esther asked him, breaking into his thoughts.

'I think so,' he said. 'More questions than answers though.'

'Well, go along then. I'll prepare this poor little chick so she can go home to Mother.' She began rearranging Leah's skirts.

Rees stepped outside into the warmth of spring. Only then did he allow the tension and the focus that allowed him to examine a body to drain away. He began shivering and gulping in the fresh pine-scented air.

NINE

Daniel was waiting for Rees outside the stable. Unaccustomed to idleness, he shuffled his feet and looked around impatiently. But his nervous movements ceased when he saw Rees approaching. 'Let's go to the office,' he said, gesturing to the Dwelling House across the street. Rees thought the Shaker Brother still looked pale and the dark shadows under his eyes betrayed his sleepless night.

Daniel did not speak as he preceded Rees upstairs to the office. Elder Jonathan was already inside and, when he saw the two men appear at the door he pushed the ledger aside and stood up. He was a rigid and rule-bound man and so he and Rees frequently butted heads.

As Jonathan took the first chair down from its peg, Daniel said, 'I'll fetch the Sisters.' The sound of his feet clattering down the stair echoed loudly into the office. Frowning, Jonathan shook his head in exasperation.

'Daniel is young,' Rees said, lifting two additional chairs from their pegs. As he lined them up opposite those Jonathan had placed on the floor – men and women sat on opposite sides, although far enough apart so that there could be no accidental touching – he wondered why he felt the need to defend the young man.

Without replying, Jonathan added another chair to each end of the rows. Then Rees and Jonathan took seats on the men's side and waited for the others to arrive.

Daniel returned with Sister Agatha, the older of the two Eldresses. 'I couldn't find Sister Esther,' he said.

'She may still be at the icehouse,' Rees said. 'I saw her there, preparing Leah's body for burial.' He stumbled over the final word. He did not want to think of that child's body disappearing into the earth.

After a moment of silence, Jonathan said, 'Of course. She will be here directly. And Leah is the reason we wished to speak with you, Rees. We have need of your special talents.'

'I'll be glad to help in any way I can,' he said.

'When you first visited us,' Jonathan said in his slow precise way, 'you were able to discover the murderer of one of our Sisters. Since then . . .' His voice trailed away.

Rees wondered if Jonathan was recalling the other murders that had occurred here in this community. Although Rees had successfully identified the culprits every time, the resolutions had not always been to everyone's liking.

He thought back to his first visit here more than two years ago. Although he'd seen some of the members of this community as individuals, he'd been naïve enough then to believe they were alike in their beliefs and usually in total agreement. Since he'd lived among them, however, he was aware of the subtle signs of disagreement. Now, for example, Sister Agatha's lips were pursed as though she'd been sucking on a lemon. Rees guessed she did not concur with the current course of action. She probably had not ever consented to his presence here and if pressed would argue that he had been mistaken in the past when he'd identified the murderers.

'Now another of our number has met a violent end,' Jonathan continued. 'This time the victim is a child. Will you look into the death?'

'I will,' Rees said quickly. He had intended to do so anyway. Zion had done so much for his family – from the time David had fled here as a boy to the most recent past when Rees had brought his family to this refuge – that he could refuse them nothing.

At that moment, he heard someone hurrying up the stairs. When he turned he saw Esther. Although her eyes were red and puffy she forced a smile when she saw him looking at her.

'Our concern, of course, is justice,' Jonathan continued when the sister was settled. 'But we are most anxious that none of our number be accused.'

'None of our Family would ever commit such a heinous crime,' Agatha said. 'No matter who might think so.' And she shot Rees a look before dropping her eyes to the hands folded in her lap. He bit back the retort that sprang to his lips.

'Although we want to ensure none of us are unfairly accused,' Esther said, emphasizing the word 'unfairly', 'we must also assist the search for the villain who treated Leah so cruelly. Her mother assigned Leah to our care. We broke our promise to her. And we failed Leah. It is our responsibility to make this right.' She looked around at her fellow Elders.

'Of course, that is so,' Jonathan muttered.

'Do you suspect anyone?' Daniel asked Rees.

'The constable has already settled upon one of the circus performers,' he replied.

'Well then,' Agatha said, 'this incident is for the World to handle.'

'I'm not entirely convinced of the man's guilt,' Rees said.

'If the murdering villain is one of us, don't you want to know it?' Esther asked, speaking into the silence. 'Do we wish to protect a wolf who is stalking our flock?'

'Do you think the murderer is one of us?' Agatha asked Rees, staring at him in dislike.

Put on the spot, now Rees considered the question seriously. 'No, I don't,' he conceded. 'But it's possible.'

The Elders glanced from one to another, some unspoken communication passing among them.

'Very well,' Brother Jonathan said at last. 'Please undertake this commission for us. Now we have only the question of payment to discuss.'

'Payment?' Rees said in surprise.

'This will be taking you from your farm chores,' Jonathan said.

Rees saw the slight twitch of Agatha's face and recognized it as contempt. Still, Rees thought, Jonathan was correct: searching for a murderer would take Rees away from the necessary work that would feed his family. These people did not have to know how happy he was at that prospect. 'I owe you far too much to take money from you,' he said. 'I was promised some help plowing and seeding my fields. Is that still possible?' If he could prevail upon his son David to lend a week as well – that might be enough help.

'You already have the child Annie helping over there—' Agatha began.

Esther put a hand upon her Sister's and she instantly stopped talking.

Jonathan and Daniel exchanged a glance. Although Rees could not read Jonathan's face he thought Daniel was relieved. After several seconds of silence Jonathan nodded.

'We will be happy to do so. We don't want to see your family starve.'

'Thank you,' Rees said.

'And keep me informed. I don't want the constable arriving to arrest one of my Brothers without warning,' Jonathan added sternly. Rees simply nodded.

The four Shakers rose as one now that the business was concluded. While the Sisters made their way to the Women's stairs, Jonathan and Daniel accompanied Rees down the Brother's steps. Rees heard Esther say to Agatha, 'He is of the World, Sister. It is better he investigate this wickedness than one of us.'

Rees wondered if he should feel insulted.

When he stepped out of the Dwelling House he found the street thronged with members of the community making their way to the big white Meeting House. Of course, he thought, it was time for prayers. The noon dinner would be served immediately after. He could smell cooking meat, lamb, he thought.

He realized he was hungry too and Lydia would be waiting for him. He crossed the road to the stable. One of the Brothers had fed and brushed down Hannibal and placed Rees's wagon tidily to one side. He hitched the gelding between the traces and climbed into the wagon seat knowing there would be no moving until the crowd of people in the street reached the Meeting House. Idle, his thoughts jumped around like a cricket on a hot pan. He couldn't erase the image of Leah's body from his mind. Dumped in the buckwheat field like garbage, her young life snuffed out before she even had time to live. He shuddered and closed his eyes.

But mixed in with that horrible scene was the memory of Bambola smiling up at him in the jail. Her clear, pale skin against those dark eyes and hair and those dimples! This time when he shivered it was for an entirely different reason.

Suddenly realizing all was quiet, he turned to look at the street. It was empty. He could hear the strains of the first hymn emanating from the Meeting House. He backed away from the barns and drove up the dirt road, heading north to home. As Hannibal trotted onto the Surry Road, Rees experienced an involuntary lift of his heart at the prospect of going home to his family.

TEN

Humming as she set the table Jerusha uttered a squeak of protest when Rees embraced her. He had come straight inside, and seeing his oldest daughter engaged in her domestic chores had inspired in him a surge of protectiveness. 'I'm busy,' she said, pushing him away.

'Did you speak with the constable?' Lydia asked, smiling at him.

'I did although he is going to be no help at all. He's convinced the circus rider . . .' Rees stopped, glanced at Jerusha, and then continued again after a second's pause. 'Rouge thinks he's solved the case already. Then I went to Zion—'

The crack of shattering crockery interrupted him. When he looked over Annie was staring down at one of Lydia's treasured teacups broken on the floor. 'I'm sorry,' she said. 'I'm sorry. It just slipped from my hand.'

Sister Agatha's sharp comment flashed into Rees's mind. Now that he thought of it, he realized that he had seen Annie here quite often lately. Rescued from a brothel in Salem, she had been living with the Shakers for the past two years. He guessed she did not care for the Shaker lifestyle. But then she'd always said she was waiting for the boy she knew in Salem to return from the sea. His letters arrived only sporadically and Rees thought Annie's dream would never come to pass.

'Won't the Sisters be looking for you?' he asked the girl now.

'Maybe,' she said. 'But I had permission to help Miss Lydia for a few hours . . .'

Rees looked at her, really looked at her. He did not think William would recognize her. No longer the scrawny malnourished girl she'd been, Annie had grown almost as tall as Lydia. And she was heavier, with rosy round cheeks. But dark circles framed her eyes and she'd bitten her nails bloody. 'Did you know Leah?' Rees asked gently.

She nodded. 'She was like me, you know. Not quite an orphan. And not one of the Family either.'

Rees threw a quick glance at Lydia. She did not look surprised and Rees had the sense some conversations had gone on without him knowing. 'Tell me about Leah,' Rees began but Lydia put a hand on his arm to halt the flow of words. When he looked at her in surprise she jerked her head at Jerusha, leaning forward and listening for all she was worth. Rees covered his sudden grunt with a cough and said instead, 'Don't you like living with the Shakers?'

Annie bit her lip. Finally, as the silence stretched on and on, she said, 'I don't dislike it.'

'But what?'

'It's just that I'll never make a Shaker.' Now she looked up at Rees, meeting his eyes with directness. 'I know that. I want to get married, have my own family.' Sharon let out a wail, almost as though she'd been listening, and smacked Joseph with his wooden horse. Annie began to move toward them but Lydia shook her head.

Breathing out an exasperated sigh, she separated the children. 'After dinner, naps for both of you,' she said to her two youngest.

'I'm a big boy,' Joseph said. 'I'm too old for naps.'

'We'll see,' Lydia said.

'I'd like to ask you a few questions about Leah,' Rees said to Annie under the cover of the wailing from the children.

'I don't know anything.' Tears filled her eyes and began spilling down her cheeks. 'She didn't tell me she was going to town. I should have been with her.'

'You couldn't have done anything,' Rees said, sharper than he intended. All he could imagine just then was Annie, lying dead in the field beside Leah.

'But I would have liked seeing the circus too,' she said wistfully. 'When I was in Salem I saw the strange beast brought from the Orient – the elephant. I was just a little girl then.'

'Only men are permitted to attend the circus,' Rees said, trying to speak softly. Although Annie did not seem aware of the danger she'd avoided, he saw it only too clearly. 'Did Leah have any other friends in Zion?'

'We are not supposed to have friends,' Annie said. 'That was why she . . .' she stopped and started again. 'She liked Shem and was always being scolded for slipping away to speak with him.'

Rees nodded slowly.

'Enough talk about such a disturbing topic,' Lydia said. 'It's time for dinner and civilized conversation.'

After the noon meal was finished, Lydia sent Jerusha and Annie upstairs to put the younger children in for their naps. Then, as she began picking up the dirty plates and carrying them to the sink, she said, 'Did Brother Daniel find you? He came here looking for you.'

'He did,' Rees said. 'And I went to Zion. The Elders want me to look into Leah's murder.'

'As if they could stop you,' Lydia said with a smile.

Rees grinned. 'I know. And they promised to help with the planting.' He saw some of the tension in her shoulders drain away and knew she'd been worrying about the farming chores. 'I also thought I'd ask David to visit,' he added. 'I'd like to see him anyway.'

'Good.' Lydia turned, the dishtowel in her hands. 'I know you prefer to weave and identify murderers than plow.'

'But my family needs to eat,' Rees finished the thought, speaking more sharply than he intended. He would dutifully do his farming chores but he didn't have to like it.

Lydia bit her lip and Rees felt a spasm of shame. But he did not apologize and several seconds passed in an awkward silence. When she spoke again it was about the murder.

'You began telling me about the man Constable Rouge thinks is guilty?'

'Yes.' Rees was relieved by the change in topic. 'Rouge arrested one of the circus performers; the trick rider I told you about.'

'Do *you* think he's guilty?' Lydia took a dishtowel, one of Rees's weaving failures, and put it on the counter next to the dishpan.

'I don't know. Maybe.' He thought back to the man peering through the bars. 'Maybe not. He told me he saw a man, one of the Shakers, following Leah and Shem.'

'I hate to think the murderer could be one of the family,' she murmured. One of her Shaker Family she meant. 'Maybe the Brother was just going into town and happened to be on the road at the same time.'

'Maybe but unlikely. The Shakers don't leave their community.' He stared at Lydia until she sighed and nodded. 'And I got the sense Boudreaux thought the man was following the kids. I'll ask him though. And I'll speak to the Reynard boy again. He saw Boudreaux. He would have noticed the Shaker as well.'

'What about Shem?' Lydia asked the question reluctantly. 'Could he be the murderer? He was with Leah.'

Rees pictured Shem. A lanky boy with a shock of dark hair, he was several inches taller than Leah. But he was also very skinny. And it looked as though he had grown several inches recently; the sleeves of his shirt did not quite reach his wrists. 'I'm not sure he would be strong enough,' Rees said. 'Besides, her body was positioned as though she were thrown from a height.'

'As though from horseback?' Lydia asked.

'Exactly,' Rees said with a nod, 'I thought so at first, anyway, but now I'm not so sure. There were some odd scrapes on her back.' He paused, recalling those burn-like injuries. 'I'll question Shem again. I think he has more to tell me. He was close-lipped when I spoke to him before.'

'He is probably afraid he would be scolded by the Brothers,' Lydia said.

'Yes,' Rees agreed. Wiping his mouth on his napkin he stood up. 'I want to spend a few hours weaving and then I'm going back into town.'

'Back into town?' Lydia's voice lifted in surprise.

'To see the circus. Mr Asher invited me. I'll stop at the Reynard farm on the way.' He stopped speaking as Lydia's body had stiffened into that stillness he recognized as disapproval.

'It's Friday night,' she said. 'Many of the farmers will be driving into town.'

'Yes, it will be a rowdy evening,' Rees agreed. 'But I want to question Mr Asher and some of the other performers as well after the performance.'

'I wish I could join you,' Lydia said softly. Now Rees knew it was not disapproval Lydia felt but envy.

'I know,' he said, crossing the kitchen to drop a kiss on her forehead. 'But you would not be permitted entry anyway.' Eyes downcast, she nodded. 'Perhaps you can accompany me when I return to Zion to speak to Shem,' Rees suggested. Lydia sighed and said nothing. Rees knew his offer was a poor one, especially when compared to a circus, but it was all he could think of to propose.

Leaving her to finish cleaning the kitchen, Rees went upstairs to the weaving room. The sun poured through the southern facing window in a hot bright flood and, despite the cool breeze outside, the room was warm. He peered at the cloth on the beam. He thought he'd made a few mistakes but, with the varying thicknesses of the yarns, he couldn't be sure. He prepared a few more bobbins and then he sat down to weave.

The sounds of the children giggling in the other room faded from his consciousness. Gradually the emotions connected with Leah's murder – the horror and the grief – began to ease. He was able to visualize the body without wanting to turn his eyes aside. As he recalled the bruises around her neck, especially the thumbprint, he pondered the murderer's hands. Who among the men he'd met had such large hands and long nails? He would make a point of looking at everyone's hands when he attended the circus this evening.

It wasn't much but it was something to go on.

Why was her body dumped in the buckwheat field? Anyone on the road or walking down the lane could have seen the murderer throwing her body in the field. It was not a clever hiding place. Even in the worst case her body would have been discovered within a week or two. At the most. Why hadn't the murderer deposited the body in the strip of forest running along the other side before the turn-off to North Road? He would have been less noticeable. It could have taken weeks – maybe months – before her body was discovered and by then the circus would have left town.

A sudden wail from the room next door levitated him from the bench and the shuttle flew from his hand. Sharon was awake. Rees looked at the window. The flood of midday sun had diminished to low, honey-colored rays. He'd lost track of time and now it was mid-afternoon. As Lydia's footsteps hurried up the stairs, Rees picked up his shuttle and put it on the finished cloth. Another few sessions would complete this commission and he was glad. He would use his free time to look into the murder.

He joined Lydia as she carried Sharon into the hall. He smiled at them and took Sharon from his wife. They walked down the stairs in a companionable silence. Annie was still in the kitchen. Weren't they expecting her in Zion? As she took Sharon from him and expertly tied a napkin around the child's neck, Rees looked at Lydia and raised his brows in surprise. 'With Jerusha in school,' she murmured, 'I can use the help.' Rees wondered what Sister Agatha would say about that.

'I'm leaving later than I intended,' he said, experiencing a sudden spasm of guilt. 'I won't have time to milk Daisy . . .' His voice trailed off. He wouldn't blame Lydia for reacting with annoyance. But she nodded without apparent anger.

'I'll take care of the cow,' she said. 'You'd best be on your way.' Glad to see she'd recovered from her pique, and relieved as well, Rees grinned at her. 'But I want to accompany you when you go to Zion,' Lydia said with mock sternness. 'You won't leave me home tomorrow.'

'I look forward to your company,' he said. 'We'll catch Shem right after he comes out of breakfast. Otherwise, no telling where he'll disappear to.' He paused for a few seconds. 'I think I'll stop at the Reynard farm and speak to the Reynard boy today, before I go into town. I want to confirm Boudreaux's story before I begin questioning the Shaker Brothers.'

'That's wise,' Lydia said. They both knew that although Zion's Elders had asked Rees to look into the murder, they would resist him if he even implied one of their fellows was the murderer.

ELEVEN

By the time Rees approached the Reynard farm it was going on three thirty. As he'd hoped, the Reynard boy was in the buckwheat field, a gunnysack looped across his chest. He walked up and down the rows, scattering seed. And when Rees stared across the other fields, he saw the entire family out. He sighed. Lydia was correct; he had fields of his own to plant. Sowing seed was not the farm task Rees hated the most but he didn't love it either. Not for the first time, he wished his son David was here. He would have organized everything and been well on his way to finishing the planting. Rees sighed again. He missed his son. The child he had left behind when he escaped to the roads on his many weaving trips had grown into a man. With most of the quarrels between them smoothed over, David had become not just Rees's son but his friend as well. Would he be willing to come for a visit? And help? Since the Maine interior was colder than the farms closer to the coast, he might have only just started working on his own farm and have some time.

Pushing away his longing and regret, Rees pulled over to the fence. 'Boy,' he shouted, climbing down from the seat. 'Boy Reynard.' What was the lad's name? He looked up in surprise. 'Remember me? I met you last night.' The boy approached the fence.

'I remember. What do you want?'

'What's your name, son?'

'Paul.'

'All right, Paul. I want to ask you a few more questions.'

'What do you want to know?' he asked. He leaned his lightly tanned arms on the topmost rail of the fence, seeming quite willing to talk as long as Rees wished.

'Was this the field you were in?' Rees asked, looking around. Additional rows had been freshly plowed and the scent of damp earth perfumed the air. 'When you saw the horseman?' The boy nodded again. 'What time was that?'

'Just after noon dinner,' Paul replied promptly. 'Two o'clock maybe.'

'And when did you see the boy and girl?' Rees asked.

'Same time,' Paul said. 'I was here.'

'Did you see an older man on the lane, maybe following the children?'

'I seen him,' said the boy. 'He had gray hair. And I could see his clothes real well.' He looked at Rees with bright, clever eyes, adding, 'He was one of them from Zion for sure.'

So, Boudreaux had told the truth, Rees thought. And we are back to the man.

'Did you see anything else?' Rees asked. 'Anyone else besides the boy and girl and the old man? Anyone from the circus perhaps?'

The boy ruminated in silence for a few seconds. 'Well, traffic picked up some later,' he said finally. 'Lots of men on horseback; people going in to see the circus. I recognized most of them. And no one was walking.'

'Anything unusual?' Rees asked.

'I saw some carriages coming off Surry Road,' the boy said. 'Nob's carriages. Both brown with red wheels.'

'And when was that?' Rees asked.

'After I'd been working in the field a little bit. The lady who come down the lane waved to me.'

'Was that before or after you saw the Shaker Brother?'

'After. Long after. Late afternoon, I think. Fourish. Maybe towards supper time.'

'You're sure?'

'Positive. It was right after my mother come out to the fence with a pail of water.'

Rees couldn't see how that carriage could be important. 'And the other one?'

'You won't be interested in that one,' Paul said, flapping his hand dismissively.

'Why not?' Now Rees was interested.

'That one belongs to the magistrate. Magistrate Hanson, that is.'

'I see.' Rees said, feeling surprise ripple through him. 'And was that near supper time too?'

'Yes. I saw the magistrate's carriage after the other one. Maybe it was closer to five than four?' Paul Reynard glanced involuntarily at the sky. 'He was going into town for the circus.'

'Thanks.' Rees spoke automatically. Although he knew Hanson had attended the circus, he was startled to realize the magistrate had been near the field where Leah's body had been dumped and at the right time too. 'Did either of the carriages stop?'

Paul shook his head. 'Didn't even slow down,' he replied.

Another dead end. 'Were there any wagons going out of town?'

The boy promptly shook his head. 'Not much traffic going out. All the farmers were driving in.'

Rees stared at the sky, thinking. A flock of geese flew north, honking as they passed overhead. 'And you watched the circus trick rider,' he said at last. 'He did not stop as he rode up and down the road?'

Paul shook his head. 'Not once.'

'Thank you,' Rees said. 'You've been a great help.' The boy's cheeks went pink and he grinned.

Rees turned back to his wagon. He could not understand how the murderer could have thrown Leah into the field with no one seeing him.

By the time Rees pulled up next to the circus wagons he figured he had less than an hour before the performance began. This time he did not walk around the front gate but pulled up next to the circus vehicles. They were drawn together and enclosed a small yard dotted with canvas tents. Rees paused to admire the insignias on the doors. The rearing horses on the fancier carriages were of sculpted metal or beautifully carved wood, both shining with peeling gilt. The painted horses on the plainer, shabbier wagons were not so carefully done but then these conveyances, although roofed and with windows, were not as elegant as the others either. Rees guessed that the more elaborate the insignia, the more important the performer.

Leaving the wagons behind, he entered a world of strange oddities. The same dwarf he'd seen the day before, recognizable because of the small, white dog and the pig, was crossing the yard. He wore his costume of short, white breeches decorated with colorful dots, bright red stockings and crimson jacket. His hair, combed into a brush of bristles, was dyed the same red as his jacket. Garish paint – carmine lips and red triangles over his eyes – was daubed on his whitened face.

Both animals wore costumes as well. A pink ruff encircled the dog's white neck. And the pig! He wore a black shirt and a white wig. Rees couldn't help but stare. When the clown caught Rees's look, he winked. With a stick, he tapped the pig's trotters. Obediently the animal rose to his feet and began mincing forward. The black shirt was revealed as a robe and in the wig lent the pig an astonishing resemblance to Magistrate Piggy Hanson. Rees burst out laughing. The dwarf grinned. Rees guessed that these circus folk disliked the magistrate as much as he did.

As a groom led two horses toward the entrance to the ring, two young women in identical short, red costumes followed, laughing and chatting. Their skirts ended at the knees and Rees had a clear view of shapely calves, covered only by thick white stockings. No one else seemed at all surprised by the equestriennes' shockingly short skirts. The clown, glancing at these women, scurried after them. He called for Jeanne but they did not slow down.

To his right Bambola, already dressed in a white dress sparkling with crystal beads, sat at a small table. She had covered the table with a white cloth and upon that she had laid out a pattern of colorful cards. 'Monsieur Rees,' said the girl, waving him over, 'how wonderful to see you again.'

'Miss Mazza,' he said.

'Call me Bambola,' she said. 'Everyone does.' She fanned the brightly painted cards upon the table and gathered them up again. 'Have you ever seen the Tarot before?' Rees shook his head as he bent over to peer at them. 'I use them to tell the future. May I tell yours?'

'I–I . . .' Rees cleared his throat. 'I don't believe in such silliness.'

'Well then, let's pass a few minutes in pleasant conversation while I lay them out.' She gestured to a nearby chair. 'Please, sit and we shall see what the cards say.'

Rees pulled the chair closer to the table and sat. What would Lydia say if she saw him now, sitting before a scantily clad woman with only a thick pack of heathenish cards between them.

Bambola scooped up the cards and placed the pack in front of him. 'Shuffle,' she directed as she smoothed her gloves. 'And think of the problem in your life to which you want an answer.'

'Well, that's simple,' he said, with a laugh. 'I want to know who killed Leah.'

'Of course,' she said with a faint smile. 'But I think the true question is who are you that you care so much, hmmm?' Taking the cards from him, she dealt them in a cross with some of the cards lying over others and four in a line to her right.

She turned over the first one, the colorful image of a young man with a sword and dressed after the Italian fashion. 'The Page of Swords. You, Mr Rees, are perceptive and a quick thinker. You have some connection with the law.' She regarded him gravely. 'Yes? Perhaps that explains your interest in the recent death.'

She turned over the next card. This one had a picture of a young man in armor. 'Ah, the Knight of Rods. You are a traveler, an explorer, if you will. You are also a passionate man. You must always

struggle to keep your passions from causing trouble.' She smiled
suggestively and Rees felt heat rise into his neck. With a thoughtful
frown, Bambola tapped the card a few times. 'You may be changing
your residence in the near future.'

Rees shook his head at that. He doubted that was likely to happen.

'Maybe sooner than you think,' Bambola added with a smile. She
turned over the third card. This one she laid at the top of the Knight
of Rods. It was an old man, facing Rees but standing upside down
to the ropedancer. She raised her dark eyes to meet his and her
admiration was like a warm hand on his cheek. 'You are the protector
of victims, those who have no other guardian. But be careful; if you
hesitate this time you will fail in your current quest.' She turned
over another card.

'That looks bad,' he said, trying to make a joke of the blindfolded
and bound figure on the card.

'Not necessarily. The eight of swords is reversed. Change is
coming. Something in your past requires resolution else it will haunt
you all your days. You must face it and solve it.' Flipping the bottom
card, another reversed card, she said, 'You are still suffering from
a recent unreasonable legal decision.' She bit her lip. 'Connected
to the other problem, perhaps? It is something very important.'

Rees involuntarily nodded as he recalled the reasons for his and
his family's flight from Dugard. Lydia had been accused with witchcraft and he still sometimes dreamed of the constable's son pulling
the rope – intended for Lydia's hanging – through his hands and
grinning. An involuntary shudder shivered through him.

'Your trouble is not over,' Bambola continued, turning another
card. 'The Knight of Cups, reversed. You should beware of a
charming rogue. He does not have your best interests at heart. Be
careful.'

'No idea which charming rogue I should be watching for,' he
said, trying to make it a joke.

Bambola shook her head without smiling. 'He is dangerous to
you,' she warned as she turned another card. Another old man,
reversed.

'This card is about you and your character.' Now she smiled. 'It
indicates you are unconventional and frequently defy the rules.
Always with the best intentions, of course. We know that is true,
don't we?' The next card, again upside down, was of what he took

to be a juggler. Bambola frowned. 'You must be careful in whom you put your trust. I see deception ahead for you.'

'That's always true,' Rees observed dryly.

The next card, right side up for a change, depicted an angel blowing a trumpet. 'Well, Mr Rees, it appears you have some serious reflection ahead of you. It is time to forgive those who have done you wrong and put those affronts behind you. You have an opportunity here to make a fresh start.' She turned the final card to reveal a bright sun and a baby – no, a cherub. 'But I see success in your future. Your decisions will bring you happiness and contentment.'

Rees stared at the brightly colored cards, each one a small work of art, with their Italian inscriptions. He found them disturbing. Miss Lucia Mazza should not have been able to read his character so well. When he raised his eyes to meet the dark, liquid gaze of the woman sitting across the table, she smiled.

'I see you are startled. I can only assure you the cards never lie.'

'Mr Rees?' He jumped and looked up. He had fallen so deeply under Bambola's spell he had lost all awareness of his surroundings. Mr Asher, resplendent in a scarlet jacket and white breeches, stood a few feet away. 'I see Lucia has drawn you into her fanciful little hobby.'

'The cards never lie,' Bambola repeated in a sharp voice as she swept the cards from the table. Clearly annoyed, she gathered the cloth and the cards and huffed away.

'You must forgive her,' Asher said. 'She is from an old Gypsy family; her grandmother told fortunes and Bambola believes in all manner of magic and superstition.'

'How did she become a ropedancer?' Rees asked.

'Her mother. Bambola was meant to join her father's act; he threw knives and shot pistols with deadly accuracy, but she demonstrated an early gift for rope dancing.'

'I'm sure there is no harm in her little hobby,' Rees said.

Asher laughed condescendingly and shook his head. 'I hope your presence here means you plan to attend our show this evening,' he said.

'I expect to enjoy it,' Rees said, rising to his feet. 'I also congratulate you on your wagons. They are far more elaborate than the vehicle I own.'

Asher smiled. 'Thank you. I saw something like them when I

lived in Europe. I adapted the design so all of them double as living space. They make traveling more bearable.'

'How is Monsieur Boudreaux doing?' Rees asked, changing the subject. 'I didn't visit today.'

'As well as can be expected. At least Mr Rouge has agreed to feed Pip if I pay for the meals.' Asher gestured at the arena a short distance away. 'Come. I'll show you the best place to stand for a good view.'

'I hope Boudreaux will not remain in the jail for very much longer,' Rees said as they crossed the muddy field. 'I have someone I want to speak to tomorrow and after that I'll talk to the constable again.'

'Damn! That's another day at least. I wanted to leave as soon as possible,' Asher said. 'It is unusual for us to stay in a town this small for more than a night. There isn't the custom, you see.'

'Are you reserved at the next town over?' Rees asked.

Asher laughed. 'Reserved? Of course not. We travel on until we see a likely village. We send in one of our criers to post signs and then go through town announcing us. A day later we follow up with a parade.' He paused and looked around, his gaze going over the tops of the wagons. 'We've never come this far north before. I thought we could expand our circuit.' Rees thought of all the names on the posters and nodded. 'But we're all eager to move on,' Asher added.

As they spoke, they crossed the scarred ground to the flimsy wooden walls. Asher gestured Rees through the curtain. 'Stand by the wall. You'll have a good view from there. I'll be starting the show soon.'

Rees positioned himself by the wall as instructed. Directly across from him stood a cluster of men and boys behind the stones that marked the ring. They were mostly farmers by the look of them, but the crowd also contained a scattering of townsfolk. He recognized some of the men from Rouge's tavern. They smiled and talked, their voices loud with excitement. 'Here he comes,' one said. Rees's breath quickened.

TWELVE

'Gentlemen.' Asher's voice boomed voice out as he strode into the ring. With a flutter of wings, the birds roosting on the arena walls took flight. 'Prepare to be amazed.' As he began detailing the joys that were to come, the two equestriennes, clad in their short red frocks, rode into the arena. They passed right next to Rees, so close he could hear the women's faint grunts as they jumped to their feet. Standing erect on the backs of their mounts, they cantered around the circle. They had added plumed headdresses to their costumes and with the high feathers dancing in the breeze the women looked very tall and graceful.

Sometimes riding in unison, sometimes opposite one another, they wheeled and turned in an elaborate pas de deux. At one point the ladies, both standing on the horses' backs, held hands across the gap while the animals thundered forward beneath their feet. They left the ring to loud applause.

Rees looked around. Asher had disappeared. But through the opening at the back of the arena stepped a figure in a black cloak. When he reached the center of the ring, he dropped the cape, revealing a jacket and breeches sparkling with gold embroidery and glittering gems. On his head he wore a tall conical hat. Although Asher's mustache had been tamed and darkened, Rees recognized him. He suspected the rest of the audience, blinded by the resplendent clothing, did not.

Asher made a big show of removing his white gloves and, talking all the while of the magic of metal, began with coin tricks. He delighted a child by pulling a shiny ha-penny from his ear – and delighted the boy's father by letting him keep it. Pennies appeared from pockets and then from the air in a shower of copper. Rees, who had seen other street performers, admired Asher's skill. But of course he had large hands. Unusually large hands striped with scratches. Rees stared at them in sudden surmise. Could this performer, who Rees had already begun to like, be Leah's murderer?

The magic with coins over, Asher gestured to someone at the

edge of the ring. The tall heavy-set man with a bald head carried a table and a box of props into the ring. The magician took a metal stand from the box and placed it on the table. Although it had been polished until it shone and looked like silver, Rees didn't believe it. What would a ragtag outfit like this circus be doing with silver props?

A glass dome went over the stand and over that went a black velvet cloth. Asher put on his gloves. 'I learned this feat of magic in the Orient,' he said, pitching his voice a tone deeper than normal. 'It was taught to me by a magician in the Chinese emperor's court.'

And not one word of that is true, Rees thought. But when he looked at the rest of the audience he saw they were completely entranced.

Asher put a small dish before the shrouded glass dome and held up a goblet. The gems inset into the gold – probably paste, Rees thought – sparkled in the golden rays of the late-afternoon sun.

'If my assistant would bring out a bottle of wine?' Asher turned toward his assistant as he carried out the bottle. Again, speaking all the while about the excellence of this wine, the magician made a production of the simple act of opening the bottle. When it was open, he poured a bit of wine into the goblet and sipped, smacking his lips for effect. Laughter rippled through the crowd. Then he invited one of the farmers up to also take a drink. Rees could smell the wine's heavy sweetness.

'That's wine all right,' the sunburned fellow said as he returned to the audience.

And probably better stuff than he's ever had in his life, Rees thought.

Asher poured a generous measure of dark wine into the small bowl. Instantly a cloud of steam billowed up from the dish, completely hiding the velvet-shrouded dome behind the white fog. The audience audibly gasped.

As the mist faded, Asher said loudly, 'From the secrets of the mysterious Orient,' and whisked the black cloth from the dome. Oranges filled the dome to the top and when Asher removed the glass one of them fell and rolled across the table. Asher grabbed it before it could fall and with a flourish offered it to a boy at the front of the crowd.

Thunderous applause followed the few seconds of shocked

silence. And Rees, who accounted himself the most skeptical of men, was as flabbergasted as anyone.

After many bows, Asher picked up his table and his stand and left the stage to a raucous ovation. Rees stared after him, two questions warring in his mind: how had Asher done that last trick and could he be Leah's murderer?

A roar of laughter brought Rees's attention back to the center of the arena. He had missed the entrance of the dwarf clown and his animal companions. Now the dog was riding on the pig as she trotted around the clown in a circle. He held up a hoop and the dog jumped right through it and landed perfectly on the pig's back. Rees heard one of the farmers wondering aloud if his pigs could be trained to carry a dog on their backs.

But the shouting and loud clapping was nothing compared to that which occurred when the pig jumped over the dog and then went through the hoop as well. Bowing, the dwarf and his companions exited the ring.

The dwarf winked at Rees as he went past him.

Asher, once again in his white trousers and scarlet jacket, ran through the curtain and took up a position in the center of the arena. 'Still to come,' he announced swinging his arm in a grand gesture, 'our world-famous equestrian who will amaze you with his horsemanship.' Rees stared at the ringmaster's hands but they were now gloved and told him nothing. 'From Europe, the strongest man in the world. Prepare to be astonished by Otto. He is so powerful he can lift a full-grown man.' A rumble of disbelief greeted this assertion. Asher smiled. 'Otto is so mighty he can lift a full-grown cow but, since we have none here, he will prove himself with a pig and one of you. If someone here is brave enough to volunteer.' He stared for a long moment at the audience before continuing his oration. 'Then, for your wonder and pleasure, Bambola the ropedancer. Trained in Italy and as graceful as an angel, she will prance across the rope no bigger than your thumb over your heads. Finally, we will close with an inspiring pantomime.'

Rees suddenly wished David were here to see these marvels. What was the boy doing now? Milking must be almost over.

With a wide expansive gesture, Asher shouted, 'First our equestrian.' A male rider in tight white trousers rode in and, like the female riders, rose to a standing position on his horse's saddle. He was just a boy; slim and no taller than Lydia. As the gelding began galloping around the ring, the performer shifted his weight to his right leg and elevated the left behind him. He bent from the waist over the horse's head and spread out his arms as though they were wings. A murmur of astonishment rippled through the audience. Rees, who had seen Boudreaux ride, was not impressed. The Frenchman rode as though he and his horse were one. After a few minutes watching the less skilled rider, Rees's thoughts drifted to Asher and his large hands. Scarcely aware of the rider and horse and the tricks that drew forth gasps of admiration from the others in the audience, Rees did not come to full attention until Asher introduced Otto the strong man.

The large man – and he was both exceptionally tall and heavy – lumbered into the ring. He had none of the flash of Asher or the charm of the clown. Otto was dressed in gray breeches and a loose gray shirt, limp and faded from many launderings. Although he was not the kind of easily remembered figure, Rees recognized him. He had brought out Asher's props and worn a clown's costume in the parade. The backs of his large hands were marked with old scratches. Rees stared hard at them.

Otto began with a pallet of bricks. Rees had seen other men lift the heavy wooden square with its even heavier load, although no one had handled it with such ease. The silence from the rest of the audience told Rees that the other men were as unimpressed. They were all accustomed to heavy work.

Asher wheeled out a cart. Otto struggled for a few seconds before he arranged the vehicle to his liking. Then, with Asher steadying the back end, he lifted the cart over his head. Rees grunted in involuntary surprise. The heavy wood and iron-banded wheels weighed several hundred pounds at least.

When Otto lowered the cart, several men pushed out a black-smith's anvil. It left a long groove in the soil. But Otto, once he put his hands underneath, brought it first to his chest and then, not so easily as the first two items, over his head. Someone whistled in surprise and scattered applause broke out among the audience.

Asher pulled a pig into the ring. Although this pig had no identifiable features Rees guessed it was the clown's pig. She stood there patiently while Otto lifted her over his head and held her there for several seconds.

'Will you look at that?' someone from the audience said in amazement.

At the same time Rees admired the man's strength – the pig had to weigh five hundred pounds or more – he was very aware of those massive hands under the pig's belly. Subduing Leah would have been easy for Otto.

When the strong man lowered the pig to the ground Rees had an opportunity to study the wide palms and long fingers. His fingernails, although jagged and rimmed with dirt, were long. They could have cut the crescents in Leah's skin as he held her down.

Otto required further and more intensive investigation.

In a heavy accent – German, Rees thought – Otto called for a volunteer. Several farmers stepped forward. He pointed at the heaviest. After some initial arm-wrestling contests, which Otto easily won, he directed the farmer to the cart. When the man was securely seated, Asher lifted the back end of the vehicle. Otto slid his hands underneath. For a few seconds he moved them around, adjusting them, and then he nodded at Asher. As the ringmaster backed away Otto lifted the cart – and the man – high above his head. This time he grunted with the effort and perspiration popped out on his forehead. After a few seconds he lowered the cart, almost dropping it the last few inches. The farmer climbed out with alacrity. Rees could see the man was trembling.

Now the applause went on and on. Otto bent from the waist, as stiff as a wooden toy. And he never smiled. Rees thought that was odd. After two reluctant bows, Otto put the anvil in the cart and pushed it from the ring.

Asher walked into the ring and waited until the clapping subsided. 'Now,' he said, pitching his voice so low the audience had to strain to hear him, 'the jewel of our company. Prepare to be amazed by our own ropedancer – Bambola.'

Clad in her sparkling beaded gown, Bambola rode sidesaddle into the ring. She circled the arena, waving to the crowd and, to Rees's combined embarrassment and pleasure, throwing a kiss at him. When she dismounted on one side and her horse was led away, two tumblers ran in. As they turned somersaults in the air, threw balls and pins and finally flaming torches to one another, two men climbed the ladders to tighten Bambola's rope. They took turns stepping on the rope, testing the bounce, until finally the tautness

met with their approval. Then they climbed down from the poles
and nodded at the ropedancer. To raucous applause, the tumblers
disappeared through the back.

Even Rees held his breath as the young woman, whom he had
just seen engaged with a pack of fancy cards, climbed the ladder
to the rope. Like the equestriennes, her costume ended at the knee.
She picked up a parasol and, twirling it above her head for all the
world like a young miss on a stroll, stepped upon the rope. Rees's
heart began pounding in his chest; he was so afraid this girl would
fall and plunge to her death upon the ground. Delicately she
traversed the narrow line to the other side and turned around.
She curtseyed to the enthusiastic applause. Rees clapped so vigor-
ously his hands began to sting.

Smiling, Bambola waved at the men below her. She dropped the
parasol to a waiting companion. He lifted a long pole with two
baskets dangling from hooks. She tied them upon her feet with
ribbons over the ankles. Then, her short skirt swaying and every
bead sparkling, she danced out upon the rope. Rees could hear her
singing, some foreign air that directed her delicate steps. Except for
the tinkling of her voice, there was not a sound within these wooden
walls. It seemed to Rees that everyone held his breath, just as he
held his.

Once at the landing on the other side of the rope she removed
the baskets and passed them to a man below. He lifted up a small
wheelbarrow. She placed it upon the line and then, balancing the
tool, she began pushing it to the other side. Rees gasped as she
navigated the narrow line overhead and, when she reached the safety
of the landing, he burst into spontaneous applause. Shouts and
whistles of approval erupted from all sides. Rees realized he was
bathed in clammy perspiration, just as if he had run a race around
the track. How could this young woman traverse a narrow rope,
dancing and performing these tasks so effortlessly?

Bambola curtsied gracefully from her position on the high and
very small platform. She waved at him before beginning her climb
down the ladder. Rees could not help the small flush of pleasure
that swept over him. Once on the ground Bambola, smiling and
waving at the men around her, danced across the ring toward the
back. Asher began extolling the wonders of the next offering, a
pantomime with an uplifting message, but Rees doubted anyone

was listening. He certainly wasn't. When he glanced around him, he saw every face turned toward the ropedancer disappearing through the curtain at the back.

Wait. Was that David? It couldn't be. But when he looked at the battered straw hat, the shabby vest and breeches that had been washed so many times they were faded and worn, he was sure it must be. Those were David's clothes. But the face did not belong to David. It was Lydia. And she was staring at him in hurt dismay.

THIRTEEN

When Lydia saw Rees looking at her, she turned and fled through the crowd.

What was she thinking? Rees wondered as he stared after her. Now he realized why she had so cheerfully seen him off; she – and probably Jerusha as well – had planned this. Loud cursing and a few slaps revealed Lydia's squirming path through the crowd toward the back exit. Rees pushed his way toward the curtain and waited until she reached him. His expression must have been ferocious. She gulped and visibly straightened her shoulders. He held the curtain open for her and followed her through it. 'What are you doing here?' he demanded as soon as they stepped into the yard.

Asher, who was congratulating Bambola, stopped mid-word and turned to look. Lydia, her face flaming, frowned at her husband.

'What were *you* doing?' she hissed. 'Besides ogling the rope-dancer, I mean.'

Asher nodded at Bambola and hurried away. Smiling, she approached Rees and Lydia. 'How did you enjoy the performance, Mr Rees?' the ropedancer asked, her dark eyes resting with unexpected sharpness on Lydia. 'And this must be Mrs Rees.'

'Amazing,' Rees began.

But Lydia stepped forward, not at all abashed that Bambola had recognized her as a woman and began speaking. 'Truly the most incredible performance I have ever seen,' Lydia said in a syrupy voice. 'Captivating. Astonishing.' Rees, who had never heard his wife speak in such a manner, turned to stare at her.

'I'm so happy you enjoyed it, Mrs Rees,' Bambola said. The two women sized each other up.

'How ever did you learn how to do that?' Lydia asked. 'So unusual to see a lady performing before a crowd of men.' Her pointed insult was barely disguised by her sweet tone. Rees's eyebrows shot up but Bambola simply chuckled.

'I am from a circus family, Mrs Rees. My mother was a ropedancer before me. You might say I was born to this life.' She extended a gloved hand. 'Lucia Mazza. How lovely to meet you.' Nothing in her voice or manner revealed any awareness of Lydia's rudeness.

'Lydia.' She swallowed. When she spoke again she sounded more like herself. 'How difficult is it to learn such a craft? Is everyone here born to the circus?'

A faint frown shadowed Bambola's expression. 'Learning these skills takes time. But no, many of our performers were not born for the circus. Many came to this country as refugees. You know that Corsican general for the French Army attacked Italy, do you not? That Bonaparte?' She almost spat the name. Lydia took an involuntary step backward. 'He is a monster,' Bambola continued. 'I weep to see what he has done to my country.' She took a breath and when she spoke again she was calmer. 'Others among us, such as Billy, have no other place to go.'

'Billy?' Rees and Lydia asked in unison.

'The clown with the pig. Even his parents didn't want him. But he has found a place here. We are his family now.'

Another roar of approval sounded from the arena and Bambola tipped her head toward it. 'The pantomime is soon beginning. I must change. Forgive me.' Inclining her head, she turned to go. But before she'd taken a step, she looked back over her shoulder. 'I hope you return. Please, accompany your husband one day. I must do a reading for you.' She smiled up at Rees. 'And another for you, I think.'

As Bambola walked quickly away, Lydia turned to her husband. 'What does she mean? A reading?'

'She tells fortunes with cards,' Rees explained. 'Total nonsense.' Taking her arm, he hurried her to the wall of circus wagons. None of the other costumed performers paid them the slightest attention. Some of the circus folk were already lining up for their few minutes in the ring while others talked to themselves, running over their roles. Rees urged Lydia through a gap in the wall of circus wagons and back to ordinary life once again.

Once on the other side, Rees turned to his wife. 'How could you do this?' he asked, gesturing to the boy's clothes. Calmer now, he was able to speak quietly.

'I thought it might be my only chance to see something so exotic,' Lydia said. 'Instead I saw my husband exchanging kisses with a ropedancer.'

'It meant nothing. She is a performer,' Rees said dismissively. 'What you saw was just part of her act.'

'No wonder ladies are not permitted to attend if this is what the performers do,' Lydia said. 'Flirt with all the men.'

'It meant nothing,' Rees repeated. Seeking to distract her, he asked, 'How much of the show did you see?'

'Almost all of it.' She sighed with happiness. 'I arrived just as the magician was beginning his act. It was enchanting. I will never, ever forget it.'

'Yes, it was,' Rees agreed. He too felt as though he were leaving a brighter and shinier country. He sighed. Back to the dull and gray world of farming chores for him.

'It must be so difficult for your trick rider to languish in jail,' Lydia said. Rees directed a look of surprise at her. 'He is accustomed to traveling all the time. Now he is penned in a ten by ten square. It must be torture for him.'

'You're right.' He paused. 'Maybe I should visit Boudreaux while we're here.'

Lydia hesitated. 'May I come?'

'Of course. What else would you do? I'm not leaving you here, by yourself.'

She smiled and together they began walking toward the jail. Just a man and a boy walking in the dusk.

They were still a distance from the jail when they heard angry shouting. Rees lengthened his stride and Lydia had to trot to keep up. Glass shattered with an ugly sharp sound and a gunshot split the air, momentarily quieting the violent roar. Rees turned a desperate look upon his wife and broke into a run.

Rouge was standing in front of the jail door, facing the mob. '. . . to put this man before the magistrate,' he was saying.

'He's a French spy,' a man shouted.

'He should be hung for that reason alone,' another man agreed.

'Not until he's gone before the magistrate,' Rouge said again. He sounded as though he'd repeated this statement over and over.

'Who's going to stop us from stringing the villain up?' another man jeered.

'Me,' said Rouge.

'One man?'

'And you've already shot one of your pistols,' another shouted. Rouge brandished another pistol and lifted a rifle over his head.

'I'm here,' Rees said, pushing his way through the crowd to join Rouge at the front. Lydia followed, sticking close by his side.

'Two men and a boy?'

Rouge handed Rees the rifle and Lydia the empty pistol. 'You know how to load a gun and shoot, boy?' he asked. Although Lydia, a proper lady from Boston before she'd become one of the pacifist Shakers, had no idea how to use a gun, she nodded. He handed her the shot bag and turned back to the mob. 'Go home,' Rouge shouted.

'You're French too,' a man said, his words slurred by drink. 'You're prob'ly a spy too.'

'Go home,' Rouge said wearily. 'You've known me all your life. Go home.'

The drunken man, more daring than the rest, pushed his way out of the crowd. Brave with the crowd at his back, he stumbled toward Rees.

Rees's breathing increased and his heart began to pound. His left eyelid began to twitch. His mind filled with the memories of facing down the mob in Dugard as he stepped forward. This time it was Lydia beside him, not their children, but his anger was the same. He would not allow anyone to menace his family.

Even in the dim light, the man saw the rage in Rees's expression and froze. At the same instant Rouge fired the second pistol over the heads of the throng.

'All of you have families. No point in making any of your wives widows,' he said. 'Go home now.'

For a moment, as Rees held his breath, the mob hesitated. He knew these men could choose either course: rushing the jail or obeying the constable. A few seconds that felt like an hour passed and then two of the men turned and stumbled away. Others followed and in a few minutes the yard in front of the jail was empty.

Lydia collapsed upon the ground as though her legs wouldn't hold her. Rouge expelled a noisy breath. 'That was close,' he muttered.

'Boudreaux might not even be guilty,' Rees said. Oh no, his voice was shaking. He took in several deep breaths and tried to control the trembling that now had spread to his limbs. 'Paul Reynard saw him riding on the road just after dinner. Leah hadn't even left Zion then.'

Rouge turned to look at Rees. 'Are you sure?' He nodded.

'I told you I didn't kill anyone,' Boudreaux shouted in a shaky voice through the barred window. Both Rees and Rouge ignored him.

'Ask the boy yourself. He said he saw a Shaker following Shem and Leah into town.'

'I told you,' Boudreaux yelled. 'I see him too.'

It was now so dark Rees could see only the faint shine of Rouge's eyes and teeth. 'We must hide him' – Rees jerked his head at the jail – 'somewhere.'

'I know,' the constable agreed. 'None of that lot' – and he gestured at the yard where the mob had recently stood – 'will listen to reason. Especially when they are liquored up and ready to brawl.'

'But where?' Now that he felt steadier, Rees took the pistol from Lydia and handed both firearms to Rouge.

'Not at the farm,' Lydia said, speaking for the first time. Rouge peered at her, shocked to hear a woman's voice from this boy.

'Mrs Rees?' he said in disapproving surprise.

'I won't have the children put in danger. Not again,' she said.

'Then Zion?' Rouge suggested hopefully.

'No,' Rees said. 'Even if I wanted to suggest it, they won't agree. When they took in your niece last winter, one of the Sisters was murdered in her stead. Jonathan won't be willing to risk that again.'

'I can't leave him here,' Rouge said. 'What if the mob comes back? They might break down the door and hang the poor bastard.'

'Why are you asking me?' Rees said unsympathetically. 'You told me not to meddle, remember? You specifically told me not to involve myself in this investigation. Lucky for you, I did, otherwise the hanging of an innocent man would be on your conscience.'

'We don't know he's innocent,' Rouge said.

'This problem is yours,' Rees said. Turning, he held out a hand to Lydia.

As they began retracing their steps toward the circus – and their wagon – Rouge called out behind them, 'Wait. What shall I do?'

Rees walked a few more steps before turning to face Rouge. 'Why don't you take him to that papist church you attend,' he suggested. 'It's out of town and I'll warrant most of these men don't even know where it is. You can guard him there. I'll see you tomorrow morning.'

'All night? By myself? *Merde*,' Rouge said with feeling.

FOURTEEN

Once out of earshot of the constable, Rees turned to Lydia and said furiously, 'What were you doing? You put yourself in jeopardy with this little stunt.'

'I was in no danger until you rushed forward like St George on a white horse,' Lydia replied just as angrily. 'Why did you think you needed to do that?'

'You should have been home with the children,' Rees said, knowing as soon as the words left his mouth that that was the worst thing to say.

'And maybe you should have been too instead of running off every chance you get,' she retorted. Since this was exactly what David had said more than once Rees could think of no reply. Despite his anger he recognized a certain validity to her accusation. After a few seconds of silence, he turned to look at her and saw her inhaling several times.

'I don't want anything to happen to you,' he said.

'It was a very frightening experience,' she said finally, in a much calmer voice. 'Will, please, let's not quarrel now when our emotions are running so high.'

'Why didn't you at least stay back?' Rees asked in what he thought was a reasonable tone.

'I thought I would be safer with you,' she said.

Rees paused, pleased and a little scared too by the trust she placed in him. He pulled her into his arms. The top of the battered straw hat scratched his neck and chin. 'I don't know what I would do if something I did harmed you,' he said in a low voice.

'Will, Will,' she said, her involuntary laugh catching in her throat. 'You are not responsible for everything in this world.' She pulled herself from his arms. 'I wanted to see the circus and despite what happened after I will never regret it. Let's go home. Jerusha must be wondering what has happened to us. And anyway, if someone saw us they'd wonder why you were embracing a boy with such affection.'

'You make a very pretty boy,' Rees teased.

Lydia laughed and, clapping the hat upon her head, began running down the street. Rees easily caught up and they walked together in a companionable silence to the wagon.

Rees sat up in bed gasping, his body cold with nervous sweat. The angry faces of a mob facing him, one man drawing a rope through his hands, as they approached. He looked at Lydia, sleeping peacefully beside him with her braid across the pillow, and slowly eased himself out of bed. His heart was still pounding in his chest and he was trembling. With the passage of time, the nightmares had come less frequently but after yesterday's experience the old terror had returned.

In his dream the mob had been made up of men from Dugard as well as from the mob in front of the jail and this time they caught both Lydia and Rees. He tried to escape, tried to save Lydia, but the harder he struggled the more the air around him held him tight.

He pulled on his breeches and shirt and wrapped a quilt over his shoulders. He couldn't help peeking into the bedrooms, just to make sure the children were safe, before going down the shadowed stairs to the kitchen. He stirred up the fire and watched the sparks rise to the chimney a few seconds before setting up the coffee pot. This is what he did every morning, just not quite so early. Although only the first gray of morning was beginning to creep through the kitchen window, he could hear Daisy mooing in the barn. The birds were beginning to wake up and chirp. The sheer ordinariness of his surroundings calmed him.

Realizing he was hungry – he and Lydia had arrived home late last night and had eaten more of a snack than supper – he tore off the heel of a loaf of bread. Jerusha had put the younger children to bed and, unable to just sit, she had made bread and set it to rise. It had just come out of the oven when Rees and Lydia had walked through the door the previous evening.

'Really, Will,' Lydia said from the doorway, 'use your knife.'

'I didn't want to wake you,' he said, glancing over his shoulder.

'Cutting bread with a knife?' she asked, stepping into the kitchen. 'Although I admit I had a little trouble falling to sleep. The excitement, I suppose.' Rees said nothing. He would not have called the confrontation at the jail 'exciting'. But Lydia did not know how terrible it had been in Dugard – he had kept the worst from her – so she did not realize how much he was reminded of it by the mob at the jail.

'Did Jerusha ask you about the circus?' he asked instead.

'Yes,' Lydia smiled. 'She was particularly interested in the ladies and their short dresses.'

'Yes. Shocking. But I imagine Miss Mazza would have had trouble crossing the rope in a long gown,' he said.

Lydia sighed. 'Indeed. I wish I could always wear breeches.'

'What's happening with Annie?' Rees asked, changing the subject. 'She's been spending a lot of time here. So much so Sister Agatha remarked on it.'

Lydia hesitated and then replied in a rush. 'She does not want to become a Shaker.'

Rees nodded. 'Annie told me that herself.'

'She wants to live with a family, with children.'

Rees dissected Lydia's statement in silence. 'She wants to live here?' he asked finally.

'Yes,' Lydia said, adding sadly, 'I think she has given up the hope that her young man will find her. She hasn't received a letter in some time.'

'I never expected that to succeed,' Rees said. 'They were both very young. And now the boy has been away at sea for several years. Why, we don't even know if he's alive. Sailing on a merchant ship is a dangerous profession.'

'I think she suspects he's dead,' Lydia admitted, 'but please don't suggest that. She is upset enough.' Rees nodded, glad he did not have to involve himself in these feminine vapors. 'You know she'll be here again this morning? She'll watch Sharon and Joseph for me while I join you when you question that boy. Shem.'

'I suppose that's the silver lining,' Rees said as he pulled on the boots.

'I can't deny she's a great help,' Lydia said. 'But don't worry, she won't be coming to live here. At least not for now. I think it best she remains in Zion for the time being.'

Rees nodded, distracted. He knew Lydia would not want to hear his plan. 'After I bring you home I plan to return to the circus.' Lydia directed a stare of dismayed surprise at him. 'Leah was strangled,' he went on, hurrying to speak so his words tripped over one another, 'by someone with large hands. I noticed yesterday that both Asher and Otto have large hands. I want to take another look at them. I forgot last night – in all the excitement.' Grinning at her, he put on his old coat. She did not smile back.

'I'd like to come,' she said. Although Rees nodded, he experienced a curious revulsion. He did not want her with him.

'Would Annie stay so long?' he asked, smiling. She shook her head and did not speak. He interpreted her silence as acquiescence. Although Bambola had invited Lydia to visit and promised to read the cards for her, Rees found himself reluctant to invite his wife along on his next visit.

He stepped onto the porch and breathed in the chilly air. Although the calendar would soon turn the page into May, frost glittered on every surface. But the sky was flushed with light and he knew that with the sun's rise the day would warm. He crossed the yard. As he entered the barn he began to whistle. He pulled the milking stool and pail over to the cow. Usually he hated farm chores of any kind, but today pressing his head into Daisy's warm flank and hearing the milk hiss into the pail relaxed him. The remaining fear and the desperation left by the last night's dream faded.

He heard the children come outside for their chores: Jerusha to fetch water, Nancy to collect eggs and Judah to gather firewood. Annie was already here, he heard the lower tones of her voice among the other higher sopranos. All the Shakers rose early but she must have left Zion before breakfast. Rees hoped she had told someone where she was going before she walked to the farm.

When he carried the brimming pails back into the house, Lydia was dressed in a sober dark-blue gown, her hair confined to a cap. Rees smiled at her. He vowed he would never ever tell her how desirable she'd appeared in her boy's clothing, her limbs exposed in breeches and stockings.

They ate breakfast quickly. Lydia gave Annie some last-minute instructions, draped a light shawl over her shoulders, and then they were on their way. Now that the sun had been up for a few hours the temperature was rising – just as Rees expected. The frosty ground had become mud.

'This is my favorite time of year,' Lydia said, looking around her with pleasure. 'Soon everything will be green.'

'Not mine,' Rees said. 'I prefer the summer, when all the planting is done and the harvest still in the future.'

'Hmmm,' Lydia said with a sideways glance. 'One would almost believe you a lazy man.'

'I am,' Rees said. 'Laziest man this side of the Atlantic.'

'We'll all starve then,' Lydia replied. She did not sound as if she were joking but Rees laughed anyway.

'Don't worry, I'll start planting the buckwheat as soon as I get home. And I'm sending a letter to David asking him to come.' A pleat formed between Lydia's brows and her mouth opened as though she would speak. But instead she closed her mouth and directed her gaze to the chapped and work-worn hands clasped at her waist. 'I'll have money from my weaving,' Rees reassured her. 'We can hire help. And I see some things sprouting in your kitchen garden. Peas, I think. We won't starve.' Lydia did not smile.

'Peas and greens,' she said. 'Soon I'll put in the beets and turnips.' As she described how she would lay out her garden, Rees's thoughts began to drift. How had Rouge and Boudreaux fared during the night? Had the trick rider admitted anything to the constable? Would he allow Boudreaux to return to the circus?

Once Rees thought of the circus his thoughts were drawn inevitably to Bambola. For him, she would always be the angel dancing overhead in her sparkling dress, untethered to the mundane world below. Her world was one of magic and enchantment, not the workaday world of farming chores.

'You aren't listening to me,' Lydia said, putting her hand on Rees's wrist.

'Yes, I am,' he lied.

'No, you're not. Nobody looks that excited about beets. What are you thinking about?'

'Nothing. Just wondering if I'll have to give evidence in front of the magistrate.' That was not untrue; he had thought about it. Lydia's brows rose.

'You seem surprisingly pleased about that.'

'I'm not. Piggy will now know where we are. He might try to send us back to Dugard.' And Rees would fight him every step.

'Don't you want to go home?'

'Maybe. But not if the warrant is still out for your arrest. You could be put on trial for witchcraft.'

'Surely not,' she said hopefully. 'I must believe all of that distrust has faded.'

Rees did not know how to answer her. His anger had barely diminished and when he thought of Dugard and how the town had turned on him and his family he was furious all over again.

'We left almost two years ago,' she continued. 'And once your sister moved to Rumsford . . .' Her voice trailed away as she stared around at Zion's crowded main street. 'What are all the Shakers doing outside?'

Rees looked around. Usually, by this time of the morning, most of the community was busy working. The street should be almost empty.

'Something's happened,' he said, throwing a worried glance at Lydia. He slapped the reins down on Hannibal's back. Whatever crisis had taken these people away from their chores and into the street could not be good.

The wagon rattled past the Meeting House and into the center of the village. As soon as they reached the Dwelling House and began to slow down, Daniel ran over. Grabbing the reins, he pulled the horse to a stop. 'Where's Shem?' he demanded. 'Is he with you?'

'Shem?' Rees repeated. 'No, we haven't seen him.'

'I hoped since Annie went to your farm that Shem—' Daniel's words lurched to a stop.

'Annie came to us but not Shem,' Rees said, turning to look at Lydia. 'In fact, that's why we're here. I wanted to speak to the boy, ask him a few more questions.'

'Well, you can't,' Daniel said, sounding angry.

'Why not?'

'He's gone,' Daniel said. 'Disappeared. We don't know where he is.'

FIFTEEN

Although both Aaron and Daniel told Rees they had searched the room Shem shared with another boy and found nothing, Rees insisted on searching it once again. He also found nothing, not so much as a scrap of paper. But then Shem, who had only lately come to Zion, probably did not read or write.

'The Brother who sleeps in the adjoining room swears Shem did not leave,' Daniel said.

Rees, who had noticed the open window, looked out of it. 'He probably went out to the tree branch and shimmied down the trunk,' he said.

'One thing.' Daniel stopped and rubbed his hand over his chin.

'Yes,' Rees said impatiently.

'He left his clothes here.'

'He went out naked?' Rees said in surprise.

'No, no, that's not what I meant. He left the clothes we gave him here. But he took his old clothing. See?' He pointed to the breeches and white shirt draped over the end of the bed.

Rees examined them thoughtfully. Shem must have been desperate to escape. 'Does anyone have any idea when he left?' he asked. Daniel and Aaron shook their heads. 'What about the boy who sleeps in the other bed?'

'He said he doesn't know anything,' Daniel said. 'But you can ask him yourself.'

While Daniel left to fetch Shem's roommate, Rees joined Lydia by the wagon. In a few words he summarized Shem's disappearance.

'So, he ran away,' she said.

'Looks like it.'

'Is it possible he hurt Leah?' she asked.

'Of course it's possible. But Shem's hands aren't that big. And I don't think he's strong enough,' Rees said.

'Here they come,' Lydia said. Rees turned. Daniel, a skinny boy by his side, was approaching. To Rees's surprise Aaron trailed behind them. And why, Rees wondered, is Aaron not occupied with his own chores?

This boy looked younger than Shem and was probably not more than twelve. Sandy-haired and freckled, he was so painfully thin his wrists were all knobs. His clothing hung on him like the rags on a scarecrow. When he saw Rees the boy's eyes began darting fearfully from side to side. Rees exchanged a glance with Lydia; this boy had had a hard time on the road.

'We aren't going to hurt you,' he said. The boy nodded but involuntarily shrank back.

'We just want to ask you some questions,' Lydia said. The boy turned to her and offered her a tentative gap-toothed smile.

Rees stepped back half a pace and nodded at his wife. She would get more information from this child than he would.

'We are looking for Shem,' she said.

'He runned away,' the boy said.

'Did you see him go?' she asked with a nod.

He shook his head. 'He snuck out last night.'

'Do you know where he was going?' Lydia persisted.

The boy shook his head again. 'He didn't like it here. Too much work, he said. Too many rules.'

'But you like it here?'

'Sure do. I don't mind the work. And we eat regular.'

Lydia paused for a moment, thinking. 'Did he talk about any special place?'

At first the boy shook his head but then, with a hopeful grin, he said, 'The circus since it come to town.'

Lydia turned to Rees. 'That's it then. He's run away to the circus.'

'As I figured.' He caught a fleeting grimace cross Aaron's face. 'You knew,' Rees accused the other man. 'You knew Shem ran away to the circus.'

'No, I didn't,' Aaron said. 'I didn't know.'

'But you guessed. You knew Shem was captivated by the trick rider.' Rees paused, the pieces falling into place. 'You were the man who followed them into town,' he said, taking two involuntary steps forward. Rees had suspected it; now he was sure. 'Weren't you?' Unlike most of the Brothers who would give ground so as not to engage in a brawl, Aaron stood defiant and unmoving.

'What if I did?' His voice rose with outrage. 'She was a foolish female who disobeyed the rules.'

Daniel, appalled, stared at Aaron. 'You knew those children left the village? You followed them. And yet you did not protect Leah?'

'She knew better than to leave Zion,' Aaron said. 'But, like Eve, she was tempted by earthly pleasures. And her punishment was swift and sure.'

'She was a child,' Rees began, his voice choked with rage.

'She was one of us. How could you be so heartless?' Daniel demanded.

'I knew that girl would lead Shem straight to Hell.' Aaron planted his feet and attempted to stare the other man down.

'You are as guilty as she was,' Daniel said. 'You also disobeyed our rules. You weren't supposed to leave the village either.'

'It was necessary. I had to keep Shem safe.'

Daniel inhaled but, bereft of words, did not speak.

'Leah is dead,' Rees shouted, stepping forward. 'Don't you under-stand that?' Lydia put a hand on Rees's forearm. He shook it off.

'If she had stayed in Zion she would not be,' Aaron said, his eyes shifting away.

'Did you see Boudreaux, the circus performer, riding down the main road?' Rees asked.

'I saw him.' He looked at Rees and added in disdain, 'But I'm not interested in the goings on in the World.'

'Boudreaux might be hung for a murder he didn't commit,' Rees's voice increased in volume.

'He wasn't on the lane,' Aaron said. 'I didn't pay much attention to the road.'

'What happened with Leah?' Daniel asked, his face flushed. Rees could see the Elder was holding on to his temper with an effort.

'I don't know. She and Shem watched the circus parade through the town – pure wickedness I tell you – and then Shem went to talk to that trick rider. Leah must have gotten bored because she left.'

'But Shem stayed?' Daniel said.

'Yes.'

'And so did you?' Rees clenched his hands tightly by his sides so he would not strike the other man. Aaron nodded again.

'You let Leah go by herself?' Daniel's voice rose and broke.

'I didn't think anything would happen to her. It was a main road,' Aaron said defensively.

'Did Shem see you?' Lydia asked. 'In town, I mean.'

'Of course not,' Aaron said. 'I didn't want him to know . . .'

'This explains why no one saw you that afternoon,' Daniel said. 'You seeded fewer rows than expected. I'll tell Jonathan and we'll have to decide . . .' He stopped abruptly, realizing both Rees and Lydia were listening to him. 'Please go inside the Dwelling House,' Daniel said. 'Right now.'

Aaron looked as though he would refuse but then, scowling, he turned and marched away. Rees thought he heard the Shaker Brother muttering under his breath.

'If we want to speak to Shem,' Lydia said, putting her hand on Rees's wrist, 'we'd better go. We may find him at the circus.'

Rees shook his head. He hadn't asked Aaron all of the questions he wanted and he suspected that the Shaker Brother knew more than he was telling. 'How could he have done that?' he asked.

'You're too angry to question him now,' Lydia said, lowering her voice.

'Leah was a child.'

'He knows. He's blaming her to make himself feel better. He'll keep.'

Rees hesitated. 'All right,' he said. Fixing his eyes on Daniel he said, 'I'll return later to speak to Aaron.'

A rueful smile twitched at the corner of Daniel's mouth. 'Of that I have no doubt,' he said. He turned to follow Aaron but looked back over his shoulder. 'And please, bring Shem back. I want to at least speak with him before he leaves us.' He turned and strode away.

'I'd like to be a fly on the wall when Daniel speaks to Aaron,' Lydia murmured, watching them walk away.

Nodding, Rees helped her into the wagon seat and clambered up to join her. Neither spoke until they were almost out of the village. Then Lydia turned to Rees, her forehead furrowed, and said, 'Aaron could have followed Leah when she left.'

'I know,' he said. 'He certainly had the opportunity. And if Shem never saw him . . .' His voice trailed away.

'He could have left when Leah did and accosted her in the field,' Lydia said, adding reluctantly, 'maybe his baser instincts just overwhelmed him.'

'But surely someone would have seen something,' Rees said, arguing out the puzzle. 'I know the main road was busy.'

'Yes,' she agreed. 'Why didn't he take the North Road? Woods line that street. He would have had privacy.'

'We're still missing something,' he said. He lapsed into silence, pondering the facts as he knew them. He couldn't make them come together and finally he gave up the attempt. 'To my mind,' he said, 'Aaron is even more likely to be Leah's murderer than Boudreaux.'

Lydia bit her lip and nodded. 'I hate to think it. Poor Jonathan,' she said in a soft voice.

Rees had chosen to drive north on the Surry Road and turn left onto the main road into town. They joined the other farmers and their wives heading into Durham. Rees thought the traffic was not so heavy as it had been the previous two afternoons. It was too early for circus traffic and he was able to drive straight through town to the fairgrounds.

But even before they reached the field Rees knew something was wrong. Where was the arena with the flags blowing so gaily from the poles? It should have been visible from all the streets around.

And where were the circus wagons? Rees pulled Hannibal to a stop where the circus vehicles had made a wall around the back of the arena and stared around in disbelief. Climbing down, he walked around the empty expanse. There was nothing here except horse droppings and the long grooves left by wagon wheels.

Deep holes remained where the stakes that held up the stadium had been placed, but of the building itself there was no sign. A torn bill blew across the empty field and plastered itself against Rees's calf. Automatically he peeled it off his leg and put it in his pocket.

There was no question about it. The circus had fled during the night.

SIXTEEN

After a few minutes, although it felt like an hour to Rees, Lydia climbed down from the wagon and joined him. 'Look. They're gone,' he said.

'Yes, I see that. Perhaps Constable Rouge freed Monsieur Boudreaux,' she suggested hopefully. Rees shook his head.

'I don't think so. Last night the constable was still fixed on Boudreaux's guilt. What would have changed his mind so quickly?'

'I suppose we'll have to ask him,' Lydia said.

'And he doesn't know about Shem,' Rees said. He stared around the muddy field once more. 'Let's find the constable.'

The tavern was very busy; the taproom crowded with farmers and their wives on their weekly visit to town as well as passengers waiting for the Boston stage. Rouge was behind the counter but was far too busy pouring drinks to pause and speak. Rees and Lydia waited until finally, wiping his arm across his sweaty forehead, Rouge looked at them inquiringly.

He looked terrible. Never a prepossessing fellow, today he had not shaved or even combed his hair. Dark circles ringed his eyes. 'I guess you didn't sleep last night,' Rees said.

'No. Boudreaux spent all night crying out for his brother.'

'Where were you?' Rees asked.

'I took him' – Rouge lowered his voice, darting quick looks around him to see if anyone was listening – 'to the Church as you suggested.'

'Where is he now?' Lydia asked.

'Here. In the kitchen. I thought it best to keep him busy. And out of sight. Besides, my cousins are angry with me right now and I don't dare leave them alone. So, I put Boudreaux to work,' he said. He sighed. 'Are you certain he is innocent?'

'Of course not,' Rees said. 'He could still be guilty. I doubt it though. Why?'

'He may have killed his brother. He kept saying he had anyway. Over and over. All night.'

Rees nodded. He understood what the constable was saying. Once one murder was committed a second always seemed easier. 'The timing doesn't work. Boudreaux was heading back to the circus while Leah and Shem were walking on the lane.'

Rouge turned a look of disfavor upon Rees. 'I know. I spoke to the Reynard boy. He corroborated your story. But Boudreaux could have gone out again, couldn't he?' He sounded hopeful. Rees recognized the statement for what it was, a man grasping at straws.

'Maybe. But no one saw him riding on the lane if he did,' Rees said. He waited a few seconds to see if Rouge understood. The road had been busy that day; someone would have seen him. 'And I saw him performing around four thirty.'

"There's still an hour unaccounted for,' Rouge argued.

'Do you think Boudreaux would have had time?' Rees asked. 'In an hour?' Rouge scowled and did not answer. 'I think the boy Shem might know something more.' Rees hesitated. Should he tell Rouge that Brother Aaron was the man who'd followed the children to town? Did he really want to send Rouge to Zion? He knew the sledgehammer tactics the constable preferred.

'That doesn't mean another of those circus villains isn't guilty,' the constable said, changing tack.

'Yes,' Rees agreed. 'That's true.' He paused and took a breath. 'Did you know the circus has left town?'

'What? No!' Rouge glared around him at his customers. 'Nobody told me.'

'We won't know if another member of the circus is guilty unless we question them,' Rees said. 'I hope Boudreaux knows where the circus is headed.'

'He's in the back.' Rouge looked around at the crowded bar. 'Come with me.'

As Lydia and Rees followed the constable, Rees wrestled with his conscience. Finally, he said carefully, 'Did Paul Reynard tell you a man followed Shem and Leah into town?'

Rouge turned shrewd black eyes on Rees. 'That sounds like you know who that man was.' When Rees continued to hesitate, Rouge said accusingly, 'Are you protecting a murderer?'

'No.' Rees sighed. 'Not knowingly. It was Brother Aaron from Zion.'

'I promise you, he followed those children from the best of intentions,' Lydia said, jumping in.

Rouge glanced at Lydia and grunted doubtfully.

'Aaron says Leah left for home before Shem and he didn't see her after that,' Rees said.

'He stayed with the boy?' Rouge said, shocked. 'He let a young girl go off by herself?'

'He did,' Rees said.

'So, he could have followed Leah,' Rouge said. Both Rees and Lydia nodded in unhappy agreement.

'Especially since Shem did not know Aaron was there,' Rees said. 'The boy wouldn't have seen Aaron go after Leah.'

'Aaron could be guilty,' Rouge said with a wolfish grin. He knew the combative and obstreperous Aaron from the past.

'He says not. Don't assume he is,' Rees warned. He knew Rouge would enjoy questioning Aaron.

'Have you questioned Shem again?' Rouge asked.

'Shem isn't at Zion,' Rees said. 'He ran away, we think to join the circus, and now . . .'

'He's with them and of course we don't know where,' Rouge said as he threw open the door. '*Merde*.'

Until the French became suspected as traitors and worse, most of the cooking in the tavern had taken place at the fireplace in the taproom. But once Rouge's cousins had come down from Canada, he had moved the cooking into this back room. Its fireplace used the same chimney as the larger hearth on the other side of the wall. Rees, who had never seen the storeroom before, looked around curiously.

The aroma of roasting meat permeated the air and an earthenware bean pot baked on the hearth. A new crock of pickles had been opened; pickled beets by the look of them. Rees was so tired of pickles after the long winter he didn't think he could face even pickled beets, a condiment he loved.

A table had been pulled in and lined up against a row of shelves and Boudreaux was up to his elbows in the dishpan placed on it. Rouge's cousin Thomas, who was usually responsible for washing dishes, was sitting in a chair drinking coffee. Rouge frowned at him before turning to Boudreaux.

'We have questions for you. Turn around.'

Boudreaux did not even try to pretend he didn't understand the English. He turned around and stared at the people facing him. 'Where did the circus go?' Rouge barked at him. Rees watched shock spread across the performer's face.

'Go?' he repeated in a tremulous voice. He reached up to brush back his dark hair. A ring of brown color followed his hair line; it looked as though the dye was leeching out of his hair and staining his white skin. Rees looked at Boudreaux's hands. They were large, large enough to have made the bruises on Leah's neck, but his nails were short and jagged and no recent scratches marred the backs.

'Yes.' Rouge did not soften his tone.

'The fair grounds are empty,' Rees said.

Boudreaux's mouth fell open but he did not speak.

'You didn't know they were leaving?' Rees asked. Boudreaux mutely shook his head. Rees felt a flash of sympathy for the other man. He knew how it felt to be accused of murder, alone in an unfamiliar town and surrounded by strangers. 'Do you know where they went?' he asked gently. Boudreaux shook his head once again.

'Stop lying,' Rouge shouted.

'I'm not,' Boudreaux said. 'We go until we see a town.'

Rees nodded. He thought that made sense, especially here in Maine where the towns were small and widely scattered. Remembering the torn bill he'd picked up at the grounds, he pulled the crumpled ball of paper from his pocket. Under the advertisement – *AMAZING FEATS OF HORSEMANSHIP, ASTONISHING ROPE DANCING* – was a line of town names. Most of them had been marked out with an X and others, like Durham here, had been written in. He held it out to Boudreaux. 'Does anything look familiar?' he asked. Boudreaux looked at the paper blankly and Rees realized the groom couldn't read, not English anyway.

'In what direction were they going?' Lydia asked.

'West. Then south again,' Boudreaux said. Rees looked at Rouge.

'What's the largest town to our west? Within a day's travel, say?' Rees's hometown of Dugard was located to the west of Durham but it was at least two days away. Surely Asher would prefer to stop as soon as he could and make some money.

Rouge hesitated. 'Well,' he said, 'there's Elliott. Couple of little towns before then, I think.'

Rees looked at Boudreaux. 'Does Elliott sound familiar?'

'Maybe.' He paused a few seconds and then burst out, 'I ride horses. I go where Mr Asher tells me.'

'Oh, come on,' Rouge said, sneering. 'You might be hanged for murder. Are you sure you want to protect the people who abandoned you here like garbage?' Boudreaux flinched.

'Don't,' Thomas said, rising from his chair. Rees, who'd forgotten he was there, jumped. 'He may be a wizard with horses but he's slow. He's not going to know anything, no matter how hard you push him.'

Rouge turned to his cousin and addressed him in French. Rees didn't understand all of the words but the ugly tone told him everything he needed to know. Thomas responded with a 'pfft' and a rude hand motion.

'Is Rouge keeping you fed?' Lydia asked Boudreaux. Rouge stepped forward as though he would intervene, but Rees halted him with an upraised arm.

'*Oui.* Uh – yes.' Boudreaux's response was weak.

'I saw some of the show,' Lydia said. 'It was extraordinary.'

'But the gentleman on the horse was nowhere near as skilled as you are,' Rees said.

'He is . . .' Boudreaux paused, searching for the word. 'Um. My second?'

'Ah. Your assistant,' Rees said.

'Yes.'

'Don't worry. I'll continue investigating,' Rees said now. 'I'll get to the bottom of this. And if you're innocent, I'll do my utmost to have you released.' Boudreaux's desperate expression did not change and Rees did not want to promise anything further, not until he was absolutely certain he could prove the groom's innocence and identify the guilty. Leah deserved justice as well and Rees would make sure she got it.

'Finished?' Rouge asked, turning to Rees. 'He needs to get back to work.' Rees nodded.

'And we need to find that circus,' Rouge added.

Yes,' Rees agreed with a grin. How quickly Rouge's command not to meddle became 'we'. 'Maybe we should take this discussion into your office,' he added, glancing at Thomas. His ears were practically lengthening so he could listen.

'Get your sister out to the bar,' Rouge told Thomas. 'We'll be in my office. And get to work.'

'Wait,' Thomas said, following them from the kitchen. He carefully shut the door behind him. 'Boudreaux didn't tell you everything.'

'What?' Rouge said rudely.

'What happened?' Rees asked.

'Mr Asher was here,' Thomas said.

'Here? At the tavern?' Rees asked. Thomas nodded.

'I didn't see him,' Rouge said, impatience in every line of his body.

'He came around to the back, to speak to Boudreaux. They argued,' Thomas said.

'About what?' Rees asked.

'Mr Asher wanted Boudreaux to return to the circus,' Thomas said. 'But he didn't want to.'

'I wouldn't want to either,' said Rouge with a dismissive flap of his hand. 'Come on, Rees.'

'Thank you,' Rees said. He did not see what importance the argument had right now but one never knew. As he turned to follow the constable, Thomas reached out and grabbed Rees's sleeve.

'Boudreaux is scared of Mr Asher. Don't know why, he was polite even when he was arguing. But Boudreaux came back into the kitchen trembling.'

SEVENTEEN

'Questioning Aaron should not be difficult,' Rouge said when they were all seated in Rouge's crowded office. 'He's in Zion. But the circus—'

'And Shem,' Rees interrupted the constable. 'Aaron may have nothing to do with this.'

'Do you have a map of the area around Durham?' Lydia asked Rouge.

'Why?'

'Well, some of the towns Mr Asher wanted to visit are listed on the poster,' Lydia said. 'And Boudreaux said the circus was traveling west and the town of Elliott sounded familiar to him. So, if we examine a map and compare the towns on the bill with the area around Elliott we might see . . .' She stopped. Rouge had leaped to his feet and was sorting through the rolled-up documents on the shelf over his desk.

As Rees pushed several stacks of books and ledgers aside on the table Rouge spread out the map. 'This is Elliott,' he said, pointing with his thick finger. Rees traced a line from Durham to Elliott. 'There's a number of smaller towns between Elliott and Durham,' he said.

'There's a lot of them,' Rouge said, 'but most are so small they're lucky if they have a general store.'

'Here's Grand Forks,' Lydia said, tapping her finger on the map. 'That's on the bill.'

'Metinic Lake and Squapan Falls are between Durham and Higgins Springs,' Rees said. 'Almost in a straight line.'

'Grand Forks is the largest village in that area,' Rouge said. 'Of course, Asher might have taken his circus in a different direction.'

'True,' Rees agreed. 'But right now this is the best lead we've got.' He straightened up. 'How many days drive are those towns?'

'Grand Forks is probably less than a day,' Rouge said. 'I don't know how far Metinic Lake is past that.' He paused and added, 'Are you planning to go there?'

'If I want to question Shem, I must. Don't you agree?' Rees looked at the constable who nodded reluctantly.

'There's something else,' Lydia said, raising her gaze to meet Rees's. 'I wonder if Leah was the murderer's first.'

'What do you mean?' Rees asked although he thought he knew.

'I'm not sure myself,' Lydia admitted. 'It's just that – well, everything was so well planned no one saw anything. If the devil who murdered Leah is a member of the circus, he could be doing the same thing in every town in which the circus performs.'

Rees exchanged a glance with the constable.

'She's right,' Rouge said reluctantly. 'I'll need that bill – I should write to the constables in all the towns the circus has visited.'

Lydia touched Rees's hand. 'I don't believe Brother Aaron is guilty of this. I know he's difficult. He doesn't follow all of the rules and he resents the Eldresses. But he is so passionate about celibacy that he doesn't even attend Union.'

'And that's exactly why I think he might be guilty,' Rouge said. 'It's not natural for a man to deny his natural urges.'

'How can you even say that?' Lydia asked with a flash of temper. 'Your own priests are celibate, are they not?'

Rouge's mouth dropped open. 'Now wait,' he said and stopped, unable to find any other words.

'He followed Shem and Leah,' Lydia said, turning to Rees, 'because Aaron is very protective of children. You know that to be true.'

Rees nodded slowly, remembering Aaron's devotion to the boy Calvin and his terrible grief at the child's death. 'He's protective of

the boys,' he said. 'But we can't be sure he's innocent until we
finish looking into this.'

'Exactly,' Rouge said. 'Aaron must be questioned.'

Rees looked from Rouge to Lydia and back again. 'And I have
to follow the circus. No one else can do it.'

Rees and Lydia left the tavern and started for home, stopping on
the way to post Rees's letter to David at the General Store. After
wasting several hours on this fruitless journey, they would be rushing
all day to catch up.

Nonetheless, at the end of the main road where it turned into
Surry, Rees did not take the left. He turned right, driving down
toward Zion. Lydia turned a look of surprise upon her husband. He
smiled at her. 'We're out already,' he said. 'We might as well try
to question Aaron. I'd like to be the one to question him – at least
before the constable does. His tactics are not always the most
productive.'

'You mean because he frightens the other person into silence?'
Lydia asked acidly.

'That. And he doesn't always ask the necessary questions.' Rouge
tried to pull out the truth with intimidation; Rees preferred a subtler
approach.

The main street in the Shaker village was already crowded with
people heading toward the Meeting House. 'It's later than I thought,'
Rees said.

'I'm positive Annie has everything well in hand,' Lydia said. But
she didn't sound sure and when he looked at her, he saw the worried
pleat between her brows. Since Jerusha's abduction the previous
year, she could not be easy leaving her children.

'We'll be home soon,' he said reassuringly.

He pulled the wagon to a stop in front of the barn and tied
Hannibal to the rail. 'I don't see Jonathan anywhere,' Lydia said.

'Or any of the Elders,' he agreed, looking around at the silent
villagers. 'Maybe they're already inside the Meeting House.'

'Maybe,' she said, her eyes roving over the crowd. 'Wait, there's
Esther.' Lydia pointed to the Eldress poised on the steps of the
Dwelling House. Lydia waved to catch her attention and they
threaded their way through the crowd to meet her. 'Did you find
Shem?' Esther asked.

'The circus has left town,' Rees said.

'And Shem with it,' Lydia said.

Although no sound escaped Esther's lips, her mouth formed a round 'o'.

'So, I want to speak with Aaron again,' Rees said.

'You can't,' Esther said.

'What Sister means,' Jonathan said, coming up behind Esther, 'is that Aaron isn't here.'

'Where is he?' Rees asked.

'You'd better come inside to the office,' Jonathan said as he and Esther exchanged a glance.

Rees already knew this would be bad news.

Once inside the office Jonathan said, 'Aaron is gone. And a cart and horse are missing.'

'We don't know where he's gone,' Esther said, adding grimly, 'although we can guess.'

'He's gone after Shem,' Lydia said. 'Of course.'

'But how did he know where to go?' Rees asked. And then, as he thought it through, he added emphatically, 'God damn!'

'Will,' Lydia said in reproof.

'Don't you see?' Rees asked, turning to face her. 'Aaron knew all along Shem was running away to join the circus. He lied to us.'

Jonathan looked as though he wanted to swear too. 'We can't be sure,' he said. 'I hope Aaron wouldn't do that.'

'It doesn't make sense,' Esther said. 'If he knew Shem was planning to run away, why wait to follow him?'

'That's right,' Jonathan said with a nod. 'Why didn't they go together?' No one spoke for several seconds.

'Because Aaron didn't know, at least he didn't when Shem left,' Rees said finally. 'So how did he find out?' He thought for a moment. 'I want to see Aaron's bedchamber.'

Jonathan looked at Rees. 'Why?'

'Because Aaron found something that told him where Shem went,' he said.

Jonathan looked skeptical and Rees could see the Shaker wanted to say no. But he didn't. 'Very well,' he said at last. 'Come with me.'

Rees followed Jonathan into the hall and down the stairs to the first floor. Rees knew this hallway well. When he'd come here from

Dugard over two years ago he'd stayed in a room at the front. Aaron's chamber was by the back door and he too occupied the room by himself. 'He's difficult,' Jonathan said as though he heard Rees's thoughts. 'And we have an uneven number of Brothers so . . .' He lifted his shoulders in a slight shrug.

Rees nodded, brushing past Jonathan and knocking him into the doorframe in his eagerness to get inside. 'Sorry,' Rees said, still in too much of a hurry to even look at the Elder.

Like all the bedchambers Rees had seen, this one was small and sparsely furnished. A single bed occupied most of the space. A table with an ewer and a jug was positioned in one corner and a small desk sat next to it. A chair, presumably for the desk, was suspended on the wall from a peg with a coat hung nearby.

Rees looked around. One of the Sisters had draped the bedding over the foot rail to air and swept the floor. Nothing appeared unusual in any way. 'When did you discover Aaron was missing?' he asked Jonathan.

'He didn't turn up for his morning chores.'

'So, we don't know when he left,' Rees said, glancing over his shoulder.

Jonathan shook his head. 'We don't but I think we must assume he left immediately after you did,' he said.

That meant, Rees thought, that Aaron had a sizeable head start. Hopefully, he did not know exactly where Shem was going.

Rees systematically began to search. He found nothing but a few items of clothing in the chest of drawers. Only a Bible reposed upon the bare desk. Rees turned his attention to the bed. First, he shook out the bedding. Nothing. He slid his hands under the mattress and then he lay on the floor to peer up at the ropes. There was nothing slipped between them.

'What do you expect to find?' Jonathan asked.

'I don't know,' Rees replied. 'I'll recognize it when I find it.' Jonathan's mouth flattened into a thin line but he said nothing.

Rees went through the pockets of the coat hanging on the peg. Still nothing.

'Maybe Shem did tell Aaron where he was going,' Lydia said from the doorway. Her training as a Shaker still prevented her from entering a man's bedchamber unless she was cleaning it. 'Surely Aaron isn't roaming the countryside with no destination in mind.'

'He might be if he is worried enough about Shem,' Jonathan said. 'I doubt he knows anything. Surely he would have said . . .' He bit his lip.

Rees swept his eyes once more around the room. He had searched everywhere with no result. Maybe he was wrong. In desperation he picked up the Bible and flipped through the pages. Nothing. But then the tome fell open at a middle page. The corner had been turned over and from the looks of the greasy paper Aaron had read this section many times. But that was not what caught Rees's interest. A torn piece of thick paper had been tucked into the spine.

'What's that?' Jonathan asked, peering over Rees's shoulder. He answered his own question. 'It looks like Aaron was moved by the Spirit and chose to draw something to honor Him,' he said in a wondering tone.

Rees looked at the faint pencil sketch; the left side of the Tree of Life. He could not imagine the dour Aaron drawing anything so ethereal. 'Where's the rest of it?' he muttered, trying to remove the paper. It was firmly fixed. No wonder Aaron had torn the sheet when he'd tried to remove it. 'And why is it here?'

'Brother Aaron was particularly fond of that Psalm,' Jonathan said in a repressive tone.

Rees took his thumbnail and gently pried up one end of the drawing. Then slowly, oh so slowly, he teased out the rest of the scrap. He never knew what impulse inspired him to turn over the paper but he did. '"Gon to",' Rees read in clumsy block printing. 'God damn it,' Rees said emphatically and very loudly.

'Rees, please,' Jonathan said. 'Such language.'

'Don't you see,' Rees bellowed, turning on the man beside him. 'Shem left a note.'

'He couldn't have,' Jonathan said. 'Shem is illiterate.'

'So, you tell me then why did Aaron leave?' Rees demanded. He didn't care he was shouting. 'Aaron knew all along that Shem was running off to the circus.'

'Will, Will,' Lydia said. 'Stop shouting. The constable can probably hear you in town.' Jonathan watched her in dismay as she entered the bedchamber. 'What's the matter?'

'Look at this,' Rees said, handing his wife the slip of paper. 'Shem left a note. And Aaron kept it without telling anyone.'

'That seems unlikely,' Esther said, also stepping into the room and peering over Lydia's shoulder. 'Even if Shem knew how to read and write some, these chicken scratches make no sense.'

'Yes, they do,' Rees said. 'Look.' He pointed at the top line of pale letters. '"Gon to" – it doesn't take much imagination to see it means "Gone to circus".'

'And these,' Lydia said, pointing at the marks on the bottom, 'these are letters. See?' She ran her finger over the first one. '"L".'

'That means nothing,' Jonathan said.

'I think it does,' Lydia said. 'These are the letters: L. E. A. T.'

'Leat?' Esther repeated. 'What does leat mean?'

'No,' Lydia said. 'It's L, E, Ah, T.' She looked up and met her husband's eyes. 'It's Ellio—'

'Elliott,' Rees said, understanding in a flash. 'Aaron is following the circus to Elliott.'

Lydia nodded. 'Shem knew where the circus was going and left a note. He probably didn't want Aaron, or anyone else,' she added, her eyes moving to Jonathan, 'to worry.'

'Aaron has at least half a day's head start,' Rees said.

'I don't understand why Aaron would lie,' Jonathan said miserably.

'I'll have to leave right away,' Rees said. Lydia bit her lip.

'Yes, I suppose you do if you want to catch them.'

'I just hope the circus stopped along the way,' Rees said.

EIGHTEEN

The children playing were outside when Rees and Lydia arrived home. Lydia's mouth turned down at the corners and she shook her head in silent disapproval. But Annie had swept the kitchen floor and both wood and water had been fetched. 'Bread is rising on the board,' Annie said. Lydia began to smile. Rees decided he was glad Annie came often to the farm. She worked hard and would be company for Lydia when he was away.

'Annie and Jerusha have everything well in hand here,' Lydia said, turning a meaningful look upon her husband. 'I want to accompany you.'

He shook his head at her. 'It may be dangerous,' he said.

She fixed her clear blue eyes upon him. 'Dangerous? You're going after a Shaker Brother and a boy,' she said. 'How dangerous could it be?'

'I'll be sleeping rough,' he said. 'Camping by the side of the road.'

'But it will only be for a day or two,' she argued.

'One of us should stay here,' he replied. 'And I can travel faster alone.'

Lydia stared at him for several seconds. Seeing that he would not yield she sighed but did not protest again.

Rees left as soon as he could. He packed a change of clothes and Lydia handed up a basket of small beer, her prize-winning cheese and Annie's fresh bread. Excitement warred with reluctance; he hated to see the disappointment on Lydia's face. But the anticipation and the joy he felt at being on the road won. By the time he left the outskirts of Durham behind, he was smiling. Even a sudden rain shower could not dampen his pleasure. He felt as though a great weight had slid from his shoulders. This short jaunt felt like a holiday from all his cares.

He had not expected to reach another town until nightfall but with the early start he was almost in Grand Forks by late afternoon. Just outside of town he spotted some activity in a field by the road. A number of men were congregated in a farmer's meadow so like the Reynard's buckwheat field Rees experienced a second of dislocation. The sense he'd seen this before tingled through him, igniting his curiosity. With sad certainty he knew what those men had found, parked his wagon and jumped the fence into the field. Of the four men in the field, two were standing with their backs to him. The other two were kneeling by the body: doctor and coroner, Rees guessed.

The fellows who were upright turned in unison to stare at the interloper and, after a few seconds, walked forward to meet him as he crossed the pasture. 'I'm a deputy constable from Durham,' Rees said, shading the truth slightly. 'We had a murder a few days ago and thought it might be connected with the traveling circus. I'm following them now. I saw you and wondered?'

Both men listened carefully and one said, 'So you think one of the circus folk is going around killing people?' He was a short, burly man with a belly that hung over the waistband of his breeches. His companion, a tall, skinny man with thinning, mouse-brown hair eyed Rees doubtfully but said nothing.

'Yes, I do,' Rees said, extending a hand. 'Will Rees.'

'Constable MacGregor,' said the heavier of the two men. Rees peered down at the body on the ground, trying to see around the broad backs of the two people who were kneeling. The only things visible were a straw bonnet, blown some distance away by the breeze, fair hair spattered by red blood, and muddy boots at the other end.

'This the victim?' Rees asked.

'Yes.' The short man turned pale-blue eyes on Rees.

'Was the circus here?' Rees asked.

The constable nodded. His deputy said, 'Circus just left this morning.'

'I didn't allow them to stay,' Constable MacGregor said. 'Don't want their kind here. Thieves and whoremongers, the lot of them. What happened in Durham?'

'The body of a young girl was discovered while the circus was in town,' Rees said, involuntarily falling into the constable's laconic style of speech. 'A young girl, violated, strangled to death and dumped in a field. We think there might be more victims. I'm following the circus to get some answers.'

MacGregor did not remove his light eyes from Rees until he'd finished speaking. 'This murder isn't connected.'

'But—' Rees began, staring at the woman's bonnet blowing through the field.

'This is a young boy,' MacGregor said. 'Beaten to death.'

'Boy?' Rees took a step back.

'Couple of years ago we had a murder of a young girl, just as you describe,' said the tall man. Despite his colorless appearance his voice was deep and resonant. 'Remember, Mac?'

MacGregor nodded. 'I do. But there was no circus then. No strangers in town at all that I remember.' He looked at Rees but he was too surprised to speak.

'I dread telling his mother,' the constable said. 'Young Jesse here was the baby of the family, the last one home.'

'If you're tracking the circus,' the deputy said to Rees, 'they were heading west.'

'Either of you gentlemen know the best way to go?'

'South and west,' said the deputy. 'Probably towards Elliott.'

'Come back to my office,' the constable invited Rees. 'I'll show you a shortcut on the map.' He turned to the man still kneeling on the ground. 'You all right, Doc?'

'Yes. Send back a wagon. We'll have to bury the boy in a closed casket. His own mother wouldn't recognize him now. It's a shame – he was her youngest. Now who will care for her in her old age?'

Rees turned and strode through the field to his wagon and climbed into the seat. He couldn't shake the certainty there was something odd about the boy's death. But, after pondering it for a few minutes, he put it out of his mind. Although the puzzle tantalized, this death had nothing to do with Leah's.

Once within the village limits, he began looking for an inn or tavern where he could park his wagon. And ask some questions; innkeepers usually knew most of what was happening in their communities.

The first establishment he found was nearer to the center of the village. Rees worried that since it was Saturday the inn and stable might be full, but the ostler said no. 'Most of them farmers keep their nags and wagons at the market with 'em. I got room.' So Rees unhitched Hannibal and pushed the wagon to one side. He watched the ostler lead the gelding into the stall. Although the man spoke poorly through his missing teeth and was layered in grime, he crooned as he urged Hannibal into the stall. This inn would do.

Rees went through the back door to the ordinary beyond for some supper. A few slices of bread and cheese were not sufficient for a man of Rees's size and his stomach was growling. The savory aromas permeating the stable yard had tantalized him as he spoke to the ostler and the sweet smell of roasting meat was even stronger inside. Rees found a seat by the door and gestured at a busy serving girl. Some kind of potpie seemed the popular meal of the day so when the girl finally stopped by his table he was able to point to it. It turned out to be beef potpie, the beef probably left over from yesterday's joint, but the pie was hot and delicious. Rees cleaned his plate and followed it up with coffee and a slab of cake.

By the time he stepped out on to the main street, it was growing dark. The streets were congested with wagons, mostly sunburned farmers and their wives on their way home. Rees turned to accost the next gentleman who passed by, an elegantly clad man in a gray frock coat, to ask for directions to the constable. And found himself staring into the face of Piggy Hanson! Both men gaped at one another in astonishment.

'Piggy Hanson!' Rees said.

'Rees!' the magistrate said at the same moment. 'I've asked you one hundred times not to call me Piggy.' He nervously touched the frothy cravat at his throat. Rees recalled the clown's pig and involuntarily smiled. Piggy looked startled. 'What are you doing here?'

Rees hesitated but couldn't think of any reason not to reply honestly. 'Looking for Asher's circus.'

'Did they leave Durham?' Hanson asked.

'They left yesterday.'

Hanson eyed Rees. 'So, you were in Durham also?'

Cursing himself for his thoughtless honesty, Rees chose not to reply. The magistrate nodded as though he understood everything now.

'I should have guessed your wife would run to that religious village.' He smiled and Rees read knowledge and cruelty in Piggy's expression. 'What's its name?'

Rees pretended he didn't hear. As magistrate, Hanson had signed the warrant for Lydia's arrest on the charge of witchcraft. Rees wondered if someone from his hometown – like the superstitious Farley – would pursue Lydia and try to arrest her now that Piggy knew where they lived.

But Hanson did not continue that topic. Instead he said, 'Well, the circus has been here and gone. Why are you following them?' He began to slap his silver-headed cane against his boot and turned his gaze away from Rees as though not much interested in the answer.

'A young girl was found murdered and it is possible one of the performers is guilty.' Rees chose his words very carefully; he didn't want to accuse Boudreaux or anyone else of such a crime, not without being certain anyway. Besides, look where his honesty had gotten him – now Piggy knew where they'd taken refuge.

'Ah. The girl's body was found after the circus left town then?'

'No.' Rees shifted his weight uncomfortably. 'One of the performers was suspected.'

'And you let him go?' The magistrate laughed. 'Wasn't enough evidence to satisfy you?'

Rees wanted to strike the other man. This was more like the

Hanson he knew, a mocking bully. 'It wasn't like that,' he said through gritted teeth and keeping a tight rein on his temper.

Hanson shook his head. 'What happened? Did the constable free them? Or did they sneak out in the middle of the night?' he asked. Since this was exactly what had happened, Rees gaped in surprise. 'Circus people can't be trusted,' Hanson said. For a moment he stared into space as the cane slapped at his leather boot. 'We've never gotten along, you and I,' he said at last. 'But we are on the same side. We both fight for justice in our own ways.' He paused. Rees inclined his head very cautiously, not sure where this speech was going. 'Both of us want to see the murderer of that young girl caught. So, I'm going to pass along a tidbit of information I heard from a casual acquaintance – that the circus is going to stop over in Elliott. I can't promise it will still be there, but if it isn't there perhaps someone will offer a new direction.'

'Thank you,' Rees said, almost too astonished to speak. In fact, he could not have been more surprised if his horse had spoken.

'See that you make the most of it,' Hanson said sternly. He turned and held one hand in the air. As his carriage came up the street behind them, he added, 'Farley is no longer the constable in Dugard. I think you should know that.'

Rees stared at Hanson in bewilderment as the coachman pulled the elegant equipage to a stop and jumped down to open the door. Rees had a good view of the inside with its upholstered seats. Although the curtains were tied back now, the ribbons could be loosened and the cloth panels closed over the windows.

Unsettled by the interchange, Rees watched the carriage pull away. Now why had Piggy Hanson told him all of that? To help? Or to throw suspicion elsewhere? After all the magistrate followed a regular circuit and he had been in Durham when Leah was murdered. With the curtains closed the interior of his carriage would be private. And that fine upholstery could have caused those burn-like marks on the backs of Leah's legs.

Had his stops in other towns corresponded to more murders?

Despite his dislike of the magistrate Rees didn't want to believe it. They'd been boys together. But now the suspicion would prey on him until he knew for sure.

NINETEEN

N ow the sky was growing dark and the shops were beginning to close. Most of the people on the street were young men. They all seemed to be heading to the tavern at which Rees had just eaten his dinner. Soon the streets would be filled with drunken men and fights; he wanted to be gone by then. He couldn't afford to stay at the inn and it was spring anyway; he had camped by the road in much worse weather than this. Turning so sharply he elicited a curse and a shove from the man trying to enter the inn, Rees accosted the first gentleman he saw. A portly gentleman with aspirations to town bronze, the fellow wore a fustic yellow coat and the newly fashionable white trousers tucked into glossy Hessian boots. He bobbed his head in reply to Rees's question, the feather on his high-hat fluttering. He stood out among the farmers and simple shopkeepers like a peacock in a flock of sparrows but he knew the direction and pointed to a haberdashery shop across the street.

'Besides serving as our constable,' the gentleman said, 'Mr MacGregor runs our dry goods store.'

Rees nodded his thanks and walked across the street.

An uneasy alliance between a clothiers and a jail, the front of the building boasted shelves of folded cloth and a long table for cutting the fabric. But its back room served as the lockup with a cell tucked into a corner. Rees paused in front of the three steps that led up to the back room and peered through the door. A table piled high with papers was clearly visible right across from the stairs. But the chair beside it was vacant as well.

'Hello?' Rees said.

'Oh, it's you,' MacGregor said, appearing at the top of the steps. 'Come up.'

Rees ascended the few steps to the office at the back. He had interrupted their suppers; the deputy was still eating. He nodded at Rees as MacGregor went to the back of the office. He rummaged through a bucket of rolled maps until he found the one he wanted.

It had yellowed a little with age and when the constable carried it to the cutting table and stretched it out to its full width Rees saw that it had been edited by hand. Newer darker ink delineated property lines as well as streams and bridges.

MacGregor pointed to a road dropping southwest from this town of Grand Forks. 'Follow this road by the mill stream,' the constable said.

Rees peered down at the map, following MacGregor's pointing finger. 'How far?'

'Ten miles maybe before you turn right on a road about here.' His stubby freckled finger pointed at what looked like an inkblot. 'It'll cut off a good bit of time.'

'Most likely you'll reach Elliott before the circus,' MacGregor said as he rolled up the map.

And what if everyone was wrong and Asher had disappeared in a different direction? Then what? His doubt must have shown on his face because MacGregor grinned. 'Don't worry,' he said reassuringly. 'The circus will definitely stop there. Biggest town around.'

'Thank you,' Rees said. And then, feeling he ought to show more interest in their latest tragedy, he added, 'What will happen to the victim's mother now?'

'She'll manage,' MacGregor said in surprise. 'Besides her older boys she has several daughters.'

That explained the girl's bonnet, Rees thought.

'Jesse was almost a daughter,' the deputy said, turning his chuckle into a cough when MacGregor scowled at him.

'Jesse's older brother will take in the widow,' the constable said, putting an end to the subject.

Rees thanked them once again and took his leave.

He drove for as long as there was still light in the sky, pulling over when he could no longer see. With sunset the air quickly cooled, and Rees spent some time building a small fire. Once it was burning he sat down. For the first time since his journey began, he thought of Lydia and his children. Why hadn't he said yes when she'd asked to come? This would be a short trip and, in David's clothes, she appeared to be a boy. Annie and Jerusha could care for the younger children. Rees sighed. If he were honest with himself, he would admit he was enjoying his solitude. He felt like a young

man again, not an old husband with a bunch of children and a farm
to care for.

And Bambola waited at the end of this journey.

Despite the cold he slept well. Arising before dawn, he started his
journey once again. He expected to be traveling until well after noon
but it was barely midmorning when he went round a bend and saw
what looked like circus wagons across the rocky field. He lost sight
of them again as the road went through thick forest. But as he followed
the bends of the muddy and hilly highway, he glimpsed the cluster
of wagons again and again through the trees. At last, following the
road around a low hill, he came upon the wagons pulled up in a
farmer's field. Last year's stalks still covered the ground in spiky
rows. Good thing, Rees thought. He did not think the farmer would
appreciate all these wagons rolling over a freshly planted field.

He followed the wheeled tracks cut into the ground, his wagon
jolting over the ruts. Why had they pulled up here? There were no
villages nearby and, indeed, the circus stadium had not been
constructed. Everyone, it appeared, was gathered around a wagon at
one end. Otto had his shoulder to the wheel. 'Push,' someone on the
other side of the wagon shouted. The strong man pushed, the wagon
rose a few inches, and one of the other men pushed a mat of straw
under the wheel. Rees, who had experienced similar problems with
his vehicle, recognized the damage immediately: a broken axle.

His gaze followed the line of wagons to the very end. Separated
from the other people was a man in a flat-brimmed straw hat, white
shirt, and navy pants. That was Shaker garb. And when he turned
to speak to someone out of sight behind the wagon Rees clearly
saw his face. It was Brother Aaron.

TWENTY

Rees drove a few feet closer and then climbed down from
the wagon. Since all of Brother Aaron's attention was
focused on the unseen speaker – Shem probably – he did
not see Rees approaching until he was almost on him. He expected

Aaron to turn and flee but he didn't. Instead he shouted, 'Run.'

Rees veered to his left intending to catch the boy but Shem didn't run. He stayed where he was, only protesting when Rees grabbed his arm. 'Ow,' he said.

Rees turned to Aaron and said angrily, 'What's the matter with you? You knew I wanted to ask Shem questions and you purposely withheld his note.'

'He knows nothing,' Aaron said. 'He barely knew the girl. And he certainly did not kill her.'

'He isn't accused of murder,' Rees said. 'Do you believe he killed the girl? Or' – and now he released Shem's arm and advanced upon Aaron – 'you killed Leah. And you hope someone else – Boudreaux or Shem here – takes the blame.'

'No! Leah's murder—' Aaron began.

'Is that true?' Shem interrupted, staring at Aaron with eyes round from shock.

'Of course not,' Aaron said, his voice rising. 'I just don't want you dragged into this mess.' He looked at Rees. 'She followed Shem. And then she chose to leave Durham by herself. For all we know, that mountebank intercepted her before he met Shem in town.'

'She didn't follow me,' Shem said. 'We went together. We both wanted to see the circus.'

'Tell me everything that happened?' Rees said, turning his back on Aaron.

'We saw the circus wagons on Surry Road early Thursday morning. It was . . . amazing.' Shem's eyes began to sparkle at the memory. And Rees could easily imagine how these children, isolated within the Shaker community, would respond to the circus's color and flash.

'Leah wanted to go,' Rees murmured.

'I tried to explain that only men and boys were allowed,' Shem said with the unconscious superiority of his sex. 'But she insisted. She said she would call for one of the Brothers if I didn't take her.'

'You don't need to tell Mr Rees anything,' Aaron put in, glaring.

Rees ignored him. 'You left after dinner?' he asked.

'Yes. We crossed the Surry Road to the lane and followed it into town.'

Rees reviewed the timing once again. The two children would have reached the town probably about two fifteen or so. 'Did you see Monsieur Boudreaux riding his horse as you went into town?'

'Yes. That's why I wanted to talk to him.' Shem's voice lifted with excitement. 'Leah and I walked across the fairgrounds—'

'You spoke to Monsieur Boudreaux?'

'Yes. He wasn't back at first so I waited by the horses. And he returned just a few minutes later.'

Rees grabbed the boy's arm. 'Where was Leah?'

'She was there, of course.' Shem stared at Rees as though he were half-witted. 'The show didn't begin until five o'clock.'

'What happened then?' Rees leaned forward.

'Well, Monsieur Boudreaux came back and he was so nice and he showed me all the horses and explained how he trained them.'

'Leave him,' Aaron said, trying to insert his body between Rees and the boy.

'Do you speak French?' Rees asked, trying to absorb all that he was hearing.

'*Un peu,*' the boy replied.

'And Leah?' Rees turned his body, blocking Aaron behind him.

'She was bored. She said she was going home and would come back later. And she left. And I never saw her again.' For the first time, the realization that Leah had started walking back to Zion alone hit Shem and tears filled his eyes. 'It's my fault. I should have gone with her.'

'Would you be willing to tell Constable Rouge your story?'

'No, he isn't,' Aaron said.

As Shem began shaking his head Rees continued. 'You see, Monsieur Boudreaux has been accused of Leah's murder. But he can't be guilty, not if you were with him that afternoon.'

'I'll get in trouble,' Shem said, grimacing.

'Do you want Constable Rouge to hang Monsieur Boudreaux?' Rees asked in a sharp voice. Shem's mouth dropped open and he shook his head.

'No. No. Of course not.'

'You can't take the boy,' Aaron said belligerently.

'He has information that he needs to share with the constable,' Rees said, keeping his voice low and calm with an effort.

'You don't have to go back,' Aaron said, turning to Shem.

'I want to help,' Shem said, his voice breaking on the final word. Scowling, Aaron, retreated.

'We'll return to Durham together,' Rees promised. He paused and added, 'And you should be brave enough to speak to Brother Daniel as well, tell him openly and honestly you want to leave the community.'

'I can't do that,' Shem said. 'He'll be disappointed.'

'You must,' Rees said. 'Sneaking out is the coward's way. Standing up and telling Daniel face to face is the behavior of a man.'

Shem stared at Rees. Finally, swallowing, he said, 'I'll go back.' His voice broke and soared to a high treble. His face went scarlet.

Rees looked at Aaron. 'You should return as well.'

'Of course,' Aaron said, eyeing Rees with dislike. 'I won't let the boy go alone.'

'Mr Rees?' Mr Asher came up behind Rees. 'What are you doing here?' He was dressed in buff breeches and shirtsleeves, his jacket and cravat discarded. Rees glanced at his hands. They were badly scratched, but several of the marks were so new they were still oozing blood. They told Rees absolutely nothing except that Asher was not above working with his hands.

'How nice to see you again, Mr Rees,' Bambola said as she came up behind Asher.

'I came to fetch the boy,' Rees said as he turned. 'His testimony should free Boudreaux.'

Asher's brows rose. 'Free him? I thought he'd be hanged by now.'

Rees shook his head. Deciding he did not want to confide the entire sorry tale, he said only, 'He's not even in jail.'

'Where is he then?' Bambola asked.

'Working in the kitchen of a local tavern,' Rees said.

Bambola glared at Asher. 'You said they were going to hang him.'

'I thought they were.' He chewed his lower lip. At last he looked at Rees and said, 'As you see, we are stopped, probably for at least the rest of today. A broken axle that must be repaired before we continue. And Elliott is still some distance away. If Pip Boudreaux is a free man, as you say, I'll return to your town and collect him.' He offered Rees a faint smile. 'When we heard the gunshot that last night we thought he'd been killed. And we did not want to be attacked as well.'

'Of course,' Rees said in understanding. 'But the constable prevented any harm from coming to your man.'

'I owe him a debt of gratitude then,' Asher said with a bow.

'Thank you, thank you,' Bambola said, leaning forward and putting her hand on Rees's. He could feel the warmth of her hand through her glove. He cleared his throat but found he could not speak. 'He is one of my greatest friends and I am so grateful to you.'

'I'm sure Mr Boudreaux will be glad to see you return for him,' Rees stammered.

'And when we're in town,' Bambola added, smiling at him from under her straw bonnet, 'I must do another reading for you.'

'Of course,' he said. He knew he should make his excuses, say he would be too busy and that superstitious claptrap made him uncomfortable. But he did not. Instead, with the prospect of seeing her again dangling in front of him, he executed a clumsy bow. 'I'll look forward to it,' he said in a strangled voice. His face felt as though it was on fire.

'In fact,' Mr Asher said, clapping Rees on the shoulder, 'why don't you join us for our noon meal.' Rees hesitated. 'There is no town around us,' Asher continued persuasively. 'Nowhere to stop.'

'Shem and I won't run away, if that's worrying you,' Aaron said in a sour voice. Rees, who hadn't been concerned about that, shot him a hostile glance.

'Very well,' he said to Asher. 'I'm delighted to accept.'

While Hannibal was pegged out with the circus horses, Asher brought Rees to the makeshift camp on the other side of the wagons. Inside a circle cleared of last year's stalks, a fire burned enthusiastically under a bubbling pot.

'Sit by Billy,' Asher directed, pointing to the dwarf.

Billy was sitting next to the strong man, his eyes fixed on the woman stirring the soup. As Rees found a seat, Billy said, 'You are so graceful, Jeanne. Even stirring the soup is poetry.' She smiled politely and handed him a wooden bowl filled with fragrant stew.

'You are wasting your time,' Otto said, in such a thick accent Rees could barely understand him.

'It's my time,' Billy said.

'But you have so little of it left,' Otto retorted as he took his bread and put it in his soup.

Rees tasted his bread. It was so stale and hard he quickly followed suit.

'We bought the bread in Grand Forks,' Billy said conversationally, turning to Rees.

'Did you put on a performance?' Rees asked, knowing they hadn't.

'We planned to. But the constable asked us to leave before we'd even begun building the arena.' Billy forced a lopsided smile. 'Maybe it was for the best.'

'What do you mean?' Rees asked. Billy did not reply. Putting down his barely touched bowl, he coughed. The first brief sound rapidly became a relentless grinding cough from deep in the chest. Scowling at Rees as though this was his fault, Otto helped Billy to his feet and they moved away. Rees saw the blood on Billy's lips and fingers with a spasm of pity.

'He has the white plague,' Asher explained as he sat down. 'It comes and goes.'

'Will he return to his family?' Rees asked, staring after Billy. He'd known others, too many in fact, who had died of the disease.

'*We* are his family,' Asher said, turning to look at Rees. 'He was born on a farm near Philadelphia. His small stature made him unsuited for farming and when he got sick his birth family expelled him. We found him, half-starved, begging by the side of the road.'

'He was lucky you took him in,' Rees said.

'We were the fortunate ones. He is popular with the audiences.' Asher smiled. 'We are a family of misfits. My father disinherited me. Of course, the old sot had already gambled away everything that wasn't entailed. Boudreaux is French, the scion of one of the noble houses that met their end at the guillotine. He still has nightmares almost every night.'

Rees nodding, understanding all too well. The past, especially one bound up with fear and guilt, frequently came back to haunt one in the wee hours of the morning.

Asher pointed to a group of young men, all dark and with enough resemblance for Rees to suspect they were related. 'They are from Italy, Jews running from that Devil's spawn Napoleon. And Otto, he killed a man. Accidentally, in a tavern brawl.' Rees turned to stare at Otto, who had returned to finish his dinner. His hands were enormous, as befitted a man Otto's size, and Rees could see several bloody scratches. So, the strong man had killed someone, that was documented. But no one had seen him on the road when Leah met her end.

'And Bambola?' he asked finally.

'Ah. It is different for her. She is from a circus family. Fortune smiled upon me the day I met her.' Asher looked at Rees. 'But what of you? Why did you follow the boy? We have had other boys run away to join us' – he pointed to a group of ragamuffins clustered around Shem – 'but rarely does someone come looking. Especially not two men.'

'I had questions to ask,' Rees said, purposely vague. He turned to examine Asher's hands once again. They were extraordinarily large, well able to circle a girl's neck and squeeze, and as he'd noted before covered with scratches. But the nails, now rimmed with dirt, had been chewed down to the quick and the cuticles were ragged and bloody. Rees felt himself relax; Asher could not be Leah's strangler.

'About the girl's death?' Asher asked, looking puzzled. 'You surprise me. Why not accept Boudreaux as the murderer? In every other town every other constable would believe he was the guilty man.'

'*You* don't believe it,' Rees said.

Asher stared, his dark brows rising almost to his hairline. 'You are correct. I know him too well to believe he's guilty. He is too softhearted.' He paused and took a bite of stew. 'Is there someone else you suspect?'

'It's too early to say,' Rees said. 'Besides, shouldn't the search for the truth be more about protecting the innocent rather than punishing the guilty?'

'You are a very unusual man,' Asher said in surprise. 'Most people wouldn't blink at hanging one of us circus folk.'

'Doesn't make it right,' Rees said. Asher turned to gaze at Rees before breaking into a wide smile. He clapped Rees on the shoulder and they finished their meals in a companionable silence.

TWENTY-ONE

The sun had barely crossed the zenith when Rees, followed by Brother Aaron and Shem, left the circus encampment to return home. At first worried that Aaron might decide to veer off and try to escape, Rees was pleased to see the Shaker Brother keep up. They made good time. They passed the village of Grand Forks mid-afternoon without stopping and Rees began to think they might make it all the way to Durham in one long day.

The sun was beginning to set when they approached Durham. Rees knew he would have to travel the remainder of the way home in darkness, but he was on familiar roads now. Even Hannibal, who'd walked more and more slowly as he tired, began to move a little faster now that he knew his barn and his supper waited.

Although he yearned to continue to home, Rees pulled into the inn yard behind Rouge's tavern. He wanted to make sure Shem spoke to Rouge before running away again. And he probably would if Daniel tried to keep him at Zion. Shem, it was clear, would not make a Shaker despite Aaron's attentions, and Rees thought the boy would be happier with Asher's circus.

Constable Rouge greeted their arrival in his tavern with surprise. 'You found the boy.'

Rees looked around. Since it was now past seven o'clock at night and on a Sunday, there were few customers. 'This lad has something to tell you,' Rees said, pushing the boy forward.

Shem stumbled into speech and gradually, as Rouge understood what he was being told, the amused smile dropped from his face. 'Are you telling me, boy, that you were speaking with Boudreaux while that girl you came into town with was being murdered?'

Shem went white.

Rees grabbed the constable's arm. 'Really Rouge,' he said disapprovingly, 'must you terrify the boy?'

Rouge threw down his rag upon the scarred bar. 'Wait. Just wait.' He stamped away, bellowing for his cousins.

'Doesn't he believe me?' Shem asked.

'He's an honest man. He'll do what's right.' Rees added half under his breath, 'I hope he does.'

Rouge returned with Thomas in tow.

Rouge gestured Rees and Shem to an empty table in a corner. Aaron trailed after them. 'All right,' Rouge said, 'tell me the whole story again. Slowly this time.' Shem stumbled through his tale once more.

'Look,' Rees explained impatiently, 'Shem and Leah left Zion immediately after dinner at noon. They took the lane and arrived in town probably between a quarter after two and half past.'

Rouge nodded. 'That follows,' he agreed.

'Well,' Rees continued, 'Boudreaux had already departed on his ride down the road. If he rode to the junction with the Surry Road, as Paul Reynard said he did, and rode back, he could not have arrived back in town until two thirty, two forty-five.' Rouge nodded reluctantly.

'Leah was still with Shem.' Rees glanced at the boy, who nodded. 'When Boudreaux returned, Shem and Leah spoke to him. But Leah did not want to stay.'

'She was bored,' Shem interjected in a low voice.

'So, she started home.' Rees paused, gathering his thoughts. 'Are you with me so far?' Rouge did not speak. 'Instead of following the lane – I'm not sure why, maybe she saw Aaron and was afraid or couldn't find it, she took the road. Someone approached her there. That's where her body was found. Shem stayed with Boudreaux talking until when, Shem?'

'He showed me some tricks,' Shem said, his face lighting up with remembered pleasure. 'But then he had to get ready for the performance. And it was getting late. Maybe four thirty? Or after. So I left.'

'He arrived in Zion for supper,' Aaron said.

'Just because you wish Boudreaux guilty does not make it so,' Rees told Rouge emphatically.

'But how could the villain not be seen?' Rouge asked in frustration. 'Or heard? I'm certain she was screaming all the while . . .'

With a gasp, Shem slid limply to the floor.

'Oh no,' Rees said, reaching down to pick up the unconscious boy.

'I forgot,' Rouge said in a guilty voice. Turning, he shouted at his cousin, 'Whiskey.'

'No,' Rees said. 'Not for him. He's from Zion.'

'Ah yes.' Rouge grinned at Rees. 'Fortunately, I know you don't drink whiskey either and I had the girl put on coffee for you. Or is he not permitted to drink coffee either, Mr Rees?'

'Coffee would be fine,' Rees replied, ignoring Rouge's mockery. He wrestled Shem, who weighed more than his skinny body would suggest, into the chair. He had regained consciousness but remained white and shaky. By then the barmaid had slopped coffee into three large mugs. Rees poured cream into one and sugared it heavily before putting it into Shem's hands. 'Drink,' he said. 'You'll feel better.' Aaron put his hands around one of the mugs but did not drink.

As Rees doctored his own coffee and took a sip, Rouge poured out a glass of the amber whiskey. Frowning in thought, he took a drink. This time Rees had the sense to keep silent.

At last Rouge exhaled in acceptance. 'All right, maybe Boudreaux could not have murdered the Shaker girl. I'll release him.'

'The circus will be returning for him,' Rees said helpfully.

'But someone killed that girl. And that someone could still be one of those circus people. You say they're coming back? Good. I'll tell that Mr Asher and his crew of villains to stay in Durham until we find the murderer.'

Rees knew the circus master would not enjoy obeying that directive but did not say so. After all, Rouge was correct. Someone had murdered Leah. And if Boudreaux was not the guilty party, then the killer was still out there, free to kill again. 'And by the way,' Rouge said to Rees as he and his companions prepared to leave, 'come by tomorrow. I have something to tell you.'

Something that the constable did not want anyone else to know, Rees guessed. 'First thing in the morning,' he promised.

By the time Shem finished his coffee and followed Rees and Aaron from the tavern, it was quite dark. Only a few threads of light still streaked the sky. Shem, swaying on his feet, climbed up to the seat. That was when Rees realized he had to light the lanterns on each side of the wagon – it was too dark to travel without light – and rather than struggle with his tinderbox he went back inside the inn to borrow a coal. When he returned he found Shem asleep in the wagon bed.

Aaron had been waiting patiently, seemingly content to drive to Zion in the dark. He glanced at Shem without comment and climbed into his cart.

They started off. Since Aaron had not brought his own lantern, he followed Rees closely behind, almost too closely Rees thought.

They arrived in Zion long after supper was over. Since most of the Sisters and Brothers had retired for the night – daytime chores began early – few candles illuminated the windows of the Dwelling House.

Rees went up the steps and into the building. It was silent and felt almost empty despite the number of people living behind those closed doors. He opened the front door and peered inside. The entire first floor was dark but candlelight glimmered from one of the rooms at the top of the stairs. Rees hurried up the staircase and tapped lightly on the door.

'Come.'

Jonathan was sitting at the desk, the light from a solitary candle spilling over the papers spread across the surface. He looked up at Rees without speaking. 'I found them,' Rees said. 'And brought them back. They're downstairs.'

Jonathan sighed and rose to his feet, rubbing the bridge of his nose. He gestured for Rees to precede him down the staircase. When they stepped outside, Rees found that Aaron had awakened Shem. The boy was standing by the wagon looking both drowsy and confused.

'What happened?' Jonathan asked.

Shem launched into a confused, and confusing, explanation. Finally, Jonathan held up his hand. 'I am not sure I understand entirely,' he said, 'but I gather you accompanied Leah into Durham. While there you engaged in conversation with one of the circus performers, the one currently accused of Leah's death, and you were still talking to him when she left town to come home.'

'Yes,' replied Shem in a hesitant voice. 'I know I'm in trouble.'

'I'm disappointed in you,' the Elder said. 'You would have saved us all a lot of grief by telling the truth in the beginning.' The boy hung his head. 'However, you've returned now and are making an attempt to put things right.'

'It was the girl's disobedience that caused her death,' Aaron said suddenly.

Rees turned and stared at the other man, shocked into an appalled silence. He heard the faint rustle of Elder Jonathan's movement. 'Surely you are not implying, Brother Aaron,' Jonathan said in a soft voice, 'that Leah deserved to die.'

'No. Of course not. But just because Shem was with her—' Aaron began.

'After all,' Jonathan continued, overriding Aaron's truculent protest, 'Shem was disobedient as well.'

'Just because Shem was talking to that groom, it don't mean he's innocent.'

'Enough.' Jonathan's voice was no less quiet but the coldness in it could have put frost on the ground. Aaron started to say something else but Jonathan held up his hand. 'Please go inside, Brother Aaron. After Shem has been fed and put to bed, we will discuss *your* punishment for disobedience. This was the second time in as many days that you left without permission.'

Aaron hesitated as though he might want to argue. Then he turned on his heel and stalked into the Dwelling House.

TWENTY-TWO

It was close to midnight when Rees finally turned down the drive to his farm. The moon floated high and there was enough silvery light for him to see his way to the barn. He unhitched Hannibal and released him into the pasture. Tomorrow Rees would give the gelding a bag of oats – he'd earned it. But now Rees was so tired he could barely stay upright.

He picked his way cautiously up the porch steps and went into the silent kitchen. Save for the dull red glow of the banked fire, it was totally dark inside. He began to feel his way through the kitchen, past the table. He banged into the chair at the end with a clatter. As pain shot up his thigh he uttered an oath. Limping, he made for the door to the hall.

'Stop right there.' Illuminated only by the glow of the banked fire, Lydia came around the corner. She was clad in a voluminous white nightgown with a shawl draped around her neck. But Rees's attention focused on the old musket she held to her shoulder. 'If you come any closer, I vow I will shoot you.' Only a slight quaver betrayed her fear and Rees had no doubt she would do exactly as she threatened. Or try to; he doubted the musket was loaded.

'It's me,' he said.

'Will?' She lowered the musket with a gasp. 'What are you doing home? I didn't expect you for at least another day, maybe more.' Rees stepped forward, removed the musket from her grasp and hugged her tightly. It felt so familiar. 'You didn't find them?'

'Aaron and Shem are back at Zion,' Rees said. 'And the circus is returning to collect Boudreaux.'

'Returning here?' Lydia pulled free of Rees's embrace. Although he couldn't see Lydia's expression in the dim light he could tell by the tone of her voice she wasn't pleased.

'Only until they collect their fellow,' Rees said. Although he had nothing to be ashamed of – at least that was what he told himself – guilt colored his voice.

'Are you hungry?' Lydia asked after a few seconds. She collected the candle from the draining board in the kitchen and used it to light the tapers on the table. Golden light flooded the eating area.

'Ravenous,' he admitted, adding, 'don't bother heating something up. Is there anything cold?'

Lydia brought out cheese and bread and two pickles for him. 'Not even coffee?' she teased.

Rees shook his head. 'It's too late. But I'll take a glass of small beer.' He carried his plate to the table. Lydia followed with his glass and sat down across from him.

'So, what happened?' she asked.

'Well,' Rees said, taking a huge bite of bread and cheese and washing it down with a large gulp of beer, 'I met Piggy Hanson in Grand Forks.'

Lydia's mouth dropped open. 'Did he see you?' she asked in a hushed tone.

'He did,' Rees said. 'It was strange. He offered me a direction to the circus.'

'I know you were worried that he might find us. Did you tell him where we lived?'

'He guessed,' Rees said. 'Of course, he knew your connection to Zion . . .' His voice trailed away. Lydia bit her lip.

'Well, there's no help for that now,' she said.

'Perhaps he won't care we're here,' Rees said hopefully. 'He seemed more interested in Leah's murder.' He paused. 'There were several odd things about our conversation. I don't know what to make of it.'

Giving herself a little shake, Lydia said, 'So the circus did stop at Grand Forks, as the constable thought they might. And Brother Aaron and Shem were with them?'

'They were. But the circus didn't stop at Grand Forks. The constable wouldn't allow it. Circus folk are troublemakers, you know.'

'Was one of their young girls murdered?' Lydia asked anxiously.

'No,' Rees said. 'Curiously, the constable was investigating a murder when I first met him. But it was the murder of a boy. There was family conflict, I understand. No, the circus was still four hours distant from Grand Forks and I likely would not have caught up with them there but for a broken axle on one of their wagons. But I'm glad I followed them. Shem's account pretty much exonerated Boudreaux.'

'Not entirely?' Lydia asked with a teasing smile.

Rees responded with a grin of his own. 'You know I'm never happy until I understand everything,' he said.

Lydia rose to her feet and picked up his empty plate and cup. 'It is very late,' she said.

'I know. And I must be up early for chores,' Rees said.

'You may have a surprise tomorrow morning,' Lydia said.

'What surprise?'

'It wouldn't be a surprise if I told you.' Lydia picked up the candle and put her hand on his arm to lead him upstairs. Rees was suddenly very glad he was home.

Rees discovered what Lydia meant by a surprise when he stumbled out to the barn to milk Daisy. It was closer to five in the morning instead of four and overcast and he still felt as though he hadn't slept nearly enough.

When he stepped inside the outbuilding he found Annie. She had already finished the milking and had released Daisy and her calf into the pasture. The water buckets, filled at the stream, waited for her to carry them inside. He stared at the girl in shock.

She smiled at him now in return. 'Jerusha and Nancy are hunting for eggs,' she said. 'Those chickens will stray.'

'What are you doing here?' he asked.

'I stayed over last night,' she replied airily. 'To help Miss Lydia.'

Rees stared at her for a moment before picking up the yoke with the buckets hanging heavily from the hooks. 'I'll bring in these,' he said. He did not know how he felt about this new development. But he wished Lydia has said something to him.

Lydia already had eggs and bacon and a mug of steaming coffee waiting. 'Surprised?' She asked with a smile.

'Yes,' he said, sitting down.

'Annie will help with chores,' Lydia said, 'and you'll have more time for the investigation.' Feeling churlish for his earlier bad temper, Rees nodded his thanks. But he still wished she had discussed this change with him.

He intended to leave for town as soon after breakfast as possible, but Lydia threw his plans into turmoil. She announced very calmly, just as though he should have anticipated it, that she planned to accompany him. 'What?' he said. The last gulp of coffee went down the wrong way and he choked. 'You want to do what?'

'There can be no question of danger now,' she replied. 'And with Annie here I won't worry. She'll watch the babies and is fully capable of starting dinner.' She waited a few seconds and then asked challengingly, 'Why? Don't you want me to come?'

Rees hesitated. Although he had missed Lydia on the trip to Grand Forks he did not want Lydia to join him in town. With her he felt like an old married man. Without her he felt young and free; not tied down with the responsibilities for a farm, a wife and five children. He knew it was an illusion, but it was one he wanted to live in for a few hours.

'You don't want me to come?' Lydia's voice broke on the last word.

'Of course, I want you to come,' Rees lied. 'I'll enjoy your company. But what about . . .?' He swung his arm around the kitchen to indicate the waiting chores.

'I have ironing but if we return for dinner, I'll certainly be able to finish it this afternoon.' Her eyes took on a faintly mocking gleam. 'And you, husband mine, should spend the afternoon planting.'

Rees could feel his lips drooping into a sour grimace. He loathed farm work, although planting was not the worst of it. But the back-breaking chores on a farm had to be done if they were to eat. 'I should finish the weaving first,' he said. 'It is the last commission I have at present. Once that is completed, I'll turn my attention to the planting.'

He knew, with the money from the finished cloth, he could hire some day laborers, the rootless men that roamed the roads from spring to fall looking for work. He hoped that by the time the fields were planted in buckwheat and rye – the corn would be put in a month from now – he would have obtained additional weaving commissions. He would rather spend all day, every day, at the loom than out in the fields.

'How much time do you think that will take?' Lydia asked.

Rees hesitated. 'A few hours, no more. I can start the planting tomorrow.'

'Don't be so unhappy,' she said, smiling at his glum expression. 'Sister Esther told me Jonathan plans to send a few Brothers to help out.' Relief swept over Rees and he grinned. Jonathan had promised some help but Rees hadn't known when it would come.

'And I wrote to David,' he said. He shook himself, almost like a dog coming out of the water, and said, 'Let's leave after breakfast.'

TWENTY-THREE

Since it was early on a Monday morning the tavern was almost entirely empty. Rouge stood at his usual place at the bar reading the newspaper. He looked up when he heard the door and abandoned his reading. 'Come with me. I have something to show you.' Shouting at Thomas to come out and mind the bar, he preceded his two visitors toward his office down the hall. The small room was no less messy than it had been a few days earlier.

Rouge went directly to the desk and rummaged among the papers. 'Sit down,' he said. Rees looked at the two chairs. Their seats were covered with bills and a blue jacket had been dropped over the back of the nearest one. He scraped the ledgers from one of the seats and added the books and papers to the piles on the table.

'I'll stand,' Rees said as he gestured Lydia to the newly available chair.

'I wrote to all the constables I know,' Rouge said. 'And I rode to some of the nearer villages. Besides that, I put classified advertising asking for information about Asher's Circus in the papers of more distant towns.' He turned and shoved a fistful of papers in Rees's direction. 'These are the responses I've received so far.' His eyes flicked to Lydia and he added reluctantly, 'It looks as though your wife was right. The villain who murdered Leah has been doing this awhile.'

Rees suspected Rouge had only done so much because he wanted to prove Lydia wrong. He did not like admitting a woman had solved a piece of this more quickly than he had.

Rees took the sheaf of letters from the constable and began to look through them. Some were written in smooth educated prose, others with misspelled words and ink blots. But almost all missives told the same story: the body of a young girl was discovered either while the circus was in town or after the show's departure. One of the constables went so far as to describe one of the performers, a tall lanky horseman much praised for his abilities to stand on a running horse's back. Although the letter described the man as possessing pale blond hair, Rees knew that performer was Boudreaux.

'Still think he's innocent?' Rouge asked Rees.

Rees shuffled through the papers once again. 'But Boudreaux couldn't have murdered Leah,' he said, distracted by the letters in his hand. Most of the letter writers assumed the murderer was a member of the circus, primarily because the deaths occurred when the show was in town. Rees went through the missives again and then handed them to Lydia. 'I don't see any evidence,' he said.

'What do you mean? Those murders took place while the circus was in town or shortly thereafter,' Rouge argued.

'The circus performers are outsiders,' Rees said. 'That alone makes me question these assumptions.' As a traveling weaver, he was an outsider in all the places he visited – and he'd been accused of crimes too many times to accept the convenient belief that it was always the stranger. 'We know Boudreaux is innocent of Leah's murder. Not only do the times not work but he was either seen by someone or engaged in conversation during the afternoon when the crime was committed.'

'Then the murderer is someone else from the circus,' Rouge said with the confidence of one for whom no other conclusion was possible. 'Maybe that Asher fellow. Or one of the clowns.'

Rees shook his head but did not reply. He reviewed the letters once again, this time paying particular attention to the villages in which these constables served. He cast his mind back to the bills he'd seen posted on the walls of the temporary amphitheater. He thought most of the towns listed on the bills were the same as those from which these letters came but couldn't be sure. Oh, how he wished he'd paid more attention to the names crossed out on the posters. 'Do you have the circus bill?' Rouge handed the crumpled and dirty paper to Rees. Some of the names were illegible but at least one of them was not represented in the packet of return letters Rees held in his hand.

'Do these constables represent all the neighboring towns?' Rees asked as he handed the packet to Lydia.

Rouge shook his head. 'Too soon to hear from everyone.'

A slight hesitation in his reply ignited Rees's suspicion. He looked at the constable in sharp surmise. 'And?' As Rouge's gaze darted involuntarily to his desk. Rees followed the constable's gaze to a stack of papers. 'There weren't murders in all the towns where the circus stopped,' Rees guessed, his hand snaking out and scooping up several letters.

'One or two,' Rouge blustered. 'That doesn't mean anything. Not compared to that.' He gestured to the stack in Lydia's hand. Rees grunted but did not reply, his eyes fastened upon the replies from towns that had had no similar murders. He did not recognize all the names of the villages but several were listed on the bill. In fact, one letter had come from Constable MacGregor of Grand Forks.

'Asher's circus visited these towns,' Rees said, holding the papers aloft. 'And there were no murders.'

'That don't mean anything,' Rouge said. 'Just because Bou . . .' He glanced at Rees and rephrased his words. 'Just because the murderer skipped a town or two don't mean he wasn't murdering girls in the other ones.'

'That's true,' Rees admitted.

'Monsieur Boudreaux would be the first circus performer anyone would see,' Lydia said, speaking for the first time. When the men turned to her, she added, 'When he was exercising the horses. He'd be memorable.' Rouge nodded, conceding her point. 'Doesn't mean he's guilty.'

'Well, someone in that traveling wickedness is guilty,' he said. Although Rees did not speak he could not help thinking of Otto, the circus strong man, and those large hands. Those large, scratched hands.

'I agree with the constable,' Lydia said.

'You do?' Both men turned to her in surprise.

'The correspondence from these neighboring towns does make the situation look extremely bleak for Asher's Circus,' Lydia said.

'Since I don't trust them to come back to Durham, despite Asher's promise,' Rouge said, gesturing emphatically, 'I'm going after them. I'll just pull in the whole crew. And we'll keep them here until we identify the guilty party. Maybe I'll just hang the lot of them.'

Rees and Lydia left the tavern in silence. The ground underfoot was slick with mud but the sky was a beautiful clear blue and the air felt soft on bare skin. The warm sun beamed down, a harbinger of the summer to come. Lydia lifted her face to let the sun shine on her cheeks and sighed happily.

'Watch out,' he warned. 'Your face will take on an unflattering bronze.'

'I don't care,' she said.

Rees understood. The winters here in Maine seemed to last forever. Sometimes it felt as though he waited forever for summer and then it passed in the blink of an eye.

He collected his horse and wagon and assisted Lydia into the seat. Once they turned onto the main road his thoughts reverted to the murder. If Boudreaux was innocent, and he certainly seemed to be, the murderer must be someone else traveling with the circus. Rees considered all of the people he'd met, and the ones Asher had described: the refugees from the wars in Europe. Rees didn't want to believe any of them guilty but what did he know about them anyway?

'You know,' Lydia said, breaking into Rees's thoughts, 'other people travel.'

He looked at her. 'Like me, you mean?' he asked with a bleak smile.

'I was thinking more of people with a regular route.' Lydia

hesitated and then continued reluctantly. 'The Shaker Brothers regularly make selling trips throughout the area. And Brother Aaron was one of the men who went out most. He enjoyed traveling.'

'Probably when the rules of the community began to wear on him,' Rees said. In this, he understood Aaron.

'For most of us in the Family, the community is a refuge,' Lydia said. 'But for Brother Aaron, well, I think sometimes the rules feel like more of a prison.' She had once been a Shaker and she continued to feel a close bond with the faith and the people in it.

Rees recalled his journey west through Maine and his final arrival at the circus. Aaron, already there, was clearly very comfortable traveling through the world outside Zion. 'How often did Aaron travel?' he asked.

'Often, especially during spring and summer,' Lydia replied. 'And I heard him say he followed a regular route.'

Rees turned to look at his wife. 'We need to speak to him again as soon as we can,' he said.

TWENTY-FOUR

When they reached the junction of the main street with Surry, Rees turned, heading for Zion. It was mid-morning now and, as they passed the fields, Rees saw the Shaker Brothers laboring among the neat rows. He wondered where Aaron was. His specialty appeared to be cattle so Rees hoped he would have a short walk rather than a long one to find the man.

Zion's main street was empty of people; everyone was working at this time of the day and would not reappear until it was time for prayers before the noon dinner. Rees pulled Hannibal to a stop and jumped down. He peered in the barn but saw no sign of anyone.

Lydia climbed down as well and came up behind him. 'I expect most of the men are working in the fields today,' she said. Turning to look over her shoulder she continued, 'But at least some of the Sisters will be in the kitchen. I'll ask there.'

Rees watched her cross the road, her skirts belling out in the breeze, until she disappeared behind the Dining Hall. How many times had he stood here, in the street, his gaze following her as she disappeared into this community that had once been her home. He knew she missed the peace she'd found in this faith but thought – hoped – that this emotion had faded with time. Especially now that she had a child of her own.

Lydia was gone longer than he expected and he was beginning to feel anxious when she suddenly appeared, not from the Dining Hall, but stepping out on the steps of the Dwelling House. Sister Esther followed her. Neither woman looked happy and Rees guessed he was about to hear news he would not like.

'Aaron is gone,' Lydia said when she was still several feet distant.

'He ran off again,' Rees said, aghast.

'Not exactly,' Esther said. Rees looked at her. Her mouth was pressed so tightly together it formed a thin line and the skin of her face was stretched over her cheekbones. 'He was expelled.'

'What?' Rees looked at Lydia for an explanation, but it was Esther that spoke.

'He's disobeyed our rules more than once and indicated his disdain for some of our practices. This time he left Zion without permission and then lied about it. We could not ignore his transgressions any longer.'

Rees could feel his dismay spreading like a cold wave throughout his body. 'But he . . . I wanted to speak to him.'

'Do you really believe Aaron guilty of Leah's death?' Esther sounded like she just couldn't force herself to pronounce the terrible word 'murder'.

'I don't want to believe it,' Rees replied, choosing his words with care. After all, he had known Aaron for some years now. 'But I cannot ignore any possibility. And,' he added reluctantly, 'Aaron was on the lane. Without permission. And without anyone knowing he was gone.'

Esther nodded, her gaze drifting over Rees's head to the barn and the blacksmith's building beyond. When she spoke again her voice was flat, lifeless, as though all the hope had been drained from it. 'Lydia and I looked at the record of Aaron's journeys. Although I can't tell you where he went, the dates he was on the road overlap with some of the dates of those other murders.'

'The ones I remember,' Lydia interjected.

'And the record sometimes has a notation – gone south toward

Massachusetts,' Esther added, 'so some of the general locations match as well.'

Rees looked at Esther, pity sweeping through him. 'This doesn't mean he's guilty,' he said gently. 'All we know for sure is that it is possible he is the culprit.'

'Besides being difficult, Brother Aaron has always been secretive,' Esther said, lowering her eyes to the dusty street. 'Unfortunately, I'm all too certain he could be the guilty man. This is not the first time I have seen sin masquerading as sanctity.'

'What of his past then?' Lydia asked. 'Do you know anything that might reveal his character?'

Esther turned a haunted expression upon the other woman. 'We don't know. We don't ask about people's pasts. We assume the Lord has brought them to our door. But even here, most of us drop hints about their lives. It is impossible, I think, to entirely forget one's past. Only not Aaron. Never Aaron. So, although we can speculate, we know nothing about him.' She looked at Rees before turning and walking away.

Rees and Lydia exchanged a glance, both speaking aloud their thought at the same moment. 'We have to find Aaron.'

It was nearing noon when Rees and Lydia pulled into the farmyard. He released Hannibal into the pasture and followed his wife inside. Only two children, Joseph and Sharon, were seated at the table their heads together. The older ones would remain at school until three or so – at least for another month. Lydia had taken off her bonnet and was now tying on her apron. The yeasty aroma of fresh baked bread perfumed the air; Annie had made it to accompany last night's stew. Rees stifled a sigh. It seemed as though they'd eaten nothing but stew, and sometimes bacon, for months. He was very tired of both.

After the meal, he released Daisy and her calf into the field and checked on his very small sheep flock. Several of the ewes had given birth to lambs but there were too many males among them. He would have to cull out the excess, a job he hated even more than all the others. He could hardly bear to kill them, and always ended up leaving more alive than he needed. But on the positive side, he reflected, lamb would be a welcome change to the family's diet.

He'd also begun shearing the sheep but even with Lydia's help could hardly manage. When it seemed likely he would cut the sheep if he kept on, he abandoned the job until he could get help. Damn! He'd meant to ask Jonathan if some of the Brothers would help him with the shearing for a day or two. Especially with the ram, a big and very strong male that was as likely to break Rees's arm as anything else.

He went to the sheep pen. Most of the lambs seemed sturdy; there were only a few weak ones. He would cull those first, feeling guilty the entire time although it was necessary for the health of the flock. But not today. Today he would weave. Feeling as though he were on his way to a few hours of leisure, Rees went upstairs to finish the cloth on his loom. He inspected the remaining warp and decided that he had told Lydia the truth: a few more hours would complete this yardage. He would probably be able to cut it from the loom the next day and bring it to his customer shortly after.

This was his final commission for the winter. He hoped at least some of the farm wives had worked at spinning and would now have many skeins of yarn for him to weave into cloth. With the increased availability of fabrics imported from the Orient, some women had gladly abandoned spinning, weaving and dyeing and purchased their dress goods.

Rees sat down on the bench and began. He had spent so much of his life weaving that now he did not have to think about it at all. His hands and feet knew what to do without conscious thought and his mind began to wander. At first, he thought of farm chores. Spring was always a busy time and there was a lot to do. But then his thoughts detoured to the murders. So much had happened that it seemed like months instead of just over a week since Leah's body had been discovered in Reynard's buckwheat field. And now, sadly, Leah's death had been shown to be one of several. Rees's thoughts danced from the responses to Rouge's inquiry to the body of the boy in Grand Forks. But he wasn't part of this; Grand Forks hadn't seen the murder of a young girl. So why did that murder niggle at Rees?

'Are you going to be much longer?' Lydia's voice made him jump. His concentration broken, he turned to look at her.

'What?'

'Do you want me to have Annie milk? Daisy's in distress.'

'I'll be done in just a few minutes,' Rees said. Turning to look at the amount of warp left on the beam he added, 'Maybe fifteen minutes.'

'I'll ask Annie to milk then.'

As her footsteps receded down the stairs, Rees looked out the window. The long rays of the sun shining golden through the window told him it was well past milking time. The final push to finish this commission was taking longer than he expected. He didn't want to stop now. And now that he looked at the cloth he saw he'd made a slight mistake earlier in the cloth. Rees wondered if he should rip out the few inches and redo them but decided, with the varying thicknesses of the yarn the mistake was almost unnoticeable.

Rees stepped on the treadle. As the shuttle went from side to side, he tried to pick up the thread of his thoughts. He'd been thinking of the circus but of course the murderer might not be from the show. Brother Aaron could have followed the same route as the circus or, at least, intercepted it at certain points. Although the Shakers themselves were considered peculiar, a gypsy performer would more likely be suspected of murder, wouldn't he? Of course, he would. Rees paused with his shuttle held aloft. Committing rape and murder within proximity of the circus would be an intelligent scheme for deflecting suspicion. And Brother Aaron, although difficult, was intelligent.

What about Grand Forks? The constable there had expelled Asher's circus from the village. But Aaron must have traveled through that hamlet when he'd been pursuing Shem and no young girl had fallen victim to the murderer. Still, something about Grand Forks bothered Rees. What was it? He prodded the itch. The name of a fellow traveler, someone no one would suspect but who followed a circuit through this area several times a year, bubbled up from the depths of his mind: Piggy Hanson. He had been in Durham and in Grand Forks; Rees had seen him. And who would suspect a magistrate of such a heinous crime?

Rees recalled the magistrate's carriage; those wide upholstered seats and the curtains. With them closed the interior of the carriage would be private. Few would dare disturb the magistrate if the carriage was pulled aside into a secluded area. And Paul Reynard had seen the magistrate's carriage at the proper time.

Hanson was as likely a murderer as Aaron. In fact, the more Rees considered his old nemesis, the more likely he appeared. 'I just have to confirm his circuit,' Rees said to himself. But he was already sure Hanson's circuit would match up to the route the circus had taken.

TWENTY-FIVE

'Are you mad?' Rouge shouted when Rees presented his latest theory the following morning. They were seated once again in the constable's messy office. Rees had insisted on privacy; his suspicions were too explosive to discuss in public. Rouge had reluctantly agreed. 'Magistrate Hanson?' he said now. 'Impossible. I think your wife is correct and the murderer is Aaron. It's just not natural for a man to live celibate. A man's urges can't be denied; anyone would snap.' Since Rees, who had heard this diatribe more than once, was not listening, the constable paused. Taking a breath, he asked, 'What does your wife think?'

Rees hesitated. The irony of Rouge asking for Lydia's opinion was not lost on Rees but he did not want to answer. She had been so annoyed he was leaving the farm again that she hadn't been willing to listen. 'I didn't tell her,' he admitted. 'I will, though.'

'I thought you told her everything,' Rouge said mockingly.

'Listen,' Rees said, suppressing his flicker of guilt. He did usually tell Lydia everything. Her irritation had made a wedge between them. 'Hanson can travel around his territory without anyone questioning him. And is there anyone who would believe a magistrate *could* be guilty of these crimes?'

'Exactly,' Rouge agreed. 'Who would believe it? I know some of your most outlandish ideas have been proven true. But this time – no.'

'You don't know Piggy the way I do,' Rees said. 'He's cruel and vindictive.'

'So you've said,' Rouge said with a frown. 'But that doesn't make him a killer.'

'I just have a hunch,' Rees said.

'That isn't good enough, especially if you're going after a wealthy and powerful man.' Rouge blew out his breath. 'Look. I'll get you a list of the towns on the magistrate's circuit. We'll start there. But you better have a lot more than a hunch if you're going to prove him guilty.'

'Yes, I know,' Rees said. 'I won't ignore Brother Aaron – once I find him – or the circus performers either. When I finally accuse someone, I'll have all the proof you need to back it up.'

Rouge blew out another breath, his gaze resting on Rees almost in admiration. 'I can't decide if you're courageous or just a fool,' he said.

'Maybe both,' Rees said. But he was on the hunt now and would not stop until he knew all the answers.

'Constable.' A lean and wiry man, a farmer already sunburned from days in the fields, knocked at the door as he poked his head inside. 'That circus – one of the wagons is broke down out on West.'

'They were having trouble with an axle,' Rees said.

'Looked like a wheel to me,' the farmer agreed.

'Guess we'd better go and see what the problem is,' Rouge said. 'Damn! It's impossible to make an honest living. Someone always dragging me away from the tavern.'

'You wanted them here,' Rees pointed out. 'Now here they are.'

'How far out are they?' Rouge asked. 'Do I need my horse?'

'Nah. They're just past the market.'

Glancing at one another, Rees and Rouge rose to their feet at the same instant.

They walked to the fairgrounds. The circus wagons were visible but were stopped a mile distant on West Road. 'I guess they'd better pull into the fairgrounds,' Rouge said, sounding irritated, as he broke into a trot. Rees jogged along by the constable's side.

The problem was immediately obvious; despite the iron band circling the wheel, the wooden sections had begun to fracture. With the added strain, even the iron had bent. The wagon tilted danger- ously toward the ground. And when Rees crawled under the other side, he saw that the repairs to the axle, consisting of several boards nailed to the shaft in what looked like a random manner, had begun to fail. Crawling out again he said to Asher, 'You need a new axle and probably a new wheel now.'

The blood left Asher's face. 'How much will that cost?' Today

he wore a shabby wrinkled shirt and blue breeches with a necker-
chief tied around his throat. He looked like one of the rowdy
laborers.

Rees shrugged. 'You'll have to talk to the wheelwright.'

'For now,' Rouge said, shoving himself into the conversation,
'all the wagons will have to park at the fairgrounds.' He gestured
behind him.

'How will we get this one there?' Asher asked.

As several men spoke up, each with a different idea, Rees walked
around the wagon and examined it. Unlike his large wagon with
low sides and no roof, this vehicle was more like a small box on
wheels. Each side boasted a window and when Rees passed the
open door he saw that the inside had been set up as living quarters:
a small bench that probably doubled as a bed, a chair, and a curtained
area at the other end. A tiny incised metal object was affixed on the
right side of the door. He leaned forward to peer curiously at the small
object. Through one of the holes he spied something that looked
like paper. He could not imagine what it might be but then he
supposed it was something circus people did.

When he straightened up he caught the eye of a woman dressed
all in black. She did not look familiar but then even the performers
he'd seen looked unrecognizable out of costume. She stared at him,
her eyes wide and her skin pasty with fright. He smiled at her. She
took two steps back, uttering a low keening, and disappeared around
the corner.

Rees stared after her, unsettled by the encounter. That woman
had seemed completely terrified. What had he done to frighten
her so?

TWENTY-SIX

I n the end, they needed rollers and two oxen borrowed from a
nearby farmer, to shift the circus wagon. The horses simply
weren't powerful enough. Then several men, Rees included,
heaved the wagon onto the rollers. Even Otto was not strong enough
to do this on his own. The oxen pulled, the wagon moved forward.

The wagon was shoved upright so the second roller could be placed underneath. The oxen pulled and the wagon moved forward. Several men pushed the wagon up so the free roller could be placed underneath. The process was repeated over and over. Rees lost count. It was hard and sweaty work and the men took it in turns.

On one of his rest breaks, Rees looked over to see Asher standing by the fancier of the carriages. Bambola leaned out of the open door and shook her head. Although Rees could not hear what they said, enough of the tone floated to him to persuade him they were arguing. He drifted toward them. As he approached Asher turned and spoke. 'I think the women should go ahead, to the fair grounds. Do you agree?'

Rees turned to look at the ropedancer.

'Some of the women are afraid,' she explained. 'We don't often meet a warm welcome.'

'Persuade her, will you, Mr Rees?' Asher clapped Rees on the shoulder and turned. 'I've got to get back.'

'I wanted to apologize for one of our members,' Bambola said as Asher trotted away. 'I believe you met Sarah?'

'Who?'

'It is her wagon that broke down.'

Rees recalled the strange incident. 'The woman in black?'

'Yes.' Bambola waved Rees closer. 'I saw her discourtesy toward you. You must forgive her. She has suffered mightily, poor thing.' She paused for a moment and then added in a low voice, 'She is a Jew and her experiences have left her frightened of strangers.'

'That must make it difficult while traveling with the circus,' Rees said in a dry tone. By now, without quite knowing how he got there, he had taken hold of the heavy carriage door and leaned in toward the woman.

'She is a seamstress and stays at the back, in the camps. I doubt she sees many strangers from one month to the next. You do not seem, how shall I say it, shocked or appalled?'

'That she's a Jew?' Rees shook his head. 'I travel too, to New York and Philadelphia among other cities.'

Bambola smiled. 'Of course, you are more worldly than many we meet. Sarah wishes me to apologize to you on her behalf.'

'You're sure she was talking about me?' Rees asked.

'She described you, of course,' Bambola said with a smile. Her sparkling eyes and mischievous grin told him the description had been less than flattering.

'Big, red-haired devil,' he guessed.

Miss Mazza laughed. 'Just so.' Leaning forward, she rested her gloved hand on his arm. 'We were fortunate to meet you. That was something we could never have foreseen.' Rees felt the warmth from her fingers spread through him like a hot and tingling wave. He began to perspire. 'Do you believe we'll be safe if we go on ahead? To town, I mean?' she continued. 'I trust you and will do as you suggest.'

'Um,' Rees said, flattered. For a moment he couldn't think. 'The constable wants you in town. It's daylight.' Realizing he was stammering, he took a deep breath and tried to concentrate. As he shifted his stance, the sculpted metal horse on the door beneath his hand seemed to move and he stepped back. Removed a few paces from Bambola's distracting touch, he was able to think more clearly. He was panting like a racing horse. After a few seconds, he said in a calmer voice, 'Yes, I think you and the other women will be safe. Go on.'

Bambola smiled. 'Very well. Will you ask Mr Asher to send one of the men to drive my carriage? I must go first; the others will follow me.'

'I'm here,' grunted one of the laborers. As he climbed up and whistled to the horses, Rees leaned against the heavy carriage door to push it shut and stepped back. Bambola waved and the driver started forward.

Excited and embarrassed – and also ashamed – by the feelings she called up in him, he was almost relieved to see her go. Turning, he started back toward the damaged wagon. Otto was standing a few feet away and watching Rees with a hostile expression. Rees approached the strongman, although after the passage of a week, he did not think he would see anything meaningful on Otto's huge hands. And, sure enough, they were covered with new bloody scratches that occluded the older healing injuries.

'I did not touch that girl,' Otto said, so suddenly and so belligerently Rees took an involuntary step backward. Otto began clenching and unclenching his hands. Rees took another step backward, all the while keeping his gaze fixed upon the big man. 'You are mixing in to something you don't understand,' Otto said. 'It is not safe for you. Go home to your family.'

And then, before Rees could manage even a word, Otto lumbered away.

Rees realized he was shaking. He had no doubt at all that Otto was dangerous.

'Rees,' Asher called. 'Come on.'

Rees went down the slope to join Asher, saying as he approached, 'Bambola is going to the fairgrounds.'

'Good. The women will only get in the way here.' Asher gestured at the broken wagon. 'They need you.'

By the time the wagon reached the fair grounds it was almost noon. The men deposited the vehicle on the very edge of the field. No one had the strength to move it any further. Rees joined the line for water and after gulping down several dippers full, he looked around for either Asher or Rouge. He spotted them finally, talking to one another, and crossed the muddy field to join them. As he approached, he heard Asher saying in irritation, 'Of course I'll stay in town. I can't very well leave until the wheel is repaired.' He walked quickly away, in such a temper he brushed past Rees without acknowledging him.

Rouge nodded as though satisfied. 'I have to return to the tavern,' he said. 'I've left it too long as it is.' He glanced at Rees. 'You going home?'

'Probably,' he replied. The reluctance in his voice sparked a quick glance from Rouge but he said nothing. With a wave, he started across the muddy field. Rees sighed. He knew Lydia would be cross. He hadn't finished the weaving yet, as he'd promised, and he had to begin planting and there were still the lambs to attend to. Then he'd disappeared from the farm for the entire morning. Oh yes, Lydia would definitely have something to say. And Rees did not want to hear it.

'Why, Mr Rees,' said Bambola from behind him.

Rees turned with a clumsy bow. 'Miss Mazza.'

'Thank you for your assistance.'

'You're welcome. But I did no more than most of the men.' Rees's expansive gesture included circus workers, townsmen, and the few remaining farmers who'd been involved in the transport of the wagon.

'May I perform another reading for you?' She smiled up at him from under the brim of her hat. 'We owe you that much, that and much more.'

'I really should go home,' he said, not moving.

'It will take only a few moments,' she coaxed.

He looked at the sky. Noon already; no doubt his family had already begun eating dinner. 'I'll be late anyway,' he said. He didn't believe in magic but the reading would pass a few minutes of pleasure before the drudgery of his life began again. Besides, he was curious. Bambola's first reading had struck close to home on several points – unsettlingly close. How had she guessed all of that?

The little table had already been set up. The box that held the cards rested on one side. Rees guessed she had been doing readings for some of her fellow circus performers. As she took out the colorful squares, Rees sat down in the chair across from her. 'Shuffle them,' she directed. This time she removed her gloves. She had smooth white hands with long carefully tended nails. 'And think about what you want to know.'

'The murder, of course,' he said with a chuckle, shuffling with single-minded intensity. He wanted these cards to come up randomly so they meant nothing. Bambola watched him with a smile and he suspected she knew exactly what he was doing. At last he handed her the deck. She dealt the cards, in the same strange configuration as before. She turned over the first card. Seven circles incised with pentacles.

'You are working hard,' she said. 'But you need to work harder.'

'Discouraging,' he said.

Catching the mockery in his voice, she darted him a quick glance. 'Perhaps this next card will help,' she said, turning it over. She stared at the pictured moon. 'This one offers a warning. Be careful of dishonesty. You've met someone who is attempting to mislead you . . .' Her voice trailed away.

Rees stared at the card but quickly dismissed his quiver of surprise. Of course he was dealing with deception; when one investigated a murder one had to expect it. There was no great talent in seeing that.

Bambola glanced at him from under her lashes and turned over the next card. Five golden chalices marched across the pasteboard.

'This speaks to your past, a more distant past. Something happened to sever a relationship but see, it is reversed, so there will be a reunion. It is possible that this relationship can be repaired.'

She flipped the next card. Rees stared at the hanged man and repressed a shudder. She smiled. 'This is not always a dangerous card but one of change. Before any reconciliation can occur, you need to make some effort to transform. It is important for you to step back and consider yourself.'

'What relationship is this?' Rees asked.

Bambola shrugged and fixed him with her dark eyes. 'I don't know. But there is something in your past that you need to reflect upon.' Her forefinger tapped the card. 'The Hanged Man is reversed; that speaks to a certain unwillingness to change.' She turned over the next card. This one was a king framed by seven sticks and a lion. 'You're strong and you keep after something until it has been completed to your satisfaction. You are honest and dependable but also very stubborn. Don't allow your stubbornness to prevent you from seeing the truth. Only by conquering your obstinacy will you succeed.'

Again, Rees experienced that flash of discomfort that she had so clearly seen a part of his personality.

She revealed the next card, a knight with more of the five-pointed stars. 'This card reveals something about you. The Knight is a responsible fellow. He always sees his projects through to the very end.' Her brows drew together, almost as though this card dismayed her. She quickly flipped the other card: a magician with a wand and a chalice. She bit her lip.

'What?' Rees asked in spite of himself. 'What's wrong?'

She smiled. 'Nothing. This is another warning. You need to be careful whom you trust. Deception and trickery are all around you.' She turned the next to the last card and said under her breath, 'Judgment.' Rees stared at the angel. 'You need to forgive someone. Only then can you move forward.'

'What does that have to do with the murder?' Rees asked. 'And who am I supposed to forgive?'

'The cards don't say,' she said. 'But something is unfinished. And it is affecting your investigation.'

'That's ridiculous,' Rees said.

'We'll see.' She smiled slightly, her sharp white teeth catching at her lower lip. 'Remember what the cards said – I think you may find they foretold the truth.' She turned over the final card and said to herself, 'Seven of swords.'

Rees was glad to see this card seemed fairly benign.

'You will be partially successful in your quest,' Bambola said. 'You will not achieve something that you currently seek.'

'Any idea what,' Rees said.

The ropedancer shook her head. 'The cards are only a guide. It is up to you to take their message and heed the lesson.'

Of course, there was no true information. These tricksters always resorted to hints. 'Uh, thank you,' Rees said insincerely. He rose to his feet. 'I must leave now. My wife will be waiting for me.' His angry wife.

Bambola darted him a quick glance from her velvety eyes. 'Please bring her with you some time. I'd like to do a reading for her as well.'

'Of course,' Rees lied. He had no intention of bringing Lydia here. Ever. Why, the whole scene was an exercise in foolishness and one he hoped never to repeat. He had allowed his attraction to Bambola to sucker him in. She had managed a couple of lucky guesses, that was all her reading had been. There could not possibly be any truth to it.

TWENTY-SEVEN

As Rees crossed across the muddy field he spotted Asher and detoured to meet him. Asher paused. 'You know that your constable is an ass,' he said by way of greeting. His shirt was streaked with mud and dirt rimmed his bitten fingernails.

'He can be,' Rees agreed. In this case, though, he thought Rouge was right to keep the circus nearby.

'You looked unnerved while Bambola was doing her reading,' Asher said, peering into Rees's face. 'Surely her parlor trick didn't frighten you.'

'Of course not,' he said, not altogether truthfully.

'She truly believes those paper squares have mystical powers,' Asher said with fond dismissal.

'You don't believe?' Rees asked.

Asher laughed. 'Of course not. But she enjoys it. It's a harmless pastime.'

'Maybe not,' Rees said, his mind returning to the previous summer. Lydia had been accused of witchcraft and some believed it because she had once been a Shaker. 'She should be careful,' he said now. 'There are those who still believe in witchcraft.'

'Witchcraft!' Asher shook his head. 'Some men will believe anything.'

'Her readings are sometimes unsettlingly close to the truth,' Rees said.

Asher lifted one shoulder in a shrug. 'Even a broken clock is correct twice a day. Besides, Mr Rees, you are not that complicated. I'm sure she tells you facts about yourself that anyone would know.'

Rees stood there in silence, feeling like a total fool. Asher was right; Bambola's predictions were only clever guesses.

'Are you haring off, still bent on discovering the identity of the murderer?' Asher asked.

'Why did you run away?' Rees, stung, responded with a question of his own. 'You must have known that hasty departure would make you look guilty.'

Asher nodded. 'I did. But you must understand . . .' He hesitated. 'This new country welcomes both Catholics and Jews.' He forced a smile. 'At least by law. That is not the same as tolerance, of course. But the Old World carries on a long history of persecution. Especially toward the Jews.'

Rees nodded. Although there were no Jews in Maine, as far as he knew, there were many Catholics. Like Constable Rouge they kept quiet about their faith. As Asher had just said, the law was not the same as tolerance.

'They expect the same persecution here,' Asher continued. 'Several of the people who travel with us are from Austria and France. And now that Bonaparte is pressing into Italy, we've acquired some Italians. It's all right for Miss Mazza; she belongs here. She's from a circus family. But some of our number are refugees and expect only the worst.' He shook his head in disbelief. 'You mark my words, Mr Rees, no country is safe from that Corsican madman.'

'The circus hardly seems a safe haven,' Rees said, feeling vaguely ashamed. How many times had he complained of being an outsider? At least he spoke the language and knew the customs of this country.

'True,' Asher said, nodding in agreement. 'We must keep on the move. In some towns we are accused of all manner of vile crimes before we've even parked our wagons. But at least those who have found refuge with us have a family and some protection of sorts.' He shook himself. 'Does that answer your question, Mr Rees? That is why we fled, leaving behind one of our own, a man who is like a brother to me. We were afraid. Still are.'

Rees could think of nothing to say. When Asher walked away, Rees continued to his wagon, his thoughts so jumbled he could scarcely string two coherent ideas together.

He was almost at the corner when he saw a tall and lanky man watching him from the alley across the street. Disguised by the shadows, unshaven, and wearing a battered straw hat pulled down well over his brow, he nonetheless looked very familiar. He looked like Brother Aaron. Rees started to cross, threading his way through the wagons and other vehicles thronging the road. A large carriage rattled by in front of him, just narrowly missing him, and causing him to jump back. When the way was clear again, the man had vanished. But Rees was sure he had just seen Aaron. And what was he still doing in town?

By the time Rees returned home it was well past dinnertime. 'Wash your hands,' Lydia said, her face stiff with annoyance.

'I'll finish the weaving today,' Rees promised as he dipped his hands in the basin of tepid water. They were quite dirty after a morning spent heaving rollers around and lifting wagons. He saw with dismay that his shirt and breeches were also streaked with grime.

Lydia dipped her head a fraction and lifted the lid from the kettle. The steam carried with it the fragrance of cooking chicken, onions and sage. 'Fricasseed chicken,' Annie said in satisfaction, distributing the plates around the table. 'With dumplings.'

'My favorite,' Rees said truthfully, keeping one eye on his wife. She did not appear mollified.

'I've fed the children already,' Lydia said as she filled the plates from the kettle and brought them to the table. Rees could barely control himself; he was so hungry it was all he could do to keep his hands from his fork. He raced through saying grace and earned another frown from Lydia.

'Where are the children?' he asked as he picked up his fork.

'Napping,' Annie said, shooting a quick glance at Lydia.

'This is an unexpected treat.' Rees tried again to start a conversation. 'Chicken? And mid-week too.'

'The hen was no longer laying,' Annie said when Lydia still said nothing.

'Well, I'm glad of it,' Rees said, aware as soon as he began speaking that he sounded far too hearty.

Annie looked at him and then at Lydia. 'We weren't sure when you would return from town,' Annie said, sounding puzzled and uncomfortable both.

'The circus is back,' Rees said. 'They pulled into town on a broken axle. Me and Rouge and most of the men from the circus had to manhandle the wagon to the fairgrounds. It took longer than I expected.' He was glad to see Lydia's expression soften.

'I'd love to see a performance,' Annie said wistfully.

'Oh, I don't believe they'll be here long enough for that,' Rees said, trying to console her. 'They've come to fetch Mr Boudreaux. And now, of course, they'll remain until the wagon is repaired.'

'And was the ropedancer there?' Lydia asked. She still sounded vexed but Rees could see her ill temper fading.

'She was,' he said. 'But we men were all busy. The women went ahead.' Now why had he said that?

Lydia's brows drew together. 'Yes?' There was a tone to her voice he did not understand. 'So, you didn't see her?'

'No, I did. From a distance.' Rees grinned at his wife but she did not smile. And he did not feel happy with himself. He had always promised himself that he would never lie to his wife. But this time the falsehood just slipped out.

'Will you be returning to the circus tomorrow?' Lydia asked. She sounded wary.

'No,' Rees said. 'I don't plan to. Although I need to speak to Rouge.' Lydia bit her lip and began crumbling her bread. Rees stared at her nervous hands. 'What's the matter?'

'Nothing. It's just – well, there is so much to do around here.'

'After dinner,' he said, 'I'll finish cutting the bolt from the loom so the cloth can be delivered tomorrow. And then I'll work in the fields. I don't believe the Shaker Brothers finished seeding the north-west buckwheat field.'

Lydia forced a smile. 'Good.'

'I think I saw Brother Aaron in town,' Rees said, changing the subject.

'You think?' For the first time, Lydia sounded like her usual self.

'He wasn't in his usual clothing. And he ran off before I could speak with him.'

'I guess he is not the murderer then,' Lydia said, rising to clear the plates.

'Why do you think that?'

'If he was, he would be far away from Durham now,' she said.

Rees was not convinced although he thought Lydia's comment had merit. There were plenty of reasons why a murderer might not flee. But he did not want to argue, so he pushed his chair back with a clatter and rose from the table. 'I'll be in the weaving room,' he said.

He wove the final few rows and then spent the better part of an hour tying off the warp and removing the cloth from the beam. He folded it neatly and left it on the bench where it would be safe from the dirty hands of his children. With the exception of Jerusha, who was quickly becoming a passable weaver herself, the children were forbidden to enter the weaving room. Tomorrow he would bring the finished cloth to the widow and collect his fee. Perhaps he would stop by the circus, just to see what had happened with the axle and the wheel. In spite of the flutter in his chest, he assured himself that Bambola had nothing to do with it.

Rees put on his clogs and straw hat, looped the bag of buckwheat seeds over his shoulder and went out to the field. He saw immediately the side of the field where the Shakers had stopped; one side was a neatly plowed field while the other was still a mess of muddy clods and rocks. The larger stones had been tossed into a pile and Rees thought he probably had enough for a stone wall. He started at the nearest end and began walking slowly past the first row, casting the seeds as he went. It was too early to plant wheat – too cool – but buckwheat and rye could go in.

Back and forth Rees went. At first this was a pleasant job. The damp soil smelled fresh and enjoyably earthy. The sun touched his shoulders with warmth and the walk was easy. But, as the planting continued, he began to find this task monotonous. Nonetheless, he was determined to finish this field. The Shaker Brothers had put in a small field of rye so, once the buckwheat was planted, only the wheat and corn were left and he still had a few weeks before it would be warm enough for that.

At milking time Annie came by to tell him she would do it so he kept on. Late afternoon was transitioning into evening by the time he finished. The sack was almost empty and Rees was tired. The rough clogs, which had grown heavier with mud as he went through the field, had worn blisters on his feet and his back was sore from stooping. But the field was entirely seeded and the soil raked over the rows. Staggering with fatigue, he walked up the track to the house. He left his clogs on the porch and padded into the house on bare feet. Lydia turned to look at him.

'My God,' she said. 'Perhaps you should go into the pantry to change your clothes. I don't want you tracking mud all the way up the stairs.'

Rees looked down at himself. Mud coated him from head to toe. He plodded into the pantry. Except for cheese and today's milk, the shelves were largely empty. Those bare shelves explained his work today; his family counted on bountiful fields to refill them before next winter.

Lydia reappeared with clean clothes – old and faded but clean – and a basin of warm water for him to wash in. As he stripped off his muddy shirt and breeches, Rees wished he could spend all his time weaving.

TWENTY-EIGHT

Early the next morning, as soon after chores as he could manage it, Rees wrapped the woven cloth in paper and left for town. The widow, pleased with the cloth despite what Rees saw as flaws, paid the eighteen shillings owing. Most of it would go into the strongbox under the bed, joining some of the money still unspent after previous weaving commissions. He always tried to keep some money aside – just in case.

Although he knew he should go straight home, he decided to stop by the circus. Just to see if there was news, not to see Bambola. It would be only for a few minutes.

The circus had settled in to the fairgrounds, spreading out to occupy most of the western half. Rees stopped the first man he saw. 'Is Monsieur Boudreaux here?' he asked.

'No,' said the man, averting his eyes and hurrying away. Unsettled by the fellow's rudeness, Rees walked around the wagons to see if he could find someone else to speak to. Most of the circus folk gave him a wide berth. But a few tumblers in drab practice clothing were rehearsing, somersaulting over one another, in a crudely marked circle filled with straw. When Rees asked for Mr Boudreaux they shook their heads without really looking at him. Rees began walking away and then turned back. 'Mr Asher?'

One of the tumblers pointed north. So, Rees followed the line of wagons around to the other side.

A rough circle had been pounded down through the stubble and, to the delight of three farmer's boys, a horse was cantering around it. Asher, in his shirtsleeves, shouted instructions to the rider. Rees thought they must have been here for some time; the horse's hooves had worn the straw away and turned the ring into bare dirt. With an exclamation of disgust, Asher threw down his whip and crossed the battered ground to speak to the boy on the horse's back. The discussion was not a pleasant one; although he could not hear Asher's words his tone was sharp. Rees looked at the boy. It was Shem; he'd returned to the circus. Tears glittered in his eyes.

Asher turned back to cross the field once again. When he saw Rees he offered a brusque nod. Rees waited until the circus master was once again in position and the horse was galloping around the circle before speaking.

'So, what are you doing here?' Rees asked curiously, waving his hand at the horse and rider.

'Boudreaux is not certain he wants to rejoin us.' Asher flicked Rees a glance. 'Without him, I need another horseman.' He abruptly stopped talking and shouted at Shem. 'No. No. No. You stand on him with no more grace than a bushel of potatoes. You must imagine yourself flying through the air. Try it again.' He flicked his whip, the horse started abruptly into his gallop and Shem, startled, fell off, landing with a thud on the ground.

'Well, he flew,' Rees said with a chuckle.

Asher groaned. 'Get up,' he told Shem. 'Get up. Enough practice for today. We'll start again tomorrow.' He turned to Rees and said in a low voice, 'I doubt this fellow has the talent to become one of my equestrians.'

Rees, who couldn't imagine himself standing on a horse at all, said, 'He looked pretty good to me. I'm sure he'll improve with practice.'

'Fortunately, I have the time to work with him,' Asher said. 'The wheelwright expects the repairs to the wheel and axle to take two or three days more.' He sighed. 'I just hope the boy improves – at least to the point where he doesn't embarrass us.'

'Boudreaux is exceptionally talented,' Rees said. 'Shem won't attain that expertise in just a few days.'

'That's true,' Asher agreed. 'I hope Pip Boudreaux chooses to stay with us. He would be a sore loss.' Turning, he glanced at Rees. 'But what are you doing here?'

'I was nearby and thought I'd stop,' Rees said, feeling heat rise into his face. Asher nodded. To Rees's guilty eyes, the ringmaster's expression indicated mocking understanding.

But Asher said only, 'I hope you don't still suspect Boudreaux of the murder?'

'No,' Rees said. 'But, if not Boudreaux, maybe someone else.' As soon as the words left his mouth he wanted to snatch them back.

Asher scowled at him. 'I see. We must be guilty because we are traveling show people?'

'I didn't mean that at all,' Rees said. He put his hand on Asher's shoulder. 'I probably understand better than anyone what it means to be the traveler, the outsider, who, by the very nature of his fleeting visits, is always suspect. But there is no ignoring the fact that your stops in many of these towns have been accompanied by the murder of a young girl.'

Asher pushed his hat back and scratched his head. 'I don't know anything about that,' he said. Rees shook his head sternly at the other man.

'You knew there were other murders and that Boudreaux might be suspected of them,' he said. 'You had to know. Boudreaux dyed his hair.'

Asher sighed and nodded. 'He was too visible with that white blond hair. Too recognizable. And because he likes to ride down the town roads rehearsing, he is the one who is remembered and accused.' He shook his head. 'I thought if someone came looking for a man with blond hair we would have only one with black. But now the dye is fading into red. I suppose we will have to wash it out anyway. That must sound foolish to you.'

'Not at all,' Rees said, recalling all the times he'd wished he were not so instantly recognizable with his height and flaming red hair.

'Anyway, I know there are others of us you might consider,' Asher continued, turning his sharp brown eyes upon Rees.

'There are,' Rees agreed. Otto the strong man for one. 'But there are other suspects beside circus people.' Brother Aaron, who seemed to have the ability to leave Zion whenever he wished and travel around. And now of course, untethered from the Shakers, he could now do what he wanted. Then there was Piggy Hanson, the magistrate. Rees was trying to conjure a clever question about Hanson without fully displaying his suspicions when he heard Piggy's voice nearby. Just as if Rees's thoughts had summoned him.

'I'm looking for Mr Asher. I understand he has a guest? Mr Rees. A tall man with red hair?'

'Not a friend of yours, I daresay,' Asher said, looking at the expression on Rees's face.

'No,' he said. He'd known Hanson since they were boys and Piggy had been vindictive even then. Adulthood had not changed him.

'Go behind the wagon over there,' Asher said. 'I have no love for the magistrate. He's dogged our travels and been at almost every stop we've made. I'll speed him on his way.'

Rees hurried across the field and crouched down behind a wagon. All he could see of Asher was his lower legs. Just a minute or two after Rees had hidden himself, a pair of smart black breeches came into view, accompanied by footsteps crunching across the straw. 'Mr Asher,' Piggy said.

'Magistrate.'

'I'm looking for Mr Rees. Tall man with red hair.'

'I don't know him.' Asher sounded indifferent.

'Who was that fellow I saw running away?'

'Monsieur Boudreaux. They do resemble one another, don't they?'

'Ah yes, I'd heard he was returning to your circus.' Hanson slapped his cane against his boot. 'If you know Rees resembles your friend, you must know who he is. Have you seen him?'

'If you are speaking about the constable's friend, I have not. Have you tried the tavern?'

'I did. Constable Rouge said he had not seen Rees today.' More slapping. 'All right, thank you.' Rees heard Piggy's footsteps crunching away.

When he was sure his nemesis was truly gone, he left the shelter of the wagon. 'Thank you,' he said to Asher.

'You're welcome. And I wouldn't walk into town if I were you. That's where the magistrate was headed.'

Rees nodded his thanks and very carefully walked the other way, taking a roundabout route to his wagon. He saw no sign of Bambola at all and was embarrassed by the surge of disappointment that swept over him.

As he climbed into his wagon, he thought he saw someone running between the wagons. Too tall to be Lydia disguised in David's old clothing, the young man looked like David. Heart leaping, Rees almost called out. But a second later reality reasserted itself. David could not be here; he was still in Dugard with his wife. The hurt of the separation burned through Rees all over again, just as if they had recently parted. David was one of the few people he truly trusted. He missed him every day. Wondering if his son had received his letter, he sighed and picked up the reins.

TWENTY-NINE

When Rees started east on the main road he was surprised to see Shem trudging along the side. Now assuming the boy he'd seen running through the circus had been Shem, he pulled up. 'Shem,' he said. 'Where are you going?'

Shem kept his head down. 'Back to Zion.'

'Oh?' Rees saw enough of the boy's face to know he'd been crying. 'I'll give you a ride.'

Shem hesitated and then, wiping his tattered sleeve across his eyes, he climbed into the seat.

'Changed your mind about the circus?' Rees asked.

'I don't want to join anymore,' Shem said. 'Mr Asher is mean.'

'The world needs farmers more than they need men who can stand on galloping horses,' Rees said. 'And Daniel will be glad to see you.'

Aaron would be happy too. Would he leave town now that Shem was safe once again within the Shaker village?

Rees dropped the boy off on the outskirts of Zion and headed home.

Because Rees saw several Shakers working in one of his pastures when he turned down the lane he did not enter the farm yard. Instead he followed the muddy track as far as he could before climbing down and crossing the field toward Daniel.

The Shakers were working in an overgrown field that had not been cleared or planted for many years and so had become a meadow. Daniel saw Rees coming and crossed the field to the edge of the tall grass to meet him. 'Jonathan thought you might want another field of rye,' he said.

'Maybe.' Rees was surprised. Surely the Shakers had enough to do on their own farm. Of course, they expected to take possession of this property eventually. If Rees and his family had not been so desperate after their mad flight from Dugard, this farm would already be part of Zion's holdings.

'And it looks like we might have rain tomorrow,' Daniel continued, 'so we thought we would make a start today.'

Rees examined the other man's face. Although Daniel was a young man, still in his twenties, dark rings circled his eyes. 'Not sleeping well?' he asked sympathetically.

Daniel shook his head. 'I keep seeing Leah . . .' He stopped and took in a deep breath. 'Are you any nearer to finding the brute who murdered her?'

'No,' Rees said in a regretful voice. 'I've found several possibilities but nothing certain yet.'

'I heard the circus is back in Durham,' Daniel said.

'Yes. They've come to fetch Monsieur Boudreaux.' Rees decided not to share Rouge's plan to keep the circus in town until the murderer was caught.

'Are you certain, absolutely certain, he's innocent?'

'I'm never absolutely certain,' Rees said. 'But I don't think he's guilty.' Daniel sighed and turned his gaze upon his Brothers. 'It would be easier if the murderer were Boudreaux, I know. But you wouldn't want an innocent man to take the blame, would you?' Rees said. 'Besides, the real murderer would still be out there. And,' he added half under his breath as he thought of the letters Rouge had received, 'he won't stop murdering young girls.'

The silence lasted so long that Rees, assuming that the conversation was over, had turned away. Then Daniel said, 'Do you know that Brother Aaron was expelled from the Family?'

'Yes,' Rees said. 'Do you know where he is?'

Daniel looked directly at Rees. Instead of replying, he asked another question. 'Is he one of the men you suspect?'

Rees hesitated. He didn't want to tarnish the man's reputation if he was innocent. Still, he needed to find him and question him. 'Yes,' he said.

Daniel nodded several times as if this was no more than what he expected. 'I'm sure he was just trying to protect Shem,' Daniel said.

'I thought I saw him in town,' Rees said, and guessed when Daniel bit his lip that he knew something more. 'Do you know where he is?' he asked again.

Daniel hesitated. 'He's working for the Perkins family on North Road,' he said at last, after a break of several seconds. 'As a day laborer.'

'Thank you,' Rees said. 'I'll speak to him.' He paused, wanting to offer some assurance that Aaron was not guilty. But he couldn't. 'Good news. I brought Shem home to Zion. He's given up on the circus.'

Daniel's expression lightened. 'That is good news. I'm glad he saw how foolish joining that carnival would be.' Smiling, he turned back to the field.

Rees climbed into his wagon and drove the few yards to the farm gate. He parked in front of the barn, unhitched Hannibal and gave him a quick rubdown before releasing him into the pasture. Then he went inside.

Lydia turned from the dishpan with a smile. She was pink-cheeked and a little breathless and her cap was askew but she sounded just as usual. 'Did you get paid?' she asked.

'I did. The full amount.' He looked around. 'Where's Annie?'

'Upstairs.' A smile touched her lips. 'Did the widow say anything?'

'She was pleased. I'm optimistic there will be other housewives with commissions now.'

Loud footsteps sounded on the stairs. 'I have a surprise for you,' Lydia said just as David burst through the door.

'I got your letter,' David said. Rees, his eyes moistening, reached out and hugged his son with all his strength.

Lydia put out bread and cheese. David declined coffee but accepted some of Lydia's home-brewed beer. 'How long are you staying?' Rees asked, wiping his eyes on his shirttail.

'Just a few days,' David said. 'Although I've done most of the necessary chores at home, there'll be more waiting.' He smiled. 'My wife and Simon are in charge and a friend is looking in on them. But I don't want to leave them alone too long, especially with the planting coming up.' He paused. 'It looks as though you've done a fair bit already.'

'The Shaker Brothers are helping,' Rees said. 'But the lambs still need to be dealt with.'

'I stopped at the circus to see you,' David said.

Rees was very conscious of Lydia's startled glance toward him. He did not know why he felt so guilty; he'd done nothing wrong.

'I stopped briefly,' Rees said. So, he had seen David running through the wagons. 'Mr Asher said Boudreaux might not rejoin the circus.'

Lydia inclined her head, her body stiff. 'Did you see Bambola?'

Rees shook his head and said truthfully, 'No, I didn't.'

David, watching the interchange between his parents, said in annoyance, 'Is that why you need my help? Because you are spending all your time at the circus?'

'One of the Shaker girls was murdered,' Rees said. 'Elder Jonathan has asked me to look into it.'

'Your father thinks Boudreaux – the trick rider – is innocent,' Lydia said.

David looked at his father. 'And you would much rather probe the ugly side of human nature than attend to your farming chores.'

Rees would have liked to contradict his son but both David and Lydia would know he was lying. 'Someone needs to reveal the truth,' he said. 'And find justice for the victim.'

David shook his head in disbelief. He had never understood his father's passion for unpeeling the layers of deception and human evil, even if it resulted in identifying murderers. Rees, for his part, found David's love of farming, even the tedious chores, beyond comprehension.

David pushed away from the table and stood up. 'I'll go look at the new lambs,' he said.

'The Shakers are working outside,' Rees said. 'You may meet some old friends.' David had been only a boy when he'd run away to the Shakers. Now he was a man, as tall as Rees himself, and married with a baby of his own. 'If they even recognize you,' he added.

David smiled. 'I have many happy memories of my time in Zion,' he said.

His departure left an uncomfortable silence behind. Lydia turned back to the dishpan and made a great show of washing dishes. Although Rees understood his wife was afraid for the security of her family, he was perversely angry with her for her suspicions. He had done nothing wrong! Before he could speak to her and profess his innocence, someone knocked at the door. 'Must be Brother Daniel,' he said, striding across the room. But when he flung the door wide, it was not Brother Daniel.

Piggy Hanson, his cane upraised, stood on the step ready to knock again. Shocked, Rees fell back a step. For a moment they stared at one another. Then Rees demanded, 'What the Hell are you doing here?' He had never thought Piggy would track him to his home.

'I must speak with you, Will.' Hanson looked at Rees's expression and backed up a few steps. 'This is important.'

'I am not giving you the opportunity to menace my family again,' Rees said, his voice rising into a shout. The magistrate's coachman turned to stare. 'Haven't you done enough? Go away.'

'Will,' Lydia said, coming up behind him and putting her hand on his sleeve. 'At least hear him out.'

'I know we've had our differences,' Piggy said. 'But I—'

'Get off my porch right now,' Rees bellowed.

'I'm very sorry for what happened in Dugard,' Piggy said. 'But now we need to work together.'

'No, we don't,' Rees said. 'You allowed a superstitious fool to come after my wife and family.' He barely heard Annie's footsteps thudding down the stairs behind him.

The magistrate's pink and white complexion went even pinker.

'I know. I'm sorry. But you managed to set everything to rights, didn't you? And I put your friend Caldwell back into the position of constable.'

'Put everything to rights?' Rees repeated at such a loud volume a flock of birds in a nearby tree rose screeching into the air. 'We're living here because Lydia is still accused of witchcraft in Dugard.' He realized he was shaking with rage.

'I said I was sorry,' Piggy said, his own temper fraying. 'I can't keep apologizing. Now we need to work together.'

'No,' Rees shouted, shoving the magistrate with all of his strength. Piggy lost his balance, went down a step and fell full length into the mud at the bottom.

'You arrogant, pig-headed . . .' Piggy struggled to his feet. Dirt covered his fine, black trousers and snug-fitting, gray jacket. Mud had even splashed his lacy cravat. He inhaled, clearly trying to master his fury. 'If you change your mind I'll be at the tavern in town.' He stamped back to his coach and climbed in. Although Rees could hear Sharon wailing behind him, he waited on the porch until the carriage drove away.

He went back into the kitchen and shut the door. Lydia had picked up Sharon. Over the child's curly, red hair, Lydia glared at her husband, blaming him for the baby's tears. 'Was that necessary, Will?'

'It's all right,' Rees said, reaching out for his daughter. Sharon turned her head away. She had never seen him so angry and now she was frightened. He felt guilty but annoyed as well. No one understood exactly what had happened in Dugard. No one appreciated his struggles to protect his family. Lowering his voice so Annie would not hear, he said to Lydia, 'Piggy may be the murderer. He travels a circuit as well.'

'Well then,' she said tartly, 'you need to find out what he wants. How will you ever know if he's guilty if you avoid him?'

Rees did not want to agree. 'Likeliest, he'll only lie to me,' he said.

Lydia's mouth tightened but she did not argue. Instead she said, 'We've learned one thing at least.'

'What's that?' he asked.

'If Magistrate Hanson did commit' – she glanced at the children – 'the crime, he might have had help.'

Rees looked at her in perplexity. 'How do you figure?'

'He goes everywhere in his coach. The coachman would have had to know something.'

Rees stared at her. 'You're right. I may have to speak to Piggy's coachman.'

'But wouldn't the Reynard boy have seen the magistrate's coach?' Lydia asked. 'It is very distinctive with its bright red wheels and that pretentious insignia on the doors.'

Rees nodded slowly. 'He did see it. I'll have to speak to him again as well.'

Annie, who had seemed a little startled herself by Rees's outburst, came forward to take Sharon from Lydia's arms. 'Who wants some bread and butter with sugar on it?' she asked with that forced cheer mothers and nannies used with children.

'Me.' Annie led Sharon to the table.

'Brother Daniel told me Aaron is working out on North Road,' Rees said to Lydia. 'After dinner I'll ride out and ask him some questions.'

'Dinner isn't for another hour or so,' Lydia said. 'What will you do until then?'

Rees offered her a lopsided smile. 'Help the Shaker Brothers in what will be another field of rye.'

She nodded, her forehead furrowed. 'Will, I have something to tell you.'

'Yes?' He paused with his hand on the door.

'When I went to the circus in David's clothes the other day, everyone thought I was a boy. One of the crowd of boys. Anyway, I heard people talking.' She hesitated.

'And did you discover something?'

'I did. It didn't mean anything to me then.' She paused and took a breath. 'Miss Mazza, Bambola, you know, and Mr Asher are . . .' She hesitated, searching for the word. 'Connected.'

'Connected?' He had not seen any affection between the two.

'Yes. They occupy their own wagons, it is true, but they frequently spend the night together. I couldn't hear all of the rest, they lowered their voices then. But Miss Mazza had a baby.'

'She did?' Rees said.

'I thought there might be something there,' Lydia said, turning her face away. She added very quickly, 'She likes you.'

'Bambola?'

'Yes.' Lydia kept her face averted from him.

Warmth swept up Rees's neck and into his cheeks. As he thought of the readings she'd done, and his eagerness to see her when he visited the circus, his body prickled with both embarrassment and guilty pleasure. 'There's nothing between Bambola and me,' he said truthfully as he pulled his wife into his arms. Truthfully for now.

THIRTY

When Rees drove out to the Perkins farm, he found Aaron, just as Brother Daniel had promised. As itinerant help Aaron had been given one of the worst jobs; shoveling manure out of the barn. Rees tied his handkerchief over his face and approached upwind, pausing within shouting distance. He really did not want to go any closer. 'Aaron,' he said.

Aaron threw a spadeful of the scrapings from the barn floor into a pile and turned to face Rees. 'What do you want?'

'Shem is safe,' Rees said. He thought he might soften up the irascible Shaker but Aaron only nodded. 'He left the circus.' Rees paused. 'What is Shem to you? Son?'

'Who told you that?' Aaron stopped working and leaned on the handle to stare at Rees.

'No one. It's obvious there's a connection there. Why keep it a secret?'

'Huh. Even if he is my son I couldn't say. We aren't supposed to have special family, are we?' Aaron spat to the side. 'You, of all people, should know that.'

Rees inclined his head, acknowledging that as the truth. 'So, what is he to you?'

'My son. On one of my selling trips I took him from that Jezebel, my sister. I knew she'd ruin him.' Startled by Aaron's frankness, Rees stared. Aaron retrieved his shovel and returned to work.

'He doesn't remember you?' This was not a guess. Rees was unsurprised when Aaron inclined his head in affirmation.

'No. I joined the Millennial Church when he was still a baby.'

'But you kept an eye on him.'

'Have to, don't I?' Aaron began shoveling as rapidly as he could and when he spoke again his voice was muffled. 'I failed to keep Calvin safe.' Rees nodded involuntarily. The disabled boy had been Aaron's particular charge until he'd been murdered. At last Aaron paused in his frantic shoveling and stood up, wiping his eyes with his sleeve. 'When I saw that girl, Leah, speaking to Shem I knew she was up to mischief. So, I kept a close eye on the pair of them.'

'But Shem . . .' Rees began. He stopped and took a breath. Shem had admitted to making several journeys to town without Leah in tow. Aaron had a blind spot where his son was concerned. 'You must have seen Monsieur Boudreaux then?'

'Yes, I saw him. Showing off. Well, pride goeth before a fall.'

Rees regarded the other man in distaste. Aaron was unlike any other Shaker Rees had ever met and he wondered how he had lasted as long as he had in that community. Trying to keep his voice even, he asked, 'What happened then?'

'I followed them into town. Lost them in that warren of alleys that the townspeople call roads. By the time I found them again, they were talking to that circus rider. The girl was whining that it was boring and she wanted to go home. But Shem wanted to stay, keep talking about horses.' Rees waited for Aaron to continue. For the first time the Brother seemed ill at ease. His eyes shifted from side to side and although the silence between the two men rapidly became awkward he didn't speak.

'You saw Leah leave?' Rees finally asked.

'Yes.' Only the one word but it revealed a depth of shame Rees had not suspected. Once again Aaron began shoveling manure as though his life depended on it.

'And then?' Rees asked.

Aaron paused and stood. 'Well, I went back home when Shem left.' He began speaking very rapidly, his forehead beading with sweat. 'I had to, didn't I? I had chores. And I'd already been gone a couple of hours. I knew Shem was safe . . .'

'And where was Leah?' Rees asked. Despite his attempt to remain neutral, his voice rose.

'Don't know.' Aaron's gaze shifted away from Rees. 'She'd left. Said she was going home. And that's where I thought she was.'

'So, you did see her?' Rees said, leaning forward on the balls of his feet as though he might charge the other man.

'No.' Aaron shook his head vehemently. 'No. Shem had the devil of a time finding his way back to the lane and even if I was willing to let him know I was there I didn't know the way either.'

'What time was this?' Rees asked.

'Around four, I think,' Aaron said, averting his eyes. 'I swear, I didn't see hide nor hair of the girl the entire time I was walking back home.'

Rees thought it must have been about four thirty when he drove past Reynard's farm and he had not seen the girl. Or either Aaron or Shem. Of course, Rees had been on the main road and not looking.

'Did you see anyone else on the lane?' he asked.

Aaron shook his head. 'Just the boy in the field. Couple of farmer's carts and a carriage.'

'The magistrate's carriage?' Rees asked in excitement.

Aaron shook his head. 'No. I would recognize his vehicle. It's not fitting for a magistrate to ride in a carriage with red wheels and a fancy design on the door. This one was plain.'

'So,' Rees said, 'let me see if I understand.' Aaron took a step backwards from the anger in Rees's voice. 'You knew Boudreaux was innocent but you said nothing. Moreover, although you'd followed Shem and Leah into town, you did not announce your presence or offer to escort a young girl home. You do realize that, by the time you reached the lane, Leah was either already in her killer's clutches being assaulted. Or dead.' Rees's voice rose until he was shouting.

'It was her fault,' Aaron shouted in return. 'She shouldn't of gone to town. She was disobedient. And she certainly shouldn't of left Shem.'

'She was a child,' Rees bellowed, not realizing this argument had a witness until someone took him by the arm. He shook off the farmer's restraining hand. 'This was her first time in town. She didn't know how to find her way to the lane, just as you didn't, so she took the road. And that's where her murderer found her.'

'Hey, what's going on here?' the farmer asked, inserting himself between Rees and Aaron.

'Nothing,' both men answered in unison.

'It didn't sound like nothing to me,' Mr Perkins said. He looked at Aaron. 'After you finish here, collect your pay and go. I don't want any trouble.'

'He's not in any trouble,' Rees said in reluctant defense. 'I thought he might know something.'

'Then let him finish his work,' Perkins said to Rees.

'Very well.' Rees took a few steps back as though he were planning to leave. But instead he waited until the farmer had left the barn. 'Will you go home to Zion now?' he asked.

Aaron shook his head. 'Women are fools and the men who listen to them are bigger fools,' he said. 'Best I don't go back.'

'Shem went home,' Rees said.

'Thank the Lord and all His angels,' he said, closing his eyes. 'But no.' Rees nodded and turned to go. As he approached the door Aaron said from behind him, 'I swear I didn't kill that girl and I didn't see the man who did.'

Rees looked back over his shoulder but he didn't speak. A man could swear anything. It didn't mean he was telling the truth.

THIRTY-ONE

When Rees left the Perkins farm he thought he might stop and visit with Rouge. But the circus – and Bambola – drew him like a moth to a flame and he found himself turning his wagon toward the fairgrounds. As he approached the field he heard the banging of several busy hammers. Although the wheelwright was there – Rees parked next to the repairman's wagon – he was not the source of the hammering. The circus roustabouts were erecting two tall poles while Bambola watched. She turned with a warm smile. 'Why, Mr Rees, how lovely to see you.'

Rees felt heat sweep over his body. To hide his face he executed a clumsy bow. 'What are they doing?' he asked as he returned to an upright position.

'Oh, the axle won't be repaired for several more days at least,' she said with a pout. 'So, I thought I would practice. I have something new in mind. I've gone through the steps several times on the ground but now I need to see how it will work in the air.'

'You have a dangerous trade,' Rees said.

She smiled. 'My mother began training me when I was five. Rope dancing does not seem so dangerous to me.' She looked back at the half-completed posts. 'They won't finish today.' She fixed Rees with an impish smile. 'We have time for another reading.'

'Oh no,' Rees said. But hadn't he known all along, even though he had not admitted it to himself, that she would want to tell his fortune again? 'Why me? There must be many here whose fortunes can be told.'

'Indeed yes,' she said with a trill of laughter. 'But I have read the cards for most of them more times than I can count.'

'Most of them?'

'Some do not believe. Mr Asher for one.' She sighed. 'And others are frightened.'

Rees nodded, understanding both emotions. In Dugard she would surely have been hanged as a witch. As for Rees, well, he did not believe either. But he went willingly and sat across the table from her. He enjoyed watching her small graceful hands lay out the cards and hear her charmingly accented voice as she spoke. It did not even matter what she said.

Once again he shuffled, unable to remember for a few seconds why exactly he had come here. Then, remembering the gossip, he asked, 'Do you have any children?'

'Me?' She uttered a laugh that sounded forced to Rees's ears. He looked up. She was shaking her head, her face set in a grimace. 'No, no children. Pregnancy would throw off my balance and I would not be able to dance across the rope.'

Very quickly she laid out the colorful pasteboard squares and flipped over the first one, signaling the end of the previous topic. 'The lovers,' she murmured. After a short silence she said reluctantly, 'This card expresses your situation right now. Infidelity can lead to marital problems, separation or worse. Be careful to behave wisely.'

Rees felt the blood race into his cheeks and hoped Bambola did not notice. She flipped the second card. She stared at it, biting her lip. Rees lowered his eyes to the card and gasped. It pictured the Devil.

'This card illustrates immediate influences,' she said. 'You face some bad habits, some old ways of thinking. You must fight against them to achieve success. Otherwise you will fail.' She turned over the third card. 'Justice, reversed. This indicates prejudice or unreasonable beliefs. Pay attention to what people say. Some are lying to you, attempting to deceive you.'

'I know that,' Rees said, trying to mock the emotions the first two cards had raised within him.

Bambola flipped the fourth card. Again, it was upside down. 'Three of Rods,' Bambola said. 'Someone has a hidden agenda. Be very sure any offers of help are genuine. Someone is trying to lead you away from the truth.' Rees involuntarily nodded, his mind going to Piggy Hanson.

'This card reveals the recent past,' Bambola said, turning over the next one. 'The King of Rods. You are strong, dependable, honest. Strong enough to prove your ideas. Don't be swayed by others.'

Rees found himself hanging on the ropedancer's every word. He did not believe, he certainly did not. But what Bambola said hit uncomfortably close. She turned over the sixth card.

'Strength. Again. But this card warns you about the future. Use your head and not your heart. Restrain yourself from impulsive actions. Hold your power in reserve. Your courage and fortitude will bring success.' The hand holding the next card began to tremble.

'Miss Mazza,' Rees said anxiously. She quickly turned the card over and put it on the table. This one pictured the moon.

'You are a man with great intuition,' she said. 'Rely upon it. All deceptions will be unmasked.' She turned the next card, a young boy with a sword. 'The Page of Swords. You will meet an old friend again. Rely upon him. If you do, the outlook is hopeful.'

'Rely on Piggy?' Rees said involuntarily. That couldn't be correct. Bambola turned the next to the last card.

'Eight of Swords. You are facing a difficult situation. Don't ignore it. Face it head on.' She revealed the final card. 'Temperance. Reach into the past for help. Only then will you find the answer you seek.'

When she finished, Bambola stared at the cards for a second or two. 'Your choices in the next few days will result in success or failure, Mr Rees, with success the more likely. Be careful.' She hastily gathered up the cards and returned them to their box. Rees nodded and rose to his feet. He turned back as though he would speak to her, perhaps ask her why she suddenly seemed so frightened, but her expression warned him off. She had closed in on herself, excluding him.

When he turned he saw Otto watching. The strong man shook his head and disappeared between the wagons.

Why was Otto following him? Recalling the strong man's large hands, Rees shuddered. If only someone had seen Otto on the road Rees would be certain of the killer. But no one had.

Worrying at it, Rees walked back to the poles for Bambola's rope. It still was not up. The men had not succeeded in moving any further forward. 'What's the matter?' Rees asked Billy.

'We need Pip Boudreaux,' the dwarf said. 'He's the only one who knows how exactly to finish this. And he's tall.' He turned to eye Rees. 'You're tall enough as well.'

'I don't know what to do,' Rees said hastily. He did not wish to climb the post; he could too easily imagine himself falling. And the knots at the top looked much too complicated for him to even guess at.

'Maybe if one of us talked you through the task?' Billy suggested. Rees shook his head in emphatic denial. 'It is not a difficult job exactly.'

Over his head, between the wagons, Rees spotted Bambola speaking to Asher. She looked very upset, almost in tears. But Asher? Rees read his expression more as condescension. He regarded the ropedancer with a slight smile as though she amused him. At last he put a hand on her shoulder and, shaking his head, spoke a few soft words. Then he turned and approached Rees and Billy with Bambola trailing behind.

'Oh no,' Rees muttered involuntarily, wondering if Asher planned to take him to task after that conversation with Bambola.

'I'm trying to persuade Mr Rees here,' Billy said to Asher, 'to help us with the rope.'

'An excellent idea,' he said, examining Rees in his turn.

'No,' Rees said.

'Perhaps Boudreaux would be willing to return and finish this small job for us if you were here to assist,' Asher continued, just as if Rees had not spoken. 'It will only take an hour or two. He could accomplish the more difficult bits – the ones only he knows – and you could hand him what was required.'

Rees almost said no once again. But Bambola clasped her hands together and smiled.

'Please,' she said.

And he was lost. 'Very well,' he said gruffly.

'Could you come tomorrow?' Asher asked. 'Pip is still at the tavern. I don't know why he prefers such a menial job when he could be here, with us. But he'll be willing to join us tomorrow afternoon, I'm sure.'

Rees nodded. 'Tomorrow then.' He turned to leave.

'One more thing,' Asher said.

Wary, Rees spun around to face the ringmaster.

'There were two men looking for you,' Asher said, drawing Rees away from the others and lowering his voice to a whisper.

'Who?' Rees said in surprise. That was not what he expected to hear.

'Not the magistrate but two others. Rough men. One short with eyes like a weasel and carrying a knife. Clearly the brains – he did most of the talking. A right villain.'

'Farley,' Rees muttered, recalling the constable in Dugard who had pursued Lydia so relentlessly. Would Farley travel so far from home in pursuit?

'That may have been the name,' Asher agreed. 'The other: big, tall, heavy-set. Broad face. Dirty. He didn't speak much and when he did, I could barely understand him. A simple-minded fellow.'

Rees shook his head, not recognizing the description. 'Anything else?' he asked.

'The clothing worn by the smaller man was too big, and ill-fitting as though he'd borrowed someone else's for the day. Like a costume, you know? But that knife was no costume.' Asher suddenly shuddered. 'He kept touching it, as a man would touch a woman. He frightened me, I don't mind telling you. Especially when he walked through our camp looking for you. What are you mixed up in?'

Rees shook his head. 'Nothing,' he said. 'Nothing here anyway.'

'Watch yourself, Mr Rees. I think they mean you harm,' Asher warned.

'Thank you,' Rees said automatically. Farley here? Everything Piggy had said when he visited Rees's farm was a lie. Like it or not, he knew he had to speak to the magistrate now and tell him to call off his dogs.

THIRTY-TWO

When Rees entered the tavern he found Rouge standing in his usual place at the bar. Although he was listening to a group of men discussing the circus his face was carefully devoid of all expression and Rees couldn't tell what the constable thought. Rees moved closer.

'What if another of our girls goes missing?' asked one man, his vest stained with at least a week's worth of meals.

Rees found it ironic that the Shaker community had always been suspect but now, in light of Leah's death, the townsfolk of Durham were taking the Shakers as their own.

'Villains, all of them,' agreed his companion.

'Why don't you just hang 'em outright?' a third inquired of Rouge.

Rees thought that maybe the circus folk had good reason to be afraid of the people in these towns. He looked at Rouge, hoping the constable's sense of justice was enough to prevent the wholesale execution of innocent people.

'They've got some fine horses,' said the first speaker.

Rouge turned and stared at him. 'We're not horse thieves,' Rouge said. He turned to look at Rees. 'What do you want?'

'Looking for the magistrate,' Rees said.

Rouge hesitated. 'I know there's bad blood between you,' he said at last. 'I don't want any trouble.'

Rees might have told him about the two men Asher described but with an audience he elected not to. 'Fine,' he said. 'No trouble.'

Rouge nodded to the back corner of the room. 'There.'

Rees turned and scanned the crowd. Sure enough, Magistrate Hanson was seated with his back to the wall and a large plate of steak and eggs in front of him. Rees started for him, threading his way through the mostly empty tables. Piggy looked up, his knife held halfway to his mouth. He lowered his cutlery with an expression of mixed hope and wariness.

'Why did you send two men after me?' Rees asked, pulling out a chair and sitting down.

'What two men?'

'Farley and a friend.' Rees leaned forward.

'Farley?' Hanson sounded confused. 'What does Farley have to do with anything?'

'Did you hire them to kill me?'

'I don't know what you're talking about,' the magistrate said, eyeing Rees with growing distress.

'I know you hate me,' Rees said. 'First you went after my family. Now murder?'

'What?'

'I'm warning you to stop.' Rees thumped the table. 'Right now. Because if anyone in my family is hurt, I will come after you.'

'Now Rees,' Rouge said from behind Rees's chair, 'I told you not to cause any trouble.'

'No trouble,' Rees said.

'We are just having a conversation,' Piggy agreed, shocking Rees into silence. 'A very impassioned conversation,' the magistrate added. Rees turned around to look at Rouge. He appeared utterly confused and suspicious both.

'Very well,' he said, backing up a few steps. 'For now.'

'We need to speak,' Hanson said, leaning forward across the table. 'But not here.'

'I've said my piece,' Rees said, rising to his feet. 'Remember what I told you.' Brushing past Rouge, Rees stamped out of the tavern. He felt the eyes of everyone burning holes in his back.

He drove home in a foul temper. Why did everyone take Piggy's side?

'What did Brother Aaron say?' Lydia asked when Rees stepped through the door. She left the dishes and approached him, drying her hands on a towel.

Rees cast his mind back. His conversation with Aaron already seemed days ago, not hours. At least the drive home had done some good and he had calmed down. 'He admitted to following the children into town,' he began. At that moment, Sharon screamed and both Rees and Lydia looked over. Sharon had thrown herself on the floor while Joseph stood over her with her doll in his hand. Lydia hurried over to separate them.

'What happened?' she asked her daughter.

'Mine,' Sharon wailed, pointing at the doll.

'I had it first,' Joseph said.

Lydia put the doll on the mantel. 'She stays here until you can play nicely together,' she said. She nodded at her husband to continue.

'Shem is Aaron's son,' Rees said. Lydia's mouth formed an 'o'. 'And he admitted, with some shame, that he allowed Leah to find her own way home.'

'We knew that,' Lydia said.

'Yes,' Rees agreed. 'But he says he didn't see her. I'd love to know what Aaron's crime was—'

They both heard the sound of Sharon slapping Joseph and he began to squeal. As Lydia hurried to the children she said over the ear-shattering screams, 'Jonathan might know.' It took Rees a moment to realize she was responding to his previous comment.

'That's true,' he said, his words drowned by the crying of the children as they were put into separate corners.

'I'll feed the children now and put them both down for naps.'

Rees nodded, disgruntled. 'Where's Annie?'

'In the vegetable garden. David is out in the fields.'

Rees turned and went out the kitchen door.

Annie raised a flushed face at his approach. Her sleeves and the hem of her skirt were tied up and her hands were muddy from planting. A basket with early peas and some greens stood at her side.

'We need you inside,' he said. She raised her eyebrows at his brusque tone but nodded and collected the basket.

When Rees returned to the kitchen Lydia had the children at the table with bread and cheese in front of them. Annie followed Rees inside and put the basket on the drainboard. She filled the tin bowl with water and washed her hands.

'After they eat, they should go down for naps,' Lydia said.

Now, with Annie in the kitchen, Rees did not want to talk about Aaron. He knew his wife's opinion anyway; It was unlikely Aaron was guilty. He'd sworn he wasn't but Rees did not entirely believe him.

'There's something else,' Rees said. 'Piggy is still in town.'

'You saw him?' Lydia asked.

'I did.' Rees knew Lydia wanted to hear he'd made peace with the magistrate, but he couldn't tell her that. He wrestled with himself for a few seconds before finally deciding on the entire truth. 'I stopped by to see him after I—' he began. Sharon screamed, very suddenly and very loudly. Lydia hurried to the table.

'She spilled her milk,' Annie said. 'It is not a problem.' Lydia looked at Rees.

'I saw Piggy in the tavern and warned him to stay away from us,' he said rapidly.

'Are you sure the magistrate is involved somehow?' she asked as she returned to his side.

Rees thought of the gloating expression on Piggy's face when he said he'd made Farley the Dugard constable. Piggy had known Farley would pursue Rees and his family. Then Farley and his sons had come to the farm looking for Lydia; arriving with a rope so they could hang her while she hid in the dairy shed. And later, after Lydia and the children had escaped and fled to Zion, the mob had returned so they could search again for them.

'Of course I'm sure,' he said sharply. 'I've told you what happened. Piggy allowed Farley to persecute us.'

Lydia's forehead wrinkled in thought. 'But he said he wanted to work with you,' she protested.

'He's a liar,' he said uncompromisingly. 'I'll never trust him, never.'

'But what then is the magistrate doing here? He never stays in the towns on his circuit for this long; if he did he would never spend any time at home.' She glanced at the children and returned her attention to her husband. 'Surely, if his sole purpose is to find you – which he has – he would have moved on by now.'

'He still wants to punish me.'

'But that is not what he said,' Lydia argued. 'He said he wanted to work with you.'

'Is that why he . . .' Realizing he was about to tell Lydia about the two men at the circus Rees clamped his mouth shut.

'I think you should listen to the magistrate.' With her attention once more focused on the children she did not see the angry flush rising into his cheeks. 'What do you know about Mr Asher?' she asked.

'I don't see he has any reason to lie,' he said stiffly.

'Unless he's protecting someone in the circus,' Lydia suggested.

Rees considered that for a moment. Asher was very protective of his people, that was true. Perhaps he was shielding Otto? But Asher had abandoned Boudreaux, a man he had described as like a brother, when he thought the charges against Boudreaux would put everyone in danger.

'Maybe,' Rees said doubtfully.

'I think you are allowing your fondness for those people to affect your judgment,' Lydia said.

'What do you mean?' Rees asked sharply even though he had a good idea. 'I'm not attached to anyone there.' She looked at him skeptically. 'Believe me, I've done nothing wrong.' That at least was true. But a small voice whispered in the back of his mind, '*Not yet.*'

THIRTY-THREE

While Lydia put Sharon and Joseph to bed, Rees drove Annie back to Zion for prayers and dinner with the community. He'd volunteered. He felt he needed some distance from his family right then. It was a silent ride. Annie, after one quick glance at Rees's expression, kept her mouth closed. And even Annie's silence annoyed him.

Rees hoped Jonathan would tell him what Aaron had done. But when he found the Elder he at first refused to say anything. 'When people choose to join us and sign the Covenant,' he said, 'they leave their former lives behind them. They are reborn. And we do not hold their previous mistakes against them.'

'You do realize that Aaron, for all he is one of your Brothers, could be a murderer, don't you?' Rees asked. He was still irritated from his discussion with Lydia and it showed; he sounded angry. Jonathan took a step backward and his mouth tightened into an even more obdurate line. Experiencing a sudden and very uncomfortable vision of himself as Jonathan saw him: brash, opinionated and habitually angry. Rees held up his hand in silent apology. 'Forgive me,' he said. 'This has been a difficult time.' Jonathan nodded but did not relax his wary stance.

'You and Aaron have frequently clashed,' he said. 'You are alike in certain unfortunate ways.' He did not sound critical. He was simply stating a fact and that made the sting worse.

'I know,' Rees said. He took a deep breath. 'I promise you this is not a vendetta. Aaron was there at the right time and he blames Leah.'

'He is trying to protect Shem,' Jonathan said. 'Aaron has always been protective of our young.'

Rees looked at Jonathan in disbelief. Aaron had claimed more than once that Leah's death was a consequence of her wicked behavior. But Rees, who did not want to argue with the Elder, took a deep breath. 'That may be true,' he said after the passage of several seconds, 'but you must agree that, if I am to find Leah's murderer, it is necessary for me to question everyone. And know everything that might have a bearing on her death.'

'Aaron's past sins have nothing to do with Leah's murder,' Jonathan said firmly. 'He would not—'

'Just as a previous Brother we know would not, hmm?' Rees interrupted impatiently, referencing previous murders in this community.

Jonathan's mouth fell open. 'That-that was an anomaly,' he stammered. 'If you wish to know Aaron's past you must question him yourself.' Turning on his heel, Jonathan walked away.

Cursing under his breath. Rees looked around him. Was there anyone else he could speak to? Most likely, only the Elders knew Aaron's secrets. And Rees knew that Esther, his friend and someone who might be prevailed upon to confide the truth, knew nothing of Aaron's past.

Muttering under his breath, Rees flung himself into his wagon and headed home, more determined than ever to learn Aaron's secret.

The following morning passed in a flurry of chores. With David's help, Rees succeeded in finishing everything, including clearing another field for planting, by the noon meal. He was almost tempted to leave as soon as he'd changed his clogs and muddy shirt but he didn't quite dare. He suspected if he did Lydia might tell him not to come home. And, although legally the farm was his he knew it really belonged to her. He would win in court but he did not want the farm. It was a base, no more. Besides, his rush to reach town had nothing to do with the circus or Bambola. That's what he told himself anyway.

So, he ate dinner with as much patience as he could muster before leaving. He thought Lydia might say something sharp or protest when he went out the door but she did not. Instead she kissed him and bade him good luck.

Rees crossed town to the fairgrounds and turned in, the golden straw crackling underneath his wagon wheels. He heard the hammering before he saw the posts. The two men working on it turned when they heard Rees approaching and he saw that one of the men was Boudreaux. His frown blossomed into a pleased smile when he recognized Rees. He climbed down from the landing step and ran across the field. 'You are here,' he said.

'Mr Asher asked me to come and help,' Rees said. He couldn't help staring at Boudreaux's head. The showman's dyed hair, revealed by his cap, had faded to a peculiar rusty red.

'I wasn't sure he told me the truth,' Boudreaux said.

'We are both tall, you see,' Rees said. 'But only you know how to attach the rope so Bambola won't fall.'

'And you are not here to ask questions about me,' Boudreaux said. 'You know I am innocent.'

'Probably,' Rees said, always cautious. Otto the strongman was also a strong contender, but no one had seen him on the lane. Now Rees's primary suspects were Piggy Hanson and Brother Aaron, men who traveled regularly and had been present in several towns where there'd been murders.

'Mr Rees,' Asher said, crossing the field, 'I wondered when I might see you. Those men asking for you came back.'

'They did?' Rees's belly revolted and he swallowed hard several times. 'But I spoke to Magistrate Hanson.'

Asher grimaced. 'You did? Well, maybe these men are not the ones you know. I did wonder if they might be servants. Someone's grooms perhaps? They had that air about them; obsequiousness mixed with sullen defiance. Anyway, they promised to return again so be careful.'

Rees knew many people with servants. Even his son David hired extra help to work in the fields when needed. But Rees would be hard pressed to describe any of them. 'Who trusts his help so much he sends them on a task such as this?' he said aloud.

'You are naïve if you don't believe some men will kill another for just one saulty,' Asher said in a grim tone. A penny? Rees considered that statement and slowly nodded in agreement. He had seen the same, especially in family disputes. His sister would have destroyed Rees's entire family. But she was far away now. Who else hated Rees that much? He thought again of the magistrate. He certainly had the funds to hire a killer. But would he? And then there was Aaron. He didn't hate Rees, at least Rees didn't think so, and was far too poor to hire a killer. He did have a lot to hide though. And maybe Rees was closing in so Aaron had scraped together the necessary funds.

'Anyway,' Asher continued, interrupting Rees's thoughts, 'if you're going to be here today I think you should consider a disguise.' His eyes went to Rees's bright hair. 'Something simple.'

'Hair dye like Boudreaux?' Rees said, his voice rising to a squeak. 'No. I expect to be here for only a few hours. At most.'

'Nothing so dramatic then. How about a cap? And different clothing? You'll look like one of us.'

'Why are you doing this?' Rees asked, genuinely curious.

Asher grinned. 'Simple really. You're more like us than them.' He waved his hand toward the town. 'Instead of just assuming Boudreaux was guilty, you were at least willing to consider him innocent. Not many would do that. Besides, when those fellows came looking for you, something evil walked over my grave. You're a good man. I know they aren't.'

'A cap is acceptable,' Rees said. 'I don't want my hair looking like Boudreaux's.'

Asher laughed. 'He did that himself with a mixture of indigo and henna and a soupcon of blackberry juice.' He cast a glance at Rees. 'We can't do anything about your height. But Boudreaux is almost as tall; we'll pass you off as his brother.'

For a moment Rees considered just leaving but now he was desperate to know about the men tracking him and the villain behind them.

While one of the women brought various articles of clothing for him to try on, Rees asked questions. Some arose directly from his curiosity about their lives: how did they prepare meals on the road?

(Over open fires.) Were the wagons comfortable? (Mostly but only in the warm weather.) How did they choose the towns in which they performed? (They would usually stop at any cluster of houses and put on a show, even if it were a small one.) But some of Rees's questions were more pointed as he attempted to discover where the circus had been. He planned to examine Rouge's letters and mark the connecting dots on the constable's map.

Asher also owned a map and had a circuit in mind that they more or less followed, always heading toward towns of a decent size like Elliott or Durham. Gradually Rees worked out the path they'd taken this year and last. He wished he had pencil and paper. Without those tools, he repeated the names in his mind, trying to commit them to memory, as the woman listed them. His retention of detail was usually excellent but this time there were a lot of names and he wasn't sure he could remember everything. He just hoped to recollect enough to draw out a rough approximation of the circus route.

Within half an hour Rees's clothing, his soft linen shirt and brown breeches, had been exchanged for tattered replacements. Although clean, his shirt especially looked just one step removed from the ragbag. Instead of his favorite tricorn, Rees now wore a flat cap of a grimy indeterminate shade. Since shoes of the proper size could not be found, he was allowed to keep his own. A worn woolen vest completed the costume.

He doubted even Lydia would recognize him.

When he rejoined Asher he pronounced himself satisfied. 'You look like a different person. With luck, those men will not return but if they do we're ready.' He pointed to the center of the wagons. 'Come and eat before you start helping Pip.'

Rees and Asher joined the crowd already grouped around the fire. An older woman was ladling out soup. She handed Rees a bowl without really looking at him and he sat down next to Boudreaux. Without speaking, the performer offered Rees the bread. Both men put their bread into the soup. It would have made a poor meal otherwise.

Billy and his trained pig sat across the circle, looking like two little, old, bald men. He offered Rees a friendly nod.

'We'll have to purchase more supplies,' Asher said as he joined them. 'We're getting low. Usually we purchase our food – bread, bacon, garden sass and sometimes a chicken or ham – from a farmer. And we always lay in supplies when we stop in town. But we haven't done either of those things this time.'

'The shops are open,' Rees said. 'And some of the farmers have food to sell.' He nodded toward town.

'Are they butchering?'

Rees, his mind following a different train of thought, said, 'Has Boudreaux been accused of murder before?' Rees knew the answer but he wanted to see what Asher would say.

The circus owner sighed. 'Durham was not the first town to connect our show with an unexplained death. But I don't want to discuss this here,' he said, glancing around. Rees followed Asher's gaze but as far as he could tell no one was paying any attention. Nonetheless, Rees inclined his head in assent and turned to Boudreaux with a question about the horses he used in his act.

The conversation that followed was a bit of a struggle since Boudreaux's English was not up to the task of explaining the intricacies of training a circus horse. But they managed to converse in the mixture of English and French and when the performer invited Rees to come and see his horses close up Rees agreed.

'You take them as poulains . . . um . . . babies,' Boudreaux said when they reached the pasture where the animals were pegged out.

'Colts,' Rees said, nodding to show he understood.

Boudreaux knelt by the gelding and ran his hands down the horse's legs. Rees was amazed that the animal submitted so readily to Boudreaux's touch. None of the horses Rees had employed in the last year, even the most docile, would have been so calm.

'They're here.' A breathless boy ran up shouting. Rees turned to stare at the dirty child.

'Who's here?'

'Those men. Hide. Hide.'

'Move!' Boudreaux shouted as he jumped up and ran towards the wagons. Rees started after him but realized he did not have time to follow. He could already hear Asher's voice. Besides, he didn't know where to go.

THIRTY-FOUR

After wasting several precious seconds in frozen indecision, Rees dropped to his knees with some hope of disguising his height. He picked up the horse's hoof as though he was examining it. The gelding snorted and shifted but did not pull away. From the corner of his eye, Rees watched the two ruffians approach.

They were just as Asher had described and Rees did not recognize either one. The bigger man overtopped his companion by six or so inches and looked as strong as an ox. And about as intelligent. The other man, a small scrawny dark-haired fellow with a feral grin, was as different as chalk to cheese. As he walked past the show people, he nodded, affecting a friendliness that was so patently false there was an almost universal shivery retreat away from him. Now Rees understood what Asher had meant about the clothing. While the bigger oafish fellow's shirt and breeches fit well and he wore them with easy familiarity, the smaller man wore his awkwardly. Perhaps they were not servants as Asher had thought but deserters from some army and the smaller man was accustomed to both a uniform and command.

'I told you, the man you are searching for is not here,' Asher said as he hurried behind the duo. 'Why do you think he's here?' That was the question on Rees's mind. He did not know these men and, to his knowledge, had never seen them before. Oh, the small man, and the more dangerous of the two, looked familiar but Rees suspected that was only because he knew the type.

'If I find you've hidden him here and lied to me,' that dark man said now, 'I'll make you sorry.' His fingers touched the knife handle with loving gentleness. Rees, who felt certain this villain would make good on his threat, could not repress a shudder.

The door to the wagon into which Boudreaux had fled banged and both men looked toward the sound. The smaller man began running and after a few seconds the larger of the two lumbered after him. They opened the wagon door and disappeared inside. Rees feared for Boudreaux but he must have been securely hidden. The men did not have him when they stepped from the wagon. They searched all around the vehicle, even crawling underneath, and went through the camp. Although they passed Rees several times they paid him no attention at all. Finally, cursing Asher, they moved toward the mounts tied up by the road. Rees dropped the horse's hoof and discreetly followed them.

He'd wondered why Asher and the other men had so easily allowed these men access but realized when he approached the road that they had help. Two other men, both armed, waited with the horses. Besides a blunderbuss Rees also saw a rifle and a musket. He knew these men would not hesitate to use their weapons.

The men who had searched the circus mounted and the entire band rode away, westward toward Elliott. 'I would pick up and move on to the next town if we were allowed,' Asher said, coming up behind Rees. He turned. Asher looked thoroughly spooked. Perspiration glittered on his cheeks and forehead and he kept biting his lower lip.

'It wouldn't matter,' Rees said. 'They'll follow you and keep following you as long as they think I'm with you. I'm putting all of you in danger. I should leave immediately.'

Asher shook his head. 'Oh, we're safe enough now, I think. They've already been here. You might as well remain and assist Boudreaux. But by dark . . .' His voice trailed away. After a few seconds pause he added, 'Maybe once they realize they can't find you here they'll leave for good. I can assure you I do not want to spend the rest of my life looking over my shoulder.'

Rees's gaze returned to the road and the cloud of dust hanging in the air. He was trembling.

'It's almost as though they suspect *you* of murdering that girl,' Asher said, leveling his brown eyes at Rees.

'How would they even know about Leah?' Rees said. 'No, this is about something else.' He paused. Could Piggy Hanson carry a grudge this long? Rees shook his head, trying to clear it. 'Maybe I've gotten too close to someone,' Rees said, stumbling over the words as he tried to put his vague thoughts into language. 'Maybe my efforts to clear Boudreaux is threatening someone.'

'Who?' asked Asher.

'I don't know. Yet. But I promise you I will find out.'

Asher examined Rees's determined expression and nodded. 'I think you will,' he said. 'If those two don't kill you first.'

Although Asher soon disappeared among the wagons, Rees lingered by the road watching as the dust from the passage of the four men dissipated. Before it was entirely gone Boudreaux joined him. For several seconds the two men stared at the road and then the Frenchman said, 'The rope?' With one final glance over his shoulder Rees turned and began to follow the other man. He had not gone more than a few steps when he heard a familiar voice saying, 'Father.' Rees turned. David was standing between two wagons – and this time Rees was sure the fellow in the battered straw hat was David.

'What are you doing here?' he asked.

'Lydia suggested I see something of the circus,' David said.

'I'll show you,' Rees said as he stared around, trying to see the circus through David's eyes.

Everyone was working. Although no performance was planned for the immediate future, these were busy folks. Some of the women sat outside the wagons working on costumes, mending seams torn during acrobatics, sewing brilliants or feathers over carefully darned holes in the equestriennes' riding habits, or scrubbing much worn petticoats so they would shine brightly white while on display. The men checked saddles and other leather accouterments for weak spots due to wear and the horses were examined, hooves up. These animals were critical to the circus, they pulled the wagons or provided the backs on which the trick riders rode, and none could be spared.

'Where do the people live?' David asked.

'In the wagons,' Rees said, pointing to an open door. David peered inside. Rees looked over his son's shoulder at the bench that doubled as a bed and as seating, at the basin that marked the kitchen and the built-in drawers to one side. A small table had been bolted into the space in front of the bench and a pair of silver candlesticks sat proudly on the scarred wood.

When David pulled his head back, his mouth was pressed into a narrow line. Rees knew that expression from the past; David disapproved. 'Not much room for sleeping,' he said.

'It beats bedding down in a field,' Rees said sharply, insulted on behalf of his friends.

The wagons were drawn closely together to free a large space in the center. More than one performer was practicing. Rees pointed out the children, some barely out of leading strings, who were already learning to turn somersaults or stand on a pony's back. One boy, so young he was still in a dress, was being taught to jump through the large hoops called balloons while his older sister stood on a galloping gelding that went round and round the track. Rees could just imagine Simon standing on a horse's back, eager to practice these tricks, and Nancy and Judah trying to copy their older brother.

'These children should be in school or learning the ways of a farm,' David said.

Rees turned to stare at his son. 'But this is what they are raised to,' he said.

'And what happens if they're hurt?' David asked.

Ah, Rees thought. David was speaking as a new father. He saw threats everywhere.

'They are already skilled,' Rees said, running his eyes over the crowd of children.

One of the boys seemed very familiar. Very familiar. Even from the back, Rees recognized that stance and an unwelcome suspicion blossomed in his mind. Surely Lydia had not followed him here!

But as Rees veered to the side so he could see the face, the children scattered, disappearing among the wagons. When he peered down the gaps, he saw no one.

'What's the matter?' David asked, coming up behind Rees.

'I thought I saw Lydia,' Rees said.

'Surely not,' David said, sounding genuinely horrified.

Rees glanced at his son's expression and decided not to mention Lydia's predilection for boy's clothing.

'Mr Rees?' Bambola approached Rees and said, sounding accusatory, 'Everyone is waiting for you. Are you coming?' But she smiled radiantly at him and Rees could not prevent the leap of his heart.

She looked much different now than the other times he had seen her. During the Durham performance she'd worn a costume spangled with brilliants and her hair had been curled and decorated with feathers. During the readings she had given him she'd worn her hair up, in a careless bun. Today it was tied at the nape of her neck and allowed to hang down her back in all of its ebony glory.

'Yes, of course,' Rees said, taking David's elbow and drawing him forward.

'And who is this?' Bambola looked at David and smiled. 'Could this be your son?'

'Yes. David, this is Miss Lucia Mazza,' Rees said, gesturing from one to another.

'Please call me Bambola,' she said, extending her hand to David. 'Everyone does.'

Rees watched the flush rise from David's neck, into his cheeks and all the way to the tips of his ears. 'Pleased to meet you,' David said, so fast Rees could barely understand the words.

'I hope you can stay for a few minutes after my practice,' Bambola said to David. 'I would love to see what the cards say about you.' She directed a sparkling smile at Rees. 'I'll tell Boudreaux you're coming.' Turning in a flutter of perfumed skirts, she hurried away.

'What did she mean reading?'

'She thinks she can foretell your future with a pack of cards,' Rees said. 'Superstitious nonsense.'

David gasped but although his mouth opened he said nothing. Rees realized David was too overwhelmed by all he had seen these last few minutes to respond.

They stepped out into the southernmost part of the fairground. The late afternoon sun stretched long and gold over the field. Here, on the trampled straw, the men had set up two tall poles. Rees, with David trailing behind him, joined Boudreaux and the other men. The high wire posts were in position and the rope had been attached, although it still hung slack between them. Boudreaux clambered up to the top of one of the posts. Once he reached the landing, he stomped on the wood but the post did not move. He nodded at his helper and descended, jumping to the ground with a thud. 'Be ready soon,' he called. Rees turned. Bambola waited to one side, a parasol held above her head. Rees did not think she meant to protect her skin from the sun, since she held the umbrella behind her shoulders with her face tipped up to the sky.

Boudreaux crossed the field to the other post and scrambled up the ladder to the top. A minute or so of jumping and he pronounced this post also secure.

Bambola closed the parasol with a snap and scaled the ladder. Although the rope was only ten feet above the ground, she seemed very high and very insecure on that narrow line of hemp. David clutched at his father's arm so tightly it began to throb. Bambola pushed one stocking clad foot out and then the other and for a moment she stood poised there in the air. She managed a little hop. Even Rees could see the bounce in the rope. She very carefully backed up until she felt the landing shelf behind her. When she descended the ladder she joined Rees and David.

'Boudreaux,' she shouted. 'This will not do. It needs to be tightened.' She repeated it in French for emphasis. Muttering, Boudreaux scaled the ladder and began pulling at the rope's end.

An errant breeze suddenly snatched his cap away and sent it spinning across the field. His strangely dyed orange hair glittered like fire. Boudreaux jumped as he made a grab for the cap but missed. Muttering audibly, he motioned to Bambola.

'Try it now,' he said.

At the same moment, a crack reverberated across the field. Boudreaux clutched his shoulder, an expression of astonishment crossing his face. As he fell backward from the pole bright scarlet drops flew across the yellow straw. Bambola screamed.

THIRTY-FIVE

Rees came to himself with his face pressed against the ground and his mouth full of mud tasting straw. He lifted his head. An instinct left over from his twenty-year-ago experience as a soldier had thrown him flat and he had taken both Bambola and David with him. When he cautiously raised his head, he saw that everyone had dropped flat except Asher. He was still upright and staring at Boudreaux.

'Get down,' Rees shouted. 'Get down.' He rose to his hands and knees but he did not know which way to go first. To Asher? To Boudreaux? Or toward the direction from which the shots had come? After a moment of indecision, he began crawling for Boudreaux.

Asher seemed frozen.

'Get down,' Rees hissed as he passed Asher. 'Get down now. The shooters may still be out there.'

Asher turned, his face pale. 'What the Hell are you doing?' Asher said, crouching low and screaming in Rees's face. 'This wasn't a random shooting. They thought he was *you*. Get under cover. Now.'

Rees was so focused on reaching Boudreaux that he did not listen. In fact, he barely heard Asher. Boudreaux was still alive but just barely. Blood stained his linen shirt and dribbled from his mouth. 'Asher,' he whispered.

'Don't try to speak,' Rees said as he slid his arm under Boudreaux's head. Boudreaux's fingers scrabbled at the front of Rees's shirt. 'Ash . . .' The name trailed off in a gurgle.

'I'm here, *mon frère*,' Asher said, coming up on Boudreaux's left side. 'I'm here.' He looked at Rees with tear-filled eyes before turning his attention back to the dying man. 'You'll be all right.'

But Boudreaux was already gone. Rees had seen too many dead men in his time to mistake the sudden stillness. Asher broke down, muffling his sobs against Boudreaux's body. Bambola began weeping as well, not dainty sniffles but wrenching cries that sounded as though something was being torn from her.

'This is your fault,' Asher said, turning his tear-stained face to Rees. 'Those villains, the ones looking for you, returned. They shot him, thinking he was you.'

Rees stared at Asher. 'Me?' Guilt and shame swept over him. 'No, that can't be.'

'Yes,' said Asher. 'They came here looking for you. But he's the one who was shot.'

Rees swallowed and looked around. Except for David, whose face was contorted with pity, none of the circus folk would look at him. They all thought Boudreaux's death was his fault. And they were right.

He turned around and began crawling away. He couldn't face any of Boudreaux's friends right now; guilt and shame raced through him like a fever and he felt sick to his stomach. When he reached the circle of wagons, he pulled himself upright. Were those murderers still here? He peered around the wooden wall but saw no one.

Even though Rees thought the men, their wicked deed done, had left, he kept low, scuttling over the ground like some kind of insect, until he reached the road that ran north to south. He saw exactly where the gang had congregated; hoof prints marked the ground and a fresh pile of horse excrement lay in the dust.

Rees dared then to stand up and look around. The wagons screened most of the circus people from view. But once Boudreaux was high up on the post by the tightrope he was a perfect target. The rifleman would have had a clear shot, especially if he were seated on horseback. Hot tears of rage and remorse filled Rees's eyes.

'It's not your fault,' David said from behind. Rees turned around. David's mouth was pressed tight into a thin line.

'Those men.' Rees pushed back the cap and rubbed his forehead. 'They were looking for me.'

'Mr Asher said. Why?'

'I don't know. But I suspect Piggy Hanson had something to do with it.'

'The magistrate? But he—'

'I suppose those monsters are gone,' Asher said, coming up behind David. The circus master's eyes were red-rimmed and as Rees watched moisture gathered and began running down his cheeks.

'They probably ran as soon as they saw Boudreaux fall,' Rees said. 'The cowards.'

'I owe you an apology,' Asher said. 'Please forgive me for what I said, I am so grief-stricken . . .' He gulped and turned his face aside.

'You're right. This is my fault, I am so sorry,' Rees said. He fought the thickness at the back of his throat until he could speak again. 'I should leave.' He brushed his arm across his eyes.

'This isn't your fault,' Asher said. He reached out and put his hand on Rees's sleeve. 'While it is true the killers mistook Boudreaux for you, they might have murdered him even if you weren't here.' He paused. Even though Rees knew Asher was trying to comfort him, every word struck him like a stone. 'The question is why,' Asher continued. 'And only you can answer that.'

Rees felt the weight of grief and guilt settle upon him until he felt too heavy to move. 'But I don't know,' he said, his voice rising with angry despair. 'I didn't know that girl Leah. And it all started with her.'

'Did it?' Asher asked. 'That's when you became involved. But you told me there were other murders. Did anyone know that before you began investigating?'

'No,' Rees said. 'I guess if I hadn't started meddling, Boudreaux would still be alive.'

'Probably,' Asher agreed. He turned and started back to the tightrope, the posts clearly visible over the field. After a moment Rees followed, David trailing behind. The group of circus people congregated around Boudreaux's body came into view. 'He was my first performer,' Asher said, his voice breaking. 'Not a smart man by any means, but a wizard with horses.' He couldn't continue. Burying his face in his hands he sobbed. Rees stood in an awkward silence, knowing there was nothing he could say. 'My fault, my fault.' The words reverberated through his head like a drumbeat.

When Asher and Rees rejoined the crowd around Boudreaux's body, Rees saw other faces streaked with tears. But none of the circus people had approached the victim. Rees pushed through the crowd and knelt by the dead man, pulling down the lids. Boudreaux's eyes were beginning to film over and his skin was growing cold.

'We'll bury him here,' Asher said.

'We must inform Constable Rouge,' Rees said.

Asher hesitated. 'We're not on good terms with the constable.'

'This is murder and Rouge has to know.'

'Will he make it possible for us to bury Boudreaux in sanctified ground?' Asher asked skeptically.

'Maybe,' Rees said. Rouge was Catholic and had sheltered Boudreaux in the church. 'I'll ask him.' Rees could do no less.

'I'll go with you,' David said.

As they started across the field, Rees said to his son, 'You go home. I'll speak to the constable. This is my responsibility.' David eyed his father's expression and veered off.

Rees glanced over his shoulder. Most of the circus folk were staring after him. He knew they blamed him for Boudreaux's death; he could see it in their faces. And he knew they were right.

THIRTY-SIX

Both Rouge and Thomas were serving customers in the tavern but it was the latter who saw Rees run in. Thomas nudged his cousin. Rouge turned, looked at the red-faced and agitated arrival and raised an eyebrow. Breathless and sweating, Rees shouldered his way past the few farmers lingering at the bar and leaned over the wooden surface. 'Boudreaux has been shot,' he said in a low voice.

'What?'

'He's dead.'

'Well, *merde*,' Rouge said with feeling.

'Oh no,' Thomas said, shaking his head sorrowfully. 'He was frightened, you know. That's why he did not want to return to the circus. He felt safer here.'

'Who was he frightened of?' Rees asked, momentarily diverted. Thomas lifted his shoulders in an emphatic shrug.

'Well, I guess whoever scared Boudreaux found him after all.' Rouge blew out an angry breath.

'They weren't after Boudreaux,' Rees said, choking on his guilt. 'They were after me. From a distance, with his height and dyed reddish hair, he looked enough like me that they . . .' His throat closed up and he had to stop.

'We have to talk. Not here.' Rouge gestured to his cousin. 'You take the bar while I look at the body.' Thomas, who seemed more grieved by Boudreaux's death than Rouge, wiped an arm across his eyes and nodded.

'Tell me what happened?' he said as they left the tavern.

'Two men have been looking for me,' Rees said. 'Asher warned me.'

'Are you sure?' Rouge interrupted. 'They didn't come to the tavern.'

'They came to the circus,' Rees said.

'You saw them?' Rouge asked. Rees nodded. 'Who were they?'

'I don't know. I saw them for the first time today while they were searching the camp. Asher succeeded in running them off and I thought I was safe. But then Boudreaux . . .' His throat closed up. After taking several deep breaths he continued. 'They shot Boudreaux.'

'I can't believe they were looking for you,' Rouge said. 'There's no reason.'

Rees turned a withering glare upon the constable. 'Isn't it obvious? I've gotten too close to Leah's – and the other girls' – killer.' When he did not speak Rees added emphatically, 'It has to be Piggy Hanson.'

'Why him? Why not that Shaker man Aaron?'

'Where would he find the money to hire murderers?' Rees knew Rouge did not deserve his scorn but he was too angry to control himself.

'How do we know he didn't?' Rouge asked with a frown. 'We know very little about him. Maybe he has family here. Maybe he hid money somewhere. You remember?'

Rees sighed. He had solved a murder not long ago in which a member of the Zion community had done just that.

'You're right,' he said.

'I found him by the way,' Rouge said.

'Who?'

'Aaron Johnson. He's in the jail right now.'

'Now?' Rees, who was walking very fast, slowed. 'Where was he?'

'I caught him skulking around town last night.' Rouge paused and then went on. 'And don't tell me he couldn't have hired those men; he could have done so days ago.'

Rees nodded but that was not what he'd been thinking. He needed to question Aaron once again.

'Then there's the circus folk,' Rouge went on. 'Did you see that big strongman around when Boudreaux was shot? How do you know he didn't do it? And that circus clown? The dwarf? I've wondered about him from the beginning. He's a freak. No woman would want him. Maybe he went after Leah.'

'I'm not forgetting them,' Rees said. 'Maybe Otto. But not Billy. He's too short to do anything. I doubt he could overpower even a young girl. His hands are very small, too small to make the marks on Leah's throat. Besides, I saw him on the field when Boudreaux was shot.'

'He could have hired those villains,' Rouge said with the air of a man who knew all the answers. 'Or he and the strongman are working together. Maybe *they* hired the villains who shot Boudreaux.' He paused and looked at Rees, who nodded reluctantly. Rouge had suggested a plausible scenario. 'Help would be easy for them to find,' Rouge continued. 'These vagabonds stick together.'

While Rees had considered Otto himself, he didn't want to suspect Billy. He'd grown fond of the dwarf. 'How would Billy have gotten to Reynard's field?' he asked now. 'He couldn't walk that distance. His legs are too short.'

'I don't know. Maybe the strongman carried him. Anyway, he has a wagon, doesn't he?' Rouge said.

Rees thought of the brightly decorated vehicles. 'Too recognizable,' he said. 'But I'll speak with Paul Reynard again.' He couldn't believe the boy had missed a wagon with red wheels and a rearing gilt horse emblazoned on the sides. Then there was Aaron's report; his account had corroborated the boy's in almost every detail. Even if Aaron was lying, well, Rees saw no reason for Paul Reynard to shade the truth.

'One other thing,' he said as they reached the eastern edge of the fairgrounds. 'We'll need to bury Boudreaux. Would the priest in your church . . .?' He turned to look sidelong at the constable. Rouge quickly looked around them to confirm no one was in earshot. Although tolerated in this new country, many people still found Catholics suspect. For their own protection they worshipped secretly.

'I'll speak to the priest,' he said, lowering his voice although no one was nearby.

They threaded their way through the cluster of wagons to the far side. Boudreaux still lay prone on the ground with Asher kneeling beside him. Weeping, he was sponging off his friend's bloody face.

Rouge glanced at the body. 'It's pretty clear what killed him,' he said.

Rees, startled by the coldness of the constable's tone, turned a disapproving look upon him before realizing Rouge was fighting his own emotion. Of course. he had gotten to know Boudreaux these past few days while he worked in the tavern's kitchen.

After a few seconds Rouge looked over his shoulder, his eyes taking in the two poles, the rope between them and finally Rees's borrowed clothing. 'From a distance, maybe . . .' he muttered.

'I told you,' Rees said.

'The coroner needs to be called,' Rouge said.

'And then what?' Asher asked, looking up. His face was flushed and mottled with tears.

'I'll make sure he's properly buried.' Rouge turned to look at Rees. 'And you – you better go home. I don't want *your* dead body in front of me.'

Rees glanced at Boudreaux's body. 'Please,' he said to Asher.

'Let me know when the funeral will take place. I'd like to be there.'

Asher nodded and wordlessly clapped Rees on his shoulder.

When Rees entered the farm's gate, Lydia came out to the porch to greet him. Very aware of her eyes resting on him, Rees unhitched Hannibal and walked him around the yard. He found himself reluctant to speak to her. He knew she hadn't wanted him to go into town and no doubt David had told her everything about the circus. But no matter how reluctant he was to go inside, he could not walk the horse forever. At last he released Hannibal into the pasture and went to the porch.

'David told me what happened,' she said. Rees nodded. 'I am so so sorry. I know you liked Boudreaux.' Rees looked at Lydia. She must have been washing dishes; her sleeves were turned up and she held a white towel in her hands. 'David told me they – the circus people that is – think Boudreaux was shot in your place.'

'Stop,' Rees said, holding up his hand. 'I can't talk about this now.'

'But it might not be true—' she began.

'I just can't.' He forced the words past the emotion clogging his throat. Lydia bit her lip. He knew he had hurt her feelings but even if he'd wished to talk about the tragedy he couldn't. Besides, he knew her. She was so loyal she would defend him even when his actions were indefensible. She could not understand. Although they were but a foot apart, he felt as though he were looking at her over a wide and unbreachable gulf.

'All right,' she said. 'I kept your dinner warm.' Rees did not think he could eat a morsel but he followed her inside. Sharon and Joseph were playing some noisy game beside him but he hardly noticed. He sat at his place and picked up his fork. When Lydia put the warm plate before him he only pushed the potatoes and the lamb around and around. At last he put down his cutlery.

'I'll see if David needs help,' he said. Lydia said nothing as she watched him leave the kitchen.

But spending time with David was no easier than it had been with Lydia. He too, just as Lydia had done, watched his father from the corner of his eye until Rees wanted to shout at him.

Rees suffered through the regard for nearly half an hour before he threw his seed bag to the ground. 'I need to go back into town,' he said.

'What? Why?' David looked at him.

Rees hesitated. Why indeed? He had promised Boudreaux he would be safe and failed. Rees wasn't sure he wanted to continue looking into Leah's death. He feared he would fail at that as well. But what else could he do?

'I'm going to talk to Aaron,' he said. 'Rouge put him in jail and I have some questions.'

David did not speak but Rees felt his son's eyes following him as he walked away.

THIRTY-SEVEN

B ruises darkened Aaron's jaw and a scabbed cut slit one eyebrow. His all black clothing was torn. He'd been roughed up, probably by Rouge, but it had not diminished his truculence. 'What do you want?' he demanded of Rees as he clutched at the bars and pressed his face against them. Although he had been involved in a fistfight, his hands were not marked at all. The Shakers were pacifists and Aaron had not fought back. Not this time anyway. Rees remembered when a grieving Aaron had attacked another Shaker. 'I told you I didn't murder Leah. Or anyone else.'

'I want to ask you something else. Why did you join the Shakers?' Rees asked.

Aaron blinked. 'What?'

'I've been told that joining the Shakers saved you from your criminal past. What did you do?'

'Criminal past?' Aaron uttered a short bark of laughter. 'I was a farmer. Not some city nob.' He turned and shuffled to the stone bench.

'Wait,' Rees said.

'You're wasting time,' Aaron said. 'While you question me about my past, the murderer is out there.'

Rees stared at the prisoner. He knew Aaron could be as stubborn and as contrary as any mule and if he did not want to speak he would not. More certain than ever that Aaron had something to hide, Rees swore he would stay here all day if he had to.

'Let me think,' he said. 'What could you have possibly done? Blackmail? No, I can't imagine you as a blackmailer.' Aaron displayed an outspokenness that would not serve a blackmailer well. 'Not thievery surely. The Elders trust you to take horse and wagon on selling trips and return with the money. That leaves murder. You must have killed someone.'

It was a shot in the dark but his guess hit its mark. Aaron still did not speak but Rees saw him flinch, a movement so slight that if Rees hadn't been looking for it he would have missed it. 'Who did you murder?' Although he asked the question aloud he did not expect an answer. Instead, he tried to think the problem through. What did he know of Aaron? 'Your wife!'

'Who told you?' Aaron asked in a hoarse voice. His hands clenched the bars so tightly his knuckles went white.

'No one had to. What happened?'

'I came home early, found her with one of the hired men,' Aaron said after a short pause. 'Shem screaming out his lungs in the cradle next to the bed.' He rose to his feet and began pacing. 'I was on my way to the barn when I heard the baby, couldn't understand why no one was tending to him. Went inside.' His voice roughened and he shook his head in remembered disbelief. Rees felt a stirring of pity. All these years and Aaron's wife's betrayal still hurt. 'Tried to kill that bastard with her but he moved fast. So fast.' He sighed and absently rubbed the cut on his eyebrow. The wound opened up again and he looked at the blood on his fingers as though he didn't know what it was. 'I was carrying a shovel.' He grinned mirthlessly. 'Swung it with all my strength but he ducked and jumped out the window with his shirt tails flying. I hit my wife instead.' He looked away from Rees but not before he saw Aaron's face twist. 'Killed her stone dead.' He heaved a sigh. 'I took Shem to my sister and ran. Few years later I found the Shakers. Figured Mother Ann Lee had it right: sex is the root of all evil. Haven't looked back since.' When Rees did not speak Aaron said, 'What are you going to do now?'

'Nothing,' Rees said. 'Not unless I find you had something to do with Leah's murder.'

'I didn't.'

'What about the two villains who tried to shoot me? Did you hire them?' Rees asked although he was almost certain of the answer.

'What villains?' Aaron's surprised bewilderment seemed entirely genuine. 'What are you talking about?'

'I'll speak to the constable,' Rees said. 'Maybe get you out of here.' He doubted the Shaker could dissemble so effortlessly so at this moment he didn't believe Aaron was guilty of either Leah's murder or the shooting of Boudreaux. But Rees couldn't be sure. After all, Aaron had killed someone in a fit of anger once before. And once that line had been crossed, taking a human life again was easier.

Although both Lydia and David attempted several times that day and later into evening to talk to Rees he refused. He didn't know what to say. He couldn't describe his feelings even to himself and Lydia's questions felt more like harassment than consolation. As soon as he could, he retreated to his weaving room and spent several hours at the loom. But the comfort he'd always found there took a long time coming. He spent more time staring out the window than weaving until, finally, the familiar magic took hold and he found the relief he sought.

Next morning, after all the chores were done, he fled into town. Uncertain where else to go, he landed at Rouge's ordinary. Rees was afraid to go to the circus. He was consumed with guilt; more even than grief and did not want to face the accusing eyes of the circus folk.

Especially Bambola. He didn't think he could bear the anger, the disappointment, and the disgust he was sure to see in her face.

Rouge hailed Rees as soon as he stepped through the door. 'I was hoping to see you. In fact, I was planning to ride out to the farm later and tell you Boudreaux's funeral is set for this afternoon.'

'This afternoon?' Rees repeated.

Rouge nodded. 'Yes. I told the priest I might not be able to attend. I expect a busy day in the tavern. And both my cousins wish to pay their respects.' Rouge offered a sour grin. 'But he said he wouldn't be here for two weeks or more and no one wants to leave the body that long. Since he is here now – he'll be officiating at Mass on Sunday – the funeral has to take place today.'

'Too bad,' Rees said automatically. He felt his distress lessening in the constable's company. Rouge was so concerned about his own pursuits and cares that he did not notice Rees's pain. The indifference was curiously relaxing. 'At least it will soon be over,' he said. Maybe then he could begin recovering from the guilt.

'Do you want to drive with me?' Rouge swished the grimy rag over the bar. 'I can show you the way. You won't find the church by yourself.'

'Maybe.' Rees hesitated. 'Will the service be in French?'

'Some of it,' Rouge admitted. 'Most of it though will be in Latin.'

Rees rolled his eyes. 'A language I understand even less of than French.' he said. 'I think I'll follow you in my own wagon.' That way he could arrive late and leave when he wished. Funerals gave him the willies.

'Planning to bolt early?' Rouge guessed with a grin.

Since this was true Rees chose not to reply. 'Do I need to contribute some money?' he asked instead. Many people began saving up for their funeral and burial when in their teens but he doubted Boudreaux was one of those.

'Mr Asher is paying for it,' Rouge said. 'He said it was the least he could do for a man as close to him as a brother.'

'Where is the body now?' Poor Asher, Rees thought.

'At the church,' Rouge said in surprise. 'I brought it to the church yesterday, after the coroner took a look at it. We held the vigil last night.'

Rees nodded although he was not sure he completely understood what the constable was talking about. The church in which Rees had grown up worshipped God in a much simpler manner, including the language of the service – English.

He decided not to drive home and back to town in the few hours remaining before the funeral. He had the time, he knew he did, but he told himself he didn't want to waste it. He did not want to admit the truth; he didn't want to go home. He drifted around town for the rest of the morning, always returning within sight of the fairgrounds. Although he circled the open space he did not stop there. Not even at the few farmers' stalls that were opened on the edges, several yards distant from the circus wagons. But he watched from the shadow of a store's front porch as the circus folk went about their business. He even saw Bambola a few times, passing back and forth.

When the sun reached its zenith he returned to the tavern for dinner. When Rouge and his cousin Thomas, who had known Boudreaux and seemed genuinely upset, left for the funeral Rees followed them.

THIRTY-EIGHT

T he Catholic church was a distance away from town. Tucked into a small hollow, the stone structure was concealed by fir trees. Rees suspected the hidden site was not an accident; occasionally a burst of anti-Catholic sentiment flared up, even here in the District of Maine where a significant part of the population boasted French ancestry.

Several other wagons, mostly the circus vehicles with the gaudy rearing horses on the doors, were pulled up in front of the church. Rouge tied his horse up at the side of the church. He waved at Rees before he and his cousin hurried inside. Rees pulled up beside one of the circus wagons and climbed out. But he did not enter the church. The sonorous voice of the priest floated out to the clearing, chanting in a foreign language that he assumed was Latin. The tones were strangely hypnotizing and he listened for a few seconds before beginning his walk around the grounds.

The hill behind the small building was steep, a rough surface made up of granite bedrock and trees clinging to the spaces in between. Last year's fallen leaves carpeted the entire area. The whitewashed church stood out, very white against the gray stone, russet leaves and the bright green of new growth. The cliff was so tall and so steep it put the small stone structure into deep shadow.

Rees followed the hollow around to the north. Tucked into a minute, flat space beside a ravine lay the cemetery. On the other side of the ditch another hill took off, rising toward the sky with even taller cliffs behind it. He stood in the foothills of the very same mountains behind his farm; the mountains where lumber was cut and floated down to Falmouth.

Several gray stones dotted the area within the fence. A new grave, a ragged hole shoveled into the moist spring soil, had been dug near one side of the fence where a maple tree would throw shade upon it. Billy the clown was perched on the exposed tree roots.

'Funny,' he said, looking at Rees. 'I thought I would be the one buried here.'

Rees eyed the clown. Despite the warmth of this bright April day a heavy wool blanket swaddled him up to his neck.

'Does knowing that you will not be laid to rest here comfort you?' Rees asked. 'Or make you feel worse?'

Billy ruminated for a few seconds. 'Worse,' he said. 'I'm sick; that's God's way. But Pip – well, it wasn't his time, was it? The rest of his life was stolen from him. Why, he might have lived well into his dotage.' He coughed, a hacking cough that hurt Rees to hear it. Blood sprayed from his mouth.

'That's true,' Rees agreed as Billy thrust a grubby handkerchief over his lips. After a few seconds, the terrible grating sound ceased. He panted for a few seconds until he caught his breath.

'Why aren't you inside?' Rees asked.

'Not a papist,' Billy said. 'Raised Congregational. Don't understand either Latin or French.' He paused and Rees held himself still, expecting another burst of coughing. But after a few gasping breaths Billy recovered. He made his way to a large stone and sat down upon it, patting the space beside him invitingly. Rees joined him and they sat in a companionable silence.

The chanting inside the church ceased and Rees could hear just the faintest threat of sound as though the priest was speaking.

'Mr Asher spent some time here last night,' Billy said abruptly. 'Keeping vigil, he said.'

'He was very close to Boudreaux,' Rees said just as the church doors opened. He jumped to his feet and looked for Bambola in the crowd. There she was. Dressed in black silk with matching black hat and gloves, her face was swollen with crying. She leaned on Asher's arm. He also was clad entirely in black except for the lacy white cravat at his throat.

Rees's left eyelid began to flutter, a nervous tic. He attempted to smooth it but as soon as he removed his finger the involuntary movement began again.

Otto and two other circus men – Rees vaguely recognized them – carried out Boudreaux's cloth-wrapped body to the cart waiting outside. Asher detached Bambola's hand and leaped forward to help.

No horse or mule was hitched between the traces; instead Asher and Otto each grabbed one of the long wooden pieces and began to pull. Rees hurried forward. He would take responsibility for his dreadful task. He had to; Boudreaux would not have been shot if those men had not been looking for a tall, red-haired man named Will Rees.

The linen sheet fell away from Boudreaux's gray face. One of the women moved forward to pull the linen sheet back over the body. She lifted up his torso to tuck the sheet under his shoulder, handling his weight easily despite her delicate appearance Although all the women wept not one succumbed to the vapors. Rees, however, thought he would have nightmares from this awful scene until the end of his days.

Since neither of the men pulling the cart seemed disposed to give up their places, Rees wondered if he was even welcome here. But Asher gestured to the back of the cart. 'Maybe you can push?'

Rees went to the back as directed and shoved so forcefully the cart juddered forward, rocking back and forth over the uneven ground. One of the wheels got stuck on a stone; he gave a mighty heave and the cart tipped over. Boudreaux's linen-wrapped body slid out, flipping face forward onto the ground.

'Oh,' said the priest in dismay.

They all stared at the linen shape on the ground. No one wanted to touch the body. At last Rees stepped forward. 'But I can't lift him alone,' he said.

'I'll help,' Asher said, removing his hat and linen jacket and stepping to Rees's side. After a few seconds' hesitation Otto also joined them. Rees threw a pointed glance at Rouge. Reluctance in every line of his body, he stared back, his resistance palpable. Finally, he too came forward. As Asher and Rouge lifted the feet Rees and Otto each took one of Boudreaux's arms. The body sagged in the middle. Otto threw a scornful glance at Rees and shouldered him aside. The strongman lifted Boudreaux from under the armpits, straight up, while the other two struggled with the limp weight of the corpse's legs and feet. Together they wrestled him into the cart. Rees noticed how Otto's enormous hands gripped Boudreaux under the armpits, those long fingers and sharp nails pressing through the linen shroud and to the soft skin just below his shoulders. He shuddered convulsively.

The body was finally in place. The three men stood around the cart breathing hard.

With the body once more in the cart, Asher nodded at Rees to take up his place at the back of the cart. The funeral vehicle began its slow and bumpy ride to the graveyard. Save for Billy, the entire circus family walked behind.

Rees successfully positioned the cart with its rear toward the hole but the body still had to be eased into the grave's waiting earthen arms. Asher tried to grasp the body, but Boudreaux, although tall and appearing spindly, proved too heavy to hold. His weight tore away from the hands grasping him and with a rustle the body slid from out of the sheet and dropped into the hole.

'We can't leave him like that,' Asher cried, staring down at the crumpled body. Rees guiltily jumped down and tried to straighten Boudreaux's limbs. The body had passed through rigor and was now flaccid. But Rees did his best to lay out the body and cover him with the shroud so that Boudreaux would go to his Maker with some dignity. Knowing that he had done what was necessary, Rees felt better.

He climbed out of the grave and took up a position among the circus people. He noticed with a start that those nearest to him shifted away. Although he was aware of the dirt covering his breeches and hands, he did not think that the grime was driving these people away. No, he knew with absolute certainty that they blamed him for Boudreaux's death. And he should be blamed, shouldn't he? Rees raised his head and looked around at the other mourners. To an outside observer he no doubt appeared as one of them. He wore the same battered clothing and flat cap Asher had given him. But he knew he didn't belong here and he wished suddenly he had asked Lydia to accompany him. Just to have a friendly face beside him.

The priest began speaking, first in Latin and then in a mixture of French and English. Rees could barely understand either. It was as though his mind had lost its ability to focus. Asher uttered a sudden and involuntary moan, his face working. He left Rees's side to pick up a handful of dirt. 'Although my name is on the circus,' he said, 'Boudreaux was just as big a part of our beginning. Truly, we began the circus together. He was an equestrian of great skill. In between his acts, I performed magical illusions. Gradually, we added a ropedancer, acrobats and other performers.' He threw his handful of soil on the top of the body. '*Au revoir, mon frère,*' he said, his words trembling with grief.

Openly sobbing, Bambola followed him to the side of the grave but she was too choked up to speak. Then Billy and Otto and the other circus folk followed her. When all who wished had paid their final respects two of the men began shoveling dirt into the hole. The crowd began to disperse.

Swallowing, Rees turned and walked rapidly from the graveyard. He reached his wagon and paused for several seconds, attempting to control his breathing. Then, finally, he grabbed the reins and climbed into the seat.

'Are you leaving?' Asher asked from the side. Rees turned. The ringmaster, with Bambola just behind him, stood next to the wagon. Billy was approaching as quickly as he could on his short legs.

'Yes.' He heard Asher inhale.

'That sounds like you're giving up,' he said, putting his large hand on the rough wagon side. Rees, who had expected sympathy, gaped at Asher in astonishment. 'You can't just wallow in your self-pity. Yes, I think we all know that Boudreaux was shot in your stead. But you can't just run away.'

'Aren't you going to find his killers now?' Bambola asked. 'You owe him that much.'

'We know who murdered him,' Rees argued weakly. 'Those villains. You saw them. And they are probably several leagues away by now.'

'I understand you're afraid of those brutes,' Asher said. 'But please, urge the constable to investigate. There are several questions still outstanding.'

'I'd think you would want to know who wishes to kill you,' Bambola said, the harsh words sounding odd in her sweet voice. 'And Boudreaux is more important than your hurt feelings.'

'I won't ask you to pursue those men yourself,' Asher said. 'Although you are not so longstanding a friend as Boudreaux, I count you as one and don't wish to see any harm befall you.' Rees, moved by this surprising statement, felt his eyes moisten. 'It's true,' Asher said. 'Both of us' – and he darted a glance at Bambola – 'count you a friend. We don't have very many. So please, don't put yourself in jeopardy. But don't allow the constable to put Boudreaux aside either. Would you do that for us?'

'Of course,' Rees said immediately. 'Although Rouge, with the best will in the world, may have little luck. Those assassins are probably miles away by now.'

'No doubt,' Bambola agreed. 'So maybe you should stop whining and begin searching for them.' Both Asher and Rees turned startled glances on her.

'Surely you don't want Rees to be murdered,' Asher said, disapproval coloring his voice.

'Of course not,' she said. She turned a look of such affection on Rees he felt his knees go weak. 'But Boudreaux is every bit as important as that Shaker girl and you're looking into her death.'

'I will do what I can,' Rees promised.

'Without putting yourself in danger,' Asher said. 'We don't want that. And now,' he clapped Rees on the shoulder, 'we're having a little celebration for Boudreaux back at camp. You're almost a part of our family. Come and have something to eat and drink with us.'

'Are you sure?' Rees asked.

'Of course,' Asher said.

At the same time Bambola said, 'I want you there.'

'Of course, you should come,' Billy panted as he reached them. Leaning over, he began coughing.

'Come for Billy,' Asher said, lowering his voice. Both men glanced at the clown. Rees, who'd wanted to come but felt he shouldn't, knew Billy didn't have much time left.

'For a few minutes then,' he said. 'For Billy.'

'We'll be leaving town soon after,' Asher said. 'And frankly I can't wait. This place has been unlucky for us.'

THIRTY-NINE

Although Rees had agreed to join the circus folk at their camp after the funeral, he did not accompany them as they left the church. Instead, he followed Rouge and Thomas down to the village. He could not have found his way by himself. With some vague notion of preventing idle gossip – he knew Rouge would say something if he went directly to the fairgrounds – he parked his wagon in the tavern yard and handed Hannibal off to the ostler. If Rees could have gone to the fairgrounds from there he would have but Rouge called to him and he could think of no reason to refuse the invitation.

Therese glared at them when they entered the tavern. Although the traffic had begun to ease, the establishment was still busy. Besides the men waiting for service at the bar, the dirty tables and piles of crockery bore mute witness to the hectic hours that had come before. Both Rouge and Thomas immediately put on their aprons and hurried behind the bar. Rees planned to slip away then but Rouge sent Therese to make coffee. 'You look like you need it,' he said to Rees.

'I'm fine,' he said.

'You don't look fine,' Rouge said. 'I guess I didn't understand how attached you were to Boudreaux.'

'I didn't know him well,' he said, evading the implied question. 'You knew him better than I did.'

'Not really,' Rouge said. 'I know he barely escaped the Terror in France with his life.'

'He was minor nobility,' said Thomas. Both Rouge and Rees turned to him in surprise.

'What? He talked, mostly to Therese. He had a tendre for her.'

'Well, go on,' Rouge said.

'He fled with his younger brother. They literally ran for their lives. But the boy couldn't keep up and . . .' Thomas stopped and swallowed. 'Boudreaux kept running. He never forgave himself for not saving his brother.'

'Then he died here in Maine because of a shot meant for me.' Rees took a deep breath and expelled it very slowly. 'He deserved better.'

Rouge said nothing for a moment, his brow creased. 'The problem is,' he said at last, 'that although it seems likely you were the intended target, we don't know that for certain.' He directed a lopsided smile at the weaver. 'You're always the one who tells me not to jump to conclusions but to follow the evidence. Maybe you should examine the murder more closely before you take all the blame.'

Rees stared at the constable in stunned silence for several seconds. 'You're right.'

Then he had to wait for the coffee and drink it. So, by the time he left the tavern, it was going on five. He parked his wagon behind the circus vehicles and jumped down but then, finding himself suddenly shy, he just stood there. The sun had begun to drop toward the western horizon and the long rays touched the wispy clouds feathering the sky with shades of peach and copper. He could smell cooking food; the circus folk had returned some time ago. Suddenly wishing he hadn't agreed to come he almost – almost – climbed into his wagon and fled. Surely no one would miss him.

But just as he began to turn away from the cluster of circus wagons, Bambola walked through one of the alleys made by the vehicles. 'I hope you aren't going,' she said. She had changed from her black gown to a soft gray and looked very feminine and desirable.

'I wasn't sure I should be here,' Rees admitted, blushing with awkwardness.

'But no,' she said, reaching out to grasp his hand. 'You are part of our family. You must stay.'

'But won't they' – he gestured toward the other performers – 'resent me?'

'Of course not,' she said. 'Besides, I want you here.' The pleasurable warmth that spread through Rees was quickly followed by shame as he thought of Lydia and his family. But he did not pull away from her grasp. 'We'll be leaving soon,' she continued. 'Now that Boudreaux . . .' She stopped and bit her lip. 'Anyway, I wanted to give you something to remember me by.' She held out a brightly colored card. Rees looked at it. He had seen it before. It depicted a man holding a sword and a set of scales. Justice.

'I can't take this,' he said. 'It will leave you one card short.'

'I have several packs,' she said. 'I have always been afraid of losing one.' She smiled. 'Is there time for a reading, do you think?' Rees shook his head. She held out the card. 'Please take it. This card represents justice. That is one of your primary qualities; your passion for justice and your search for the truth. It is why you do what you do.' She inhaled a sobbing breath. When Rees moved forward as though to comfort her she held up a hand to stop him. She struggled with her emotions for several seconds before saying quickly, 'Boudreaux should not have died. He was one of us. He was loyal, how you say, to a fault?'

'Yes,' Rees said. He felt worse than ever. Now she moved forward to lay a hand on his sleeve.

'Find the murderer, Mr Rees,' she said passionately. Although her eyes were reddened with tears, Rees thought she looked even more beautiful than ever. 'Find him and bring him to justice. You owe Boudreaux that.' She spun around in a rustle of skirts and hurried away, leaving just the faintest trace of perfume. Rees stared after her. Of course he could not refuse.

Whistling, he put the tarot card very carefully in his pocket. Although reluctant to examine his happier mood, he picketed Hannibal with the other horses and followed Bambola toward the campfire. Everyone was gathered there, save for Asher. Some glanced casually at Rees but most paid him no attention. Only Otto regarded him with antipathy from flat, hard eyes.

'Come inside and take a seat,' Billy said, waving. White and sweaty, he was tightly wrapped in his quilt. Rees couldn't think of any reason to refuse the dying clown. He made his way to Billy's side and lowered himself to the grass. 'Listen,' Billy said, 'I'm going to tell you something. I can see you tearing yourself up over Boudreaux's death, but it wasn't your fault.'

'Why do you say that?' Rees said doubtfully.

Billy inhaled and then, as though he were sharing some great secret, he said, 'He might have been shot anyway, even if you weren't here.'

'But the shooters knew I was here, with the circus,' Rees argued. 'That was why those brutes searched the camp.'

Billy bit his lip and looked as though he were struggling to keep silent. 'I like you,' he said at last. 'I think I should warn you . . .' A fit of coughing interrupted him.

Bambola approached them, her face creased with worry. 'Don't make him talk, Mr Rees.'

'I'm fine,' Billy said. 'I'm fine.' He chuckled a little breathlessly. 'We were speaking about my pig. I've had her since she was a piglet.' Rees blinked at the clown in surprise. 'She's a smart girl. Everyone loves that bit, where she mocks the magistrate.'

'You mean Hanson?' Rees grinned, distracted. 'I saw that the first day.'

'He's not a popular man. In some towns he's known as Hanging Hanson. Did you know that?'

'No,' Rees said, recalling the events of the last summer. He already knew Hanson was a vindictive cuss. 'But I'm not surprised.'

'Show life is a good life,' the clown said abruptly. 'Travel around, see a bit of this new country. See all kinds of people too. Some of these new faiths call us the devil but I see plenty of men sneaking in, even though they're doing something they're ashamed of.'

'Here in Maine also?' Rees said, thinking of Brother Aaron. 'Shakers? Flat straw hats, white shirts?'

'Yes, I've seen some like that. Couldn't swear to what they call themselves though.' Another fit of coughing interrupted him and this one went on so long Rees became anxious.

'Can I fetch you a cup of ale?' he asked.

'No, no.' More coughing. 'I'm fine. Fine.'

'Find Asher,' Bambola told Rees.

He nodded and leaped to his feet. As he stared around the fire, trying to spot Asher among the faces, Rees considered Brother Aaron. Like Leah, the lure of the outside world pulled him into it. Did the Shakers' insular and celibate community inspire such desire in Aaron that he used his travels to satisfy himself on the young girls he met? Rees didn't entirely believe it.

'Never mind Asher.' Bambola caught at Rees's sleeve. 'There isn't time. You must help me now.'

Billy was laying on the straw, quilt drawn up to his chin. Blood spotted his waxy skin and he was too weak to wipe it away. 'He shouldn't be lying on the cold ground,' Bambola said. 'Help me bring him inside his wagon.'

Rees picked up the small man and followed the ropedancer to a wagon. As befitted a popular performer, Billy had a better wagon in which to sleep, but he shared it with another man. By the size of the boots lying carelessly by one of the benches, Rees though Billy's roommate might be Otto.

'Put him here,' Bambola directed, pointing at the smaller of the two benches.

Rees carefully laid Billy down.

'Thank you,' Billy said in a faint voice. 'I just need to rest . . .' His voice trailed away and he closed his eyes, turning his face to the wall.

'You'll be better soon,' Bambola said in a hearty voice. But tears poured down her cheeks. 'Take a good nap, Billy. You'll be better . . .' She stifled her sob with a hand pushed into her mouth.

Sorrowfully, Rees went to the door and down the steps. He held up a hand to assist Bambola to the ground and she took it. 'Thank you,' she said. 'I know Billy doesn't have long but . . .' She stopped, her mouth trembling. Rees held her hand while she fought her tears. After a few seconds, she added, 'I don't think I could bear another death so soon after Boudreaux's.' She inhaled and wiped her eyes with a handkerchief. 'I'll find Otto. He'll know what to do.' Forcing a smile, she squared her shoulders and released his hand. Head high, she joined the other performers. Rees twisted around to watch her. And there, standing on the other side of the field was David. He leveled a shocked and accusatory stare at his father before turning and disappearing behind the wagons.

After a few seconds of frozen dismay, and the realization that David had completely mistaken what he'd seen, Rees burst into a desperate sprint. He caught up to his son at the edge of the fairgrounds as he climbed into Lydia's cart. The mule was overwhelmed by the activity around her and kept shuffling back and forth. David was trying to calm the animal with soothing noises. Rees put his hand on the mule's bridle and began stroking the animal's neck. 'Look,' he said to David, 'I'm not sure what you think you saw but—'

'I know what I saw,' David said in a harsh voice. 'How could you?'

'It was nothing,' Rees said. 'All I did was—'

'Huh! You came out of that wagon hand in hand! I saw the way you looked at her. And the way she looked at you.'

'I didn't do anything wrong,' Rees said, his voice rising. There was enough truth in David's accusation to sting. 'Yes, Bambola is a beautiful woman but I am faithful to Lydia.'

'If that's true, and I'm not persuaded it is,' David said, 'how long is it going to last?' He straightened up and repeated, 'I saw you.'

'I carried an ill performer inside and put him to bed,' Rees said, struggling to control his temper. 'I would never betray Lydia.'

'Really? Is that why you keep sneaking off to this . . . this . . .?' Unable to find a good word, he gestured around at the wagons. 'It looks to me like you prefer this to your wife and family.'

'That's not true.'

'So, why are you here, day after day?' David stared into his father's eyes. 'And don't say you're investigating a murder. It was a Shaker girl; why aren't you spending more time in Zion? Or questioning that Shaker Brother? You keep talking about questioning some farmer's boy again – I know, I've heard you – but you don't. Instead you come to the circus.'

'I am questioning them,' Rees said.

'Uh huh. Are you thinking of running away to the circus? Little old for it, aren't you?'

'Of course I'm not going to join the circus,' Rees snapped. 'I told you; I'm questioning them.'

'Yes, that's what it looked like when you came out of the wagon,' David retorted.

Now really angry, Rees took a furious step toward his son. But before he did something he would later regret, he got a grip on himself and stepped back. He did not trust himself to speak.

David did not move. After a few seconds he pushed back his hat and wiped his arm across his forehead. 'I'm sorry,' he said. 'That wasn't fair.'

'Were you spying on me?' Rees snarled. 'What? You and Lydia cooked this up together?'

David eyed his father in disdain. 'No. She doesn't even know I'm here. But she's worried. I think she suspects something.' He paused. 'She expected you home hours ago. She's a good woman; she doesn't deserve this. What are you doing?'

'Nothing'

'I know you like to travel but—'

'Is this about my traveling when you were a little boy?' Rees interrupted.

'No!' David said instantly. Then he paused. When he spoke again his voice was softer. 'Well, maybe a little. I don't understand why you want to leave your home and family behind. I never have. I've begun to accept, though, that you'll never stay home. But this' – he gestured behind him at the wagons – 'is something different. This isn't traveling to make a living. This carnival is an illusion; everything in it is false. You seem swallowed up by the fakery. And that ropedancer well and truly has her hooks in you. What's happened to you?'

Rees, incapable of speech, stared at his son. After several seconds of silence David flapped his hand at his father and turned toward the cart.

'Are you going to tell Lydia? What you saw, I mean?' Rees called after him.

David looked over his shoulder. 'And say what? I don't know anything. Besides, she doesn't deserve that kind of hurt.' He climbed into the cart and drove away.

As David disappeared into the streets of Durham, Rees began to think of all his counter arguments. First, he would strongly refute any connection between himself and Bambola. Wasn't it true that they were only cordial to one another? And he had to question these circus folk, didn't he? But mostly he wanted to explain to his son how remaining at the farm and working every day on tedious farm chores made him feel as though a heavy weight rested on his shoulders. To be energized, to be the person he knew he was, he needed to escape the relentless drudgery of a farm on a regular basis. If Rees was honest with himself, he couldn't understand people who *didn't* feel that way.

By the time he thought all of this, David was out of sight.

Sighing, Rees climbed into his own wagon and started home.

He said little to Lydia when he arrived home. He just couldn't talk about the funeral and what came after quite yet. So, while David worked in the barn, Rees used the last rays of the setting sun to carry the brush from the newly cleared field to the pile. That was almost done. Then he milked Daisy, fetched some water, and finally climbed the stairs to the weaving room. No new commissions had come in so he found a bag of scrap wool and began the tedious process of winding the warp. The wool was white, although it was a variety of thicknesses, so if he obtained another job using either wool or linen, this warp might do.

All the while the events of the morning and afternoon played in his head. It had been an emotional day. For everyone, he thought, recalling David's shock and anger. Rees's own feelings had been scraped raw and it took a long time for them to settle. Even after the light faded, he lingered in the silent room, thinking. Not of the argument with David; the feelings brought up by that were still too fresh and painful. Instead he considered the funeral and his subsequent visit to the circus. As he recalled the conversations he'd held with the circus people, he began to realize something was off. But what? Something Billy said? Rees wasn't sure.

'Are you coming for supper?' Lydia called up the stairs. Rees realized the weaving room was almost completely dark. He'd been here for hours. Lydia had delayed dinner until she couldn't wait any longer. He hesitated. Was he ready to meet his family? Yes, he was. Although he'd made no progress on identifying the murderer, he realized he was calmer.

'Yes. I didn't realize it was so late,' he said. Her soft footsteps descended the stairs.

When Rees arrived in the kitchen a few minutes later only David and Jerusha were there. Both were in front of the fire. David had his boots off and seemed to be dozing while Jerusha worked on homework. 'Where are the other children?' he asked.

'In bed,' Lydia said.

When Rees looked at the clock he saw it was almost eight. 'It's later than I thought,' he said apologetically. Lydia gestured at the table.

He sat down and stared at his plate. Cold lamb, something he did not care for. But Lydia had collected garden peas and they were still bright green and sweet. He wasn't very hungry anyway. He'd eaten heartily with the circus people.

Lydia handed him the gravy and then the plate of fresh biscuits, especially delicious with freshly churned butter melting into the bread.

It was a silent meal. Rees found himself missing the chatter of his children. And Lydia, although she seemed on the verge of making a comment or two, did not speak until Rees had cleaned his plate.

'What happened?' she asked at last. 'You look . . .' She paused a moment, searching for the proper word. 'You look ragged. Was the funeral very difficult?'

Rees nodded. 'Boudreaux fell out of the cart on to the ground. And then he had to be laid out in the grave.'

Lydia waited for him to continue speaking. When he did not, she said, 'That can't be all that happened.'

When Rees did not immediately respond David said, 'I think I'll turn in.' He almost ran out of the kitchen door. His boots thudded up the stairs. Lydia stared after the boy in surprise.

'Did you and David quarrel?' she asked, turning her attention back to her husband.

'Bambola gave me one of her cards,' Rees said, almost at random. He did not want to talk about David right now. Lydia tensed. Rees placed the brightly colored card on the table between them. Lydia stared at it.

'A tarot card,' she said. 'Why did she give this to you? Was it to remember her by?' The tone in her voice sent a wave of heat through Rees's body.

'Of course not,' he lied, now wishing he had kept it secret. 'She gave me *this* card because she thought it was about me. It's Justice, you see. And she asked me to find Boudreaux's murderer.' Lydia stared at her husband for a moment. He met her gaze squarely, striving for an appearance of innocence. At last Lydia dropped her eyes.

'Was she close to Boudreaux?' she asked, her tone softening.

'I think so.' Rees let out his breath in relief. 'But of course, they worked together for years.' He paused. He had accepted the rope-dancer's desire to find the murderer uncritically but now he wondered. She had seemed genuinely upset. And angry.

'What about Mr Asher?'

'He asked me as well. Ordered me almost. He told me that Boudreaux's life was every bit as important as Leah's. But he also expressed some concern that I would be making myself a target for the men who shot Boudreaux.' Rees paused. 'I've made a mess of this entire investigation. Honestly,' he admitted in a low voice, 'I've been considering abandoning it.'

'My word,' Lydia said, but she sounded relieved more than star-tled. 'What does the constable say?'

'I haven't told him.'

'And what do you want to do?' Lydia asked, fixing him with an intent stare. Rees thought about it. He wasn't sure. 'You were desperate to find Leah's murderer once,' she added.

'Yes,' Rees agreed. But somewhere along the way his investiga-tion had become muddled with the circus. And then there was Piggy Hanson. The magistrate's arrival on the scene, and Rees's loathing of the other man, had complicated his feelings even further.

'I think you should talk to Magistrate Hanson,' Lydia said, just as though she could read his thoughts. 'He didn't come here to threaten you. He just wanted to talk. Maybe he can help.'

'I doubt that,' Rees said. 'Hanson is a tricky bastard.'

'He may know something,' Lydia persisted.

Rees felt his temper begin to rise. 'Don't nag. Don't you see he might be behind the murders,' he said in a chilly voice.

Lydia's nostrils flared and when she spoke again her voice was cold. 'Don't you think that's even more reason to question him?'

'You don't understand this at all,' Rees said shortly. David, he recalled, had said something similar. 'It's really none of your business.'

'None of my business? I suppose that . . . that circus woman does understand you?' Lydia snapped.

'I haven't discussed this with her,' Rees said in a stiff voice, realizing as soon as the words left his mouth that he'd implied regular conversation with Bambola.

'You surprise me. But then maybe you're too busy to talk.'

'What? Has David—?'

'David knows? He told me nothing. Surely you don't think I am too stupid to realize she's the reason you've run off every single day to the circus.'

'She has nothing to do with it,' he said angrily.

'You know I'm right,' Lydia said.

Rees turned on his heel and walked out of the kitchen, slamming the door behind him. He paused on the front porch, taking in deep lungfuls of air. Except for the sounds of night – frogs singing loudly in the pond and the hooting of an owl – everything was silent. He felt his anger and his tension begin to seep away. As he revisited his quarrel with Lydia he was suddenly very glad none of the children had witnessed it. He had not set a good example and he was ashamed of that now.

Rapid hoof beats drew Rees's attention to the lane outside the gate. He took the lantern down from its hook and held it up. Rouge appeared in the circle of light. He'd been riding hard; his boots and stockings were splattered with mud and the filth coated his horse all the way to the belly. Rees felt his stomach plummet.

'Bad news?' he asked as Rouge pulled the bay to a stop.

'Get your wagon,' Rouge said. 'You need to come with me.'

'Why?' Rees looked around at the shadowy farm yard. 'Can't it wait until tomorrow? It's too dark to see.'

'No.' Rouge hesitated and even in the dim light Rees could see the constable chewing his lower lip. 'Bring a lantern. I need you to identify two bodies.'

'Two more bodies?' Rees asked in dismay.

'They were murdered,' Rouge said.

'Of course they were else you wouldn't be here. Who are they? Not Asher or one of the circus people?'

'No.' Rouge sighed audibly. 'I think they may be the men who shot Boudreaux. That's why I need you to look at them; I never saw their faces.'

FORTY

About halfway to town Rees began to feel both guilty and ashamed. Angry, he had not returned inside to tell his wife he was leaving. Instead, he'd harnessed Hannibal to the wagon and followed the constable from the farm. She would have no idea where he was.

Now that he'd begun to cool off, he realized he'd behaved in a spiteful and petty manner, punishing her for fearing her husband would go to another woman. His hand went involuntarily to the card in his vest pocket. Lydia was right to worry. He loved her, he really did; loved his entire family, but if he were honest he had to admit Bambola attracted him. She was a beautiful woman and she had a way of looking at him with teasing admiration that was as unlike Lydia's cool, level gaze as chalk to cheese. While Bambola represented freedom, Lydia meant responsibility. Farm and family. Rees groaned.

Rouge glanced over but said nothing. His mouth was set in a grim line.

They drove past the fairgrounds. The circus wagons were still there, clustered around the central campfire. Rees could see the orange and yellow flames and smell cooking meat. Rouge continued on, to West Street, following it out of town. Farms were few on this side of Durham. Maine was rocky and hilly even near the coast but a traveler going west would soon hit mountains, dramatic steep slopes with deep ravines cutting between them.

Rouge did not ride very far out of town, just far enough for the houses to disappear behind the hills. He pulled his horse to a stop outside a thick stand of trees. Rees pulled up beside him. Although the trees were not yet clothed in leaves, none of the pale light from the sky reached the ground. It was like walking into a cave. 'Light the lanterns,' Rouge said. Forgetting the constable couldn't see him, Rees nodded and after securing Hannibal to a tree he took out his tinderbox. He had to walk to the middle of the road to find enough light. Once the spark caught in the bundle he lit the first candle and then the second and put them in the lanterns. Rouge took the first one and started into the woods. Rees fell into step behind.

The ground rose steadily. For a short while they traveled over rough ground, Rees tripping over the tree roots that snarled his footing. Gradually the ground transitioned into rock and they climbed over one escarpment after another, until they reached a flat granite shelf screened by trees and underbrush. Rees held up his lantern and shone it around. Dead falls and downed branches were so plentiful the slope below was almost invisible.

The bodies were stuffed half in, half outside a thicket. Some attempt had been made to cover them with a blanket of last year's leaves and pine branches. One of the corpses was in a sitting position but had fallen forward so that his face hung over his knees. The other, larger figure was sprawled face down with one puffy hand protruding from the leafy carpet. Rees stared at them. Although he could not see their faces, he was already sure he recognized them by their size and clothing.

'Who found them?' he asked Rouge.

'Over here,' the constable said loudly and a man moved into the light. He was unfamiliar to Rees but Rouge seemed to know him. He carried a musket and Rees guessed he'd been out hunting for tonight's supper.

'How did you find them?' Rees asked the man.

'I hunt here all the time. Could tell something was off.'

'At dusk?' Rees asked in some surprise.

The farmer hesitated. 'It wasn't just the seeing. It smelled different,' he said finally.

Rees stepped forward and pulled back the head of the sitting man so that the face was visible. The body had not been here very long – damage from the animals was minimal – and despite his pallor Rees recognized him. It was the smaller of the two men who had come to the circus. He held the lantern closer so that it shone fully on the face. A dark necklace of bruises circled the corpse's neck. Although blurred the marks were clearly from someone's hands. Unusually large hands. Rees was almost positive the bruises would match those around Leah's throat. He would have to take a closer look when the light was better.

He stepped over and removed the pine boughs from the body on the ground. Turning over this cadaver was much more difficult but when the larger form was stretched out on the rock his cause of death was obvious. A bullet hole pierced his forehead, over the left eyebrow.

'That's a pretty small wound,' Rouge said, peering over Rees's shoulder.

'Not a hunting rifle,' Rees agreed.

Rouge exhaled and looked at the other fellow. 'Go on home. I know where to find you if I need you.'

The hunter turned and disappeared silently into the woods.

'What do you think? A dueling pistol?' Rees asked.

'Or a muff pistol,' Rouge said.

Rees nodded. 'The Ladies' Protector,' he said. The small pistol fired only one shot and although women carried the pistol, which was small enough to hide in a muff, it was also used by gentlemen who slid it into their pockets.

This victim had been dragged to the side and covered up immediately after death; the pine boughs and the rock underneath the head were stained with blood.

'Are these the men you saw at the circus?' Rouge asked.

'Yes.' Rees inhaled, recalling one of his mother's favorite expressions: those who lived by the sword, died by the sword. 'I wager the man who hired them murdered them.'

'You think he didn't want to pay?' Rouge asked.

'Or because they made such a serious mistake, killing Boudreaux instead of me,' Rees said.

'That makes sense,' Rouge agreed. 'But why come here? In the middle of nowhere?'

'He didn't want anyone to see him,' Rees said. 'Clearly.' He turned to look at Rouge. 'This was someone who is easily recognizable. And with a lot to lose.'

'Surely you aren't thinking of the magistrate,' Rouge said incredulously.

'Why not? He is exactly the sort of gentleman who would carry a small pistol.'

Rouge, his mouth agape, stared at Rees. In the yellow lamplight, the constable's skin looked puffy and discolored, his eye sockets deep-set and hollow. He slowly shook his head.

'No. He isn't strong enough to overpower two men, especially when one was so much larger.'

Rees turned and looked behind him. The sky was fully dark now and he could barely see the bodies. 'You're right. And I can't think of anyone who could overpower two such villains. Not without trickery.'

'Or help,' Rouge said. 'There had to be two people.'

Rees nodded slowly. 'Except . . .' He paused, thinking. 'What if these villains came here to be paid? The murderer shoots the bigger man and then overpowers the smaller man and strangles him.'

'And what was the smaller man doing while his companion was being shot?' Rouge asked doubtfully. 'Just standing there?'

'Maybe the smaller fellow shot his companion thinking he would be paid the full sum?' Rees suggested. 'There is no honor among thieves.'

Rouge shook his head, unconvinced. 'Perhaps. We'll sort this out later. We need to get these bodies back to town.'

'In my wagon,' Rees said, casting a sour look at the constable. Now he knew why Rouge had told him to bring the wagon – to carry the bodies. He was beginning to think his wagon was being used to transport the dead more often than his loom.

'There's nothing else,' Rouge said. Rees grunted. That was true, but he didn't like it.

Guessing correctly that he would be able to carry the smaller of the two men Rees slung the body over his shoulder and started down the slope. The thicket where the two men had been dumped wasn't far from the road although protected from view by heavy vegetation. No doubt the murderer had expected the bodies to remain hidden at least until autumn. With Rouge holding both lanterns to light the way, Rees trudged one step at a time over the rough ground. The section of the path tangled with the tree roots was the worst. He stumbled over the thick knots, alternately tripping and almost losing his balance or sliding into a hollow and fearing he would twist an ankle. The flat ground felt like mercy. He hurried to the wagon and dropped the body inside, shuddering when the head bounced off the wood panels with a thud.

The heavier, taller man proved more of a struggle. Rees couldn't carry this body by himself so Rouge had to help. But how to carry a heavy body and the lanterns as well? Finally, each man took one of the body's arms in one hand and the lantern in the other. Step over step, they carefully began backing down the slope, the corpse's booted feet dragging on the ground. Jerking him over the roots made for a stop-go, stop-go journey.

This man was heavy! His linen shirt began to rip from the strain. Finally, Rees wound his arm around the body's shoulder and began to drag him. After a few seconds Rouge copied Rees. Now they made some distance although they had to stop every few minutes to rest. Rees's back began to ache.

It seemed to take an hour or more to reach the wagon, but Rees thought it was probably half that. He was sweating hard; his shirt was soaked. They dropped the body by the wagon and leaned against it panting. Rouge looked at Rees and grinned. 'We did it,' he said. Rees nodded.

'Still have to get him in the wagon.'

'I'll grab the feet,' Rouge said.

'A minute,' Rees said, holding up a hand. He waited until his heartbeat slowed slightly. 'Ready.' Grasping the body by the shoulders, Rees jerked it up and into the wagon bed. Then he climbed into the wagon and when Rouge lifted the feet, Rees pulled the body inside to lie next to its companion.

Rees made his way to the wagon seat. Every movement sent a twinge of pain through him. When he finally arrived home – and he did not want to think what Lydia might say – he would beg a draught of willow tea.

Even with the lanterns throwing light on the road the going was slow. By the time they reached the town, all the roads were empty and many of the candles they'd seen from the road had been extinguished for the night. They drove past the fairgrounds. The fire had been banked and except for a few men passing a jug as they sat by it, the field was empty of people.

The coroner's house was dark but for one solitary candle burning in an upstairs window. Rouge pounded on the door until a young girl, her hair in its night-time braid and with a wrapper hastily thrown over her nightgown, opened the door. He explained why they were there. Inviting them into the front hall, the maid went upstairs. When she returned she told them the coroner would meet with them as soon as he exchanged his dressing gown for shirt and breeches and slippers for shoes. Then she retreated into the darkness.

A few minutes later the coroner came down the stairs scowling. 'What do you want?' he asked. 'Do you have any idea what time it is?'

Rouge gestured to the wagon behind him. 'We have two bodies. Murdered men.'

'You're sure they're murder victims?' the coroner asked in a surly tone.

'There is no doubt,' Rouge said sharply. 'One was shot, the other strangled.'

The coroner glanced behind him. Turning back with a sigh he said ungraciously, 'Put them in the shed. I won't have time to start them until tomorrow.'

'I want P– the magistrate to look at them,' Rees said.

'Can't this wait until tomorrow?'

'No.'

'If you think he can recognize them by candlelight,' the coroner said, 'and you can find him, bring him over.'

'I think you should wait until tomorrow morning,' Rouge advised Rees in a low voice.

'No. What if he leaves town before then?'

'But he might anyway if he knows we found these men,' Rouge argued. Rees folded his arms and shook his head.

Rouge exhaled an exasperated breath. 'Stubbornness should be one of the seven deadly sins,' he said. 'But I'll fetch him. If he sees you, he's likely not to come. And I can't say I'd blame him,' he added.

The coroner refused to help with the bodies but Rees and Rouge managed. Rees pulled his wagon up to the shed and he and the constable half-carried, half-dragged the bodies inside. Then Rees stepped outside to wait while Rouge took off at a run, quickly covering the short distance to his tavern.

FORTY-ONE

Magistrate Hanson looked as though he too had been pulled from his bed. Although he wore his fine, black jacket and carried his cane, his shirt hung untidily from the bottom and he'd dispensed with his cravat.

When he saw the man waiting for him, he took an involuntary step backward. Rees saw the magistrate steel himself for what was to come. 'What is this about?' Hanson blustered.

'Get a candle,' Rouge said to the coroner.

'We have the bodies of two men you might know,' Rees said, throwing open the door to the shed.

It was so dark inside it might have been a tunnel to the center of a mountain. Rees fetched one of the lanterns from his wagon and held it up. It illuminated only a small circle around them. He carried it to the table and held it so that the light shone upon the faces. In this yellow glow, the flesh appeared waxy pale. Hanson glanced at the bodies.

'What am I looking at?'

'Do you know them?' Rees asked, expecting to see some involuntary flicker of guilt.

'I've never seen them before,' Hanson said, looking up to meet Rees's gaze.

'The light is poor,' he said, watching a bright blaze approach. The coroner carried a candelabra with six candles, every one alight. When he entered the shed it suddenly seemed quite bright. 'Look again, Piggy,' Rees said.

Hanson bent over the bodies and examined each pallid face with care. 'No,' he said finally. 'I don't know them. Who are they?'

'These are the men you hired to kill me and who shot Boudreaux instead,' Rees said.

The magistrate looked blank. 'I hired?'

'We don't know who hired them,' Rouge said, putting a hand on Rees's arm. 'We aren't even certain these are the men who killed that circus vagabond.'

Rees wrenched his arm away. 'I'm certain.'

'Wait,' Hanson said. 'Boudreaux is dead? Who shot at you? And I didn't hire anyone.'

'Yes, you did,' Rees said. 'You've been threatening me and my family for a long time.'

'I don't understand. Boudreaux is dead?' Piggy took a deep breath. 'I thought Boudreaux was the murderer of all those girls.'

'You don't understand?' Rees laughed bitterly. 'I can't believe you are still protesting your innocence.' He moved forward.

Hanson held up his hands. 'I am no threat to you or your family,' he said. 'I offered to work with you to identify the murderer.'

'You and Farley drove me and my family out of Dugard,' Rees shouted, crowding the smaller man with his bulk. 'I should punch you right now.'

'I could have you taken into custody for threatening me,' Hanson shouted in return, shaking his cane in Rees's face.

'Farley threatened to hang my wife.' The remembered fear swept over Rees. Reaching out, he grasped the other man by his silk lapels. 'He came to my house with a rope.'

This time Rouge grabbed him from behind and held tight, pulling him backward. Rees released Piggy's jacket.

Hanson stared at Rees and then, very slowly, he lowered his cane. 'He did?'

'Don't pretend you didn't know,' Rees said.

'I didn't know.' He paused for a beat before speaking again. 'When I returned home from circuit Farley told me the murderer had been discovered. You and your family were gone. Farley, well, he and I parted ways and I put Caldwell back into the position of constable.' He looked directly into Rees's eyes. 'I told you that. When I saw you in Grand Forks I knew you could help me. You have certain skills—'

He broke off as Rees broke free of Rouge's grip and surged forward. But although Rees did not want to believe the magistrate, Hanson's story was plausible. And he certainly had made several attempts to make peace with Rees.

But Rees wasn't ready. Turning around, he stamped angrily from the shed and climbed into his wagon. By the time Rouge and Piggy Hanson followed, he had already driven several paces down the road.

'Wait,' Rouge called after him. But Rees did not slow down.

*   *   *

It was very late when he reached the farm. The moon had risen. In the silvery illumination from the moon and the fitful glow from the lanterns on the wagon Rees was able to see well enough to unhitch Hannibal and release him into the field. He left the wagon by the barn; it was too dark to see inside and the candles had burned low and were beginning to gutter out. He extinguished the last struggling flame and started for his house.

He thought everyone was asleep. But, although he saw no movement through the window, several candles burned inside. Cautiously he went up the steps and through the door. Lydia was sitting at the table knitting. She looked up and her mouth thinned into a straight line. But she said nothing. Instead she rose to her feet and went to the fireplace where the coffee pot rested by the embers. She poured a cup, brought the sugar cone and the tongs to the table and followed them up with a pitcher of milk. Still she said nothing.

'Aren't you going to ask me where I was?' Rees asked. 'And why I returned so late?'

Lydia glanced at him and quickly looked away. 'I assumed you were at the circus,' she said in a brittle voice.

A wave of heat crept up Rees's neck. 'I wasn't,' he said. He was speaking the truth so why did he sound as though he were lying? He hurried on. 'Rouge came by after supper. I suppose I should have told you where I was going.'

She nodded. Rees attempted to pull her into his arms but a wooden board would have been more responsive. After a few seconds he released her and stepped backwards.

'A farmer out hunting found the bodies of those two men who shot Boudreaux,' he said. 'Hidden in the woods. Rouge came and fetched me so I could identify them.'

He could see Lydia struggling to appear disinterested. But she couldn't resist. Turning to look at him – finally – she said, 'Did you recognize them?'

'I did. They were the ones I saw at the circus camp.'

Lydia ruminated for a few seconds. 'Where were the bodies?'

'West of town, where the forest gets thick. One was shot, one was strangled.'

'Bare hands?'

'Yes. Probably by the same man who murdered Leah.' Rees sat down and picked up his cup. When Lydia joined him at the table, he expelled a long slow breath and some of the tension drained from his shoulders. He was not foolish enough to believe the conflict between him and his wife was settled but at least for the moment they could be friends. Rees shook his head. 'Not sure how their employer managed to kill both, virtually at once.'

'You're assuming the man who hired them committed the murder?' Lydia asked.

'I think so, yes. He's tying up loose ends.'

'There were two people, of course,' Lydia said.

Rees shook his head. 'I don't think so. If the murderer is eliminating anyone who could identify him a second person would just be one more risk.'

Lydia frowned. 'But there were two of them. How would one person subdue both?'

'He shot one,' he said laconically. It didn't feel right that Lydia should echo Rouge's argument. Lydia bit her lip and Rees knew he had not persuaded her.

'So, whom do you believe is the murderer?' she asked.

'I don't know. Right now I'm leaning toward Piggy Hanson.'

'Hmm,' Lydia said. Rees could hear the skepticism in her voice. 'I really can't see Piggy wandering around the forest. For one thing, he's far too plump. And for another, he is too fastidious, too careful of his fine clothing to want to muss it.'

Rees involuntarily nodded. That was true. 'Unless he and Aaron are working together,' Rees suggested, forcing a chuckle.

Lydia did not laugh. She looked at him with her eyebrows raised. 'Really, Will,' she said disapprovingly. 'This is not a time for jokes. I think,' and she paused.

'Are you going to tell me I should talk to the magistrate again?' he asked stiffly.

'No.' She eyed him for a second. 'I think you should but I already know you aren't listening.' As she turned away she said, 'I am retiring now. It is very late.'

Rees stood in the kitchen and watched her until she disappeared. He did not follow her up the stairs but instead turned and settled himself at the table. Although he was very tired, his thoughts raced through his mind in a never-ending loop. 'She's blaming me for something I didn't do,' he said aloud. But he knew, although he didn't want to admit it, that his strong attraction to Miss

Lucia Mazza, circus performer, justified Lydia's anger and uncertainty.

He passed a hand over his damp forehead. He couldn't stop thinking about Lydia. How had they gotten to such a place? And he needed to concentrate on other problems; now there were four murders to solve. Rees moved his hand suddenly, closing his fingers into a fist, and the movement sent his coffee splashing everywhere. Cursing under his breath, he brought a rag from the sink and wiped up the puddles.

It was time for bed. He washed quickly in the sink and went up the stairs. The bedchamber was in darkness but he still had the clear sense Lydia was not asleep. He undressed hurriedly and climbed in beside her. She kept her back to him and after a few moments he folded his hands on his chest and closed his eyes.

But he did not fall asleep for a long time and when he finally drifted off he slept poorly. He did not truly slumber until close to dawn, finally falling asleep to the sound of rain dripping from the eaves. When he awoke a few hours later Lydia and Sharon were already gone and he heard voices from the kitchen. Sluggish with fatigue, he arose and followed them downstairs.

Joseph and Sharon were playing on the floor while Lydia washed dishes. It looked from the pan as though they'd eaten cornmeal porridge. But Lydia had coffee ready. She pushed it over the fire. 'I have bacon,' she said. 'And fresh cornbread.' She forced a smile. 'I rose very early today.'

Rees nodded. He felt awkward and wasn't quite sure what to say. 'David?'

'Already out doing chores.' She paused and then, keeping her eyes on the dishpan, she asked, 'What do you plan to do today?'

Rees saw that she felt as uncomfortable as he did. 'I have to go into town, inspect the bodies once again.' He looked through the window. He could see the raindrops bouncing in the mud puddles in the yard. He thought it was raining even harder now than it had been when he'd gotten up. But a brightening in the west hinted at clearing skies. 'It was too dark to see much last night.'

Lydia followed his gaze. 'This might be a good day to finish questioning the Reynard boy. You've been talking about it.'

'Or I can finish winding the warp and begin tying it on the loom.' The crackling sound and smoky aroma of frying bacon filled the kitchen. The water rushed into his mouth. He suddenly felt almost faint with hunger. 'But first, breakfast.'

Lydia put a plate full of bacon in front of Rees. Fresh cornbread came out of the oven. She cut it and put several hot pieces on his plate. He smeared them with butter and doused them liberally in the honey. As he was taking his first bite, David came inside with a clanking of the milk pail. He'd discarded his mucky boots on the porch and crossed the kitchen in his stockinged feet.

'Breakfast is ready,' Lydia said, taking the pail from her stepson. David sat down by his father.

After several strips of bacon, with Joseph standing beside his chair and hungrily watching every piece that went into his father's mouth, and two big pieces of cornbread dripping with honey, Rees felt ready to tackle the day. He broke the last fragment of bread in two and divided the honey-soaked pieces between Joseph and Sharon. 'Oh Will,' Lydia said reproachfully, 'now they're all sticky.'

'They're hungry,' he said, pushing back his chair.

'They already ate breakfast,' she said, moving toward the children with a wet rag in her hand.

'What are you planning to do today?' David asked his father.

Feeling that David was hinting, Rees said, 'I thought I might help you.'

'There's nothing you can do,' David said. 'I've finished the chores.'

Rees nodded, trying to hide his elation. 'Then I'll visit the coroner.' Just as though he hadn't been planning it. 'And,' he added with a glance at Lydia, 'I'll speak to the Reynard boy again.'

'I'm coming with you,' she said as she stripped off her apron. Rees looked at her. Although she was staring at him with her most determined and forthright expression, he saw that her hand was clenching and unclenching on her rag. He hesitated, a spark of irritation flashing through him. She didn't trust him. Although he'd been planning to stop by the circus – the pull to see Bambola felt like a rope drawing him forward – he knew he could not with Lydia by his side. But he didn't want to blatantly refuse her either. That would only add fuel to the fire.

'It's raining,' he said, hoping to persuade her to change her mind.

She glanced out the window. 'It's clearing up,' she replied.

'Rain is already stopping.' David lent his voice to hers.

'You should know I also plan to re-examine the forest where the bodies were found,' Rees said. 'It will be wet and muddy.'

'I understand,' Lydia said. 'I'll wear my boots.'

'Don't worry about the kids,' David said. 'I'll be here.' When Rees glanced at his son – why did David have to interfere? – he smiled innocently. But his eyes were alert and watchful.

'Very well,' Rees said, knowing he sounded ill-tempered. 'Let's go now.'

FORTY-TWO

Light rain continued to fall while Rees harnessed Hannibal to the wagon but as they drove toward town the sun appeared through the clouds. The Reynard boys were already outside in the fields, wet and muddy though they were. Rees stopped by the fence. The young men had already stripped the stubble from last year – the piles edged the plot in heaps of gold – and were now reseeding. Paul was working in the field where Leah's body had been discovered. Mr Reynard could not afford to be anything but a pragmatist.

Rees called to Paul. All of his brothers and his father turned to look as he left his work and ran to the worm fence. 'Mr Rees,' he said, looking eagerly up into Rees's face. 'More questions for me?'

'Yes,' Rees said with a slight smile. He jumped down from the wagon seat and extended a hand to Lydia. Leaning against the top rail, he said, 'We can now be certain Monsieur Boudreaux did not murder that girl.' Paul nodded, understanding he should be sad and horrified but excited in spite of himself. Rees thought this was probably the most interesting thing that had ever happened to Paul. 'Where did you begin your work that day? When the girl was killed.'

Paul pointed to the lane. 'We always begin on that side and work toward the main road.'

'Tell me again about the traffic on main,' Rees said. 'Besides Mr Boudreaux. I think I have a pretty good idea about him.'

'There was some,' Paul said. 'But it got much heavier later. The circus had already gone by; before noon. You should have seen it, Mr Rees. All the gold horses on the wagon doors sparkling in the sun—'

'Tell me about any wagons or carriages you saw,' Rees interrupted. He knew about the arrival of the circus.

'There were a lot of wagons,' Paul said. 'But they came by after four o'clock mostly.'

'So, they would be here for the five o'clock show,' Rees said with a nod.

'I suppose. Anyway, I recognized all the men in the wagons. All farmers from around here.'

'And the carriages on the main road?' Lydia said, speaking for the first time.

'There were only two,' Paul said promptly.

'And one belonged to Magistrate Hanson?' Rees said.

'I told you that already. He was going into town.'

'Yes, I saw the magistrate in town,' Rees said. 'Did you see a carriage on the lane?'

Paul looked at Rees, one eyebrow lifted in surprise. 'I told you I did.'

'Did you notice anything about the carriage? Anything unusual?' Lydia leaned forward to ask the question.

Paul shook his head. 'It was just a regular carriage. Nothing special about it.'

'Especially after seeing the circus vehicles, right?' Rees asked, his tone dry.

The boy nodded emphatically. 'Exactly. Boring.'

'Did you see the passengers?' Lydia asked.

'One passenger. A woman. She leaned out of the window and waved at me.' He paused and then added, 'I think it was the doctor's wife. She went to Surry to visit her daughter . . .' His voice trailed away uncertainly.

Lydia and Rees exchanged glances; another dead end.

'Was there anything else?' Rees asked, feeling a little desperate. 'Anyone else? A tall heavyset man?'

'No one on foot except the Shaker children and the man following them. First, they walked in. Couple of hours later I saw the man and boy walk home.'

'Together?' Rees asked.

Paul shook his head. 'The boy acted like he didn't know the man was there.'

'What color was the carriage?' Lydia interjected.

Paul shrugged. 'The regular color. Brown.'

'The horses?' Rees asked.

'Brown.'

'Any insignias on the doors?' Lydia asked.

Paul shook his head. 'I would have told you,' he said shortly.

Rees sighed.

'Can I help you?' Mr Reynard asked, approaching the fence.

Rees shook his head. 'Thank you, no.'

Lydia, who had stepped away from the fence when she saw Mr Reynard approaching, swept her skirts from her feet and climbed into the wagon. As Rees climbed up beside her, she said in a low voice, 'Well, I'm not sure that was useful.'

'Damn waste of time,' Rees agreed. Glancing at his wife, he added, 'Why did you press him about the carriage on the lane?'

She did not reply for a moment. 'I don't know,' she said at last. 'It's just that . . . well, the attack on Leah had to be done in private. And then her body was transported to the field.' She looked at her husband. 'Even in a wagon a body would have been visible. So, I thought a carriage . . .' Her voice trailed off. Rees waited. 'But that doesn't look possible either.'

'Unless the murderer is Piggy Hanson,' he said.

'That's just so hard to believe,' she said.

As they drove past the fairgrounds, Rees could not help glancing at the circus. To his dismay, he saw that the rope and posts erected for Bambola had been taken down. It looked as though Rouge had given Asher permission to depart. Why? Rees was not finished with the investigation. He might have more questions. He did not want to admit, even to himself, that he didn't want to see the ropedancer disappear from his life forever.

'What are you looking at?' Lydia asked in a sharp voice.

'Nothing,' he replied. 'Nothing at all.'

Rees had a difficult time finding the correct clearing. In the daylight the trees along the road all looked identical. But Lydia, seated on the passenger side, spotted the tracks of the wheels disappearing into the forest and pointed them out. Rees turned in and they climbed down from the wagon.

The clearing looked much different than it had the night before. He had not realized how closely the underbrush grew around the small opening. But there was the path he remembered following up the hill. It did not look so steep now.

'What's this?' Lydia asked, pointing to something white caught in the bushes.

'I don't know,' Rees said, staring at it. Surely it had not been there the night before. Wouldn't he have seen it in the lantern light?

Lydia pulled out the long piece of cloth and held it up. 'It's a cravat,' Rees said, joining his wife by the bush.

'A cravat?' Lydia turned to stare at the long linen scarf in her hand. 'Who wears a cravat around here?'

'The magistrate,' he replied grimly. Lydia stared at him, her eyes widening. Despite his arguments, she had not seriously entertained the possibility Hanson was guilty. 'We'd better take the cravat with us,' Rees said. Lydia nodded silently and dropped it on the wagon seat.

She followed Rees up the path. In the sunlight he could see the hard-packed earth interspersed by rocks underfoot. Lydia looked at it and said, 'I can climb this in a skirt. It is not so very difficult.'

'Follow me then,' he said.

They followed the trail up the hill. She picked her way cautiously around trees with their roots exposed to the air. Rees, recalling the difficult descent the night before, shook his head. He was surprised he and Rouge had made it.

At last they reached the junction with the flat boulders. Streaks of blood, dried black, marked the violence that had occurred here the previous day. Rees could now see how the farmer had discovered them. Another trail, even more gradual than the one he and Lydia had just climbed, looped down to a rocky field of buckwheat below.

'The bodies were found here,' he said, pointing to the crushed vegetation where they had been dumped. A blood pool marked the resting place of the big man.

'There was a struggle over here,' Lydia said. Rees followed her pointing finger. The broken stems of low blueberry bushes shone white against the green. Crushed leaves from the previous fall formed a wavering line across the granite where someone had dragged a body.

Rees stared at the trail for a moment and then turned to look at the pool of blood. 'Rouge was right,' he said. 'Two people. One shot the bigger man while the other strangled the smaller.'

Lydia, who was looking at her husband, suddenly crossed the rock. Stepping daintily around the dried blood, she pulled something from the bush behind him. Holding up several black threads, she said, 'One of the men hid here.'

Rees took the threads. 'This is silk,' he said. He put the threads carefully in his vest pocket.

'Silk?' Lydia repeated in disbelief. 'Who wears silk to an ambush and a murder?'

'The magistrate wears a black, silk jacket,' Rees said, remembering the feel of it underneath his hands the night before. 'He was wearing it when I saw him last night.' Crossing the rock, he pointed. 'Piggy hid here, in the bushes. When his confederate stepped forward to meet the smaller villain, Piggy came out of hiding and shot the big man.'

'Well, someone shot this man,' Lydia said.

'Who else wears silk here?' Rees said, sweeping his arm around him. 'Even the shopkeepers do not wear silk. It is too expensive for the likes of us.'

Lydia nodded reluctantly. 'I just can't imagine the magistrate—' She stopped. 'Why would he? He's a married man. With a position to lose.'

'I'll speak to him again,' Rees said. He was more certain than ever that Piggy Hanson was guilty.

FORTY-THREE

They drove back to town in silence. As they passed the fairgrounds Lydia said suddenly, 'I want to speak to the ropedancer.'

Rees glanced at her in surprise but she would not look at him. 'Why?' he asked.

'I want to ask her something.'

'Nothing has happened between us,' Rees said, hearing the guilty anger in his voice. Now Lydia met his gaze. Her blue eyes were so level and calm Rees felt a flush rise into his cheeks.

'My question has nothing to do with you,' she said. He wasn't sure he believed her.

'Very well. I wanted to speak to Asher again anyway,' he lied. He had some vague notion that if he claimed an ongoing connection between himself and the circus owner Lydia would lose all suspicion of Rees's attraction to Bambola.

Feeling very strange to stop at the circus with Lydia beside him, Rees pulled into the fairgrounds. He parked in the field and they walked together toward the wagons. While she went on to find Bambola, he found the circus master and begged a pail of water for his horse.

Asher, who was overseeing the packing up of his magic props, eyed Rees curiously. 'What are you doing here?' he asked as he pulled a pair of leather gloves over his scratched hands. 'I thought you were done with your investigation, especially in light of Boudreaux's death.'

'Not quite,' Rees said. 'You and Bambola persuaded me to keep looking.' He paused a moment and then added, 'The two men who shot him are dead themselves.'

'Did you . . .?' Asher stared at Rees in horror.

'I didn't kill them,' he said.

'Then how do you know?' Asher turned completely around to give Rees his full attention.

'A farmer found the bodies,' he said.

'Who killed them then?' Asher brushed his hand over his forehead. 'I'm sorry. I'm having trouble understanding all of this.'

'I know,' Rees agreed. 'It is difficult. I suspect the man that hired those men murdered them. Maybe he didn't want to pay them but I think it is more a matter of removing anyone who can identify him.'

'Ah,' Asher said. He sighed. 'I expect we will be long gone by the time you identify the murderer. As much as I want to know who murdered Boudreaux, we have to make a living. Even your constable agrees we can leave.'

'I think he is jumping ahead,' Rees began but he had already lost

Asher's attention. And Lydia was fast approaching, holding up her skirts so they did not drag in the mud.

'Mrs Rees,' Asher said with a bow.

Lydia nodded, barely polite, and took her husband's arm. Together they walked to the wagon. She did not speak and he began to wonder about her conversation with Bambola. Burning with curiosity, he said, 'Well?'

'Well what?' Lydia replied with a faint smile. He helped her up the step into her seat.

'What did Miss Mazza say?' Rees climbed in beside her.

'Nothing about you,' Lydia said, turning to look at him. Rees waited. 'I asked her if she loved Mr Asher,' Lydia said after several seconds.

'And?' Rees felt a sinking sensation in his gut.

'She said she would do anything for him.' Lydia's forehead wrinkled. 'But what does that mean? And is it even true?' She looked at her husband once again. 'I suspect she might have answered the question differently if you'd asked it.'

Rees said nothing, afraid to meet his wife's gaze. Instead he said, 'We have to show the constable the cravat and the silk threads.'

As he drove the short distance to the tavern, he knew with absolute certainty that she had not told him all she'd learned. And she wouldn't, not yet anyway, even if he asked.

When they pulled into the yard, the ostler frowned. 'Your horse is hot and sweaty,' he said accusingly.

'Walk him, please,' Rees said, handing the man a penny.

He checked that the threads were still in his pocket and picked up the white cravat. Then he and Lydia went inside the tavern.

Rouge, standing in his usual spot at the bar, nodded at them when they entered. Rees waved at him to follow and continued on to the taproom at the front.

Rees found the magistrate seated at the back wall with the remains of a large breakfast in front of him. He looked up in surprise and smiled tentatively. Rees threw the linen in his hand at the table, narrowly missing Hanson's dirty plate.

'What is this?' the magistrate asked in surprise.

'Do you recognize it?' Rees asked. 'It's someone's cravat.'

The magistrate picked it up and examined the linen. 'No, I don't recognize it.' He looked up, his eyes narrowing. 'If you're asking if it's mine, it is not. It is cheap and shabby. And worn a long time. See? It's been darned several times.' He pointed to two small areas. The needlework was so fine the darns were almost invisible, even when one knew they were there. Rees stared at the repairs in consternation. He knew Piggy would never wear anything damaged, no matter how finely the repairs had been done. Besides, now that the linen Lydia had found in the forest was held close to the cravat around the magistrate's neck, the difference was plain. Piggy's was a snowy white and starched into knife-sharp folds, against which the other appeared faintly yellow and limp.

Lydia took the linen square from the magistrate and inspected it.

'Where did you find it?' Rouge asked, peering over Rees's shoulder.

'In the woods where we found the bodies,' he replied.

'It wasn't there last night,' Rouge said loudly. 'We woulda seen it. Do you think the murderer was wearing it?'

'Maybe,' Rees said cautiously. He'd been convinced this piece of fabric tied the murders to Hanson but now was no longer sure. And who else in this small farming town wore cravats?

Hanson pursed his mouth as he thought. 'I daresay those are the bodies you dragged me from my bed last night to see? Neither one of those men would wear a cravat, even an old one.'

'I agree,' Rees said. 'But it might belong to the man who hired them.' He stared at Hanson and the two men exchanged a long look.

'That wasn't me,' the magistrate said. 'I've never seen this before. Or those men. Besides, why would I hire such villains?' As he realized what Rees was suggesting he stared at him in horror. 'We've known one another since we were boys. Surely you don't think I had anything to do with the deaths of those young girls!'

Rees stared back. God help me, he thought, I don't want to believe him, but I do.

A crack of thunder broke the silence.

'A storm is coming,' Rouge said, turning to look through the window. Rain was already streaking the wavy glass. 'You don't want to be caught out in it.'

Rees turned to his wife. 'We'd better start home,' he said. 'I'll have to take another look at the bodies tomorrow.' By then they would be beginning to bloat. In a few days their own mothers wouldn't recognize them. But the delay couldn't be helped.

FORTY-FOUR

'I think Magistrate Hanson is telling the truth,' Lydia said as they rode out of town. The light drizzle was already beginning to thicken. As thunder crashed overhead Hannibal broke into a canter.

'But he's the only one who wears cravats on a regular basis,' Rees argued.

'Do you think that shabby cravat belongs to the magistrate?' Lydia asked, turning to look at her husband. Faced with a direct question, he hesitated for several seconds.

'No,' he said finally. 'I don't.'

'And then there is this question,' Lydia continued. 'What was the cravat doing in the middle of the forest anyway? No one, not even Mr Hanson, wears a silk jacket and a cravat into the woods.'

'What do you think?' Rees said, knowing he sounded grumpy. 'You seem to have all the answers.' Lydia threw him a glance. When she didn't speak, Rees said, 'Well, go on.'

'I think someone put it there,' Lydia said. 'Neither you nor the constable saw it and you would have, even in the dark. The lantern light would have shone on the white cloth.'

'To implicate Piggy?' Rees asked rhetorically.

Lydia's explanation made a lot of sense. 'To implicate someone.'

'No honor among thieves,' Rees said. 'What if the murderer, the one who hired those two villains, is trying to incriminate his confederate? No, wait, that won't work. That man would simply accuse his associate.' He stopped, frustrated, as another crack of thunder rolled across the sky. A bolt of lightning sent a flash of blue light to the ground and the rain began to come down, so fast and hard it felt like needles on Rees's exposed skin. Hannibal whinnied and began to run, his hooves throwing up clots of mud and peppering the wagon's passengers with dirt. Rees pulled on the reins, hard, struggling to slow him down. For several seconds he could barely see the horse's brown flanks in front of him. The grooved and pockmarked surface of the road rapidly filled with water. As the wagon swayed and juddered through the puddles, the wheels splashed muck everywhere.

Rees and Lydia arrived home soaked to the skin, muddy and cold. After Rees put Hannibal into his stall he went inside to change his clothes. Lydia had already changed to a much-worn, dark-blue dress that was so old it had begun to fade in spots. She put on her apron and pulled a bowl from the shelf. The tinkling sound of the spoon hitting the bowl's edge sounded through the kitchen as she mixed up cornbread for the noon meal. She was chewing her lip and frowning. Rees recognized that look. She was brooding over something that did not make her happy.

The kitchen was noisy. David and Jerusha were trying to play cribbage, an exercise in futility as they had to keep stopping to pry the pegs from Sharon's chubby hands. Now it was a game for her and she giggled as she ran from her older brother and sister. David was laughing but Jerusha looked angry enough to chew nails. Rees guessed she was the one winning.

He kicked off his muddy shoes at the door and hurried upstairs to put on dry clothing. Then he went into the weaving room. The weather had already ended his plans to work outside. He could not resist a guilty flare of happiness that fate had taken a hand. He needed to think and weaving allowed him to do that.

As usual, he took a few minutes settling himself. But once he began weaving, the repetitive motion of throwing the shuttle allowed his mind to sink into a place where he could concentrate fully on the murders. Something had happened this morning – he'd either seen or heard something that bothered him. But Rees could not put his finger on it. After several minutes of wrestling with the elusive memory, he abandoned that puzzle and moved on.

He thought of Piggy Hanson, reflecting upon their earlier conversation. A magistrate who traveled, he'd been on the scenes of several of the murders of young girls. But not all. And he had made a concerted effort to involve Rees in the investigation. Besides, like it or not, he believed Hanson when he claimed the cravat wasn't his. Even as a boy he had been particular about his appearance. As an adult – well, Rees had never seen him less than perfectly dressed. What's more, the Hanson Rees had built up in his mind was a different man than the one he'd spoken to this morning. Rees began to wonder about his certainty the magistrate was guilty.

But who else even wore cravats and silk jackets? Not Aaron. Rees could not imagine him in anything fancy or ostentatious, even though he was no longer a Shaker. On the Perkins farm and then in jail, Aaron had been clad entirely in black.

Then there was Otto, the strong man from the circus. His large hands could have made the bruises around Leah's neck. But he wore only simple linen breeches and shirt even while performing. And silk? Far too expensive for a man who was little more than a laborer. Besides, Paul Reynard had not seen him on either the lane or the road.

Could Boudreaux have been the murderer after all? Rees involuntarily shook his head. Like Otto, Boudreaux always wore plain clothing. And that was in addition to the problem with the timeline.

At the very last Rees considered Asher. A charming gentleman to be sure, but charm could mask a villain. And he wore a cravat while in his ringmaster's costume but that article of clothing ended in a fall of lace. The jacket he wore in his role as circus master was bright red. Rees stopped, the shuttle held aloft. He had seen Asher in black. It was at Boudreaux's funeral. But although Asher's jacket was black it was not silk. It was linen. Well-cared for, to be sure, but worn to softness and very wrinkled. So not Asher then.

Then there was the question of whether two people were involved in the murder of the ruffians in the forest. Rees could see no connection between any of the men with the exception of Asher and Otto. At least they were both from the circus. He pondered that possibility for several minutes. Leah – or any of the young girls – would not have had a chance against two men, one of them unnaturally strong. But he had never seen anything that hinted at a relationship between the two men. If anything, Asher treated Otto like a servant. But Otto and Billy?

'Pshaw!' Rees exclaimed in frustration, stretching his hands above his head. Nothing fit. What was he missing?

Deciding that he had spent enough time chewing over this conundrum, he rose from the bench and went to the window. The wild storm was over, but rain pattered gently on the glass. He could smell something cooking; it must be past noon and time for dinner. Heat from the fire had risen into this small room and it was now very warm. Too warm. Sweat prickled on the back of Rees's neck. He pushed the window up to allow in some fresh air. It felt much cooler outside. After a few moments breathing in the rain-scented air he closed the window and clattered down the stairs.

The light from the candles and the fireplace cast a warm glow over the main room. Rees smelled frying meat and hot cornbread. David, who had given up on the game, was tossing Sharon in the air to loud squeals of excitement. Jerusha finished laying out the plates and went into the pantry for the maple syrup.

'You're just in time,' Lydia said, gesturing Rees toward the table. He eyed her. But she was relaxed and smiling so whatever had bothered her had been settled. As he sat down at the head of the table, David put his sister down and joined his father.

'Even though the rain has stopped,' David said, 'it's still too wet to plow or plant. I was wondering if you wanted to look at your flock of sheep with me? It will soon be time for shearing. Have you given any thought to that? Some of your ewes have exceptionally thick fleeces. Good for weaving, I would expect. Or worth a lot of cash money.'

Rees hadn't thought. 'The Brothers in Zion will be shearing their flock in a month or so,' he said, adding mendaciously, 'I thought I might ask them for help.'

His thoughts of murder, the circus, Bambola and the two bodies lying in the coroner's shed receded as domestic concerns took precedence.

FORTY-FIVE

C lad in his oilcloth cape, Rees left early the following morning. Although the sky was the color of pewter and a light rain mixed with snow was falling, a streak of blue on the western horizon promised fair skies later. He wanted to examine the bodies in the coroner's shed and perhaps say goodbye to Bambola before returning home for his farm chores. The responsibility of more farm work weighed heavily upon him and without consciously realizing it he sighed heavily several times.

The road into town was empty of traffic but he still could not travel as fast as he wanted. Pools of water pocked a surface that was a slurry of slippery mud and stones. Rees had to steer carefully around the pools as well as he was able, the wagon rocking beneath him like a living thing. Within the first few minutes mud coated Hannibal up to the belly and spattered Rees's cape.

He'd planned to stop at the tavern and share his plans with Rouge but the yard was already full of wagons and horses. He looked at the light shining welcomingly through the smoke-begrimed windows and sighed again.

The coroner's shed was cold and damp; rainwater seeped under the door and turned the dirt floor into mud. But at least, Rees thought, the cool temperature would slow the corruption of the corpses.

He left the door open despite the flood of cool, wet air and in the gray light he examined the corpses once again. The bruises around the neck of the smaller victim had come out in all their livid glory. Rees did not spend much time with them; he was already certain the large ovals printed into the man's skin were a match for those circling Leah's delicate neck.

But as he inspected the body this time he noticed that the right hand was clenched tightly upon something. Since the stiffness had passed off, Rees was able to pry the fingers open. And there clutched inside was a piece of black material, ripped from an article of clothing. Involuntarily Rees's fingers went to his vest pocket and the threads within.

Now that he was more carefully scrutinizing the body, he noticed dried blood beneath the grimy nails. This victim had put up a fight and, like Leah, had left scratches on the murderer. Rees thought of Piggy Hanson and his plump, carefully tended hands. He recalled seeing scratches on Aaron, though, and he had not been wearing Shaker garb while in jail. No, he'd been wearing black. Not black silk but still Rees wondered if Rouge had freed Aaron too quickly.

He moved on to the second body. A big man with muscles visible through the linen of his shirt, he should have mounted a serious challenge to the murderer. But there were no marks on the body other than the small, round hole placed neatly on the left side of his forehead. The pistol, Rees thought, must pull a little to the right. Deciding that this victim had nothing further to tell him, Rees returned for another look at the first body. He would have to share what he had found with the constable.

He stepped outside, glad to see the clearing skies. He had spent over an hour inside the shed and in that time the rain had stopped.

Before he went to the tavern he drove to the fairgrounds. He knew he shouldn't but the yearning to see Bambola was so strong he couldn't resist. Despite the wagons still grouped around the center, the camp already looked abandoned. The fire, which had burned for a week, had been extinguished and the field was empty of people.

The three carriages, all with the rearing gold horse proudly emblazoned on the doors, were grouped together. Rees could see even from a distance that they were empty. He looked around, realizing that he did not know which of the wagons belonged to whom. From the outside they all looked alike except for the grandeur of the horse insignia. The more important performers like Billy boasted carved wooden horses on their doors instead of painted pictures. Asher as the owner of the circus and Bambola as the featured star would certainly live in wagons that displayed their status and they would sport metal insignias. Now Rees looked around again, paying particular attention to the doors. There! The only two conveyances with gilded iron were drawn up close together. He started for them.

A woman's terrified scream tore through the camp and was closely followed by the sound of a gunshot. It sounded as though it came from Bambola's wagon. Rees froze for a few seconds and then started running.

He had a hard time pushing open the door, finally managing to shove it in. When he squeezed through the gap he understood why; Asher lay dead on the floor with a bloody hole over his left eyebrow. His sightless eyes stared at the roof.

'Oh no,' Rees said. Even though he knew the circus master was dead he knelt beside him and felt for a pulse.

'What happened here?' He stared around in shock and disbelief.

Screaming and crying, Bambola stood a few feet away, the muff gun lying at her feet. The right side of her skirt was charred black and smoking. And Lydia was bound to the built-in bench behind her.

'What are you doing here?' he gasped as his eyes took in the ragged boy's clothing she wore.

A rag had been tied over her mouth and Rees saw the beginnings of a bruise on her cheek. A trickle of blood ran down from her nose and when she looked at him her blue eyes were wide with fear. 'Oh, Lydia,' Rees said. What if Asher had killed Lydia? Faced with the possibility of losing her forever he felt the wagon walls spin around him. His stomach twisted into knots. What had he been thinking? He stepped forward, to his wife. But before he reached her, Bambola flung herself into his arms and began weeping against his chest.

Closing her eyes, Lydia turned her face away. Rees tried to push Bambola aside but she clung to him with a desperate grip.

'He made me help him,' Bambola sobbed, her voice muffled against Rees's vest. 'He threatened me . . .'

Rees shot an agonized look at Lydia. A tear formed in the corner of her one visible eye and crept down her cheek. He shuddered in self-disgust and put his hands on Bambola's upper arms to push her away. Although the soft and sweet-smelling body pressed against him was still as enticing as before, the overpowering hunger had faded. The attraction he'd felt earlier now seemed no more than a form of madness.

'Bambola, please,' he said, his gaze fixed on his wife. Lydia still would not look at him.

The ropedancer snuggled closer, her hands twisted in the home-spun of his vest.

'When he tied up your wife, I took his gun and shot him,' she said, tipping her head back so she could look into his face. 'I had to stop him before he hurt anyone else.'

Lydia shook her head.

As interested in listening to Bambola's story as he was, right now he cared more about helping Lydia. 'Please, I need to free my wife.'

'He hired those men to shoot Boudreaux.' The ropedancer's voice rose. 'I'll never forgive him for that, never!' Rees believed her.

'What the hell is happening here?' Rouge squeezed part way through the half-open door. 'I had reports of screaming and gunfire . . .' His voice trailed away as he stared at the circus master lying at his feet. He looked up, staring first at Rees with Bambola held in his arms and then at Lydia, in boy's clothes but with her long auburn hair cascading down her back.

'What the . . .?'

'How could Asher hire those men to kill Boudreaux?' Bambola wept. 'How could he be so wicked? Boudreaux was like a brother.'

'What?' Rouge asked, sounding confused. 'Why would he do

that?' he added, grasping the one piece he understood. 'Have Boudreaux murdered, I mean?'

'I don't know,' Bambola said, lowering her eyes. 'I wondered but I was not sure until today. Until she came.' She flicked a glance at Lydia.

'Here,' Rees said, attempting to thrust Bambola into Rouge's arms. 'Take her. And get Asher's body out of here. I must see to my wife.'

Bambola reluctantly relinquished her hold on Rees's vest. Casting him a reproachful glance, she allowed herself to be pulled from the wagon.

He turned to Lydia. 'Are you hurt? Did Asher hurt you?' She shook her head in denial despite the bruises on her face. 'I'm sorry,' he said as he knelt beside her. 'So so sorry.' He tried to untie the gag but the knots stubbornly opposed his efforts. At last he took out his knife and cut it. He saw with a spasm of pain the red lines on either side of her mouth where the tightly bound linen had pressed into her cheeks. 'I'll get you out of these ropes.'

'Are you leaving with that woman?'

'No, no,' he said, trying to put his arms around her. 'Never. You are the woman I love.' Her stiff body resisted him and he finally abandoned his effort to embrace her.

'Do you have any water?' she asked. He jumped to his feet and looked around. Asher had tied Lydia to the bench that also served as the bed and the chair. Across the small aisle was a wash basin in which Bambola's black dress was soaking and, next to it, a pitcher of water. Rees tasted it to make sure it was drinkable – the wash water was brown – before pouring it into a glass and holding it to Lydia's lips. She drank thirstily.

'What the hell are you doing here?' he asked when she had drained the glass. She did not speak as he began sawing at the ropes.

'Trying to save my marriage and my family,' she said. 'I had to ask Bambola some questions.'

Rees' fingers slipped on the handle and the knife clattered to the floor. 'What do you mean?' But he knew. 'There was never anything between me and Bambola,' he said. He could not meet her eyes.

'Nothing physical,' Lydia said. 'Yet.'

His ears burning, Rees picked up his knife and began struggling with the ropes once again. 'I think,' he said, trying to explain, 'that

Bambola's allure was tied up with the glamour of the traveling circus.' He knew that didn't excuse his behavior. 'I wanted to be a young man again.'

'She is beautiful,' Lydia said shortly.

'Yes,' Rees agreed. He couldn't deny it. 'And exotic. She looked like an angel dancing along the rope in her spangled costume. But it wasn't real.' And then, emphasizing it to himself, he repeated, 'It was never real.' Who had tried to tell him this was all illusion? He cast his mind back. David – but Rees had not been able to listen.

In the ensuing silence he could hear Rouge talking outside.

'I know I said I didn't want you traveling,' Lydia said at last. 'Taking your weaving trips.' She gulped in a big breath of air. 'I've changed my mind. I think you should go.'

'I should take weaving trips, you mean?' Rees repeated. 'But . . .' He stopped and started over. 'What about the farm? And the children?'

Lydia managed a smile. 'I'll manage. I'll have the children to help.'

Rees stared at her for a few seconds. 'Are you sure?' When she nodded he went on, 'If my earnings are good, we can hire help.'

'Yes, that's true. But it is not even about the money.' She darted a glance at him and then looked down at her lap. 'You aren't happy unless you take your loom and your wagon and go. I've always known that.' Tears flooded her eyes. 'I just want you to come home to me at the end of your journeys.'

'Oh Lydia,' Rees began, pulling her into an awkward embrace.

'Are you finished with those ropes?' Rouge asked, putting his head through the door. 'We're waiting for you.'

Quickly releasing Lydia, Rees said, 'Almost done.'

The circus folk were clustered around the wagon. Rouge had called for a cart and now everyone watched in silence as Asher's body was positioned in it. Not Rees's wagon for once, he thought with a touch of gratitude. He would have expected Bambola to join Billy or Otto for comfort but instead she was standing beside the magistrate. He was smoothing down the lapels of his elegant, gray jacket and re-tying his cravat into a fussy bow. The ropedancer had found no comfort there.

Lydia turned to her husband. 'Pretend you don't know Bambola,' she said urgently in a low voice. 'Think this through,' she added as the ropedancer ran to Rees's side.

'Tell the magistrate,' she said to Lydia, 'tell him I saved you.'

'Is this true?' Hanson asked, blinking at Lydia's boyish garb.

'Mr Asher was threatening to kill me,' Lydia agreed.

'So, we owe her a debt of gratitude?' Rouge said dubiously.

At the same moment Rees caught Billy's expression of mingled horror, fear, and disgust. Arrested by it, he said, 'Wait. Tell the whole story, Lydia. What happened after you arrived here, at the circus?'

'Yes, tell it,' Rouge said. 'What were you doing here? And dressed like that?'

'It's easier to travel like this,' Lydia said. 'And I wanted to talk to Miss Mazza in private.' She regarded the other woman with cold eyes. Rouge's face went through a series of embarrassed contortions and Rees realized his attraction to Bambola had not gone unnoticed. He stared at the ground as heat traveled up his neck and into his ears.

'Go on, Mrs Rees,' said Hanson evenly. He seemed to be the only one unaware of Rees's lapse. 'Did you see the ropedancer here?'

'Only from a distance.' Lydia took in a deep breath. 'I don't believe she saw me. Mr Asher approached me first. He told me he was taking me to her.' She stopped and bit her lip. Rees could feel her trembling beneath his arm.

'And did he?' Hanson asked.

Lydia nodded. 'He took me here but she wasn't in. He-he accused me of spying on him for you.' She turned her gaze on her husband. 'Mr Asher behaved as though you already knew he was guilty.'

While Rees stared at her in shock, Bambola spoke. 'And then I came in. I told him to leave you alone.'

'Yes,' Lydia said. 'That's what happened. And he said he wasn't going to bother me anyway. I was too old to be attractive.'

'But you're only twenty-six,' Rees said. Then the meaning of Lydia's words sank in.

'He-he was the one attacking the young girls?' Rouge asked then. He threw a knowing glance at Rees. 'I told you the murderer was in the circus.'

The magistrate nodded. 'I've been following them for months. I knew something was wrong.'

But I liked Asher, Rees thought, horrified.

'I swear I didn't know,' Bambola said, looking at Rees.

'How did you happen to shoot Asher?' Rouge asked her.

'He said he was going to kill her,' Bambola said. 'I couldn't allow that to happen so I shot him.'

Rees, who could not imagine Asher saying that, felt as though the world was shifting around him. He had understood nothing. Asher had performed an entire play around him and he had never realized it. 'But wait,' he said and then paused. He had no clear idea what he would ask.

'*She* is the connection to Asher,' Lydia said in a low voice.

Rees looked at Bambola. 'You loved Asher, didn't you?' he said.

Tears filled her eyes. 'Once,' she said. 'Before he became a monster.'

'Weren't you . . .? I mean . . .?' He stopped. He wasn't sure he could ask this in front of everyone.

Bambola smiled faintly. 'We were lovers. Once. And, as you might expect, I became pregnant. I was not so good on the rope anymore; my balance was off. One day I fell.' Tears began streaming down her cheeks. 'I lost the baby. Asher was glad. I would have been useless to the circus as a mother.' The resentment in her voice made Rees flinch.

'So, he . . . those young girls,' Rees said, unable to keep the censure and disgust from his voice.

Bambola nodded. 'I didn't know. I swear it. None of us did. God forgive me, I wondered if Boudreaux might be the guilty one.'

Rees hesitated. Did he believe her?

'Someone was helping him,' Rouge said. 'Had to be. For one thing, he could not have dealt with those two villains by himself.'

'I didn't know. He kept that part of his life from me,' Bambola said, her eyes wide. 'If he had help I do not know of it.' She swept her eyes around the circle. 'But it was no one in the circus; of that I am certain.'

'Why did he kill Boudreaux?' Lydia asked.

Bambola blinked. Rees was glad to see the color returning to Lydia's cheeks.

'I don't know. Maybe Boudreaux knew about him? Maybe he helped? They were very close. Or maybe Boudreaux tried to black-mail him.' She paused. Turning her gaze to Rees, she added, 'Mr Asher wanted to frighten you away. Maybe he thought shooting Boudreaux would succeed in doing so. I knew you would solve the murders, you see. My cards told me. I didn't know Asher was the guilty one, you understand. But I knew you would find the murderer and I told him that.'

'You told him?' Rees repeated.

'He laughed at me. He hit me.' She pulled back her lacy sleeve to reveal bruises on her wrist. 'He never believed in the cards.'

'Was that Mr Asher's cravat?' Lydia asked.

Bambola nodded. 'Of course. He wore it to the funeral.' She glanced at Rees from under her lashes. 'You saw him there.' Rees nodded, the image of Asher in the cravat and shabby linen jacket flashing into his mind.

'You put it in the bushes,' Lydia said. 'To implicate Asher.'

Bambola did not reply.

'Well, this all seems very clear,' Hanson said.

'Are you going to put me in jail?' the ropedancer asked, twisting her hands together. 'I did shoot Mr Asher.' Her face twisted and tears filled her eyes again. 'I didn't want to. I tried to talk to him but he wouldn't listen.'

Hanson and Rouge shared a look and then they both turned to Rees. 'What do you think?'

Rees felt the weight of everyone's eyes upon him. He turned to look at Bambola. As her large dark eyes lifted to meet his gaze she smiled tremulously and he felt a tug of familiar desire. Then Lydia stepped forward and slid her hand into his elbow. Although he didn't turn to look at her, he smelled the lavender from her hair and the ghost of David in her borrowed clothing; the odors of manure and sheep and soil. Rees realized how closely he had come to betraying his marriage vows and hurting the people he loved.

'Black silk,' Lydia murmured.

Rees remembered Bambola on Asher's arm; Bambola wearing a black silk dress.

Exhaling, he began thinking furiously.

'Just a few more questions,' Rees said.

Bambola stared at him in astonishment. 'More? You don't believe me?'

Rouge grinned at Rees as Hanson bowed. They would support him.

'Why didn't you leave Asher?' he asked her.

'And go where? Do what? Besides, I was afraid. You cannot imagine the things he made me do.' A shudder racked her small frame. Rees thought she might be telling the truth now and realized how little he trusted her.

'He made a mistake in Grand Forks, didn't he?'

'How did you know?' She stopped and took a breath. 'That boy was dressed as a girl. Asher was angrier than I'd ever before seen him.' She shuddered and buried her face in her hands. 'The worst of it is . . .' She looked at him with tear-filled eyes. 'I think at the end he preferred strangling those girls to the-the . . . other.'

'You were his partner,' he said.

'No. No. I only found out after.' She stretched out a hand but dropped it when she saw Rees's expression. He was silent as he tried to untangle the facts from her partial truths.

'You shot Asher in the head,' he said. 'It was an excellent shot.' She blinked, thrown off balance by the abrupt change in subject, and nodded warily. 'You told me your father taught you.' She nodded again. He could tell by the stiffness of her body that she no longer believed he would free her. 'Tell me again how you took the gun from Asher.'

'It wasn't in his pocket,' she replied. 'He'd left it on the counter. So, I took it and fired.' She smiled. 'I was fortunate – I was too close to miss.'

Rees looked at the charred fold on the right side of her skirt. She followed his glance. As the color drained from her cheeks, she dropped her hand to cover the blackened cloth.

'Were you close to the smaller of the two men Asher hired to murder Boudreaux?' Rees asked icily. 'That was another precise shot.'

'But I–I didn't,' Bambola stammered. 'I didn't shoot anyone.'

'That shot was positioned a little to the left, almost exactly in the same place as the shot that killed Asher. The muff gun pulls right. I think you were a willing participant in the murders. All of them. The young girls as well. Until Asher went too far and murdered Boudreaux, one of your own.'

It was a stab in the dark but when Rees saw her expression change he knew he was right.

'I knew it!' Hanson muttered.

'But wait a minute,' Rouge said. 'You argued with me. You said it couldn't be anyone from the circus because no one saw their wagons. All of them' – and he gestured around him – 'are marked with the rearing horse.'

Nodding, Rees looked over his shoulder at the carriages. Before he even knew what he would do, he was moving toward them. He felt as though his mind had been filled with fog and now, as that blew away, he could think clearly. The pieces of the investigation were falling into place. Within those twenty steps, he came up with a possible explanation. He reached out for the rearing horse and pulled. With some effort, the iron insignia came off in his hands. The wood underneath the door was unmarked, plain. This carriage now appeared unremarkable. 'It's magnetic,' Rees said. 'Both metal carvings can be removed.' He turned once again to look at the ropedancer. 'Paul Reynard saw a woman in a carriage. He said she waved at him. That was you, wasn't it?' He paused but she looked away and said nothing. 'I think you were not just a willing participant but an enthusiastic one.'

Now she stared at him, her soft velvety eyes going as hard and black as obsidian. 'You could have come with me, you know. Joined the circus.'

'And what would I do in the circus?' Rees asked scornfully.

'I would have taught you.' She smiled at him, her face softening. 'My feelings were engaged. What I felt between us was real. You're a good man, Will Rees.'

Despite the tingle that went through him, the ghost of the feelings Rees had once felt, he imagined her hands with those perfect nails clutching the girls under their armpits and shuddered.

'I love my wife and children. My life is with them,' he said. He thought of the tarot card she had given him. 'Did you read the cards for yourself?' he asked. 'You told me I was Justice. What did the cards say about you?'

She looked at him for a moment and then she spat at him.

'None of that,' Rouge said, taking her by the arm and jerking her backward.

As the constable left the field, Rees looked at the magistrate. Hanson nodded at him.

'I knew you'd solve it,' he said. 'That's your gift.'

Rees inclined his head in response. Piggy would never apologize for what he'd done, Rees knew that. But he felt they had made a step forward, away from the anger and envy that had marked their relationship since their childhood.

Inhaling a deep breath, he looked around him, first at Billy who was leaning against the wagon wheel and then at the rest of the crowd. They all looked worried; one of the women sobbed. Otto's forehead was furrowed.

'Are we free to go?' he asked.

'I believe so,' Rees said. And then: 'What are you going to do?'

'Continue on,' Otto said. 'We won't have a magician or a rope-dancer. But we will manage.'

'I know a few tricks,' said one of the men.

'You'll have a clown,' Billy said. He coughed raggedly. 'At least for a little while.'

'Good, good,' Otto said. 'Let's finish packing up. We can stop along the road and take stock . . .' His voice faded as he turned away. All of the circus folk followed him except for Billy.

'I wanted to say goodbye,' he said, coughing.

'Will you be all right?' Lydia asked, reaching out a hand.

'I don't know.' He turned to look behind him at the colorful wagons. 'Maybe Otto . . .' He shook his head doubtfully but managed a lopsided smile. 'At least we won't be fleeing from the villages in the middle of the night. Not usually anyway.'

Hearing something in Billy's voice Rees fixed an accusing stare on the clown. 'You knew Asher was murdering those girls.'

Billy shook his head. 'I didn't know. But I guessed something was going on, something not right.'

'All those young girls,' Lydia said in a hushed voice.

'Why didn't you tell someone?'

'Tell someone? Who?' Billy scoffed. He paused to catch his breath. 'Nobody would believe a circus clown.'

'Why didn't you tell me?' Rees asked. 'Don't you understand, Billy? How many of those girls could have been saved?'

'I could have been wrong,' Billy protested in a feeble voice.

'That's an excuse.' Rees passed his hand over his forehead. 'I might have caught Asher sooner.' He could not say Bambola's name. Just the thought of her participation in the murders made him nauseous.

Billy looked up at the sky for a few seconds before looking directly into Rees's face. 'And what were we to do?' he asked, waving his arm at the wagons behind him. 'This is our home. Where would we go? Where would I go? No one wants a freak like me working for them. My own family turned me out onto the road to starve. And I'm not the only one either. None of us has any other place. This circus and these people are our only home, our only family. Would you risk everything on suspicion?'

Rees stared at the little man for several seconds. Finally, he said, 'I'm sorry. But you understand I had to pursue justice for those murdered girls. I had to stop Asher. Other girls would have died . . .'

Billy nodded. 'I know. That's why no one except Asher and Bambola, not one of us' – he gestured again at the wagons – 'tried to prevent you from investigating. We wanted you to succeed.'

'Otto warned me off,' Rees said.

'He was afraid for you,' Billy replied. 'We thought it would be you lying dead on the ground.'

Rees heard Lydia gasp.

Billy looked around at the muddy field. 'With any luck, Otto will keep the circus going.'

'I hope so, for all of your sakes,' Lydia said. 'Come on.' She nudged Rees with her elbow. 'It's time to go home.'

Rees nodded and began walking toward his wagon. 'How did you know?' he asked her. 'About Bambola, I mean?'

'I'm a woman and I looked at her with a different eye,' she said grimly.

Shame swept over Rees. 'But the black silk dress? You weren't at the funeral.'

'It was soaking in the wash basin. In bloody water.'

Now he felt like a fool.

They crossed the field in silence. As she climbed into the wagon, Lydia spoke. 'I do love these clothes. It's so easy to move around.'

Rees, understanding she was offering him an olive branch, looked at her. 'The world is turned upside down,' he said, smiling but not entirely joking. 'I daresay I'll be wearing skirts next.'

Lydia turned a tentative grin upon him. 'I doubt we could make dresses in your size.'

'Yes,' he agreed. He forced a grin. 'You don't have to say it: I would make a very homely female.'

Lydia laughed out loud and he felt something inside of him relax.

Knowing that he was returning to his usual life – farming – felt bittersweet. But it was *his* life, and the lives of his wife and children.

Still, he would never forget Bambola; the murderer he had almost – almost – set free.

AUTHOR'S NOTE:

The circus has a long history. Acrobats and jugglers have their beginnings in the Bronze Age; the first known depictions of acrobats and jugglers are from approximately 3000 B.C. The ancient Egyptians taught these arts to the Greeks, and the Greeks taught them to the Romans. They spread them throughout their empire in the form of itinerant troupes known as *funambuli* or ropewalkers. The word circus is actually from the Latin for circle. (Acrobatics arose independently in China.)

During the Middle Ages, jugglers and acrobats performed at fairs all over Europe and in England. With the ascension of the Puritans in England in the mid-1660s, however, the fairs and the entertainment there stopped. They prohibited all frivolity including Christmas celebrations.

England's circus began again about one hundred years later with a retired Sergeant-Major named Philip Astley. A trick rider, he began exhibiting his horsemanship just outside of London. He performed in a circle – or circus – like most equestrians. In 1770 Astley decided to draw other entertainers to what was basically a horse show: i.e. he hired acrobats, ropedancers (wire walkers), and jugglers to attract a larger audience. He ended his show with a Pantomime that included Harlequin, Columbine, and Clown, characters from the Elizabethan stage theater which were themselves influenced by the Italian *Commedia del'arte*. They became another prominent and familiar part of the circus: the clowns. The new circus became very popular.

Like so many parts of American culture, the early circus was a transplant from Great Britain, brought over by John Bill Ricketts in 1793. Astley had built a large enclosed ring (that he called a Hippodrome) not only in London but also in France. With the brewing violence of the French Revolution, Astley fled Paris. England began preparing for war, a war that began a few years later with Napoleon's rise. So, Ricketts left for the United States, bringing some of his performers with him to Philadelphia. With the upset in

Europe more and more of the British circus folk joined him in the United States.

A few years later, Ricketts took the circus on tour. Do not imagine this early circus performing under a big canvas tent with trained elephants, lions, and other exotic animals. In the beginning they performed outside in a handy field and passed around the hat. The circus still did not have the more exotic animals like lions and elephants. The animal acts at this time consisted of trained dogs, pigs, and sometimes bears. And, of course, trained horses continued to be the stars as this was still primarily an equestrian show. Later, temporary wood enclosures, usually open to the sky, were built in the towns for the performances. The first canvas big top was not used until the mid-nineteenth century when the circus truly became a traveling entertainment.

By 1900 circuses dominated American popular culture. 1905 was the Golden Age. Then hundreds of outfits existed, playing to between several hundred and 20,000 people a night. If anyone is interested in pursuing a circus career, there are a number of circus schools around the world, (Ukraine, Germany, and France) including several in the United States.

Lightning Source UK Ltd.
Milton Keynes UK
UKHW010943081220
374816UK00002B/85